Step into a world of scandal and surprise, of stately homes and breathtaking seduction. . . . Step into the world of master storyteller Mary Balogh. In novels of wit and intrigue, the bestselling, award-winning author draws you into a vibrant, sensual new world . . . and into the lives of one extraordinary family: the Bedwyns— six brothers and sisters—heirs to a legacy of power, passion, and seduction. Their adventures will dazzle and delight you. Their stories will leave you breathless. . . .

Aidan—the brooding man of honor
Rannulf—the irresistible rebel
Freyja—the fiery beauty
Morgan—the ravishing innocent
Alleyne—the passionate nobleman
Wulfric—the mysterious head of the family

THIS IS HIS STORY . . .

Praise For The Novels Of
Mary Balogh

Slightly Dangerous

"*Slightly Dangerous* is the culmination of Balogh's wonderfully entertaining Bedwyn series. . . . Balogh, famous for her believable characters and finely crafted Regency-era settings, forges a relationship that leaps off the page and into the hearts of her readers."

—*Booklist*

"With this series, Balogh has created a wonderfully romantic world of Regency culture and society. Readers will miss the honorable Bedwyns and their mates; ending the series with Wulfric's story is icing on the cake. Highly recommended."

—*Library Journal*

Slightly Sinful

"Smart, playful and deliciously satisfying . . . Balogh once again delivers a clean, sprightly tale rich in both plot and character. . . . With its irrepressible characters and deft plotting, this polished romance is an ideal summer read."

—*Publishers Weekly* (starred review)

Slightly Tempted

"Once again, Balogh has penned an entrancing, unconventional yarn that should expand her following."
—*Publishers Weekly*

"Balogh is a gifted writer. . . . *Slightly Tempted* invites reflection, a fine quality in a romance, and Morgan and Gervase are memorable characters."
—*Contra Costa Times*

Slightly Scandalous

"With its impeccable plotting and memorable characters, Balogh's book raises the bar for Regency romances."
—*Publishers Weekly* (starred review)

"The sexual tension fairly crackles between this pair of beautifully matched protagonists. . . . This delightful and exceptionally well-done title nicely demonstrates [Balogh's] matchless style."
—*Library Journal*

"This third book in the Bedwyn series is . . . highly enjoyable as a part of the series or on its own merits."
—*Old Book Barn Gazette*

Slightly Wicked

Slightly Married

A Summer to Remember

"Filled with vivid descriptions, sharp dialogue, and fantastic characters, this passionate, adventurous tale will remain memorable for readers who love an entertaining read." —*Rendezvous*

No Man's Mistress

"This romantic and intensely emotional story will cast its spell on you from the first page."
—*Old Book Barn Gazette*

"A lively and thrilling tale." —*Rendezvous*

"Deep emotions, strong characters and an unusual plot blend to perfection into another winner for this Jewel of the Highest Water, Mary Balogh."
—*Romantic Times* Top Pick—4 1/2 stars

"A pair of strong, equally determined protagonists clash exquisitely in this lively, passionate sequel to *More than a Mistress*." —*Library Journal*

More than a Mistress

"Luscious Regency-era delight. Balogh will delight fans and new readers alike with her memorable characters and fast-paced, well-constructed plot."

—*Booklist*

"*More than a Mistress* is an irresistible story with the perfect hero and heroine, the brilliance of London high society, scandal and seduction, as well as a dash of humor here and there that make for a truly spellbinding and memorable romantic tale. Mary Balogh is a fabulous writer—like a fine wine, she just keeps getting better with time."

—*New Age Bookshelf*

"This romantic story is hilarious in spots with characters who are well-rounded and lovable. *More than a Mistress* is a surefire winner from one of the genre's finest authors."

—*Rendezvous*

"A pleasant and agreeable sensual Regency romp."

—*Kirkus Reviews*

"Mary Balogh is an exceptional talent. The complexity of her characters, the depth of their emotions and the romance and sensuality of her books are unsurpassed in the Regency genres and this book is no exception. A master craftswoman."

—*Old Book Barn Gazette*

"Assured hardcover debut. Smart, sexy dialogue."

—*Publishers Weekly*

Also by Mary Balogh

SLIGHTLY DANGEROUS

MARY BALOGH

A DELL BOOK

SLIGHTLY DANGEROUS
A Dell Book

PUBLISHING HISTORY
Delacorte hardcover edition published June 2004
Dell mass market edition / April 2005

Published by
Bantam Dell
A Division of Random House, Inc.
New York, New York

Library of Congress Catalog Card Number: 2003070091

Dell is a registered trademark of Random House, Inc., and the colophon is
a trademark of Random House, Inc.

ISBN 0-440-24112-X

Printed in the United States of America
Published simultaneously in Canada

www.bantamdell.com

OPM 10 9 8 7 6 5 4 3 2 1

SLIGHTLY DANGEROUS

*Y*OUR CHEEKS ARE LOOKING ALARMINGLY flushed, Christine," her mother remarked, setting her embroidery down in her lap the better to observe her daughter. "And your eyes are very bright. I hope you are not coming down with a fever."

Christine laughed. "I have been at the vicarage, playing with the children," she explained. "Alexander wanted to play cricket, but after a few minutes it became clear that Marianne could not catch a ball and Robin could not hit one. We played hide-and-seek instead, though Alexander thought it was somewhat beneath his dignity now that he is nine years old until I asked him how his poor aunt must feel, then, at the age of *twenty*-nine. I was *it* all the time, of course. We had great fun until Charles poked his head out of the study window and asked us—rhetorically, I suppose—how he was ever to get his sermon finished with all the noise we were making. So Hazel gave us all a glass of lemonade and shooed the children off to the parlor to read quietly, poor things, and I came home."

"I suppose," her eldest sister, Eleanor, said, looking up from her book and observing Christine over the tops of her spectacles, "you did not wear your bonnet while you frolicked with our niece and nephews. That is not just a flush. It is a *sunburn*."

"How can one poke one's head into small hiding places if it is swollen to twice its size with a bonnet?" Christine asked reasonably. She began to arrange the flowers she had cut from the garden on her way inside, in a vase of water she had brought with her from the kitchen.

"And your hair looks like a bird's nest," Eleanor added.

"That is soon corrected." Christine rumpled her short curls with both hands and laughed. "There. Is that better?"

Eleanor shook her head before returning her attention to her book—but not before smiling.

There was a comfortable hush in the room again while they all concentrated upon their chosen activities. But the silence—tempered by the chirping of birds and the whirring of insects from beyond the open window—was broken after a few minutes by the sound of horses' hooves clopping along the village street in the direction of Hyacinth Cottage, and the rumble of wheels. There was more than one horse, and the wheels were heavy ones. It must be the carriage from Schofield Park, Baron Renable's country seat, which was a mere two miles away, Christine thought absently.

None of them took any particular notice of the carriage's approach. Lady Renable often used it when she went visiting, even though a gig would have served her purpose just as well, or a horse—or her feet. Eleanor often described Lady Renable as frivolous and ostentatious, and it was not an inaccurate description. She was also Christine's friend.

And then it became obvious that the horses were slowing. The carriage wheels squeaked in protest. All three ladies looked up.

"I do believe," Eleanor said, peering out the window over her spectacles again, "Lady Renable must be coming here. To what do we owe the honor, I wonder. Were you expecting her, Christine?"

"I *knew* I should have changed my cap after luncheon," their mother said. "Send Mrs. Skinner running upstairs for a clean one if you will, Christine."

"The one you are wearing is quite becoming enough, Mama," Christine assured her, finishing the flower arrangement quickly and crossing the room to kiss her mother's forehead. "It is only Melanie."

"Of *course* it is only Lady Renable. That is the whole point," her mother said, exasperated. But she did not renew her plea for a different cap to be sent for.

It did not take a genius to guess why Melanie was coming here either.

"I daresay she is coming to ask why you refused her invitation," Eleanor said, echoing her thought. "And I daresay she will not take no for an answer now that she has come in person. Poor Christine. Do you want to run up to your room and have me tell her that you seem to have come down with a touch of smallpox?"

Christine laughed while their mother threw up her hands in horror.

Indeed Melanie was not famed for taking no for an answer. Whatever Christine was doing, and she was almost always busy with something—teaching at the village school several times a week, visiting and helping the elderly and infirm or a new mother or a sick child or a friend, calling at the vicarage to amuse and play with the children, since in her estimation Charles and her sister Hazel neglected them altogether too much with the excuse that children did not need adults to play with them when they had one another—no matter what Christine was doing, Melanie always chose to believe that she must be simply *languishing* in the hope that someone would appear with a frivolous diversion.

Of course, Melanie *was* a friend, and Christine really did enjoy spending time with her—and with her children.

But there were limits. She surely was coming here to renew in person the invitation that a servant had brought in writing yesterday. Christine had written back with a tactfully worded but firm refusal. Indeed, she had refused just as firmly a whole month ago when first asked.

The carriage drew to a halt before the garden gate with a great deal of noise and fuss, doubtless drawing the attention of every villager to the fact that the baroness was condescending to call upon Mrs. Thompson and her daughters at Hyacinth Cottage. There were the sounds of opening doors and slamming doors, and then someone—probably the coachman, since it certainly would not be Melanie herself—knocked imperiously on the house door.

Christine sighed and seated herself at the table, her mother put away her embroidery and adjusted her cap, and Eleanor, with a smirk, looked down at her book.

A few moments later Melanie, Lady Renable, swept into the room past Mrs. Skinner, the housekeeper, who had opened the door to announce her. She was, as usual, dressed absurdly for the country. She looked as elaborately turned out as if she were planning a promenade in Hyde Park in London. Bright plumes waved high above the large, stiff poke of her bonnet, giving the illusion of height. A lorgnette was clutched in one of her gloved hands. She seemed to half fill the room.

Christine smiled at her with amused affection.

"Ah, there you are, Christine," she said grandly after inclining her head graciously to the other ladies and asking how they did.

"Here I am," Christine agreed. "How do you do, Melanie? Do take the chair across from Mama's."

But her ladyship waved away the invitation with her lorgnette.

"I have not a moment to spare," she said. "I do not

doubt I will bring on one of my migraines before the day is over. I regret that you have made this visit necessary, Christine. My written invitation ought to have sufficed, you know. I cannot imagine why you wrote back with a refusal. Bertie believes you are being coy and declares that it would serve you right if I did not come in person to persuade you. He often says ridiculous things. I *know* why you refused, and I have come here to tell you that *you* are sometimes ridiculous too. It is because Basil and Hermione are coming, is it not, and for some reason you quarreled with them after Oscar died. But that was a long time ago, and you have as much right to come as they do. Oscar was, after all, Basil's brother, and though he is gone, poor man, you are still and always will be connected by marriage to our family. Christine, you must not be stubborn. Or modest. You must remember that you are the widow of a *viscount's* brother."

Christine was not likely to forget, though sometimes she wished she could. She had been married for seven years to Oscar Derrick, brother of Basil, Viscount Elrick, and cousin of Lady Renable. They had met at Schofield Park at the very first house party Melanie hosted there after her marriage to Bertie, Baron Renable. It had been a brilliant match for Christine, the daughter of a gentleman of such slender means that he had been obliged to augment his income by becoming the village schoolmaster.

Now Melanie wanted her friend to attend another of her house parties.

"It is truly kind of you to ask me," Christine said. "But I would really rather not come, you know."

"Nonsense!" Melanie raised the lorgnette to her eyes and looked about the room with it, an affectation that always amused both Christine and Eleanor, who dipped her head behind her book now to hide her smile. "Of course you want to come. Whoever would not? Mama will be there with Audrey and Sir Lewis Wiseman—the party is in honor of their betrothal, though it has, of course, already been announced. Even Hector has been talked into coming, though you know he can never be persuaded to enjoy himself unless one of us forces him into it."

"And Justin too?" Christine asked. Audrey was Melanie's young sister, Hector and Justin, her brothers. Justin had been Christine's friend since their first acquaintance at that long-ago house party—almost her *only* friend, it had seemed during the last few years of her marriage.

"*Of course* Justin is coming too," Melanie said. "Does he not go everywhere—and does he not spend more time with me than with anyone else? You have always got along famously with my family. But even apart from them, we are expecting a large crowd of distinguished, agreeable guests, and we have any number of pleasurable activities planned for everyone's amusement, morning, noon, and night. You must come. I absolutely insist upon it."

"Oh, Melanie," Christine began, "I would really—"

"You ought to go, Christine," her mother urged her, "and enjoy yourself. You are always so busy on other people's behalf."

"You might as well say yes now," Eleanor added, peering over her spectacles again rather than removing them until their visitor had left and she could return her undivided attention to her book. "You know Lady Renable will not leave here until she has talked you into it."

Christine looked at her, exasperated, but her sister's eyes merely twinkled back into her own. Why did no one ever invite Eleanor to entertainments like this? But Christine knew the answer. At the age of thirty-four, her eldest sister had settled into middle age and a placid spinsterhood as their mother's prop and stay without any regretful glance back at her youth. It was a course she had chosen quite deliberately after the only beau she had ever had was killed in the Peninsular Wars years ago, and no man had changed her mind since then, though a few had tried.

"You are quite right, Miss Thompson," Melanie said, her bonnet plumes nodding approvingly in Eleanor's direction. "The most provoking thing has happened. Hector has been his usual impulsive self."

Hector Magnus, Viscount Mowbury, was a bookish semirecluse. Christine could not imagine him doing *anything* impulsive.

Melanie drummed her gloved fingers on the tabletop. "He has absolutely no idea how to go on, the poor dear," she said. "He has had the audacity to invite a friend of his to come here with him, assuring the man that the invitation came from *me*. And he very obligingly informed me of this turn of events only two days ago—far too late for me to invite another willing lady to make numbers even again."

Ah! All was suddenly clear. Christine's written invitation had come yesterday morning, the day after social disaster had loomed on the horizon of Melanie's world.

"You must come," Melanie said again. "Dear Christine, you absolutely must. It would be an unthinkable disgrace to be forced to host a house party at which the numbers are not even. You could not possibly wish such a thing upon me—especially when it is in your power to save me."

"It would be a dreadful shame," Christine's mother agreed, "when Christine is here with nothing particular to do for the next two weeks."

"Mama!" Christine protested. Eleanor's eyes were still twinkling at her over the tops of her spectacles.

She sighed—aloud. She had been quite determined to resist. She had married into the *ton* nine years ago. At the time she had been thrilled beyond words. Even apart from the fact that she had been head over ears in love with Oscar, she had been elated at the prospect of moving upward into more exalted social circles. And all had been well for a few years—with both her marriage and the *ton*. And then everything had started to go wrong—*everything*. She still felt bewildered and hurt when she remembered. And when she remembered the end . . . Well, she had blocked it quite effectively as the only way to save her sanity and regain her spirits, and she needed no reminder now. She *really* did not want to see Hermione and Basil ever again.

But she had a weakness where people in trouble were concerned. And Melanie really did seem to be in a bit of a bind. She set such great store by her reputation as a hostess who did everything with meticulous correctness. And, when all was said and done, they *were* friends.

"Perhaps," she suggested hopefully, "I can remain here and come over to Schofield a few times to join the party."

"But Bertie would have to call out the carriage to take you home every night and send it to bring you every morning," Melanie said. "It would be just too inconvenient, Christine."

"I could walk over," Christine suggested.

Melanie set one hand to her bosom as if to still her palpitating heart.

"And arrive each day with a dusty or muddy hem and rosy cheeks and windblown hair?" she said. "That would be quite as bad as not having you at all. You must come to stay. That is all there is to it. All our guests will be arriving the day after tomorrow. I will have the carriage sent during the morning so that you may settle in early."

Christine realized that the moment for a firm refusal had passed. She was doomed to attend one of Melanie's house parties, it seemed. But gracious heaven, she had *nothing* to wear and no money with which to rush out to buy a new wardrobe—not that there was anywhere to rush *to*, within fifty miles anyway. Melanie had recently returned from a Season in London, where she had gone to help sponsor her sister's come-out and presentation to the queen. All her guests—except Christine!—were probably coming from there too, bringing their London finery and their London manners with them. This was the stuff of nightmares.

"Very well," she said. "I will come."

Melanie forgot her dignity sufficiently to beam at her before tapping her sharply on the arm with her lorgnette.

"I knew you would," she said. "But I do wish you had not forced me to use a whole hour in coming here. There is *so* much to be done. I could absolutely throttle Hector. Of all the gentlemen he could have invited to come here with him, he had to choose the one most likely to put any hostess into a flutter. And yet he has given me only a few days in which to prepare to entertain him."

"The Prince of Wales?" Christine suggested with a chuckle.

"I cannot say anyone would covet *his* presence," Melanie said, "though I suppose it would be an enormous coup to have him. This is hardly less so, though. No, my unexpected guest is to be *the Duke of Bewcastle*."

Christine raised her eyebrows. She had heard of the duke, though she had never met him. He was enormously powerful and toplofty—and as cold as ice, or so it was said. She could understand Melanie's consternation. And *she* had been chosen to balance numbers with the Duke of Bewcastle? The idea was enormously tickling until she realized that it was one more reason why she should remain at home. But it was too late now.

"Oh, my," her mother said, looking vastly impressed.

"Yes," Melanie agreed with pursed lips and nodding plumes. "But you must not worry, Christine. There are a number of other gentlemen whom you will find personable and who are bound to delight in dancing attendance upon you. You do have that happy effect upon gentlemen, you know—even at your age. I would be mortally jealous if I were not still so attached to Bertie, though he can be horridly provoking when I decide to organize one of my entertainments. He huffs and rumbles and gives me to understand that he is less than enamored with the prospect of enjoying himself. Anyway, I daresay you will not need to exchange a single word with his grace if you do not choose to do so. He is a man famed for his arrogance and reticence and will probably not even notice you if left to himself."

"I promise," Christine said, "not to trip over his feet but to keep a decent distance."

Eleanor's lips curved into another smirk as she caught her sister's eye.

But the trouble was, Christine thought, that she was likely to do just that if she was not careful—trip over his feet, that was, or more likely over her own as she passed in full view of him, a tray of jellies or lemonade balanced on her hands. She would be *far* happier remaining at home, but that was no longer an option. She had agreed to go to Schofield for two weeks.

"Now that I have even numbers again," Melanie said, "I can begin to forgive Hector. This really will be the most famous house party. I daresay it will be the talk of London drawing rooms all next Season. I will be the envy of every hostess in England, and those who were not invited will clamor for an invitation next year. The Duke of Bewcastle never goes anywhere beyond London and his own estates. I cannot imagine how Hector persuaded him to come here. Perhaps he has heard of the superiority of my entertainments. Perhaps . . ."

But Christine had stopped listening for the moment.

The next two weeks were bound to be anything but pleasant. And now there was going to be the added aggravation of having the Duke of Bewcastle as a fellow guest and of feeling self-conscious—quite unnecessarily, since, as Melanie had just remarked, he was unlikely to notice her any more than he would a worm beneath his feet. She *hated* feeling self-conscious. It was something she had never felt until she was a few years into her marriage and had suddenly become the persistent object of unsavory gossip no matter how hard she tried to avoid it. After she was widowed, she had vowed that she would never put herself in such a position again, that she would never again step out of her familiar world.

Of course, she was a great deal older now. She was twenty-nine—almost ancient. No one could expect her to frolic with the young people any longer. She could be a dignified elder. She could sit back and enjoy all the proceedings as a spectator rather than as a participant. It might be highly diverting to do just that, in fact.

"May we offer you a cup of tea and some cakes, Lady Renable?" her mother was asking.

"I have not a moment to spare, Mrs. Thompson," Melanie replied. "I have a houseful of guests arriving the day after tomorrow, and a thousand and one details to attend to before they come. Being a baroness is not all glamour, I do assure you. I must be on my way."

She inclined her head regally, kissed Christine's cheek and squeezed her arm warmly, and swept from the room, all nodding plumes and waving lorgnette and rustling skirts.

"It might be worth remembering for future reference, Christine," Eleanor said, "that it is altogether easier to say yes to Lady Renable the first time she asks a question, whether in writing or in person."

Their mother was on her feet.

"We must go up to your room right *now*, Christine," she said, "and see which of your clothes need mending or trimming or cleaning. Goodness me—the Duke of Bewcastle, not to mention Viscount Mowbury and his mother and Viscount Elrick and his wife! And Lord and Lady Renable, of course."

Christine fled upstairs ahead of her to see if perhaps a dozen or so really ravishing and fashionable garments had suddenly materialized in her wardrobe since she had dressed that morning.

WULFRIC BEDWYN, DUKE of Bewcastle, was sitting behind the large oak desk in the magnificently appointed and well-stocked library of Bedwyn House in London. He was dressed for the evening with exquisite taste and elegance, though he had entertained no guests for dinner and none were with him now. The leather-inlaid desktop was bare except for the blotter, several freshly mended quill pens, and a silver-topped ink bottle. There was nothing to do, since he was always meticulous about dealing with business matters during the daytime and this was evening.

He might have gone out to some entertainment—he still could, in fact. There were several to choose among even though the Season was now over and most of his peers had left London to spend the summer in Brighton or at their country estates. But he had never been one for social entertainments, unless his presence was particularly called for.

He might have gone to spend the evening at White's. Even though the club would be sparsely populated at this time of the year, there was always some congenial companionship and conversation to be found there. But he had spent altogether too much time at his clubs in the last week or so since the parliamentary session ended.

None of his family was in town. Lord Aidan Bedwyn, the brother next in age to himself and his heir presumptive, had not come at all this spring. He had remained at home in Oxfordshire with his wife, Eve, for the birth of their first child, a daughter. It was a happy event they had awaited for almost three years after their marriage. Wulfric had gone there for the christening in May but had stayed only a few days. Lord Rannulf Bedwyn, his next brother, was in Leicestershire with Judith and their son and daughter. He was taking his responsibilities as a landowner more seriously than ever now that their grandmother had died and the property was officially his. Freyja, their sister, was in Cornwall. So was the Marquess of Hallmere, her husband, who had neglected his duties in the House this year and not come up to town at all. Freyja was pregnant again. They had had a son early last year and were apparently hoping for a daughter this time.

Lord Alleyne Bedwyn was in the country with his wife, Rachel, and their twin girls, who had been born last summer. They were concerned about the health of Baron Weston, Rachel's uncle, with whom they lived, and wouldn't leave him. His heart had taken a turn for the worse again. Morgan, his youngest sister, was in Kent. She had come up to town for a few weeks with the Earl of Rosthorn, her husband, but the London air had not agreed with their young son, and so she had returned home with him. Rosthorn had gone home whenever he could after that until the House closed and then had wasted no time in going back to stay. Never again, he had told Bewcastle before he left. In future, if his wife and children could not accompany him, he would simply remain at home and the House could go hang. *Children,* he had said. Plural. That probably meant that Morgan too was with child again.

It was gratifying, Wulfric decided, picking up one of the quill pens and drawing the smooth feather between his fingers and thumb, that his brothers and sisters were all married and settled in life. His duties to them had been satisfactorily discharged.

But Bedwyn House felt empty without them. Even when Morgan had been in town, she had not stayed here, of course.

Lindsey Hall, his principal seat in Hampshire, was going to seem even emptier.

It was that realization, perhaps, that had led him into making an uncharacteristically impulsive decision just a few days earlier. He had accepted a verbal invitation from Lady Renable—conveyed by Viscount Mowbury, her brother—to a house party at Schofield Park in Gloucestershire. He *never* attended house parties. He could not imagine a more insipid way of passing two weeks. Of course, Mowbury *had* assured him that there would be superior company and intelligent conversation there as well as some fishing. But even so, two weeks in the same company, no matter how congenial, might well prove wearing on the nerves.

Wulfric sat back in his chair, rested his elbows on the arms, and steepled his fingers. He stared off sightlessly across the room. He missed Rose far more than he cared to admit. She had been his mistress for well over ten years, but she had died in February. She had taken a chill that had seemed relatively harmless at first, though he had insisted upon summoning his physician to her. It had developed into a severe inflammation of the lungs anyway, and all the doctor had been able to do for her was make her as comfortable as possible. Her death had come as a severe shock. Wulfric had been with her at the end—and almost constantly throughout her illness.

It had felt every bit as bad as being widowed must feel.

They had had a comfortable arrangement, he and Rose. He had kept her in considerable luxury in London during the months of each year when he had to be here, and during the summers he had returned to Lindsey Hall while she had gone to her father's home at a country smithy, where she had enjoyed some fame and commanded universal respect as the wealthy mistress of a duke. He had spent most of his nights with her whenever he was in town. Theirs had not been a passionate relationship—he doubted he was capable of passion—and they had not enjoyed a particularly deep friendship, since their education and interests were quite dissimilar. But there had been a comfortable companionship between them nevertheless. He was quite sure she had shared his contentment with their liaison. After more than ten years he would have known if she had not. He had always been glad that she had never had children by him. He would have provided handsomely for them, but it would have made him uncomfortable to have bastard children.

Her death, though, had left a vast emptiness in his life.

He missed her. He had been celibate since February but did not know how he was to replace her. He was not even sure he wanted to—not yet, at least. She had known how to please and satisfy him. He had known how to please and satisfy her. He was not certain he wanted to adjust to someone else. He felt too old at thirty-five.

And then he rested his chin against the tips of his fingers.

He was thirty-five.

He had fulfilled every one of his duties as Duke of Bewcastle, a position he had never wanted but had inherited anyway at the age of seventeen. Every duty except that to

marry and beget sons and heirs. He had been about to ful-
fill that obligation too, years ago, when he was young and
still a little bit hopeful that personal happiness might be
combined with duty. But on the very night when his betrothal was to be announced, his chosen bride had put on
an elaborate charade in order to avoid a marriage that was
repugnant to her, too afraid of him and her father simply
to tell the truth.

How could a duke choose any woman to be his
duchess and expect personal contentment out of the
arrangement? Who would ever marry a duke for himself?
A mistress could be dismissed. A wife could not.

And so the one little rebellion he had allowed himself
in the years since Lady Marianne Bonner was to remain
single. And to satisfy his needs with Rose. He had found
her and brought her under his protection less than two
months after that disastrous evening.

But now Rose was dead—and buried at his expense in
a country churchyard close to the smithy. The Duke of
Bewcastle had astonished the neighborhood for miles
around by attending the funeral in person.

Why the devil had he agreed to go to Schofield Park
with Mowbury? Had he done so only because he was not
looking forward to returning alone to Lindsey Hall—and
yet could not bear the thought of staying in London either? It was a poor reason even if Mowbury *did* have a
well-informed mind and lively conversation and there
was every hope that the other guests would match him.
Even so, it would have been better to spend the summer
touring his various properties in England and Wales, and
perhaps calling in on his brothers and sisters as he went.
But no—that latter was not a good idea. They all had their
own lives now. They all had spouses and children. They
were all happy. Yes, he believed they really were—all of
them.

He rejoiced for them.

The Duke of Bewcastle, very much alone in his power and the splendor of his person and the magnificence of the London mansion surrounding him, continued to stare off into space as he tapped his steepled fingertips against his chin.

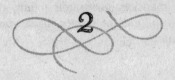

*B*ARON RENABLE'S CARRIAGE CAME RATHER early in the morning to fetch Christine to Schofield Park. Melanie, looking harried, gratefully accepted her offer to help with some final preparations. Christine made a brief visit to her appointed chamber—a small box room at the back of the house wedged between two chimneys, both of which blocked the view from the window and gave her only a narrow glimpse of the kitchen garden below—in order to take off her bonnet, fluff up her curls, and unpack her meager belongings. She then dashed up to the nursery to greet the children and spent the rest of the morning and part of the afternoon being rushed off her feet with various errands. She might have run for the rest of the day if Melanie had not suddenly spotted her in the middle of the afternoon dashing upstairs with an armful of towels for one of the more opulent guest chambers and shrieked in protest at her appearance.

"You simply *must* get dressed, Christine," she said faintly, one hand over her heart, "and do something with your hair. I said you might *help.* I did not intend that you be treated like a *maid.* Are those really *towels* over your arm? Go to your room this instant, you wretch, and start behaving like a guest."

Less than half an hour later Christine appeared downstairs clad decently if not dazzlingly in her second-best sprigged muslin with her curls freshly brushed to a shine. She positively despised the fact that she was nervous—and that she had allowed herself to be trapped into this. She could be in the middle of giving her weekly geography lesson at the school now and actually enjoying herself.

"Oh, there you are," Melanie said when Christine joined her in the hall. She grabbed one of her hands and squeezed it rather painfully. "This is going to be such *fun*, Christine. If only I have not forgotten anything. And if only I do not vomit when I see guests approaching. Why do I always want to vomit on such occasions? It is really quite ungenteel."

"As usual," Christine assured her, "everything will go so dazzlingly well that you will be declared the summer's finest hostess."

"Oh, do you think so?" Melanie set one hand over her heart as if to still its erratic beating. "I like your hair short, Christine. I almost had a fit of the vapors when you told me you were going to have it cut, but you look young and pretty again, as if someone had turned back the calendar just for you—not that you were ever *not* pretty. I am mortally jealous. *What* was that you said, Bertie?"

But Lord Renable, a short distance away, had merely cleared his throat with a long rumbling sound.

"Carriage approaching, Mel," he said. "Here we go." He regarded her gloomily, as if they were expecting the bailiffs to invade Schofield Park and haul off all their earthly possessions. "You go upstairs and hide, Christine. You can have another hour of freedom yet, I daresay."

Melanie tapped his arm none too gently and drew a deep and audible breath. She appeared to grow three inches and was instantly transformed into a gracious, aristocratic hostess who had never in her life felt a single qualm of nerves or tendency to vomit in a crisis.

Though a relapse did threaten when she looked down suddenly and realized that she had a half-full glass of lemonade in her right hand.

"Take this, someone!" she commanded, looking around for the closest footman. "Oh, gracious me, I might have spilled it over someone's boots or muslins."

"I'll take it," Christine said, laughing and suiting action to words. "And spilling it over someone sounds far more like something I would do than you, Melanie. I'll take myself and the lemonade out of harm's way."

She escaped up the stairs on her way toward the primrose sitting room, where the other lady guests were to join her. For some reason known only to herself, Melanie always kept the ladies and gentlemen apart at her parties until she was free to welcome them all to the drawing room for the tea that was the official opening of festivities.

But she paused on the landing, which curved back above the hallway so that one could look down over the banister. The carriage Bertie had heard must have been closer than he thought. The first guests were already stepping inside, and Christine could not resist looking to see if they included anyone she knew.

They were two gentlemen. One of them—carelessly dressed in a brown coat that was wrinkled and too large for him, dark blue pantaloons that bagged slightly at the knee, scuffed boots that had seen better days, a cravat that appeared to have been thrown about his neck with haste and without any reference to either a mirror or a valet, shirt points that drooped without benefit of starch, and fair hair that stuck out in all directions as if he had that moment lifted his head from the pillow—was Hector Magnus, Viscount Mowbury.

"Ah, it's you, is it, Mel?" he said, smiling vaguely at his sister as if he had expected someone else to greet him at her house. "How d'you do, Bertie?"

Christine smiled affectionately and would have called down if it had not been for the gentleman with him. He could not have been more the antithesis of Hector if he had tried. He was tall and well formed and dressed with consummate elegance in a coat of blue superfine over a waistcoat of embroidered gray with darker gray pantaloons and white-topped, shining Hessian boots. His neckcloth was tied neatly and expertly but without ostentation. His starched shirt points hugged his jaw just so. Both garments were sparkling white. He held a tall hat in one hand. His hair was dark and thick, expertly cut and neatly worn.

His shoulders and chest looked broad and powerful beneath the exquisite tailoring, his hips slender in contrast, and his thighs very obviously in no need of a tailor's padding.

But it was not so much his impressive appearance that held Christine silent and rooted to the spot, spying when she ought to have moved on. It was more his utter assurance of manner and bearing and the proud, surely arrogant, tilt to his head. He was clearly a man who ruled his world with ease and exacted instant obedience from his inferiors, who would, of course, include almost every other living mortal—a fanciful thought, perhaps, but she realized that this must be the infamous Duke of Bewcastle.

He looked everything she had ever been led to expect of him.

He was an aristocrat from the topmost hair on his head to the soles of his boots.

She could see something of his face as Melanie and Bertie greeted him and he bowed and then straightened. It was handsome in a cold, austere way, with stern jaw, thin lips, high cheekbones, and a prominent, slightly hooked, finely chiseled nose.

She could not see his eyes, though. He moved almost directly beneath her as Melanie turned her attention back to Hector, and Christine leaned slightly over the banister rail at the very moment when he tipped back his head and looked up and spotted her.

She might have drawn back in instant embarrassment at being caught spying if she had not been so startled by the very eyes she had been trying to see. They seemed to bore right through her head to the back of her skull. She could not be sure of the color of those eyes—pale blue? pale gray?—but she was not too far away from them to feel their effect.

No wonder he had such a reputation!

For one fleeting moment she was given the distinct impression that the Duke of Bewcastle might well be a very dangerous man. Her heart thudded painfully in her chest as if she had just been caught in the act of peeping into a room through a forbidden knothole in the door at some scandal proceeding within.

And then something extraordinary happened.

He *winked* at her.

Or so it seemed for yet another fleeting moment.

But then, even as her eyes widened in shock, Christine could see that he was swiping at the eye that had winked, and she realized that when she had bent forward over the rail so had the glass in her hand. She had dripped lemonade down into the eye of the Duke of Bewcastle.

"Oh!" she exclaimed. "I am so terribly sorry."

And then she turned and scurried away as fast as her legs would carry her. How excruciatingly embarrassing! How horridly clumsy of her! She had promised not to trip over his feet on the very first day, but it had not occurred to her also to promise not to pour lemonade in his eye.

She desperately hoped this was no harbinger of things to come.

She must compose herself before any of the ladies joined her, she thought after she had arrived safely in the primrose salon. And she must stay well out of the orbit of the Duke of Bewcastle for the next thirteen and a half days. It really ought not to be difficult. He probably would not even recognize her when he saw her again. And she was not the sort of person he would notice in the normal course of things.

The Duke of Bewcastle could not, despite the fact that she had inadvertently assaulted him with lemonade, be even the slightest bit dangerous to someone as lowly as she.

And why should she be so discomposed by him anyway? He was not the sort of man she could ever wish to impress.

IT WAS LEMONADE, Wulfric soon realized. But while lemonade might be a refreshing enough drink for those who did not wish to imbibe wine or something stronger on a warm day, it was certainly not a comfortable eye wash.

He did not complain aloud. The Renables appeared to have noticed nothing amiss even though the creature who had spilled it on him from the gallery above had had the impertinence to call down an apology and then scamper away like a frightened rabbit—as well she might. The Renables were busy with Mowbury.

Wulfric wiped his eye with a handkerchief and hoped it did not look as bloodshot as it felt.

But it was not an auspicious beginning to a two-week visit. No servants in any of his own establishments would remain long in his employ if they spied upon guests, spilled liquids on them, apologized aloud, and then ran away. He hoped this was just an aberration and not a sign of poor, slipshod service to come.

The creature had not even been wearing a cap. He had been given a distinct impression of bouncing curls and a round face and big eyes, though he had not, of course, had a good look at her.

Which fact he did not in any way regret.

He dismissed her from his mind. If the Renables could not control their own servants, then poor service was ultimately their concern, not his. He did, after all, have a valet with him to see to his personal needs.

He still had hopes that the house party at Schofield Park would be to his taste. Mowbury, a man in his thirties who had read voraciously and traveled extensively, especially in Greece and Egypt, had been an interesting companion during the long journey from London. They had known each other and been friends of sorts for years. The Renables greeted him affably. His room was an elegant, spacious apartment overlooking the lawns and trees and flower beds at the front of the house.

After changing into fresh clothes and sitting before the dressing room mirror while his valet shaved him, he went down to the billiard room, where the gentlemen had been asked to gather, and discovered the Earl of Kitredge and Viscount Elrick there ahead of him. Both gentlemen were older than he, and he had always found them congenial company. It was a promising sign. Mowbury and his younger brother, Justin Magnus, were there too. Wulfric had never had any dealings with Magnus, but he seemed an amiable young man.

Perhaps this was, after all, just the thing for him, Wulfric thought as he settled into conversation. He would enjoy two weeks of interesting company and then be ready to return to Lindsey Hall for the rest of the summer. After all, one could not become a hermit simply because one's brothers and sisters had all married and one's mistress had died.

And then the door opened again and he heard two extremely unpleasant sounds—feminine giggles and male laughter. Male and female voices mingled in a flurry of merry sound. The ladies went on their way; a large group of gentlemen came inside the room. And there was not one among them, Wulfric estimated, who was above twenty-five years of age. And not one of them—if he was to judge by their laughter and posturing and swaggering—who had a brain in his head.

And if he was not very much mistaken, just as large a group of their female counterparts had just walked by.

They were the very people who filled London ballrooms every Season for the grand marriage mart. They were the very reason why he avoided all such entertainments unless circumstances absolutely forced him to attend.

They were his fellow guests.

"Ah," one of their number said—Sir Lewis Wiseman, a fresh-faced, genial youngster whom Wulfric knew by sight, "it looks as if almost everyone else has arrived too. A fellow does not really *need* a betrothal party in his honor, but Audrey's sister and her mother disagree—and Audrey too, I suppose. So here we all are." He blushed and laughed while his young companions slapped him on the shoulders and made foolish and bawdy comments.

Wiseman, Wulfric recalled now when it was too late, had recently announced his betrothal to Miss Magnus— Lady Renable's sister. This was a house party in honor of the betrothal. And since both halves of the couple were very young people, most of their invited guests were also very young.

Wulfric was appalled.

He had been brought here under false pretenses to *frolic* with the infantry of both sexes?

For two whole weeks?

Had Mowbury deliberately misled him? Or had someone deliberately misled Mowbury?

He had no one to blame but himself, of course, for believing a man who was so vague in his dealings with the outside world that he had been known to put in an appearance at White's Club wearing two quite mismatched boots. It was altogether possible that he had forgotten about the recent betrothal of his sister.

Wulfric's hand curled about the handle of his quizzing glass, and almost unconsciously he assumed his most chilling, forbidding demeanor as the young gentlemen showed some inclination to treat him and the other elders with boisterous camaraderie.

He blinked a few times. His eye, he realized, was still aching slightly.

CHRISTINE'S SISTER-IN-LAW, Hermione Derrick, Viscountess Elrick, was one of the first ladies to arrive. Tall and fair and slender, she was looking as beautiful and elegant as ever though she must be past forty by now. Christine, feeling as if her heart were about to beat right out of her bosom, stood up and smiled at her. She would have kissed her cheek, but something in the other woman's demeanor stopped her and so she stood awkwardly where she was.

"How are you, Hermione?" she asked.

"Christine." Hermione greeted her with a stiff nod and ignored the question. "Melanie informed me that you were one of her guests."

"And how are the boys?" Christine asked. Oscar's nephews were no longer children, she realized, but young men who were no doubt out in the world, experiencing life on their own account.

"You have cut your hair," Hermione observed. "How extraordinary!"

She turned her attention to the other ladies present.

Well, Christine thought as she sat down again, her person was not to be ignored, it seemed, but her voice was. This was an unpromising beginning—or rather an unpromising continuation of the beginning.

Hermione, the daughter of a country solicitor, had made an even more brilliant match than Christine when she had married Viscount Elrick more than twenty years ago. She had welcomed Christine warmly into the family and had helped her adjust to life with the *ton,* including sponsoring her for her presentation to the queen. They had become friends despite the gap of more than ten years in their ages. But the friendship had become strained during the last few years of Christine's marriage. Even so, the terrible quarrel after Oscar's death had taken Christine by surprise and shaken her to the roots. She had left Winford Abbey, Basil's country home, the day after the funeral, crushed and distraught and quite penniless after purchasing her ticket on the stagecoach, intent only upon returning home to Hyacinth Cottage to lick her wounds and somehow piece her life together again. She had neither heard from nor seen her brother- and sister-in-law since—until now.

She fervently hoped that they could at least be civil with one another for two weeks. After all, she had done nothing *wrong*.

Viscountess Mowbury, Melanie's mother, small and rotund, with steel-gray hair and a shrewd eye, hugged Christine and told her she was pleased to see her pretty face again. Audrey also expressed delight and blushed and looked very happy when Christine congratulated her on her betrothal. Fortunately, Christine's troubled relationship with Oscar's immediate family had never affected her amicable relations with his aunt and cousins, who had not themselves spent much time in London during those years.

Lady Chisholm, wife of Sir Clive, with whom Christine had once had an acquaintance, and Mrs. King, whom she had also known, were polite.

And there were six very young, very fashionably and expensively clad young ladies, presumably friends of Audrey's, who clearly knew one another very well and huddled in a group together, chattering and giggling and ignoring everyone else. They must all have been still in the schoolroom when she was last in London, Christine thought. Again, she felt positively ancient. And her second-best muslin suddenly looked like a veritable fossil. It was one of the last garments Oscar had bought for her before his death. She doubted it had ever been paid for.

"The *Duke of Bewcastle* is to be one of the guests," Lady Sarah Buchan announced rather loudly to the huddled group, her eyes as wide as saucers, two spots of color high on her cheekbones.

The girl could perhaps be forgiven for believing she brought fresh and startling news. She had only recently arrived with her father, the Earl of Kitredge, and her brother, the Honorable George Buchan. But everyone already knew because it was the one piece of information with which Melanie had regaled and impressed each of her arriving guests, having apparently recovered completely from her chagrin with Hector for inviting him.

"I never saw him even once all through the Season," Lady Sarah continued, "even though he was in London all the time. It is said that he rarely goes anywhere except the House of Lords and his clubs. But he is coming here. Imagine!"

"Only one duke and hordes of us," Rowena Siddings said, her eyes dancing with merriment and her dimples showing. "Though the married ladies do not count, of course. Nor does Audrey because she is betrothed to Sir Lewis Wiseman. But that still leaves an uncomfortably large number of us to vie for the attentions of *one* duke."

"But the Duke of Bewcastle is *old*, Rowena," Miriam Dunstan-Lutt said. "He is well past his thirtieth year."

"But he *is* a duke," Lady Sarah said, "and so his age is of no consequence, Miriam. Papa says it would be beneath my dignity to marry below the rank of earl at the very least, though I had *dozens* of offers this spring from gentlemen most girls would consider perfectly eligible. It is not at all unlikely that I will marry a duke."

"What a conquest it would be to win the hand of the Duke of Bewcastle," Beryl Chisholm added. "But why should we concede the victory to you, Sarah? Perhaps we should all compete for him."

There was a flurry of giggles.

"You are all remarkably pretty young ladies," Lady Mowbury said kindly, raising her voice so that she could be heard across the room, "and are bound to marry well within the next year or two, but perhaps you ought to be warned that Bewcastle has avoided every attempt to draw him into matrimony for so long that even the most determined mamas have given up trying to attract him for their daughters. I did not even consider him for Audrey."

"But who would want to marry him anyway?" that young lady said from the complacent safety of her betrothed state. "He has only to step into a room to lower the temperature by several degrees. The man lacks all feeling, all sensibility, and all heart. I have it on the most reliable authority. Lewis says that even most of the younger gentlemen at White's are in awe of him and avoid him whenever possible. I think it was unsporting of my brother to invite him here."

So did Christine. If Hector had not invited the duke, then *she* would not be sitting here now, feeling partly uncomfortable and partly bored—*and* she would not have dripped lemonade in his eye. She felt somehow stranded between the older ladies, who moved together into a group and were soon deep in conversation with one another, and the young girls, who were closer, so that she became a de facto member of their group as they lowered their voices and resumed their giggling.

"I propose a wager," Lady Sarah half whispered. She must be the youngest of them all, Christine estimated. She looked like an escapee from the nursery, in fact, though she must be at least seventeen if she had made her come-out. "The winner will be the one who can entice the Duke of Bewcastle into making her a proposal of marriage before the fortnight is over."

"That is quite impossible, I am afraid, Sarah," Audrey said while the others stifled giggles. "The duke does not mean to marry."

"And no wager is even remotely interesting," Harriet King added, "if there is no chance of its being won by *someone*."

"What shall we wager on, then?" Sarah asked, still flushed and bright-eyed and determined not to let go of her idea entirely. "Whichever one of us can engage him in conversation? No, not that—that is *too* easy. Whoever is the first to dance with him? Does your sister have any dancing planned, Audrey? Or . . . what, then?"

"The one who can engage his undivided attention for a whole hour," Audrey suggested. "Believe me, that will be difficult enough to accomplish. And the winner—if there *is* a winner—will have earned her prize. An hour in the duke's company would be akin to an hour sitting on the North Pole, I would imagine."

There was another flurry of giggles.

But Sarah ignored the warning and looked with sparkling eyes at every member of the group—except Christine, who was not really a part of it though she had overheard every word.

"An hour alone with him, then," she said. "The winner will be the first to accomplish that feat. And who knows? Perhaps she will make him fall in love with her, and he will offer marriage after all. It would not be at all strange, I declare."

There was a pause for the inevitable giggling.

"Who is in?" Lady Sarah asked.

Lady Sarah, Rowena, Miriam, Beryl, her sister Penelope, and Harriet King all took up the challenge to the accompaniment of a great deal more squealing and giggling and indulgent smiles from the older ladies, who demanded to know what was so amusing them.

"Nothing," Harriet King said. "Nothing at all, Mama. We were merely discussing the gentlemen who are expected here."

Christine smiled too. Had she ever been this silly? But she knew she had. She had married Oscar on the strength of a two-month acquaintance, merely because he was as handsome as a Greek god—it had been a common description of him—and she had fallen head over ears in love with his looks and his charm.

"And you, Cousin Christine?" Audrey asked when the older ladies had returned their attention to their own conversation. It had been agreed upon that Audrey would hold the bank—one guinea from each of the participants, the whole amount to go to the winner or back to each individual at the end of the two weeks if no one could claim the prize.

Christine pointed at herself in some surprise and raised her eyebrows. "Me? Oh, no, indeed," she said, and laughed.

"I really do not see why not," Audrey said, cocking her head to one side and observing Christine more thoroughly. "You are a widow, not a married lady, after all, and Cousin Oscar has been gone for two whole years. And you are still not *very* old. I doubt you have reached the age of thirty yet."

The other young ladies turned in a collective body to gaze askance at someone who was close to thirty. Their silence spoke quite eloquently enough to assure Christine that at her age she had no hope whatsoever of engaging a duke's attention for a full hour.

She wholeheartedly agreed with them, though not because she was twenty-nine rather than nineteen.

"I really cannot see the attraction of paying for the privilege of being frozen into an icicle for all of one hour," she said.

"You do have a point," Audrey conceded.

"You are the daughter of a country schoolmaster, are you not, Mrs. Derrick?" Harriet King asked with obvious disdain. "You are afraid of losing the wager, I daresay."

"I am indeed," Christine conceded with a smile—the question, she understood, had been rhetorical. "But I do believe that I would be even more afraid of winning. What on earth would I do with a duke?"

There was a moment of silence and then another burst of giggles.

"I could offer an idea or two," Miriam Dunstan-Lutt said, and then blushed at her own risqué words.

"Enough of this," Audrey said firmly, holding up one hand for everyone's attention and checking quickly to be sure that no one in the other group was listening. "I really cannot allow you to preclude yourself merely on the grounds that you do not *wish* to win, Cousin Christine. I shall put in the guinea for you. I shall, in effect, wager on you. And is that not shocking when ladies are not supposed to wager at all?"

"What gentlemen do not know will not hurt them," Beryl Chisholm said.

"You will lose your guinea, I do assure you," Christine told Audrey, laughing and wondering how the Duke of Bewcastle would react if he knew what was transpiring in the primrose sitting room.

"Perhaps," Audrey agreed. "But my expectation is that no one will win, and so my money is sure to return safely to me. Of course, since the wager is not to draw the duke into a marriage proposal but only into a lengthy conversation, I could enter the competition myself, but I don't think I will. I don't think seven guineas is sufficient inducement. Besides, Lewis might be jealous, and it would be no defense to explain to him that I was attempting to win a *wager*."

A bell rang from somewhere beyond the sitting room, the signal that everyone had now arrived and that they were all expected to assemble in the drawing room for tea.

"And so," Harriet King said to Lady Sarah, "you have never even met the Duke of Bewcastle?"

"No," Sarah admitted, "but if he is a duke, he surely must be handsome."

"I *have* met him," Harriet said, linking her arm through Sarah's in preparation for leaving the room with her, "and would not normally set my cap at him. But I cannot risk being bested by the widowed daughter of a country schoolmaster who may or may not have passed her thirtieth birthday, can I?"

The two of them walked away, arm in arm.

Audrey looked at Christine and grimaced. "Oh, dear, the battle lines have been drawn, I'm afraid," she said.

"You surely cannot resist such a challenge now, though, can you, Christine? You simply must win my money back for me."

Rowena Siddings slid an arm through Christine's as they made their way to the drawing room.

"How ridiculous we *all* are," she said. "Shall you and I participate in this wager, Mrs. Derrick, or shall we keep our distance and admire the great man from afar?"

"I believe I shall keep my distance and *laugh* at him from afar if it turns out that he is as pretentious and toplofty as he is reputed to be," Christine said. "I do not admire greatness that has no substance."

"How splendidly brave of you." The girl smiled. "To *laugh* at the Duke of Bewcastle."

Or at herself, Christine thought, to have been drawn into all this secretive, girlish nonsense when all she had had to do was give Melanie a firm no at Hyacinth Cottage the day before yesterday or Audrey a firm no in the sitting room.

But she had no one but herself to blame, she conceded ruefully.

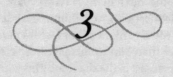

3

$\mathcal{T}$HE DRAWING ROOM WAS ALREADY FULL OF gentlemen. The house party, it seemed, had officially begun—which was just as well. It could never end if it did not first begin, could it? Was it too soon, Christine wondered, to start counting the days until she could go home?

Justin Magnus, Melanie's younger brother, was the first man she saw. He smiled and waved at her from across the room. Lady Chisholm was talking to him, and Lady Chisholm liked to talk. Christine waved and smiled back. Small—he was half a head shorter than she—and thin and quite unremarkable in appearance, Justin nevertheless had charm and humor and intelligence to recommend him. And he always dressed with exquisite taste and elegance—unlike poor Hector, his elder brother. He had proposed marriage to Christine at that first house party long ago. But after she had refused him, and after she had accepted Oscar instead, they had settled into a friendship that had deepened as time went on until for the last few years before Oscar's death he had seemed to be her only friend—the only one available, anyway. Her own family had been far away. He was the only one who had never believed the horrible rumors about her—even the last ghastly one. He was the only one who had spoken up in defense of her, though neither Oscar nor Basil and Hermione had ever believed him. He had remained her friend ever since.

Basil was the next man Christine saw. Of medium stature and slender build, with thinning fair hair and a bald patch at the crown of his head, and with a narrow face and regular, rather than handsome, features, Viscount Elrick had always been cast in the shadow by his younger brother when it came to looks. He had also been more than ten years older. But he had adored Oscar and had been shattered by his death.

He did not ignore Christine, though she had half expected that he might. He bowed with meticulous formality while she spoke his name and curtsied. And then, like Hermione earlier, he turned away to talk with the elderly gentleman Christine remembered as the Earl of Kitredge. He had not spoken a word to her.

She went in determined search of the remotest corner of the room. It was time to become the satirical spectator of humanity, a role she intended to play for the next two weeks. If she was fortunate, no one would take any notice of her in all that time.

Fortunately she reached the corner and settled into a chair there before the Duke of Bewcastle came into the room—she had been dreading seeing him again after that unfortunate incident earlier. But really—what was she dreading? That he would pounce upon her, or rather that he would direct an army of servants to pounce upon her, and have her dragged before the nearest magistrate for assault and battery upon his eye?

He came into the room with Bertie, and there was immediately a different quality to the sound in the room. The young ladies chattered more brightly and smiled more dazzlingly, and the young men laughed more affectedly and swaggered more noticeably. The older ladies preened themselves.

It was really quite amusing.

They might all not have bothered, though. If they had been a roomful of worms, he could scarcely have looked about him with a more supercilious air. His cold, aristocratic face said more plainly than words that he considered this whole scene so far beneath his ducal dignity that really it was too much trouble either to smile or to look marginally approachable.

Melanie, of course, pounced upon him in full grand-hostess style, took him by the arm, and led him about, making sure that all the lesser mortals who had no previous acquaintance with him were given the opportunity to bow and scrape before him.

Fortunately—*very* fortunately—Melanie failed to see Christine in her corner and so the very least mortal in the room was given no chance to rise to her feet in order to have the honor of making her deepest curtsy to the great man.

Satirically observing, Christine reminded herself, surely did not necessitate heaping scorn upon the head of a man she did not even know. But she instinctively bristled at the very sight of the Duke of Bewcastle. She disliked him, she scorned him, and she would be perfectly happy to be soundly ignored by him for thirteen and a half days.

Why *was* it that she reacted so negatively to him? She did not usually react thus, either to acquaintances or to strangers. She *liked* people. All sorts of people. She even liked all the little foibles of her acquaintances that drove other people to distraction.

The round of introductions complete, the duke stood, plate of food in hand, conversing with the Earl of Kitredge and Hector, who had nodded and smiled kindly in Christine's direction. The earl was a great man. He was also pompous. But she felt no animosity toward *him*.

Hector was a viscount, and she was enormously fond of him. So it was not the duke's aristocratic title that made her bristle.

And then all Christine's complacency fled as her eyes met the Duke of Bewcastle's across the room and she had instant images of jailers and jails and chains and magistrates flashing through her head.

Her first instinct was to efface herself utterly and lower her eyes in an attempt to fade into the upholstery of the chair on which she sat.

But self-effacement had never been her way of reacting to the world's ways—except perhaps in the last year or two before Oscar died. And why *should* she seek to disappear? Why should she lower her eyes when he was making no attempt to lower his?

And then he really annoyed her.

Still looking at her, he raised one arrogant eyebrow.

And *then* he infuriated her.

With his eyes on her and one eyebrow elevated, he grasped the handle of his quizzing glass and raised it halfway to his eye as if utterly incredulous of the fact that she had the effrontery to hold his gaze.

Christine would not have looked away then for all the jails and all the chains in England. So he had recognized her, had he? *So what?* When all was said and done, her only crime was to have allowed the glass in her hand to tip too far when he happened to have been standing directly beneath it.

She looked steadily back at him and then compounded her boldness by deliberately laughing at him. Oh, she did not literally *laugh*. But she showed him with her eyes that she was not to be cowed by a single eyebrow and a half-raised quizzing glass. She picked up a cake from her place and bit into it—only to discover that it was a fairy cake. She felt the cream ooze out over her lips and licked it off as the Duke of Bewcastle left his group and made his way toward her.

A path opened before him as if by magic. There was nothing magical about it, of course. Everyone stood out of his way—he probably took it so much as his right that he did not notice it happening.

Oh goodness, she thought as he approached, he really did have a magnificent *presence*.

He stopped walking when the toes of his Hessian boots were a few inches from the toes of her slippers. Danger loomed, Christine thought, her heart fluttering uncomfortably in her chest despite herself.

"I do not believe we have an acquaintance, ma'am," he said, his voice cultured, slightly bored.

"Oh, I know who you are," she assured him. "You are the Duke of Bewcastle."

"Then you have the advantage of me," he said.

"Christine Derrick," she told him. She offered no other explanation. He probably had no interest in her family tree—or Oscar's.

"Have I inadvertently caused you some amusement, Miss Derrick?" he asked her.

"Oh, yes, I am afraid you have," she said. "And it is *Mrs.* Derrick. I am a widow."

His quizzing glass was in his hand again. He raised both eyebrows in an expression that could surely freeze grapes on the vine and cause ruination of the harvest for a whole year.

Christine took another bite out of her cake—and that necessitated another lick of her lips. Should she apologize again? she wondered. But why? She had apologized at the time. Was his right eye a little pinker than the left? Or was she just imagining that it was so?

"Might I be permitted to know why?" he asked, raising his glass almost, though not quite, to his eye.

What a marvelous weapon it was, she thought. It set as much distance between him and troublesome mortals as any drawn sword in the hand of a lesser man. She rather thought she might like to use one herself. She would grow into an eccentric old lady who peered at the world through a giant quizzing glass, terrifying the pretentious and amusing young children with her hideously magnified eye.

He was asking why he had amused her. *Amused* was not quite the right word, but she *had* laughed at him—as she was doing again now.

"You were so very outraged—you *are* so very outraged," she explained, "that I failed to obey your command."

"Outraged? I beg your pardon?" Both eyebrows arched upward again. "*Did* I issue a command?"

"Indeed you did," she told him. "You discovered me looking at you from across the room, and you raised first one eyebrow and then your quizzing glass. I ought not even to have noticed the glass, of course. I should have dropped my gaze obediently long before you raised it."

"And the raising of an eyebrow constitutes a command and that of a quizzing glass *outrage*, ma'am?" he asked her.

"How else do you explain the fact that you have crossed the room to confront me?" she asked in return.

"Perhaps, ma'am," he said, "it is because, unlike you, I have been circulating politely among my fellow guests."

She felt genuine delight then. She even laughed out loud.

"And now I have provoked you into spite," she said. "It would be better to ignore me, your grace, and leave me to my chosen role of spectator. You must not expect me to show fear of you."

"Fear?" He raised his glass all the way to his eye and observed her hands through it. Her fingernails were cut short. They were also clean, but it seemed to her that he could see very well that she actually *worked* with her hands.

"Yes, fear," she said. "It is how you rule your world. You make everyone afraid of you."

"I am gratified that you presume to know me so well, ma'am, on such short acquaintance," he said.

"I suppose," she admitted, "I ought not to have spoken with such frankness. But you did ask."

"I did indeed," he said, making her a stiff bow.

But before he could turn away and leave her, Melanie appeared at his side.

"I see you have met Christine, your grace," she said, slipping an arm through his and smiling graciously. "But may I draw you away for a moment? Lady Sarah Buchan has a question she wishes to ask you, but she is too shy to approach you herself."

She led him away in the direction of Lady Sarah, who darted a look of pure venom at Christine before dipping into a deep curtsy and simpering prettily at the approaching duke.

Gracious heaven, Christine thought, that wager! Did the child seriously believe that she was already scheming to win it? But if the girl did, she was apparently not the only one. Harriet King came to stand before Christine's chair.

"A word of friendly advice, Mrs. Derrick," she said kindly. "You may be able to lure the Duke of Bewcastle to your corner once by smiling invitingly at him and neglecting to look modestly away again, but you are going to need a far more active plan if you are to keep him in conversation for a whole hour."

Well, gracious heaven, Christine thought again, and laughed out loud.

"I am sure you are right," she said. "I will have to think of something *really* enticing."

But instead of sharing the joke, the girl turned away, her kind deed accomplished.

Christine began to feel a premonition that spending two weeks unobtrusively in a corner might not prove as practicable as she had hoped. She had already drawn as much attention to herself there as she would if she had been standing in the middle of the room waving a banner. Of course, she had never been one to fade into any background—that had been half the trouble during her marriage. She was just too sociable by nature.

Those eyes! she thought suddenly. She had discovered during her brief conversation with the duke that they were pure silver. They were the most extraordinary eyes she had ever seen. They were hard and cold and quite opaque. One's own glance seemed to bounce right off them instead of penetrating through to the person within. She had been given the distinct impression either that there *was* no person within but only the hard, arrogant shell of an aristocrat or that the person within was kept well guarded and out of sight to the casual observer.

Either way they were rather disturbing eyes since, though they could not be seen into, they certainly seemed to possess extraordinary power to see right through one's head to the hair on the back of it. Seeing them from close range and *feeling* them penetrate her skull had more than confirmed her initial impression that he would be a dangerous man to provoke. *Had* she provoked him? No more than a slightly troublesome gnat buzzing by his ear, she supposed—or flying into his eye.

She sighed and finished off her fairy cake. She was licking her fingers when Justin arrived in her corner. She jumped gladly to her feet, and they hugged each other warmly.

"Justin!" she cried. "It has been forever."

"*And* a day," he agreed, grinning at her. "It was Easter, actually. I like your hair short. You look prettier than ever. You have just been making the acquaintance of the great man, I see. I'll wager Mel had a few sleepless nights after she discovered that Hector had invited him here."

"And then she came to Hyacinth Cottage to persuade me to come too so that the numbers would be even again," Christine said, grimacing. "And you know what Melanie is like when she has her mind set upon something. I did not stand a chance."

"Poor Chrissie!" He laughed at her. "And lucky me."

Christine relaxed for the first time all day, it seemed.

"CHRISTINE WAS MARRIED to my poor cousin Oscar," Lady Renable explained to Wulfric. "Perhaps you knew him? He was Viscount Elrick's younger brother. He was charming and well loved. His death was a tragedy, especially for Christine, who was forced to return to her mother's house in the village here. She was the daughter of the village schoolmaster when Oscar married her. She did brilliantly for herself. But, alas, it did not last, and now I feel dreadfully sorry for her. It is why I invited her here. She is a dear friend of mine and needs some diversion."

Her name had led Wulfric to realize that she must be a relative of Elrick's, and then when she had explained that she was a widow, he had remembered that Elrick had lost his only brother a few years back. But it would seem that she was not Elrick's dependent but was living with her mother and was forced to rely upon the charity of her friends to invite her to entertainments like this. Oscar Derrick, Wulfric guessed, had either been impoverished to start with, or—more likely—had squandered his fortune. His widow did not appear to have private means.

She was dressed far less finely than any of the other ladies. Indeed, when he had first set eyes—or eye—upon her, he had mistaken her for a servant. Her muslin dress was decent enough but not by any means in the first stare of fashion. Neither was she particularly young. She was well into her twenties, at a guess. She had a pretty, wide-eyed, rather round face, which—it had been impossible not to notice—was sun-bronzed. And, if that were not bad enough, there was a dusting of freckles across her nose. Her hair was dark and short and curly.

She looked thoroughly countrified and quite out of place among Lady Renable's guests. But then, she *was* out of place. She had indeed made a brilliant marriage, but she was in fact a *schoolmaster's* daughter—and a markedly impertinent one too. It was too bad for her that Derrick had been inconsiderate enough to die young.

Mrs. Derrick, Wulfric decided, was definitely not a lady whose acquaintance he would pursue during the coming two weeks. But then, the same might be said of almost every other lady guest too. He was beginning to realize how colossal a mistake he had made in so impulsively accepting an invitation that had been made verbally and at second hand—and via the notoriously vague Lord Mowbury.

Lady Sarah Buchan, though she had been introduced to him not half an hour since, was making him a deep curtsy again.

"I *must* ask you, your grace," she said, gazing at him with huge brown eyes, her cheeks still flushed with color, "which morning activity you prefer—riding or walking. I have a wager with Miriam Dunstan-Lutt, even though I know it is not at all the thing for ladies to wager." She tittered.

He had not been on the marriage mart for a long time, and ladies of all ages as well as their mamas had stopped courting him a number of years ago on the correct assumption that he was not to be caught. Nevertheless, though he was out of practice, he could recognize a trap when he encountered one.

"I normally write letters and conduct business in the mornings while my brain is fresh, Lady Sarah," he said curtly, "and do my riding and walking later in the day. Which do *you* prefer?"

He was already bored almost beyond endurance.

Was the chit really *flirting* with him?

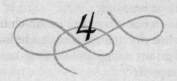

$\mathcal{M}$OST OF THE GUESTS WERE WEARY FROM traveling and used the time between tea and dinner to rest quietly in their rooms. Wulfric took the opportunity to slip outdoors for some fresh air and exercise. He did not know his way about the park, of course, but he instinctively sought out cover so that he would not be seen from the house and thus invite company. He made his way diagonally across a tree-dotted lawn and took a path through denser trees until he came to the bank of a man-made lake, which had clearly been created for maximum visual effect.

It was not very large, but it was secluded and lovely and peaceful—and completely hidden from the house. It was a pleasant day, warm if not hot, with a light breeze. This, he thought, inhaling deeply, was just what he needed— fresh air and a quiet outdoor setting to restore his spirits after the lengthy journey and the crowded drawing room during tea. There were paths leading off through the trees to either side of him, but he stood where he was, undecided whether to take one of the walks or to remain where he was, simply breathing in the summer scents of water and greenery.

He should have gone home to Lindsey Hall.

But he had not, and so there was no point in wishing now that he had made a different decision.

He was still standing there, content for the moment to be idle, when he heard the distinct rustle of footsteps on the path behind him—the path by which he had come. He was annoyed with himself then that he had not moved off sooner. The last thing he wanted was company. But it was too late now. Whichever of the side paths he took, he would be unable to move out of sight before whoever it was emerged onto the bank and saw him.

He turned with barely concealed annoyance.

She was marching along with quite unladylike strides, minus either bonnet or gloves, and her head was turned back over her shoulder as if to see who was coming along behind her. Before Wulfric could either move out of the way or alert her to impending disaster, she had collided with him full-on. He grasped her upper arms too late and found himself with a noseful of soft curls before she jerked back her head with a squeak of alarm and her nose collided with his.

It seemed somehow almost inevitable, he thought with pained resignation—and with the pain of a smarting nose and watering eyes. Some evil angel must have sent her to this house party just to torment him—or to remind him never again to make an impulsive decision.

Her hand flew to her nose—presumably to discover if it was broken or gushing blood or both. Tears welled in her eyes.

"Mrs. Derrick," he said with faint hauteur—though it was too late to discourage her from approaching him.

"Oh, dear," she said, lowering her hand and blinking her eyes, "I am so sorry. How clumsy of me! I was not looking where I was going."

"You might, then," he said, "have walked right into the lake if I had not been standing here."

"But I did not," she said reasonably. "I had a sudden feeling that I was not alone and looked behind me instead of ahead. And, of all people, it had to be you."

"I beg your pardon." He bowed stiffly to her. He might have returned the compliment but did not.

More than ever she looked countrified and without any of the elegance and sophistication he expected of ladies with whom he was obliged to socialize for two weeks. The breeze was ruffling her short curls. The sunlight was making her complexion look more bronzed even than it had appeared in the drawing room. Her teeth looked very white in contrast. Her eyes were as blue as the sky. She was, he conceded grudgingly, really quite startlingly pretty—despite a nose that was reddening by the moment.

"My words *were* ill mannered," she said with a smile. "I did not mean them quite the way they sounded. But first I spilled lemonade over you, then I engaged you in a staring match only because I objected to your eyebrow, and now I have run into you and cracked your nose with my own. I *do* hope I have used up a whole two weeks' worth of clumsiness all within a few hours and can be quite decorous and graceful and really rather boring for the rest of my stay here."

There was not much to be said in response to such a frank speech. But during it she had revealed a great deal about herself, none of which was in any way appealing.

"My choice of path appears to have been serendipitous," he said, turning slightly away from her. "The lake was unexpected, but it is pleasantly situated."

"Oh, yes, indeed," she agreed. "It has always been one of my favorite parts of the park."

"Doubtless," he said, planning his escape, "you came out here to be alone. I have disturbed you."

"Not at all," she said brightly. "Besides, I came out here

to walk. There is a path that winds its way all about the lake. It has been carefully planned to give a variety of sensual pleasures."

Her eyes caught and held his and she grimaced and blushed.

"Sometimes," she added, "I do not choose my words with care."

Sensual pleasures. That was the phrase that must have embarrassed her.

But instead of striking off immediately onto her chosen path, she hesitated a moment, and he realized that he stood in her way. But before he could move, she spoke again.

"Perhaps," she said, "you would care to accompany me?"

He absolutely would not care for any such thing. He could think of no less desirable a way of spending the free hour or so before he must change for dinner.

"Or perhaps," she said with that laughter in her eyes that he had noticed earlier across the drawing room after he had raised his eyebrow and so offended her, "you would not."

It was spoken like a challenge. And really, he thought, there was something mildly fascinating about the woman. She was so very different from any other woman he had ever encountered. And at least there was nothing remotely flirtatious in her manner.

"I would," he said, and stepped aside for her to precede him onto the path that led back in among the trees, though it ran parallel to the bank of the lake. He fell into step beside her, since the person who had designed this walk had had the forethought to make it wide enough for two persons to walk comfortably abreast.

They did not talk for a while. Although as a gentleman he was adept at making polite conversation, he had never been a proponent of making noise simply for the sake of keeping the silence at bay. If she was content to stroll quietly, then so was he.

"I believe I have you to thank for my invitation to Schofield," she said at last, smiling sidelong at him.

"Indeed?" He looked back at her with raised eyebrows.

"After you had been invited," she said, "Melanie suddenly panicked at the realization that she was to have one more gentleman than lady on her guest list. She dashed off a letter to Hyacinth Cottage to invite me, and, after I had refused, came in person to beg."

She had just confirmed what he had been beginning to suspect.

"After I had been invited," he repeated. "By Viscount Mowbury. I daresay the invitation did not come from Lady Renable after all, then."

"I would not worry about it if I were you," she said. "Once I had rescued her from impending disaster by agreeing to come after all, she admitted that even if having the Duke of Bewcastle as a guest was not quite such a coup as having the Prince Regent might have been, it was in fact far preferable. She claims—probably quite rightly—that she will be the envy of every other hostess in England."

He continued to look at her. Then an evil angel really *had* been at work. She was here only because he was—and *he* was here only because he had acted quite out of character.

"You did not *wish* to accept your invitation?" he asked her.

"I did not." She had been swinging her arms in quite unladylike fashion, but now she clasped them behind her back.

"Because you were offended at being omitted from the original guest list?" She was normally treated as a poor relation and largely ignored, then, was she?

"Because, strange as it may seem, I did not want to come," she told him.

"Perhaps," he suggested, "you feel out of your depth in superior company, Mrs. Derrick."

"I would question your definition of *superior*," she said. "But in essence you are quite right."

"And yet," he said, "you were married to a brother of Viscount Elrick."

"And so I was," she said cheerfully.

But she did not pursue that line of conversation. They had emerged from among the trees and were at the foot of a grassy hill dotted with daisies and buttercups.

"Is this not a lovely hill?" she asked him, probably rhetorically. "You see? It takes us above the treetops and gives us a clear view of the village and the farms for miles around. The countryside is like a checkered blanket. Who would ever choose town life over this?"

She did not wait for him or mince her way up the rather steep slope. She strode up ahead of him to the very top of the hill, though they might have skirted around its base, and stood there, spreading her arms to the sides and twirling once about, her face lifted to the sunlight. The breeze, which was more like a wind up there, whipped at her hair and her dress and set the ribbons that tied the latter at the waist streaming outward.

She looked like a woodland nymph, and yet it seemed to him that her movements and gestures were quite uncontrived and unselfconscious. What might have been coquetry in another woman was sheer exuberant delight in her. He had the strange feeling of having stepped—unwillingly—into an alien world.

"Who indeed?" he said.

Mrs. Derrick stopped to regard him.

"Do *you* prefer the countryside?" she asked.

"I do," he said, climbing until he was beside her and turning slowly about in order to see the full panorama of the surrounding countryside.

"Why do you spend so much time in town, then?" she asked.

"I am a member of the House of Lords," he told her. "It is my duty to attend whenever it is in session."

He was looking down at the village.

"The church is pretty, is it not?" she said. "The spire was rebuilt twenty years ago after the old one was blown off in a storm. I can remember both the storm and the rebuilding. This spire is twenty feet higher than the old one."

"That is the vicarage next to it?" he asked.

"Yes," she said. "We practically grew up there, my two sisters and I, with the old vicar and his wife. They were kind and hospitable people. Their two daughters were our particular friends, and so was their son, Charles, to a lesser degree. He was one boy among five girls, poor lad. We all went to the village school together, girls as well as boys. Fortunately my father, who taught us, was not of the persuasion that girls have nothing but fluff to keep their ears from collapsing in on each other. Louisa and Catherine both married young and now live some distance away. But after the old vicar and his wife died, within two months of each other, Charles, who had been a curate twenty miles from here, was given the living himself and married Hazel—the middle sister of my family."

"Your eldest sister is married too?" he asked.

"Eleanor?" She shook her head. "She announced when she was twelve years old that she intended remaining at home after she grew up to be a comfort to Mama and Papa in their old age. She did fall in love once, but he died at the Battle of Talavera before they married, and after that she would not look at any other man. After our father died she repeated what she had always said as a girl, though now, of course, it is only our mother she needs to comfort. I believe she is happy."

Yes, he thought, she really was from a different

world—the world of the lower gentry. She had indeed made a brilliant marriage.

She stretched out one arm and moved a step closer to him so that he would be able to see just what it was she pointed at.

"There is Hyacinth Cottage," she said. "It is where we live. I have always thought it picturesque. There was a moment of anxiety after my father died, since the lease was in his name alone. But Bertie—Baron Renable—was kind enough to lease it to Mama and Eleanor for the rest of their lives."

"On the assumption," he said, "that you will not outlive the two of them?"

She returned her arm to her side. "I was still married to Oscar at the time," she said. "His death was not pre-dictable, but even if it had been, Bertie would have as-sumed, I suppose, that I would remain with his family."

"But you did not?" he asked her.

"No."

He looked at Hyacinth Cottage in the middle distance. It looked a pretty enough home, with its thatched roof and sizable garden. It looked like one of the larger houses in the village, as befitted the home of a gentleman by birth, even if he had also been the schoolmaster.

Mrs. Derrick, standing quietly beside him, chuckled softly.

Wulfric turned his head to look at her.

"I have done something to amuse you again, Mrs. Derrick?" he asked.

"Not really." She smiled at him. "But it has struck me how like a doll's house Hyacinth Cottage looks from up here. It would probably fit into one corner of the drawing room at wherever you live."

"Lindsey Hall?" he said. "I doubt it. I perceive that there

are four bedrooms upstairs and as many rooms down-stairs."

"Perhaps the corner of your *ballroom*, then," she said.

"Perhaps," he agreed, though he doubted it. It *was* an amusing image, though.

"If we follow the path right around the lake at this pace," she said, "we may arrive back at the house in time to scrounge a biscuit or two with our late-evening tea."

"Then we will move on," he said.

"Perhaps," she said, "you did not intend to walk so far. Perhaps you would prefer to return the way we have come while I continue on my way."

There it was—his cue to escape. Why he did not take it, he had no idea. Perhaps it was that he was unaccustomed to being dismissed.

"Are you by any chance, Mrs. Derrick," he asked, grasping the handle of his quizzing glass and raising it all the way to his eye to regard her through it—simply because he knew the gesture would annoy her, "trying to be rid of me?"

But she laughed instead.

"I merely thought," she said, "that perhaps you are ac-customed to riding everywhere or being conveyed by car-riage. I would not wish to be responsible for blisters on your feet."

"Or for my missing my dinner?" He lowered his glass and let it swing free on its ribbon. "You are kind, ma'am, but I will not hold you responsible for either possible di-saster."

With one hand he indicated the path down the other side of the hill. For a short distance, he could see, the path then followed the bank of the lake before disappearing among the trees again.

She asked questions as they walked. She asked him about Lindsey Hall in Hampshire and about his other estates. She seemed particularly interested in his Welsh property on a remote peninsula close to the sea. She asked about his brothers and sisters, and then, when she knew they were all married, about their spouses and children. He talked more about himself than he could remember doing in a long while.

When they emerged from the trees again, they were close to a pretty, humpbacked stone bridge across a stream that flowed rather swiftly between steep banks on its way to feed the lake. Sunshine gleamed off the water as they stood at the center of the bridge and Mrs. Derrick leaned her arms on the stone parapet. Birds were singing. It was really quite an idyllic scene.

"It was just here," she said, her voice suddenly dreamy, "that Oscar kissed me for the first time and asked me to marry him. So much water has passed beneath the bridge since that evening—in more ways than one."

Wulfric did not comment. He hoped she was not about to pour out a lot of sentimental drivel about that romance and the gravity of her loss. But when she turned her head to look at him, she did so rather sharply, and she was blushing. He guessed that she had forgotten herself for a moment—and he was delighted that she had recollected herself so soon.

"Do you *love* Lindsey Hall and your other estates?" she asked him.

Only a woman—a sentimental woman—could ask such a question.

"*Love* is perhaps an extravagant word to use of stone and mortar and the land, Mrs. Derrick," he said. "I see that they are well administered. I attend to my responsibilities for all who draw a living from my properties. I spend as much time as I can in the country."

"And do you love your brothers and sisters?" she asked. He raised his eyebrows.

"*Love*," he said. "It is a word used by women, Mrs. Derrick, and in my experience encompasses such a wide range of emotions that it is virtually useless in conveying meaning. Women love their husbands, their children, their lapdogs, and the newest gewgaw they have purchased. They love walks in the park and the newest novel borrowed from the subscription library and babies and sunshine and roses. I did my duty by my brothers and sisters and saw them all well and contentedly married. I write to each of them once a month. I would, I suppose, die for any one of them if such a noble and ostentatious sacrifice were ever called for. Is that love? I leave it to you to decide."

She gazed at him for a while without speaking.

"You choose to speak of women's sensibilities with scorn," she said then. "Yes, we feel love for all the things you mentioned and more. I would not want to live, I believe, if my life were not filled with love of almost everything and everyone that is involved in it with me. It is not an emotion to inspire contempt. It is an attitude to life directly opposed, perhaps, to that attitude which sees life only as a series of duties to be performed or burdens to be borne. And of course the word *love* has many shades of meaning, as do many, many of the words in our living, breathing language. But though we may speak of loving roses and of loving children, our minds and sensibilities clearly understand that the emotion is not the same at all. We feel a delighted stirring of the senses at the sight of a perfect rose. We feel a deep stirring of the heart at the sight of a child who is our own or closely connected to us by family ties. I will not be made ashamed of the tenderness I feel for my sisters and for my niece and nephews."

He had the distinct feeling that he was being dealt a sharp setdown. But as with many people who argued more from emotion than from reason, she had twisted his words. He directed one of his coolest looks at her.

"You will forgive me if I have forgotten," he said, "but did I say or imply that you *ought* to be ashamed, Mrs. Derrick?"

Most ladies would have looked suitably chastised. Not Mrs. Derrick.

"Yes," she said firmly. "You *did* imply it. You implied that women are shallow and pretend to love when they do not know the meaning of the word—when, indeed, there *is* no meaning to the word."

"Ah," he said softly, more annoyed than he normally allowed himself to be. "Then perhaps you *will* forgive me, ma'am."

He moved back from the parapet and they walked on, in silence now, back among trees, though there was a clear view of the lake, which they circled about in order to return to their starting point. She set a brisk pace back to the house from there.

"Well," she said, smiling brightly at him when they stepped inside the hall, breaking the lengthy silence in which they had completed their walk, "I must hurry if I am not to be late for dinner."

He bowed to her and let her run—yes, *run*—up the stairs and disappear from sight before making his way to his own room. He was surprised to discover when he arrived there that he had been out for well over an hour. It had not seemed so long. It *ought* to have done. He did not usually enjoy the company of anyone whom he had not chosen with care—and that included all strangers.

THE DUKE OF Bewcastle did not, Christine was relieved to find, feel obliged to escort her up to her box of a room. Doubtless he was sagging with relief that he had survived such a tedious hour, she thought as she ran lightly up the stairs, forgetting all of Hermione's teaching about running being an ungenteel way of moving from one place to another.

She hurried along to her room. It would not take her long to dress for dinner, but she had left herself precious little time.

She could scarcely believe what she had just done. She had allowed herself to be goaded by a couple of silly girls, that was what. She had dashed out of the house after tea in order to steal some quiet time alone, she had run headlong into the Duke of Bewcastle—*ghastly* moment—and then, just when she had been about to scurry away from him, she had conceived the grand idea of winning the wager right there and then, almost before it had been made. *Just* to prove to herself that she could do it. Right from the first moment she had had no intention of dashing back to the house after the hour was over to claim her prize. She did not need the prize or the envy of her fellow-conspirators. It was just that she was at the nasty age of twenty-nine, and all the young ladies, almost without exception, had looked on her with pity and scorn as if she were positively *ancient*.

She still could not quite believe she had done it—and that he had agreed to accompany her. *And* that, even on the hill, when she had been assaulted by conscience and had given him a decent chance to escape, he had chosen to continue on the way with her.

She was enormously glad the hour was over. A more toplofty, chilling man she had never known. He had talked of Lindsey Hall and his other properties, and he had talked of his brothers and sisters and nephews and nieces without a single glimmer of emotion. And then he had spoken scathingly of love when she had asked him about it.

If the full truth were told, she would have to admit that

she did find him fascinating in a shivery sort of way. And he did have a splendid profile—and a physique that more than matched it. He ought to be cast in marble or bronze, she thought, and set atop a lofty column at the end of some avenue in the park at his principal seat so that future generations of Bedwyns could gaze at him in admiration and awe.

The Duke of Bewcastle was a handsome man and easy on the eyes.

She stopped suddenly in the middle of her small room and frowned. No, that was not his appeal. Oscar had been a handsome man—quite breathtakingly so, in fact. It was his looks that had bowled her right off her feet and right out of her senses. She had been a typically foolish girl nine years ago. Looks had been everything. One glance at him and she had been head over ears in love. Only his looks had mattered. She had been quite unawakened to any other appeal he might or might not have had.

But she was older now. She was awakened, knowledgeable. She was a mature woman.

The Duke of Bewcastle was definitely handsome in his cold, austere way. But he had something else beyond that.

He was sexually appealing.

The very thought, verbalized in her mind, set her breasts to tightening uncomfortably and her inner passage and thighs to aching.

How very embarrassing.

And alarming.

He was a dangerous man indeed, though not perhaps in any obvious way. He had not exactly tried to have his wicked way with her out there in the woods, after all, had he? The very thought was ludicrous. He had not even tried to charm her—even more ridiculous. He had not even cracked a smile the whole time.

But, even so, every cell in her body had pulsed with sexual awareness while she had walked with him.

She must have windmills in her head, she thought, giving herself a firm mental shake as she sat down before her dressing table mirror, to be feeling a sexual attraction to the Duke of Bewcastle, who could be placed bodily atop that lofty column at the end of that avenue in the park at Lindsey Hall and passed off as a marble statue without anyone's ever knowing any different.

And then she slapped a hand over her mouth to muffle a shriek. Windmills *in* her head? She looked very much as if windmills had been busy *on* her head. Her hair was in a wild, tangled bush about her head. And her cheeks were like two shiny, rosy red apples after being exposed to the wind. Her nose was as bright as a cherry.

Heavenly days! The man must be made of marble, all funning aside, if he had been able to look at her like this without breaking out into great guffaws of mirth.

While her cells had been merrily pulsing away with sexual attraction, his must have been cringing with distaste.

Mortified—and far too late—she grabbed her brush.

BY THE TIME Christine went to bed that first night, she felt a great deal better about the house party than she had before it began and until just after tea. She had not wanted to come in the first place, and of course it had begun disastrously. But her success in luring the Duke of Bewcastle into spending an hour with her had amused her and lifted her spirits, even if she *had* decided not to share her triumph with the other ladies.

She *did* share it with Justin, however, when she sat with him in the drawing room after dinner while the tea tray was still in the room. She told him about the whole absurd wager and about the ease with which she had won it, though no one else would ever know.

"Of course," she explained, "it was not an *easy* hour. I can understand why the Duke of Bewcastle has such a reputation for coldness. He did not *once* smile, Justin, and when I told him that I had been invited here only after Melanie had been cast into hysterics by Hector's inviting *him*, he neither laughed nor looked chagrined."

"Chagrined?" he said. "Bewcastle? I doubt he knows what the word means, Chrissie. He probably thinks it is his divine right to attend any house party that takes his fancy."

"Though I cannot imagine that many parties do," she said. "Take his fancy, that is. But we must not be nasty, must we? I am very glad that I *have* won that foolish wager to my satisfaction. Now I can happily avoid the man for the next thirteen days."

"His loss, my gain," Justin said, grinning at her. "I would love to have seen his face when you crashed into him."

But there was something else that had made Christine more cheerful by the end of the evening. She had faced something she had been dreading for two years—the moment when she must come face-to-face with Hermione and Basil again—and she had survived it. And, having done so, she had realized that there was really nothing else to fear and nothing else to inhibit her from being herself.

She had come here to Schofield determined to blend into the background, to be an observer rather than a participant, to avoid all incidents and encounters that might make her the subject of gossip. She had come here, in fact, determined to behave as she had tried to behave during the last few years of her marriage before Oscar died. It had never worked then, much as she had tried, and it had not worked now during the first few hours of the party.

She was glad her plan had failed so soon.

For her failure had made her ask the question—*why* would she behave in a manner that went so much against her nature? If the villagers knew that Christine Derrick was planning to spend two weeks at a house party sitting in a corner observing the activity around her, they would surely collapse in a heap of mirth—if they believed such an apparent bouncer.

Why should she behave so—or try to behave so—just because her brother- and sister-in-law were at the party too? They believed the worst of her anyway. They still hated her—that had been clear since the afternoon. But she was free of them now and had been for two years. Oscar was long dead.

She could be herself again.

It was a wonderfully freeing thought, even if the memories of Oscar—brought alive again with particular poignancy out at the stone bridge by the lake—and the sight of Hermione and Basil had caused a certain tight soreness of grief in her chest.

She *would* be herself.

And so she spent the rest of the evening playing charades even though at first she was not chosen for either team on the assumption, she supposed, that she was to be identified with the older generation. She was picked finally only because one team was one player short and Penelope Chisholm refused to fill the place, declaring that she was so poor at the game that soon every member of her team would be begging her to resign.

Christine was *not* poor at charades. It was, in fact, one of her favorite indoor games. She had always loved the challenge of acting out an idea without words and of guessing the meaning of someone else's efforts. She threw herself into the game with unbridled enthusiasm, and was soon flushed and laughing and everyone's favorite—among her own team members, anyway.

Her team won handily. Rowena Siddings and Audrey, infected by her enthusiasm, soon elevated the quality of their own performances, though Harriet King, who was quite hopeless at the game, pretended to be bored and to consider the whole thing quite beneath her dignity. Mr. George Buchan and Sir Wendell Snapes were soon looking upon Christine with admiration as well as approval. So were the Earl of Kitredge and Sir Clive Chisholm, who were watching from the sidelines and calling out encouragement.

The Duke of Bewcastle was also watching, a look of supercilious weariness on his face. But Christine took no notice of him—beyond noticing that expression anyway. He might have a reputation for lowering the temperature of any room that he occupied, but he was not going to chill her spirits.

By the time she went to bed, she was feeling quite reconciled to the idea of simply enjoying herself for the next two weeks and forgetting about all the duties with which she normally filled her days.

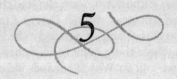

5

MRS. DERRICK, WULFRIC CONCLUDED OVER the next few days, did not know how to behave.

When the company played charades on the first evening, she became flushed and animated and laughed right out instead of tittering delicately as the other ladies did and shouted out guesses without any fear that she might outguess the men. She did not mind making a spectacle of herself when it was her turn to act.

Wulfric, who had not intended subjecting himself to the tedium of watching the game, found that he could not take his eyes off her. She was the sort of woman who was pretty even in repose, but she was quite extraordinarily lovely when animated. And animation seemed to come naturally to her.

"One cannot help admiring her, can one?" Justin Magnus said with a chuckle, having come up beside Wulfric unannounced. "Of course she does not possess the refinement many members of the *ton* expect of well-bred ladies. She often embarrassed my cousin Oscar, and Elrick and Hermione too. But if you want my opinion, Oscar was fortunate to have her for a wife. I always defended her staunchly and always will. She is a regular out-and-outer—unless one happens to be excessively high in the instep, of course."

Wulfric turned his quizzing glass upon the young man, unsure whether he was being subtly reprimanded for being high in the instep or whether he was being treated as some sort of comrade who was expected to agree that out-and-outers made more desirable companions than ladies with refined manners. Either way he did not appreciate the familiarity with which he was being treated. Despite the fact that Magnus was Mowbury's brother, Wulfric had only the slightest acquaintance with him.

"One would assume," he said in the voice he invariably used to depress pretension, "that you are talking about Mrs. Derrick. *I* was observing the game."

But no true lady had any business being so bright-eyed and vivacious and . . . rumpled when in genteel company. Her short, dark curls bounced about her head when she moved and quickly lost all semblance of refined elegance. The fact that she looked twice as pretty at the end of the game as she had before it began said nothing to the issue at all.

She ought not to have behaved so. If this was the way she had behaved during her marriage, Derrick and the Elricks had had every right to be offended.

She reminded Wulfric a little of his sisters, he was forced to admit, but she lacked the air of breeding that had always saved them from vulgarity. Not that Mrs. Derrick was vulgar exactly. She was just not good *ton*. But then, she was not, by birth, a member of the beau monde at all.

She did conduct herself with more decorum during the next few days, it was true. She spent a great deal of time in company with Justin Magnus, with whom she appeared to enjoy a close friendship. But whenever Wulfric looked directly at her—and it happened far more than it ought—he saw the same intelligence and laughter in her face that he had observed that first afternoon in the drawing room. But never again was she to be found alone in any corner of a room. She was becoming popular with the young people—a strange thing in itself. She was not a young woman. She ought not to be romping with the infantry.

Then there was the afternoon when they were all to go on an excursion to the ruins of a Norman castle some miles away and the carriages had been drawn up on the terrace and they were all out there ready to take their appointed places as directed by Lady Renable—except that it turned out when a head count was made that they were one lady short and thus the plan to pair them neatly for the journey threatened to fall into chaos. It was Mrs. Derrick who was missing—Lady Elrick was the one to point it out, her chilly tone suggesting that they all might have suspected it from the start. It took fifteen minutes of searching, during which time Lady Renable looked as if she might collapse into a fit of the vapors, before Mrs. Derrick put in an appearance.

Actually, she came dashing up from the direction of the lake, two children—a girl and a boy—at her heels, and another in her arms.

"I am so terribly sorry!" she cried gaily as she came, her voice breathless. "We were skipping stones on the water and I forgot the time. I shall be ready to go the moment I have returned your children to the nursery, Melanie."

But Lady Renable put her offspring, of whose very existence Wulfric had been unaware until that moment, firmly into the keeping of a footman, and Mrs. Derrick, looking less than pristine but really very pretty nevertheless, was handed into one of the carriages by Gerard Hilliers, her appointed partner. Within five minutes they were all on their way, and she behaved herself for the rest of the day, though she *did* climb up to the battlements of the castle with the gentlemen when all the other ladies remained in the grassy courtyard admiring the ruins from below—*and* the group of young gentlemen with whom she climbed seemed very merry indeed. It would have been decidedly unseemly if she had been a young girl, but she was not, and she was, moreover, a widow, and so Wulfric conceded that her behavior was not quite improper.

It was only a little irregular—perhaps a little indiscreet. Not quite good *ton*.

And then on the fifth day she went beyond indiscreet. They had had one day of rain and one day of indifferent weather after the expedition to the castle, but at last the sun shone once more. Someone suggested a walk into the village to see the church and take refreshments at the inn, and a sizable number of them set out.

Wulfric went with them. He was interested in old churches. And since he could never seem to deter the very young ladies from hanging upon his coattails, even if only figuratively, he walked deliberately with two of them—Miss King and Miss Beryl Chisholm—and wondered when the world had turned mad. Young ladies—and most older ones too—had been giving him a wide berth for years past, but these two chattered away in a manner that could only be called flirtatious. Mrs. Derrick walked between the Culver twins, Renable's nephews, and took the offered arm of each. There was a great deal of merry conversation and laughter coming from their group, though Wulfric was not close enough to hear anything that was said. She was wearing her usual bonnet—a straw one with a brim made floppy from age, though he had to admit that it looked very becoming on her. She also had a tendency to stride along as if she had energy to spare—and as if she had never heard of ladylike deportment.

They all went first into the church and were given a lengthy tour by the vicar, who was well informed on the history and architecture of the building and was able to answer every question posed to him—most of them by Wulfric himself. Then they all moved out to the churchyard, a picturesque, tranquil area centered about two ancient yew trees. The vicar proceeded to point out some of the more historic gravestones, though several of the young ladies were restless and impatient to move on to the inn. Lady Sarah Buchan even suggested, as she came to stand beside Wulfric, that she was quite sure she would swoon from the heat if she did not remove to somewhere shady within the next few minutes. But her brother called her a silly goose as he drew her arm firmly through his own and pointed out to her that they were standing directly in the shade of one of the yews, besides which it was not *that* hot a day.

Either George Buchan did not possess a subtle bone in his body, Wulfric decided, or he did not recognize flirtation and dalliance when it stared him in the face. Or perhaps he was just too accustomed to thinking of his sister as a child. However it was, Wulfric was grateful to him.

And then, just when they were all arranged about the plot reserved for Renable's ancestors with due reverence for the solemnity of their surroundings, and the vicar was launching into a history lesson, a child's voice intruded.

"Aunt Christine!" it screeched at the top of its lungs, and a young boy came tearing across the churchyard from the direction of the vicarage garden, a ball clutched in one hand, and hurled himself at Mrs. Derrick, who whooped with delight and swung him off his feet and around in a large circle, laughing up at him as she did so.

"Robin," she said, "you have escaped from the garden, have you? Mama will have your hide, and Papa is already frowning at you." She rubbed her nose across his as she lowered him and set him back on the ground. "But what a delightful greeting!"

The vicar was indeed frowning quite thunderously. A lady who must be the vicar's wife—and therefore Mrs. Derrick's sister—was beckoning urgently and quite ineffectually from beside the vicarage, and a young girl and boy, both older than Robin, were hurrying toward the group, clearly with the intention of hauling their youngest brother back home.

But a number of the ladies, who were doubtless bored silly with the graves, exclaimed with delight and admiration over the lad, whose blond curls and chubby cheeks set him closer to infanthood than boyhood. And one of the Culvers snatched the ball from the child's hand and teased him by throwing it to his twin over the boy's head. The second twin threw it back. The child giggled and shrieked as he tried to intercept its passage over his head.

The whole unseemly scene would have been over in a few moments. One of the twins would have given the ball back and ruffled the child's hair. The ladies would have tired of their raptures over the child's prettiness, the vicar would have said something suitably quelling to his youngest offspring, and the brother and sister would have taken an arm each and marched the child back where he belonged.

But Mrs. Derrick forgot herself—again. It appeared that she actually *liked* children and could descend to their level at the slightest provocation. She launched herself into the game, all flopping bonnet brim and fluttering sash ribbons, and caught the ball as it flew over her nephew's head. She was laughing gaily.

"Here, Robin," she called, backing up with a few

running steps, heedless of the fact that she was providing her audience with a shocking glimpse of her ankles, "catch it."

The child missed, of course—his hands met each other with a resounding slap as the ball sailed on through. But he darted after it, caught it up in one hand, and tossed it back to his aunt. Except that, with a child's lack of coordination, he threw the ball straight up . . . and up . . . and . . . It did not come down again. It lodged itself very firmly between a branch of the yew tree and the trunk and stuck there.

The child showed every sign of bursting into tears, his father uttered his name with ominous displeasure, his brother invited him to see what he had done now, his sister called him a clumsy clot, Mrs. Derrick took a step closer to the tree, and Anthony or Ronald Culver—it was virtually impossible to tell them apart—went up it.

Even then the scene might have been over soon—and really it was the fault of both Culvers that it had been prolonged in the first place. But though the one twin rescued the ball with no trouble at all and tossed it down to the ground, he could not so easily rescue himself. Somehow a sturdy twig had lodged itself up the back of his coat, and he was stuck fast.

Ronald—or Anthony—Culver would doubtless have gone to the rescue. But while he wasted precious seconds crowing derisively at his twin's plight, someone else went up to the rescue instead, and it was very apparent that this was not the first tree Mrs. Derrick had climbed in her life.

Wulfric watched with pained resignation as she put her hand right up under Culver's coat and wrestled the twig free. It was a massively vulgar display despite the laughter with which it was enacted—and she had shown a considerable amount of leg on the way up.

Culver swung himself to the ground and turned gallantly to help his rescuer down after him. But she waved him away and sat on the lowest branch to jump down instead.

"I always seem to forget when I climb trees," she said merrily, her bonnet slightly askew, her curls in a riot beneath it, her cheeks flushed, her eyes bright, "that I have to come down again. Here goes!" And she launched herself downward.

She came.

Part of her skirt did not.

There was a loud tearing sound as another offending twig tore it from bosom to hem all down one side.

Wulfric was certainly not the closest to her. He *was*, however, the first to reach her. He stood in front of her to shield her from view and kept his eyes steadily on a level with her face. Afterward, it seemed to him that he might actually have stood *against* her. Certainly he could remember her body heat and the smell of warm sunshine and woman. He shrugged as quickly as he could out of his coat—not an easy matter when it had taken all his valet's considerable strength and ingenuity to get him into it earlier—and held it open against her while she did the best she could to gather the torn sides of her dress together.

He gazed grimly into her eyes. She *laughed* back, though her cheeks were more rosy than her exertions would account for.

"How utterly, spectacularly mortifying," she said. "Do you wonder that I often embarrassed myself before the *ton*, your grace?"

He did not wonder at it at all.

There was a great deal of noise and fuss behind him, Wulfric was aware as he raised his eyebrows but did not deign to reply.

"Christine," the vicar said above the general hubbub, "I would suggest that you remove to the vicarage and allow Hazel to see to you."

"I will do that, Charles, thank you," she said, her eyes all the while laughing into Wulfric's. "I am just not sure it can be done decently." She was clutching the sides of her dress with both hands, though it was obvious that *ten* hands would have been more effective.

"Allow me, ma'am," Wulfric said, wrapping his coat around her to cover her from the waist down and trying at the same time not to touch her and cause her further embarrassment—he assumed that she *was* embarrassed, as she well deserved to be.

But it was no good. It was almost immediately apparent that there was no way she could walk the distance to the vicarage without exposing far more of herself than the ankles and leg she had displayed while in the tree.

"Hold the coat," he instructed her.

As soon as she had done so, he stooped down and swung her up into his arms. Without a word or a glance in anyone else's direction, he strode off toward the vicarage with her, wondering how on earth he had got himself into such an uncharacteristically ridiculous situation. A path opened for him—but that at least was not an unusual occurrence.

He was feeling decidedly out of charity with the world, especially the part of it he carried in his arms.

The children were cavorting along beside them, the little boy excitedly telling his brother and sister what had just happened as though they had not witnessed it for themselves. He did a fair imitation of the sound of tearing muslin.

"Oh, dear," Mrs. Derrick said, "I must be very heavy."

"Not at all, ma'am," Wulfric assured her.

"You look downright morose," she said. "I suppose you have servants who usually do things like this for you."

"Ladies do not usually jump out of trees, tearing their dresses to ribbons in the process, in the vicinity of either me or my servants," he said.

That silenced her.

They were at the vicarage a minute later. Her sister had had the presence of mind to possess herself of a large white tablecloth, which she wrapped about Mrs. Derrick as soon as he set her down on her feet in the kitchen inside the back door. A cook or housekeeper blessed her soul and returned her attention to whatever she was cooking over the fire.

"There goes my second-best muslin, Hazel," Mrs. Derrick said. "I *will* mourn it. It was my favorite, and it was only three years old. Now my third-best will have to be promoted and my fourth-best will become third and last."

"Perhaps it can be mended," her sister said with more optimism than sense. "But in the meanwhile Marianne will run along to Hyacinth Cottage to fetch you a clean dress to wear back to Schofield. All of mine will be far too large for you. Marianne, go and ask Grandmama or Aunt Eleanor to send something, will you? In the meantime do come upstairs, Christine."

It was then that Mrs. Derrick remembered that she had not presented him and rectified her error.

"This is the Duke of Bewcastle, Hazel," she said. "My sister, Mrs. Lofter, your grace. And I suppose I ought to have asked you first if you wished for the introduction, ought I not? But it is too late now."

Wulfric bowed and Mrs. Lofter, looking suddenly terrified, fluttered into an awkward curtsy.

"You would probably like to be on your way to the inn with the others," Mrs. Derrick said to him, wriggling about inside the tablecloth and bringing out his coat to hand to him. "Please do not feel obliged to wait for me."

"I will do so, nevertheless, ma'am," he said with a stiff inclination of his head. "I will wait outside and then escort you to the inn."

Though why he had made that decision he did not know since she had lived most of her life in this village and could doubtless find her way to the inn blindfolded. He waited for all of half an hour, first struggling into his coat as best he could without the services of his valet, and then making desultory conversation with the vicar while the older boy galloped around the garden with the younger one on his back.

When she came outside, Mrs. Derrick was wearing a pale blue dress that looked, closer to the seams, as if it might have been royal blue when it was new. There was a skillfully done but still quite noticeable patch close to the hem, perhaps denoting the fact that this dress too had once been the victim of an accident. Her curls had been freshly brushed and her bonnet put on straight. Her cheeks were rosy and shining, as if she had just doused her face in water.

"Oh, dear," she said, looking at him, "you *did* wait."

He made her a curt bow. How, he wondered, did such a shabby creature contrive to look not only remarkably pretty but also vibrant with life?

She turned and poked her head back into the kitchen.

"I am on my way," she called. "Thank you for sending up water and soap, Mrs. Mitchell. You are a dear."

Was she talking to the *servant*?

Her sister came outside and the two of them hugged each other. Then the children came running up and had to be hugged in their turn, though the older boy held out his right hand self-consciously instead and she shook it, laughing as she did so. She shook hands with the vicar and pecked him on the cheek. And then they all—every one of them—trooped around the house to the front garden in order to wave her on her way to the inn, which was all of a two-minute stroll distant.

It was a remarkable display.

"I never know quite how I manage to get myself into such ghastly scrapes," Mrs. Derrick said, having taken the arm he offered. "But I do. I always have. Hermione, who tried to make me into a perfect lady after my marriage, despaired of me. Oscar came to believe that I did it deliberately just to shame him. But I was always quite innocent."

Wulfric did not comment.

"Of course," she said, "if I had waited I daresay Anthony Culver would have gone up the tree to the rescue. Do you think?"

"I do indeed think, ma'am," he said curtly.

She laughed then. "Well, at least," she said, "none of Melanie and Bertie's guests will forget me in a hurry."

"I daresay, ma'am," he agreed, "they will not."

They entered the inn then, and she was soon surrounded by a group that included Justin Magnus and his young sister and the Culver twins. They all hailed her as some sort of heroine, albeit a rather comic one. There was a great deal of laughter within their group. And she laughed right along with them. At least, Wulfric conceded, she was a good sport.

But no, he decided when that interminable morning was finally over, Mrs. Derrick simply did not know how to behave. And if she was to be believed—and he had previous evidence that she spoke the truth—the disaster of the yew tree was not even entirely unusual with her.

He would be very careful to keep his distance from her for what remained of the house party.

And yet, while all the other young ladies quickly

became almost indistinguishable from one another in his mind, it was of Mrs. Derrick that he found himself thinking altogether too much. She had fine eyes and a pretty, good-humored face—even if it *was* somewhat marred by sun bronzing and freckles—that could turn to dazzling beauty when she laughed or was engaged in some strenuous activity. She had trim ankles and shapely legs and a nicely rounded figure.

And he was not by any means the only one who noticed. She quickly became a favorite with most of the other gentlemen. It was hard to explain her appeal, since she was neither elegant nor refined—nor young.

But there was that sparkle about her, that sense of fun, that bright vitality, that . . .

She was sexually appealing.

She was also, he understood, as poor as the proverbial church mouse. He had learned from a casual question posed to Mowbury that her husband had dissipated his fortune during the last few years of his life with excessive gambling and had left his widow quite destitute when he died in a hunting accident on Elrick's estate. Elrick had apparently taken care of his considerable debts but not of her. And her *second-best* day dress—the one that had been ripped beyond repair—had been *only* three years old. She had very few others.

It did not amuse Wulfric to discover himself drawn to a woman who had *none* of the attributes he found admirable in women. It positively disturbed him to find himself wondering what it would be like to bed her. He was not in the habit of looking upon ladies—or any woman, for that matter—with lascivious intent.

But he was drawn to Mrs. Derrick.

And he *did* wonder.

* * *

CHRISTINE WALKED BACK to Schofield with Justin on the day of the disaster in the churchyard.

"You had to wait an awfully long time at the inn," she said. "But I am *so* thankful that you did, Justin. Was it your idea? If you had not waited, I would have had to walk all the way back with the Duke of Bewcastle."

"I thought perhaps you would be looking on him as a kind of knight in shining armor," he said with an amused grin.

"I have never been more mortified," she told him. "If only he had stayed at the house and not been a witness to that horrible display, it would not have seemed nearly as bad. He did not crack a single smile, Justin, or utter one sympathetic word. I do not mind being laughed at under such circumstances—I would laugh if it were someone else, and indeed I cannot help but laugh at myself. But though he did all that was correct and gentlemanly, and I was and am extremely grateful for the speed with which he acted, he looked downright morose and made me feel three inches high. It is a pity I did not actually shrink to that size. I might have wrapped my tattered dress about me and slunk off to the vicarage in good order, most of my dignity intact."

"If you could just have seen yourself, Chrissie." He snorted with suppressed mirth.

"I have a lamentably vivid imagination, thank you very much," she said, and dissolved into laughter again herself.

But, goodness, she thought—oh, gracious goodness, when he had stood against her and gazed grimly into her eyes while shielding her half-naked form from the goggling eyes of their fellow guests, she had fairly sizzled with awareness even though fortunately she had been able to cover up her reactions with embarrassment over her appearance and futile attempts to make herself decent. She had been able to *smell* him. He wore some musky and doubtless expensive cologne. And she had felt his body heat like a raging furnace.

It was a good thing Justin had not guessed *those* feelings. Some things were best kept from even one's closest friends. It was not rational—it certainly was not admirable—to pant with awareness over a man whom one disliked really quite intensely.

She would have liked to escape to her little box room for a while after they returned to the house. Indeed, she would have been perfectly content to be swallowed whole and permanently into an abyss there if only the room had sported such a convenience. But the young ladies who had participated in the walk and witnessed her humiliation were not going to allow her to escape so easily.

"I would not have made such a spectacle of *myself* for all the wagers in the world," Lady Sarah said disdainfully after summoning Christine into the primrose sitting room with all the others.

"And if you think you have now *won*, Mrs. Derrick," Miriam Dunstan-Lutt said resentfully, "then I beg to disagree. Only fifty minutes passed between our arrival at the inn and yours with the Duke of Bewcastle—I was particularly watching the clock over the doorway. Besides, you were with the vicar and his wife and children for most of that time and not alone with the duke at all."

That wretched wager again!

"I am glad I do not have to award you the prize today, Cousin Christine," Audrey added dryly. "No one has yet paid me her guinea."

"One must *sympathize* with Mrs. Derrick, though," Harriet King said, sounding anything but sympathetic. "I suppose the vicar's wife had to pull that dress out of the rag bag."

"But the patch at the hem has been neatly done, Harriet," Lady Sarah observed with honeyed kindness, "and is *almost* unnoticeable."

"One must confess, though," Rowena Siddings said, "that that scene in the churchyard was *priceless*. I have never laughed so hard in my life. If you could just have seen your face when you landed, Mrs. Derrick." She went off into peals of laughter, and all the others, with the noticeable exception of Miss King and Lady Sarah, joined in.

Christine, for lack of anything else to do since she certainly did not choose to engage in any catfight, laughed—yet again. Laughing at one's own expense did begin to pall after a while.

The conversation turned to an animated discussion of how the wager was to be won.

And then the older ladies, none of whom had participated in the walk to the village, learned about the incident—it would have been a miracle of epic proportions if they had not, of course. Lady Mowbury was no problem. She simply invited Christine to sit beside her in the drawing room before dinner and tell her own version of the story—which Christine did with considerable embellishment.

Lady Chisholm and Mrs. King both avoided the subject and stayed away from Christine, as if fearful that what ailed her might be infectious and before they knew it *they* would be leaping from trees and almost leaving their dresses behind.

Hermione sat down on Christine's other side when Lady Mowbury finally turned her attention to someone else, and Basil came to stand in front of her. It was the first time since their arrival at Schofield that they had sought her out or spoken directly to her.

"I suppose," Hermione said in a low, bitter voice, "it

was too much to expect that you would behave with proper decorum for two whole weeks, Christine."

"And the first week is not even at an end yet," Basil pointed out dryly.

"Have you *no* respect for my brother-in-law's memory?" Hermione asked, her voice shaking. "Or for *us*?"

"And you forced Bewcastle of all people to come to your rescue," Basil said. "But I do not know why I was surprised when I heard of the incident."

"Whatever must he *think* of us?" Hermione raised a handkerchief to her lips and looked genuinely distressed.

"I daresay," Christine said, feeling heat flood her cheeks, "he thinks the same of both of you as he thought yesterday and the day before. And I daresay I have sunk lower in his estimation. But since I was undoubtedly very low in it to start with, I do not suppose there was much farther to sink. I will not allow the matter to interfere with my sleep."

Which was about the most ridiculous thing she had said or done all day, of course. She was, in fact, extremely upset. The incident to which they referred had been bad enough, but not sufficient in itself to rob her of appetite or sleep. Her brother- and sister-in-law's continued hostility toward her was another matter, though. They had been kind to her once upon a time. They had liked her. Hermione had even perhaps loved her. She had been fond of them. She had tried very hard to fit into their world, and she had succeeded during the first few years. She had tried to be a good wife to Oscar—she had *loved* him. But then everything had fallen apart, and now they were her bitter and unhappy enemies. They had refused to listen to her after Oscar's death. Or rather, they had listened but refused to believe her.

"I suppose," Hermione said, "you were *flirting* with the

Duke of Bewcastle, Christine. It would be hardly surprising. You are flirting with everyone else."

Christine jumped to her feet and moved away without another word. It was the old accusation! And it hurt as much now as it had ever done. Why was it that other ladies could talk with gentlemen, laugh with them, and dance with them, and be admired for having the correct social accomplishments, while *she* must always be believed to be flirting? She did not even know how to flirt—unless she did it unconsciously. And it would not have occurred to her to flirt during her marriage even if she *had* known how. She had married for love. And even if she had not, she firmly believed that a wife owed her husband total fidelity. It would not occur to her to flirt now that she was free again either. Why should she? If she wished to marry again, there were several eligible prospects among her acquaintances. But she had never wanted to remarry.

How could anyone—even Hermione—think that she would *flirt* with a man like the Duke of Bewcastle?

But before she could hurry from the room and avoid facing everyone at dinner, Melanie linked an arm through hers and smiled fondly at her.

"I know, Christine," she said, "that if there is a child to be entertained, you must entertain it and if there is someone to be rescued, you must do the rescuing even if it means climbing a tree. I was inclined to feel a migraine coming on, I must confess, when I first heard what had happened. But Bertie chose to rumble and then laugh outright when Justin told the tale. Even Hector found it funny, bless his heart, and laughed merrily. And so I followed suit. I could not stop laughing, in fact, and you must not look sideways at me now or I will start again. Only Hermione and Basil refused to see any humor in the situation, the silly things, even though Justin assured us all that you were acting out of the kindness of your heart and were not trying to draw attention to yourself, least of all Bewcastle's. I just wish I could have *seen* it."

"I will crawl off home and lie low for what remains of the two weeks if you wish," Christine offered. "I really *do* beg your pardon, Melanie."

But Melanie squeezed her arm and told her not to be such an idiot.

"Dear Christine," she said, "you must simply relax and *enjoy* yourself. It is why I invited you—so that you would not have to be so busy for a couple of weeks. It was too bad that it had to be the Duke of Bewcastle who was forced to rush to your rescue, but we must not worry about that. He will forget you before the day is out and as like as not will not address another word to you before the party ends."

"That would be a relief at least," Christine said.

"In the meantime," Melanie said, "a number of the other gentlemen are clearly smitten with you, as gentlemen always are, the earl among them."

"The Earl of *Kitredge*?" Christine asked, all amazement.

"Who else?" Melanie said, patting her hand before wafting off on some other hostessing duty. "His children are grown and he is looking about him for a new wife. I daresay you could make another brilliant marriage if you chose. Just promise me that you will climb no more trees before the party is over."

Another brilliant marriage. The very thought was enough to give Christine nightmares.

But it seemed that Melanie was right about one thing. For the rest of that day and the next few the Duke of Bewcastle avoided all contact with her—not that she made any concerted effort to put herself in his way, of course.

The very idea that he or other members of the party might think that she had been *flirting* with him . . .

Whenever she looked at him—and annoyingly she could not keep her eyes off him for more than five minutes at a time when they were in the same room—he looked haughty and coldly dignified. If ever she caught his eye—and it happened altogether too frequently—he lofted one eyebrow or both and grasped the handle of his quizzing glass as if he were about to verify the amazing fact that such a lowly mortal really had dared lift her eyes to his.

She had come to hate that quizzing glass. She amused herself with mental images of what she would do with it if given the chance. Once she visualized herself ramming it down his throat and watching it swelling the sides of his neck on its way down. She was sitting in a corner of the drawing room at the time in an attempt to resurrect her short-lived role as satirical spectator, and he caught her eye just as her imagination had reached the most graphic part. Suddenly she found herself being viewed for a brief moment through the lens of his glass.

She really was terribly attracted to him, she was forced to admit to herself on occasion.

She felt a dreadful curiosity to know what it would be like to go to bed with him.

The very thought filled her with horror. But in parts of her person over which thought held no sway—the lower portion of her insides, for example—there were unmistakable stirrings of unbridled lust.

She disliked the Duke of Bewcastle quite intensely. More, she despised him and all he stood for. She was also a little—a very little—afraid of him, if the truth were known, though she would endure being stretched to twice her height on the rack before admitting such a lowering fact to any other mortal.

And yet she wondered what it would be like to go to bed with him, and sometimes went even a little beyond just wondering.

Sometimes, it seemed to her, she needed very badly to have her head examined.

$\mathcal{I}$T DID NOT TAKE WULFRIC MANY DAYS TO realize that the young lady guests must have some sort of contest in progress that concerned him. He was not the sort of man who attracted young girls, despite the fact that he was one of England's most eligible bachelors. Yet they all fawned over him almost every weary, mortal minute of the day and used every ruse imaginable to draw him apart from the crowd.

He was not amused.

He resisted by adopting a frostier than usual manner when in the ladies' company and by associating as much as he could with the gentlemen and the older guests. Since there was nothing he could do now about avoiding this particular party, he decided that he would use it as an object lesson. For a few foolish days at the end of the session and the Season he had allowed himself to feel a touch of loneliness and self-pity, and this was the consequence. He would not let it happen again.

He had always been alone in all essential ways—since the age of twelve, anyway, when he had been virtually separated from his brothers and put directly under the care of two tutors and closely supervised by his father, who had known that his death was imminent and who had consequently wanted his eldest son and heir to be properly prepared to succeed him. He had been alone since the age of seventeen, when his father had died and he had become the Duke of Bewcastle. He had been alone since the age of twenty-four, when Marianne Bonner rejected him in a particularly humiliating manner. He had been alone since his brothers and sisters had married, all within a two-year span. He had been alone since Rose's death in February.

Aloneness did not equate with loneliness. It did not call for self-pity. It certainly did not call for scrambling to attend every house party that presented itself. Being in company could often be a great deal less tolerable than being alone.

He was feeling more than usually irritated after a lengthy afternoon ride, during which he had twice been lured away from the group, first by Miss King and then by Miss Dunstan-Lutt, on slight, ridiculous pretexts and would—both times—have become hopelessly lost along winding country lanes if he had not possessed a strong sense of direction and an even stronger instinct for self-preservation.

Were they trying to lure him into marriage?

The very idea was preposterous. Even if he was not literally old enough to be their father, he felt as if he were.

Rather than follow everyone else into the house after their return, he made his escape and headed off through the rose arbor and onto the long grassy alley beyond. It was picturesque and secluded, with its knee-high stone walls on either side and behind them long rows of laburnum trees, whose branches had been trained to grow over trellises into a high arch overhead. It was rather like a living, open-air Gothic cathedral.

It was also, on this occasion, occupied. Mrs. Derrick was sitting on the wall on one side, reading what he supposed was a letter.

She had not seen him. He might have withdrawn back through the rose arbor in good order and found somewhere else to walk—unlike that other time out at the lake, when she had collided into him. But he did not withdraw. She might have an unfortunate tendency not to know how to behave on occasion, but at least she was not silly, and she did not simper or flirt.

After he had taken a few steps in her direction, she looked up and saw him.

"Oh," she said.

She was wearing the floppy-brimmed straw bonnet again. Indeed, he had not seen her in any other all week. It was quite unadorned apart from the ribbons that tied beneath her chin. It was inexplicably fetching. She was also wearing a dress of striped green-and-white poplin with lace-trimmed square neck and short sleeves that she had worn several times before—unlike her fellow guests, who changed several times a day and rarely wore the same thing twice. The dress was neither new nor in the first stare of fashion. He wondered if it was her best or the newly promoted second best.

She looked remarkably pretty.

"I will not disturb you, Mrs. Derrick." He inclined his head to her, his hands clasped at his back. "Unless you care to walk with me, that is."

She had looked startled at first. Now she regarded him with that look that always intrigued him as much as it occasionally annoyed him. How could she smile—or rather laugh—when her face remained in repose?

"Have you just returned from the ride?" she asked him. "And were you now attempting to escape the press of humanity? And then found me disturbing your solitude as I did once before? Except that this time I was here before you."

At least, he thought, here was someone who was not

forever throwing herself in his path trying to win whatever contest the very young ladies had concocted among themselves.

"Will you walk with me?" he asked her.

For a few moments he thought she would refuse and was glad of it. Why the devil would he want the company of a woman who, in his opinion, ought not even to have been invited to this house party? But then she looked down at her letter, folded it and put it away in a side pocket of her dress, and got to her feet.

"Yes," she said.

And then he was glad of *that*.

It seemed like an eternity since any woman had stirred his blood. Rose had been gone for all of six months. It constantly surprised him to realize how much he mourned her loss. He had always thought theirs more a satisfactory business arrangement than a personal attachment.

Christine Derrick undoubtedly—and quite inexplicably—stirred his blood. He became instantly more aware of the leafy branches overhead, the blue sky visible beyond, the sunlight making patterns of light and shade on the long grassy alley ahead. He became aware of the heat of the summer day, of the light breeze on his face, of the heavy, verdant fragrances of grass and leaves. The alley was loud with birdsong, though none of the songsters were visible.

She fell into step beside him, the brim of her bonnet hiding her face from his view. She had not worn a bonnet during their lake walk, he remembered.

"Was the ride pleasant?" she asked him. "I suppose you were born in the saddle."

"That might have been a little uncomfortable for my mother," he said, and won for himself a glimpse of her face when she turned her head to smile rather impishly at him. "But, yes, thank you, the ride was pleasant."

He had never, actually, seen the point in riding about

the countryside purely for pleasure, though his brothers and sisters had done it often—if *riding* was the appropriate word for what they had done. More often they had galloped neck or nothing, jumping any obstacle that happened to be in their path.

"It is your turn now," she said after a few moments.

"I beg your pardon?" he asked her.

"I asked a question," she told him, "and you answered it. You might have elaborated for a few minutes, describing the ride and your destination and the stimulating conversation you enjoyed with the others. But you chose to answer with great brevity and no real information at all. Now it is your turn to attempt to make agreeable conversation between us."

She was laughing at him again. Nobody ever laughed at him. He found himself curiously intrigued that she would dare.

"Was your letter pleasant?" he asked.

She laughed out loud, a light, cheerful sound of genuine amusement.

"Touché!" she said. "It was from Eleanor, my eldest sister. She has written to me even though she is only two miles away at Hyacinth Cottage. She is a compulsive and amusing letter-writer. She taught my geography class at the village school two days after I came here and wonders how I can ever teach the children anything when they are so full of questions about any topic under the sun *except* anything related to the subject of the lesson. It was their little trick, of course. Children are very clever and will take full advantage of the novice who does not know any better. I shall scold them roundly when I return, but of course they will all look at me with blank, innocent faces, and I will end up laughing. And then *they* will laugh and poor Eleanor will never be avenged."

"You teach school." It was a comment, not a question, but she turned her head to look up at him again.

"I help out," she said. "I have to do *something*, after all. Women do, you know, if they are not to expire of boredom."

"I wonder," he said, "that you did not remain with Elrick and his wife after your husband died. You would have remained in the social milieu to which you must have grown accustomed and have been offered more in the way of activity and amusement than you can expect here." And as a dependent of Elrick's she would have had some new clothes in the past two years.

"I would, would I not?" she said, but she did not pursue the topic.

It was not the first time she had avoided talking about her marriage or anything connected with it. And he had noticed that the Elricks stayed away from her and she from them. They had not liked her, perhaps. It was probable that they had disapproved of Derrick's marrying her and had not accepted her gladly into the family fold. It would not be surprising.

"I could tell you more about my letter," she continued after a short pause, "but I must not dominate the conversation. Do you spend your summers going from one house party to another? It is the way of the *ton*, I know. Oscar and I did it all the time."

"This is the first I have attended in years," he said. "I usually spend the summers at Lindsey Hall. Sometimes I travel about the country, inspecting some of my other estates."

"It must be strange," she said, "being that wealthy."

He raised his eyebrows at the vulgarity of the comment. Well-bred persons did not talk about money. But it would be strange not to be wealthy. She was evidently poor. It must be strange to be poor. It was all a matter of perspective, he supposed.

"I hope, Mrs. Derrick," he said, "that was not a question."

"No." She chuckled, a low, attractive sound. "I do beg your pardon. It was not a well-mannered observation, was it? Is not this a charming alley? The whole of the park is quite, quite lovely. I once asked Bertie, when I was still married, why he did not open the park to the public so that all the people from the village might enjoy strolling here, at least when the family is from home. But he rumbled and laughed in that way he has, and then looked at me as if he thought I had uttered a great witticism that did not require a verbal response. Does Lindsey Hall have a large park? And your other estates?"

"Yes," he said. "Most of them do."

"And do you allow the public to enjoy any of them?" she asked him.

"Do you allow the public into your garden, Mrs. Derrick?" he asked in reply.

She looked up at him once more. "There *is* a difference," she said.

"Is there?" It was the sort of attitude that irritated him. "One's home and one's garden or park form one's private domain, the place where one can relax and be private, one's own personal space. There is no essential difference between your home and mine."

"Except for size," she said.

"Yes," he agreed.

He resented people who put him on the defensive.

"I believe," she said, "we must agree to disagree, your grace. Otherwise we will come to fisticuffs and I daresay I will get the worst of it. It is a matter of size again."

She was laughing at him once more—and perhaps at herself too. At least she was not one of those disagreeable crusaders who must press her argument to the point of offensiveness, especially if there were any suggestion of aristocratic privilege and injustice to the poor involved. Actually, all his homes except Lindsey Hall were open to any traveler who cared to knock on the door and ask permission of the housekeeper. It was a common courtesy extended by most landowners.

Light and shade played over her form as they walked. She was pleasingly formed, he noticed again. She had a mature woman's body rather than that of a slender girl. He tried to verbalize in his mind what exactly it was about her that was attractive to him. He knew many women who were more beautiful and more elegant—including several of their fellow guests. Certainly her slightly sunbronzed skin and those freckles made it impossible to call her a true beauty. And her hair was short and frequently looked rumpled. But there was that energy about her he had noticed from the start, that vitality. There was a sense of light and joy about her. Certainly she appeared to light up from the inside when she was animated—and she frequently was. It appeared that she loved people—and most people returned the compliment.

But he would not have expected to be attracted to such a woman. His tastes, he would have thought, ran more to quiet refinement and sophistication.

"You did not care to join the ride?" he asked her.

She flashed him a smile. "You ought to be thankful that I did not," she said. "I *can* ride, in the sense that I can scramble onto a horse's back and remain there without falling off—at least, I have never yet fallen. But no matter what horse I am mounted on, even the most docile, I invariably lose the battle for control within a few minutes and find myself on a prancing, sidling course, being led in every possible direction except the one I wish to take or the one everyone else in my party is taking."

Wulfric did not comment. All true ladies were accomplished equestrians. Most were also graceful, elegant riders. He was indeed thankful that Mrs. Derrick had chosen to remain behind this afternoon with her letter.

"I rode in Hyde Park once with Oscar and Hermione and Basil," she said. "But only once, alas. We were riding along a narrow path as a whole host of other riders approached from the opposite direction. Oscar and the others moved obligingly off onto the grass to allow them to pass, but my horse chose to turn sideways, blocking the whole path, and then to stand stock-still. It stood there like a veritable *statue*. My companions were full of apologies to the other group, but all I could do was *laugh*. The scene struck me as enormously funny. Basil explained later that the other riders were all important government officials and the Russian ambassador. They were all good sports about the incident, though, and the ambassador even sent me flowers the next day. But Oscar never invited me to go riding again when we were in London."

Wulfric, looking down at her bonnet, could just imagine the embarrassment of her party. And she had sat there and *laughed*? But the strange thing was that picturing the scene, imagining her sitting helplessly atop her statue of a horse, laughing gaily and attracting the admiration of the Russian ambassador, made *him* want to laugh. He should be feeling disdain. He should be feeling confirmed in his conviction that she did not know how to behave. Instead he wanted to throw back his head and shout with laughter.

He did not do so. He frowned instead and they proceeded on their way.

They were coming to the end of the alley, he realized after a while. They had been walking for the past few minutes in silence. It had not been uncomfortable—at least not to him—but there did seem to be a certain tension in the air about them suddenly, a certain awareness that must surely be mutual.

Was it possible that she was attracted to him as he was to her? She certainly had not gone out of her way to entice him. She did not flirt. She was not a coquette. But was she attracted? Women did not as a whole, he believed, find him attractive. His title and wealth, perhaps, but not *him*. Perhaps she was merely embarrassed by the silence.

"Shall we continue?" he asked her, indicating the upward flight of stone steps at the end of the alley. "Or would you prefer to return to the house? I believe we are in danger of missing tea."

"One eats and drinks far too much at a house party," she said. "There is a rather splendid maze up there. Have you seen it?"

He had not. He could not imagine finding a maze amusing, but he did not want to turn back yet. He wanted to spend a little more time in the aura of her light and vitality and laughter. He wanted to spend more time with *her*.

From the top of the steps he could see a wide, tree-dotted lawn stretching away into the distance. But not far away was the maze she had spoken of, its seven-foot-high hedges carefully clipped to look like green walls.

"I'll race you to the center," she said as they approached it, turning to look at him with a sparkle in her eyes. Actually, she did not just turn her head. She turned her whole body in front of his and kept her distance by taking little backward running steps.

"Indeed?" He raised his eyebrows and stopped walking. "But I daresay you know the way in, Mrs. Derrick."

"I did once upon a time," she admitted. "But it is years since I have done it. You must count slowly to ten before coming after me, and I shall count slowly to ten when I reach the center. If I can count any higher than ten, then I am the winner."

She did not give him a chance to refuse to participate. She whisked herself through the narrow opening in the outer wall of the maze, turned to her right, and disappeared from view.

He stared blankly at the hedge for a moment. He was expected to *frolic* through a maze? And he was going to *do* it? But he did not have much choice, did he, short of leaving her stranded in the center, counting slowly to three thousand or so.

One . . . two . . . three . . .

Would he have refused?

Four . . . five . . . six . . . seven . . .

He *never* played games like this.

Eight . . . nine . . .

He never played any sort of game.

Ten.

He set off grimly into the maze. The hedges, he found, were all neatly clipped. They were also all high enough and thick enough that they afforded no glimpses of the center or of the path farther in. One might wander here, hopelessly lost, for some time, he guessed. Around one corner he thought he spotted her striped skirt, but a white butterfly fluttered across his line of vision instead and soared over the hedge to his left. Around another corner he *did* see her, but with a light laugh she whisked herself out of sight, and by the time he reached the gap through which she had disappeared, it was impossible to know which way she had gone.

There was an air of marked seclusion in here, he discovered, as if the world had been left behind and nothing existed but trees and grass and butterflies and sky—and the woman he pursued.

He took several wrong turns, but eventually he figured out the pattern of the maze. Wherever there was a choice of path, one always took the left-hand one alternating with the right-hand one. It did not take him long after that to reach his destination, though he did not catch up with her on the way.

"Fifteen," she said aloud as he stepped out into the clearing at the center of the maze ten minutes or so after entering it.

There was a stone statue of some Greek goddess in the middle of the clearing, with a wrought-iron seat off to one side. She was leaning back against the statue, a living, vital goddess or nymph, looking flushed and bright-eyed and triumphant. He walked toward her.

"We could sit down and rest if you wish," she said. "But the view is not spectacular."

"No, it is not," he agreed, looking around. "Was there to be a prize? You did not mention it after issuing your challenge."

"Oh," she said, laughing, "the triumph of being the winner is enough."

And then they were stranded within a foot of each other with nothing else to say, it seemed, and nowhere else to look except at each other. The sense of seclusion deepened. Somewhere not far off a bee droned.

The flush of color in her cheeks deepened and her teeth sank into her lower lip.

He possessed himself of one of her hands and held it between them with both his own. It was warm and smooth-skinned.

"I will simply concede defeat, then," he said, and raised it to his lips.

His heart for some reason was pounding hard enough in his chest to make him feel slightly dizzy. Her hand trembled in his own. He held it to his lips far longer than was necessary.

But would even a single second have been necessary? Or wise?

She was gazing at him with wide eyes and slightly parted lips, he saw when he raised his head. She smelled of sunshine and woman again.

He leaned forward and set his lips to hers.

And felt an instant shock of intimacy and desire.

Her lips were warm and soft and inviting. He tasted her, touched her with his tongue, probed the soft flesh behind her lips, breathed in the warmth of her, drugged his senses with the essence of her. He held her hand between them and felt as if some core of ice that had always held his emotions safely imprisoned was dripping warm melted water into his veins.

He did not know if she slipped her hand from his or if he released it. But however it was, her arms twined about his neck, one of his circled her waist, the other her shoulders, and they came together in a close embrace, her soft, warm, shapely body arched in along the length of his.

He teased her mouth wider with his own and pressed his tongue deep inside. She touched it with her own and sucked it deeper.

It was a lengthy, heated embrace. He did not know how long it lasted or what brought it to an end. But it *did* end, and he lifted his head from hers, released his hold on her, and took one step back.

Her eyes, huge and blue as the summer sky, gazed into his, so open and so deep that he might well lose himself in them, he thought. Her lips looked rosy and moist and just-kissed. If ever he had thought that she was not the most incredibly beautiful woman he had ever set eyes upon, then he must surely be blind in both eyes.

"I beg your pardon," he said, clasping his hands behind his back. "I do beg your pardon, ma'am."

She continued to look at him just so.

"I do not know why," she said softly. "I did not say no, did I? Though I suppose I ought to have. And I definitely ought *not* to have challenged you to come into the maze with me. I do not always think before speaking or acting. I am famous for it, in fact—or *notorious,* I suppose I should say. Shall we go back to the house and see if there is any tea left?" She had recovered her poise, it seemed. She smiled brightly—a little too brightly—at him.

"How long has Derrick been dead?" he asked her.

"Oscar?" The smile faded. "Two years."

"You must have been lonely during those two years," he said, "and unhappy at being forced to return to the village of your birth to live with your mother and your spinster sister."

She had ended up no better off than she had been originally. Perhaps worse. She now knew what she missed.

"We all have our own separate destinies to live out," she said, putting her hands behind her to rest against the statue. "Mine is not intolerable."

"But you could do better," he said. "I could offer you better."

He heard his own words as if a stranger spoke them. He certainly had not planned them. And yet he would not unsay them even if he could, he realized. He had himself under control again, but he was still stirred by her.

Their eyes clashed and tangled. There was a lengthy silence, during which he listened to the bee droning away near the hedge and wondered absently if it was the same one as before. Her eyes, he noticed, were more guarded than they had been a minute ago.

"Oh, could you?" she said at last.

"You could be my mistress," he said. "I would set you up with your own home and carriage in London. You would lack for nothing by way of clothes and jewels and money. I would treat you well in every conceivable way."

She continued to stare at him for several silent moments.

"And I could earn all this," she said at last, "by being available to you at all times? By sleeping with you whenever you wished to sleep with me?"

"It would be a position of considerable prestige," he told her, lest she think he might be offering her the life of a common courtesan. "You would be well respected, and you could have as active a social life as you chose."

"Provided," she said, "I did not choose to have you escort me to any *ton* event."

"Of course." He raised his eyebrows.

"Well, that, at least," she said, "would be an enormous relief."

He stood looking at her. He had not mistaken the nature of their kiss, and neither, surely, had she. There had been nothing innocently romantic about it. She was no maiden. She had been married for a number of years. There had been quite open sexual awareness—and hunger—in her embrace. She must know that he was not a man to dally lightly with any woman, no matter what her station in life.

Had he offended her?

Her life would be infinitely better as his mistress than as the village schoolmaster's assistant, who was forced by widowhood and poverty to live with her mother. It would be better in material things. It would also, surely, be better for her sexually. A two-year celibacy was probably as irksome for a woman as it would be for a man. But he could not read her expression as she gazed back at him.

Surely she had not expected a marriage offer?

"A home of my own," she said. "A carriage. Jewels, clothes, money, entertainments. And, best of all, you to bed me regularly. It is an almost overwhelmingly flattering offer. But I really must decline, you know. It has never been my ambition to be a whore."

"There is a world of difference, ma'am, between a whore and a duke's mistress," he said stiffly.

"Is there?" she asked him. "Merely because a whore ruts in a doorway for a penny while the mistress performs between silk sheets for a small fortune? Yet each one sells her body for money. I will not sell *mine,* your grace, though I thank you for your kind offer. I am honored."

Her final words were spoken, of course, with clipped sarcasm. She was very, very angry, he realized, even though she showed no outer signs beyond the tone and the slight trembling in her voice. He was somewhat shaken by the vulgarity of her words.

"I beg your pardon." He made her a stiff bow and gestured with one hand to the opening in the inner wall of the hedge. "Allow me to escort you back to the house."

"I would prefer it if you would remain here and count slowly to ten after I leave," she said. "The charm of your company has worn thin, I am afraid."

He walked around the statue and stood with his back to it until he was sure she had gone. Then he went to sit on the seat.

He had totally misread the signs. She had been willing enough to indulge in a lascivious embrace but not to enter into any prolonged relationship with him—not as his mistress anyway, and that was the only position he was willing to offer. He was sorry about it. She had stirred his blood, and he had felt as if a vast, long winter were approaching the thaw of spring.

He had not expected that she would refuse. She was obviously attracted to him—*that* had not been feigned. And it was a good offer that he had made, considering her social status and financial circumstances. Of course, she had once married a viscount's son, albeit a *younger* son. And so, even though she was now an impoverished widow living with her mother and sister in a country village, she probably expected more of life than to become the mistress of a duke. She might be disappointed that he had not offered more—but that was hardly his concern.

This already tedious house party had just taken a turn for the worse, he thought. He had not needed this. He really had not.

But it was entirely his own fault, of course. His mind had jumped from a mild attraction and a hot embrace to something altogether more serious. Hers had not made a similar leap. It was quite unlike him to speak so impulsively without first thinking through all the implications of any new idea. She was, after all, Elrick's sister-in-law, though neither Elrick nor his wife appeared to have much use for her. And she was the daughter of a gentleman, even if the man had been forced to become a schoolmaster.

It was a very good thing she had refused.

Besides, she was someone of whom he disapproved, was she not?

Wulfric sat very still, staring ahead at the hedge and concentrating upon tucking his emotions neatly back inside that safe ice core.

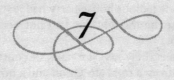

7

CHRISTINE TOOK A NUMBER OF WRONG TURNS before blundering out of the maze and stumbling across the grass and down the steps and half running along the alley, which suddenly seemed to have doubled in length. A couple of times she darted glances back over her shoulder, but he was not coming after her. What did she expect? That he would chase her down and beat her into submission with his quizzing glass?

She slowed down. She had a stitch in her side anyway.

You could be my mistress.

The absurd thing was that when he had told her he could offer her something better than her present life, she had thought he meant *marriage.*

The even more absurd thing—the absolutely *insane* thing—was that for a moment her heart had leapt with gladness. Could anyone be more of an idiot than she was?

Would the *Duke of Bewcastle* want to marry someone like her? More to the point, would *she* want to marry someone like the Duke of Bewcastle?

The answer to both questions was a resounding no.

It was a good thing—a very good thing—that what he had actually offered was something very different.

She stepped into the rose arbor and realized with a start of dismay that someone was sitting there. But it was only Justin, she saw with considerable relief as he got to his feet and came toward her, a smile on his face.

"Oh, you took me by surprise," she said, one hand over her heart.

"Did I?" He tipped his head to one side and looked closely at her. "Has something happened to upset you, Chrissie? Come and sit down and tell me about it."

But she hurried the rest of the distance toward him and took him by the arm. "Not here," she said urgently. "Let's walk out behind the house."

He patted her hand comfortingly as they walked. "I saw you strolling with Bewcastle," he said. "You had told me you were coming out here to read your sister's letter and after I thought I had given you a decent time to enjoy it, I came out to see if you wanted to go for a walk with me. But I was too late—he was here ahead of me. Did he insult you?"

"No, of course not," she said quickly, flashing him a smile.

"This is me, Chrissie," he said. "You cannot easily deceive me, remember? You were dreadfully agitated when you came into the rose arbor. You still are."

Christine drew a deep breath and expelled it audibly. Justin had been her friend for a long time, and he had remained loyal to her through the difficult years and beyond. She would trust him with her life.

"We went into the maze," she said, "and he kissed me. That is all."

"Do I need to call him out," he asked, looking up at her with a rueful smile on his lips, "and give him a lesson in manners?"

"Of course not." She laughed shakily. "I kissed him back. It was nothing really."

"I did not think Bewcastle was into the petticoat line," he said as they made their way out past the paddock behind the stables and the kitchen garden behind the house. "But I will have a word with him if you wish, Chrissie. He has obviously upset you. You are not hoping to be his duchess, are you?"

"Oh, Justin." She laughed again. "He offered something far more lowering. He asked me to be his *mistress*."

It *was* lowering. It was degrading. She had not intended to share her humiliation with anyone, but she had blurted it out anyway.

He stopped and turned toward her, dropping her arm as he did so. He looked unusually grim.

"Did he, by God?" he said, his voice shaking with fury. "Yes, I can believe it. Bewcastle would not stoop to actually *marry* anyone lower on the social scale than a princess, I daresay. But to offer *you* such an insult! It is insufferable. Chrissie, stay away from him. He is not a pleasant character. I do not know anyone who likes him or can even tolerate him. You do not want to be getting yourself mixed up with the likes of him. I am going to—"

"Justin!" She took his arm again and forced him to walk onward. "How very sweet of you to be so angry on my behalf. But I am not *very* angry, you know—only rather shaken, I must confess. Of course I do not want to be his duchess. Who in her right mind would? I do not want to be married at all. I am quite happy with the life I live. I certainly will not put myself in the position of being insulted again. You need not fear for me."

"Sometimes I do, though," he said with a sigh. "You know how fond I am of you. I would even marry you myself if I thought you would have me, but you won't and so I am quite content to be your friend. But don't expect me to stand tamely by while other men insult you."

Christine was touched—and embarrassed. She squeezed his arm.

"I am really all right now," she said. "But I would like a

little quiet and fresh air before going inside. Do you mind, Justin?"

"Never let it be said," he told her, smiling, "that I cannot take a hint. I will see you later."

And that was one thing she had always loved about him, she thought as he walked away. He would be her dearest friend, but he would never press either his time or his attentions on her when she wished to be alone. She was only sorry that in many ways it was a one-sided friendship. He rarely if ever confided in her or shared a great deal of himself with her. But, one day, she thought, that would surely change. One day he would need her friendship, and she would be there to offer it to him.

She felt weary indeed by the time she had climbed the stairs some time later and reached the door of her room—weary and emotionally drained. But she was not going to be allowed to escape even yet, it seemed.

"Mrs. Derrick!" a voice called from behind her, and she looked back to see Harriet King standing in the doorway of her own room, and then Lady Sarah Buchan poked out a blond, ringleted head from beyond her shoulder. "Do come here if you please."

It was more an imperious command than a request, though it might easily have been ignored. But what was the point? There was little privacy to be had at a house party. If she did not go now to find out what they wanted, she would have to hear it later.

"Of course." She smiled as she made her way back to the room—a spacious chamber facing the front of the house. "Did you enjoy the ride?"

All the very young ladies were in Harriet's room— Lady Sarah, Rowena Siddings, Audrey, Miriam Dunstan-Lutt, Beryl and Penelope Chisholm, and of course Harriet herself.

"You are to be congratulated," Harriet said, a sharp edge to her voice.

"I can give you five guineas of your prize money," Audrey told her. "The rest has not been paid in yet. Congratulations, Cousin Christine. I wagered upon you, but I did not expect you to win, I must confess. Or anyone else, for that matter."

"I am so glad that *someone* has won," Rowena said with feeling. "Now I can relax for the second week of the party. Much as I like to win contests, I must confess that the prospect of being in the company of the Duke of Bewcastle for a whole hour has been keeping me awake at night. Congratulations, Mrs. Derrick."

"We *saw* you," Beryl explained. "Penelope and I did. We were just stepping into the rose arbor as the duke was stepping out of it onto the laburnum alley. We were discussing which of us would follow him—or, more to the point, which would *not*—when we saw him stop to talk to you. And then you went off down the alley with him and we spoke to Mr. Magnus for a minute when he too came into the arbor. But you did not come back until now, though we have been watching for you. You have been gone for almost an hour and a half. Well done. We desperately wanted to win, did we not, Pen, but like Rowena, we did not fancy what we would have to do to become the victor."

"I would never have remained alone with a gentleman for an hour and a half for all the money in the world," Sarah said, which was strange really in light of the terms of the wager. "It would be a good way for someone to lose her reputation."

"Assuming that there were one to lose, Sarah," Harriet added pointedly.

They all spoke almost at once, a fact for which Christine was somewhat thankful. They gave her a chance to recover from her initial shock. Had anyone *not* seen her walking with the duke? And why was it that she had not thought of that foolish wager even once while she was with him?

"But you must keep the money, Audrey," she said. "You wagered on me and put in the money yourself. The whole prize is therefore yours. It really has been a rather absurd contest, has it not? But I saw my chance to win it today when the Duke of Bewcastle found me reading a letter in the alley, and I took advantage of it. I chattered away to him for a whole hour while he looked as if he might well expire of boredom, and I am quite sure that *I* would if I had to do it ever again. So, yes, I claim the victory, ladies."

She laughed and looked brightly about at all the group. Most of them, she thought, looked decidedly relieved and quite happy to forfeit their guineas. Of course, two of them were looking angry and disappointed, but both Lady Sarah and Harriet King were spoiled young ladies who did not deserve her sympathy. She had not, after all, been *trying* to win the wager. It was ironic that she had been seen this time, whereas last time, when she had deliberately set out to spend an hour with the duke, there had been no one in sight when they returned to the house together.

"Harriet and Sarah," Audrey said, "you owe me a guinea apiece."

Christine escaped soon after that and finally found refuge in her room. It was probably absurd to tell herself that she had never been more upset in her life, but she felt at that precise moment that it must be true.

You could be my mistress.

She shut her eyes tightly and shook her head.

He had kissed her. And she had kissed him. For a few seconds—or minutes or hours—she had felt a surging of passion more powerful than anything she had ever felt before.

And then he had asked her to be his mistress.
How utterly mortifying!

"CHRISTINE REALLY IS not a flirt," Justin Magnus said to
Wulfric.

Two days had passed since the debacle out at the maze.
Wulfric and Mrs. Derrick had assiduously avoided each
other during that time, though it did not appear to him
that her spirits had been dampened by the experience.
Quite the contrary. She appeared to have the affection of
most of the young ladies and she had won the admiration
of most of the young gentlemen. Kitredge too was quite
noticeably enamored of her. Although she never pushed
herself forward to dominate any of the activities of the
house party, it nevertheless might be said that she was the
life and soul of the party. Wherever the conversation was
brightest and the laughter merriest, there Mrs. Derrick
was sure to be found.

Some people might think her a flirt.

It was very obvious to Wulfric, however, that she was
not. She had a genuinely magnetic appeal. And she genuinely liked people.

"Quite so," he said as chillingly as he could. They were
walking, the whole lot of them, out to the hill by the lake
for what Lady Renable had described as an impromptu
picnic, but which Wulfric suspected was anything but
impromptu. Magnus had attached himself to his side.

"She is not conventionally beautiful or accomplished
or elegant," Magnus continued, "but she *is* attractive. She
does not even know how much, but every man she meets
feels it and is drawn to her. The thing is, though, that most
ladies feel drawn to her too. So it is not flirtation, you see.
It is simply the extraordinary attractiveness of her character. My cousin Oscar fell for her on sight and insisted

upon having her even though he could have had any woman he wanted. He looked like a Greek god."

"How fortunate for him."

They came to the clearing by the lake where Mrs. Derrick had run into him on that first afternoon, and turned in the direction of the hill. Wulfric slowed his steps slightly and hoped the young man would go on ahead, but it appeared he was on a mission. Magnus was Mrs. Derrick's friend, of course. Had he been sent with a message? Or had he taken it upon himself to deliver his own? It annoyed Wulfric that he had put himself in the ridiculous position of having to endure a scold from a stripling.

"And so the fact that Kitredge admires her," Magnus continued, "and that the Culvers do and Hilliers and Snapes does not mean she has deliberately invited their attentions."

"I daresay," Wulfric said, "you intend to explain the relevance of these remarks to me?"

"You admire her too," Magnus said. "And maybe you think that she has been flirting with you. Or maybe you think she has been flirting with all the others and is seriously trying to snare you. You would be wrong either way. It is just her friendly manner, you see. She is the same with everyone. If Oscar had realized that, he would have been far happier. But he wanted all her smiles and all her attentions for himself."

Magnus would have been well advised not to try being his friend's champion, Wulfric thought. Inadvertently, he was giving the impression that Mrs. Derrick was incapable of any deep affection or attachment, even for a husband, and that she was indiscriminately amiable to all and sundry. That, in fact, she *was* a flirt.

"Forgive me," Wulfric said, fingering the handle of his quizzing glass, "but my interest in the happiness or unhappiness of a dead man is really quite minimal. You will excuse me?"

They had reached the hill, and it was instantly clear that the picnic had been well planned in advance. Blankets were spread on the slope facing the lake and a few chairs had been set for the more elderly. Hampers of food and wine lay beside each blanket and within reach of each chair. A couple of servants stood unobtrusively among the trees at the foot of the hill.

Wulfric engaged Renable in conversation and noticed that Mrs. Derrick was at the top of the hill, the ribbons of her bonnet fluttering in the breeze, pointing out various places of interest to Kitredge—as she had done to *him* on that first afternoon. She was laughing at something Kitredge had said.

It bothered Wulfric that she had complained to Magnus. It annoyed him that he was guilty where she was concerned. Until he had kissed her—uninvited—she had not said or done anything to make him think that she would welcome either his advances or his offer. Doubtless he owed her an apology.

He was not usually either impulsive or gauche. He rarely put himself in the wrong or made himself vulnerable to any attack.

It would not happen again. He felt decidedly irritated with Christine Derrick—perhaps because he knew she was in no way to blame.

CHRISTINE HAD LAIN awake through most of the night following the distressing scene in the maze and had almost decided that she would return home in the morning. But pride and a certain stubbornness had come to her rescue. Why *should* she run away simply because the Duke of Bewcastle had offered to make her his mistress?

It did not matter that he would not have dared make such an offer to any other of the lady guests. It simply did not matter.

Why *should* it matter? She disliked and despised him more than ever. She could hardly bear to be in the same room with him—or the same *house,* for that matter. But she would stay, she had decided at last, if for no other reason than that perhaps her continued presence would embarrass him.

And so she had thrown herself into what remained of the house party with a new exuberance and had the satisfaction of knowing that she had won the friendship of several of her fellow guests, both male and female. She could do this, she had decided. She could enjoy herself *and* she could keep well out of the way of the Duke of Bewcastle, who seemed just as intent upon staying out of *her* way.

It was all very satisfactory.

She enjoyed herself at the picnic, pointing out landmarks from the top of the hill to the Earl of Kitredge, who kept her there for some time with his questions, and running down to the lakeshore after tea at the request of a group of the young gentlemen to demonstrate the art of skipping stones over the surface of the water. A few of the ladies came down there too, and a merry time they all had of it, though Christine *did* succeed in getting the hem of her dress wet when she could see perfect stones for throwing on the lake bottom just beyond reach from the bank and insisted upon getting them herself. But since she had had the forethought to remove her shoes and stockings beforehand, no great harm was done.

Sometimes she could convince herself that the past was all over and done with and her youth and naturally high spirits had been restored without any lurking shadows. But the shadows were never far away, even in the brightest light—or perhaps especially then. Subsequent events proved it.

She was one of the last to leave the picnic site, as she had to find a secluded spot in which to pull her stockings back on. She saw that Hermione and Basil were still on the hillside, and then she saw that the Duke of Bewcastle was with them.

"I confess, your grace," Hermione said to him as Christine trudged up toward them, "that Elrick and I have been determined to have a private word with you since the day before yesterday, but it is appropriate that Christine hear what we have to say. We really must apologize on her behalf."

Christine looked blankly at her sister-in-law and stopped where she was, a few feet below them.

"It was extremely foolish of the young ladies to wager upon which of them could engage you in private conversation for a whole hour," Hermione said, her voice actually shaking with some emotion that sounded very like suppressed anger to Christine, "but girls will be girls, and it is understandable that they would wish to impress someone of your rank and consequence. However, it was unpardonably presumptuous of Christine to participate in such a wager and actually to *win* it."

Christine closed her eyes briefly. That wretched wager! But how had Hermione found out about it? From Lady Sarah and Harriet King, no doubt.

Basil cleared his throat. "Lady Elrick and I do not condone such vulgar behavior, I do assure you, Bewcastle," he said.

"It is simply our misfortune that my brother-in-law became enamored of a schoolmaster's daughter and actually married her," Hermione added. "Throughout the house party so far she has done nothing but flirt with every gentleman guest and humiliate us with displays such as this." With one hand she indicated Christine's wet hem. "But that she should involve *you* and flirt with *you* is unpardonable."

Christine could not quite believe the evidence of her own ears as she listened to this outpouring. It was like being catapulted right back into the past. They both spoke with such anger and bitterness—and such injustice. She was too distressed to say anything—or simply to hurry away from there.

The Duke of Bewcastle raised his quizzing glass halfway to his eye. If he used it on her hem or any other part of her person, Christine decided, she would snatch it away from him and break it across his nose—or break his nose with it. But he directed his attention instead on Hermione.

"I beg you not to distress yourself, ma'am," he said, his voice stiff and quite, quite arctic. "Or you, Elrick. Daughters of gentlemen with an academic turn of mind are frequently better educated and therefore more interesting conversationalists than the average young lady of *ton. Was* it a whole hour I spent in Mrs. Derrick's company after inviting her to stroll in the laburnum alley with me? I confess it seemed less than half that time. And *did* I flirt with her by discussing the afternoon ride and the letter from her sister that she was reading when I came upon her? If so, I will beg her pardon and promise to be more circumspect in future."

His glass fell on its black ribbon as he released his hold on it.

He looked, Christine thought, very, very dangerous indeed, and the silence with which his words were greeted suggested that she was not the only one feeling it. He had dealt them a chilling setdown. She might have enjoyed it if she had not been so wretchedly hurt.

"Hermione!" she said softly. She merely looked at Basil,

who had so adored Oscar and yet could treat Oscar's widow so shabbily. But he would not meet her eyes.

She would probably have moved in the next moment and dashed blindly away from there if the Duke of Bewcastle had not turned his attention on her.

"Allow me to escort you back to the house, ma'am," he said. "And you may tell me if I do indeed owe you an apology."

She doubted she had ever heard his voice more cold.

He offered his arm, and since Christine could not think of an excuse not to take it, she did so. His eyes, she noticed, were like two chips of ice. Their normal charming selves, in fact. She would have far preferred to run off in the other direction, to lose herself among the trees, to nurse her wounds in private. She had not realized that there were still wounds to nurse. She had thought them long healed.

Hermione and Basil made no move to return with them.

"*Do* I owe you an apology, Mrs. Derrick?" the duke asked her when they were out of earshot.

"For making the offer you did?" she said. "You have already apologized for that."

"As I thought," he said, "though my offer must have been a rather shocking conclusion to your successful ruse to draw me off alone for a whole hour. The maze was a clever delaying touch. I trust you enjoyed claiming your prize, ma'am, and that it was worth your efforts—and perhaps even the insult you were forced to endure."

She drew a deep breath and released it slowly. Her private wounds were going to have to wait awhile yet.

"Actually," she said, "I did not claim the prize at all. Someone put in the money for me and thus wagered on me. I relinquished all claim on the prize to her. But, yes, I *did* enjoy my moment of triumph for its own sake. I won on the very first day, of course, when I lured you into walking about this lake with me, but it would have seemed unsporting to end the game so soon. And so I decided to repeat the feat two days ago." She sighed aloud and lifted her face to the sky.

"It was, however," he said, "I who invited *you* to walk with me on that second occasion."

"But, of course." She looked at him with wide-eyed surprise. "A lady ought not to invite a gentleman, ought she, especially twice within a week? But *that* does not deter *me*. There are ways of inviting a gentleman to invite me—like sitting on a wall with a month-old letter, for example, looking pensive, while a whole grassy alley looms invitingly ahead, and then pretending that she is merely reading the letter."

Perhaps wisely he held his peace. She felt a nasty satisfaction in the realization that he was maybe angry and maybe—dared she hope?—a little humiliated too.

They were among the trees. She might easily have slipped her arm free of his and would have done so if it had not occurred to her that it was precisely what he must wish her to do.

"The original wager, you know," she said, "was to entice you into making a marriage proposal. But since it was concluded that there was no fun in wagering on an impossibility, the terms were changed to luring you into an hour of conversation tête-à-tête. I might almost have won the first wager as well as the second, except that you offered me carte blanche instead of matrimony. That was extremely lowering, you know, though I daresay it had something to do with my being a schoolmaster's daughter and far too vulgar for the position of duchess. However, no lasting harm was done since I did not have to confess it to my fellow contestants."

He continued to hold his peace.

It really was quite provoking. She had never been one for quarreling and fighting with others. But she thought there would be something intensely satisfying about having a raging row with the Duke of Bewcastle. However, if her guess was correct, it would be harder to draw him into any uncontrolled, unseemly display of emotion than it would to lure him into matrimony. And that was because there *was* no emotion, no passion in the man. She quelled the memory of a certain embrace in the maze two days previous. That had not been passion—that had been lust.

She sighed aloud again. "I am glad I have won the wager—twice," she said. "Now I no longer have to cultivate your company."

"And that is my cue, I suppose," he asked her, "to assure you that I am delighted to hear it?"

"Are you?" she asked him. "Delighted, I mean?"

"I have no opinion on the matter," he said.

"Do you never quarrel?" she asked him.

"Quarreling," he said, "is quite unnecessary."

"Of course it is." She sawed the air with her free hand. "You can command obedience with the mere lifting of an eyebrow."

"Except," he said, "when someone decides to ignore the threat of either the eyebrow or my quizzing glass."

She laughed, though she was not, truth to tell, feeling vastly amused. She had been horribly humiliated, first in the maze and now on the hill, and she could not wait to crawl into her little box of a room and curl up into a ball on the bed.

"Your brother- and sister-in-law do not like you, Mrs. Derrick," the Duke of Bewcastle said crisply and abruptly.

Well, they had just made that perfectly obvious. There was no point in being upset anew at this bald statement of fact.

"They are probably terrified that I will lure you into marriage as I lured Oscar," she said as they stepped out into the clearing by the lake, where she had collided with him that first afternoon of the party. "And that later you will blame them for not warning you."

"Warning me that you are a schoolmaster's daughter?" he said. "That you are conniving?"

"And vulgar," she said. "You must not forget that. It was one of my chief sins, you know. I was forever doing things that drew attention to myself and embarrassing them. Try as I would, I could never be perfect as Hermione was. Now that you have had time to reflect on the matter, you must be very thankful that I refused to be your mistress."

"Must I?" he said. "Because you are not a perfect lady?"

They were among the trees leading to the lawn before the house.

"And because I am a flirt," she said.

"Are you?" he asked her.

"And because I might kill you as I killed Oscar," she said.

There was a short silence, during which she realized that all the defenses she did not know she had erected about herself were down and all her good humor was gone and if they did not reach the house soon she was going to quarrel with him whether he wished to quarrel with her or not. She had mental images of herself pummeling his chest with both fists, stamping on his boots with both feet, and twisting his quizzing glass into a corkscrew while screeching at him like a demented night owl. But the trouble was that they were not amusing images.

She was going to start crying if she was not careful. She never cried. There was never any point, was there?

"It would seem, then," he said, "that Elrick and his lady have some justification for their dislike."

What had she expected? That he would ask if it was true? That he would drag the whole story out of her as no one else had ever done and exonerate her of all blame? And then apologize abjectly for the offer he had made in the maze and sweep her off on his trusty steed—every knight worthy of the name possessed one of those—to be his duchess?

She could conceive of no worse fate. She really could not. Because he was *not* a knight in shining armor. He was a cold, disagreeable, haughty aristocrat.

"Absolutely," she said. "Oh, absolutely. It did not matter that I was nowhere near him when he died, did it? That was just another example of my cunning. I killed him anyway. And I am *not* in a good humor, your grace, as you have perhaps perceived. I am going to break into a run as soon as I have finished speaking and arrive back at the house all hot and panting. I do *not* expect you to come dashing gallantly after me."

But before she could suit action to words, his right hand caught her upper arm in a viselike grip and she found her heaving bosom being hauled within an inch of his chest. His silver eyes blazed with cold light into her own.

She thought for one startled moment that he was going to kiss her again.

Perhaps he thought so too. Certainly his eyes dipped to her mouth and his nostrils flared. His left hand came somewhat more gently to her other arm.

If a lightning bolt had crashed to earth between them the air could not have crackled with greater tension.

But he did not kiss her—for which fact she was mortally thankful later when she could think straight again. She would probably have kissed him back and clung to him and begged him to carry her off deep into the woods and ravish her. And the trouble was, she thought then, that she probably would really have done it too—gone with him, that was, lain with him. Maybe she would even have begged him to repeat the offer he had made in the maze.

But he did not kiss her.

"More and more," he said instead, more to himself than to her, it seemed, "I regret that I came here. And before you contrive to have the last word, Mrs. Derrick, I daresay you regret it too—that *I* came, that *you* came."

He released his hold on her, and she caught up her wet hem and fled, feeling more wretched than she had felt in two years. She really ought not to have come to this party—and that was surely the understatement of the decade. She had *known* Hermione and Basil were coming. And now she had exposed herself to the ridicule and censure of the Duke of Bewcastle, who would think that she had *killed* Oscar, for heaven's sake.

And yet if he had kissed her just now, she would have kissed him back. Yet all he had been able to say when he did *not* kiss her was that he regretted more than ever coming to this house party.

She hated him with a passion. It was an alarming thought. She would have far preferred to be indifferent to him.

She should remain outside, she thought as she arrived at the house hot and breathless and disheveled. She should confront Hermione and Basil as soon as they returned. It was high time. She had been as distraught as they during the days following Oscar's death and quite unable to defend herself properly against their accusations. But she was feeling hardly less distraught at this particular moment. And so, like the coward she sometimes was, she hurried up to her room, thankful that she met no one on the way.

She shut the door, threw herself across the narrow bed, and clutched fistfuls of the bedspread as she fought tears so that she would not have to appear at dinner with swollen eyelids and bloodshot eyes and blocked nasal passages. She had no one to blame but herself for all this, she knew. She should have refused to come. Even Melanie could not have forced her if she had said no and stuck with it.

A long time passed before she calmed down and sat up on the bed to observe her appearance in the looking glass. With a smile on her face she would perhaps look no different from usual. She smiled at her image to test her theory. Tragedy's face looked back at her with grotesquely upward curved lips. She parted her lips and added a sparkle to her eyes.

There, she thought—she was as good as new, safe behind her defenses again. Strange—she had not known she still had them, that she still needed them. She had been free for two years and happy again. Well—almost happy.

She would survive intact to the end of the party, she decided firmly, until she could go home and hide her heart again in the comfortable routine of her daily life. After all, she had survived Oscar's death.

WULFRIC FELT UNUSUALLY discomposed—again. And for the same reason—again. He had almost *kissed* her, for God's sake. A more inappropriate ending to a bothersome afternoon he could not imagine.

He had very badly miscalculated, though, he realized as he watched her run from him. In more than one way.

She was still angry with him over the offer he had made her.

Of course, he was more than a trifle annoyed himself. He did *not* believe that those two lengthy meetings between them had been wholly contrived on her part. But she *had* been a participant in that ridiculous contest and had doubtless prolonged their second encounter as long as possible. It had been her suggestion to go into the maze, after all. And he had followed her in like a puppet on a string. And then he had kissed her and made his impulsive offer.

It must have been some consolation to her when she ran from the maze to be able to rush back to claim victory and the prize.

His own ruffled feathers paled into insignificance, however, beside the fact that she had been deeply hurt by the asinine behavior of Elrick and his lady back there on the hill—as well she might. He had a previous acquaintance with those two and had never before found either of them unpleasant or indiscreet or foolishly spiteful. They had been all three today.

They had certainly aired the family linen before him in a manner that was quite unseemly. They resented her lowly origins, her vulgarity, her flirtatiousness—that word again. It came up with tedious regularity where she was concerned. He really did not want to know any of their feelings about her. He certainly did not *need* to know.

But something had obviously happened among the three of them—something concerning the death of Oscar Derrick. He did not for a moment believe that Christine Derrick had killed him, but there had been *something* to cause such lasting enmity. This afternoon he had been somehow caught in the middle of a sordid family squabble.

He deeply resented the imposition.

At the same time he had learned something interesting about Mrs. Derrick. She was made up of more than just sunshine and laughter. There was darkness in her too, deeply suppressed, though it had come bubbling to the surface while they had walked together just now. She had tried her best to provoke a quarrel with him.

He had almost succumbed—in a manner she would not have expected.

Her vulnerability was something he did not wish—or intend—to deal with. He had felt an attraction to her, he had kissed her, he had offered to make her his mistress, she had refused, and there was an end of the matter. Apart from what he had to confess was a lingering attraction to her person, he had no further interest in her or the dark complexities of her life.

And yet, annoyingly, he found his eyes drawn to her quite as much as ever during the second week of the house party.

She was a light-bringer despite the darkness he had glimpsed in her.

He was still unwillingly dazzled by that light.

8

*W*ULFRIC WENT FISHING WITH BARON RENABLE and some of the other gentlemen a few mornings in succession. He sat in Renable's library on several occasions with a small group of gentlemen, talking politics and international affairs and books. He played billiards more than once with the gentlemen who were similarly inclined. In the evenings he played cards, since only the older people were really interested in doing so. He participated in as few of the merrier events of the party as possible without being ill-mannered. He spent as much time alone as he possibly could—it was precious little. He counted the days, and almost the hours, until he might leave to return home.

There was one event he was not going to be able to escape, however, though at least it had been placed at the very end of the party as the culminating entertainment. There was to be a grand ball—or as grand as any such event could be in the country—as the official celebration of the betrothal between Miss Magnus and Sir Lewis Wiseman. A select group of neighbors had been invited, since twenty-four houseguests and two hosts could not decently fill a ballroom.

"Most of our invited guests have only a small claim to gentility," Lady Renable explained to Wulfric a day or two before the event. "However, they like to be invited, and one does feel duty bound to condescend to them once or twice a year. I do hope you will not find the company too insipid."

"I believe, ma'am," he said, raising both his eyebrows and his quizzing glass, "your taste in guests as in all things is to be trusted."

Why apologize for what could not be avoided? And why apologize to him alone? Why apologize at all? One thing about Bedwyns for which he would be eternally thankful was that they were not forever apologizing to one another.

Balls had never been his idea of pleasurable entertainment, though they sometimes had to be endured. This one was of that number. Since he could hardly shut himself into his bedchamber with a book, he dressed with his usual meticulous care, allowing his valet to spend longer than usual over the tying of his neckcloth, and descended to the ballroom at the appointed hour. He reserved the opening set with Lady Elrick, the second with Lady Renable, and hoped that after that he could decently withdraw to the card room.

The young ladies, he noticed as he strolled to where Mowbury was standing, looking awkward, if not downright miserable, were all decked out in their most opulent finery, jewels sparkling in the candlelight, plumes nodding above elaborately styled hair—perhaps a deliberate ruse to distinguish themselves from the less gorgeously clad neighbors, who had already begun to arrive.

"I reminded Melanie that I was born with two left feet," Mowbury told him, "but she would insist that I put in an appearance here and dance with *someone*. I have asked Christine—Mrs. Derrick. She was married to my cousin, you know, and is a decent sort, I have always thought, even though Hermione and Elrick don't seem to like her, do they? Tiresome things, balls, Bewcastle."

She was across the room, talking with three ladies and a gentleman—Mrs. Derrick, that was. Wulfric recognized the vicar and his wife and assumed that the other two ladies were her mother and eldest sister. Mrs. Derrick certainly had been blessed with all the looks in that family, he thought. The vicar's wife was unremarkable. The eldest sister was downright plain.

Mrs. Derrick was wearing a cream-colored evening gown with a single flounce at the hem and matching frills at the edges of the short, puffed sleeves. The neckline was deep though not immodest. Her short curls, brushed to a sheen, were threaded with pink ribbon to match the length about the high waistline of her gown. The ribbons were her only adornment apart from the closed fan she carried in one gloved hand. She wore no jewels, no turban, no plumes. The gown itself was not by any means in the first stare of fashion.

She made her fellow houseguests look rather ridiculously fussy.

"So Mrs. Derrick has agreed to dance the opening set with you," he said.

"She has." Mowbury grimaced. "I promised not to tread all over her toes. But she will just laugh at me if I do and tell me they needed flattening anyway, or some such thing. She is a good sport."

Kitredge, whose portly form was positively squeaking inside his stays, had joined her and was being presented to her family. For a moment his plump, beringed hand rested against the small of her back. Wulfric's fingers curled about the handle of his jeweled evening quizzing glass. The earl's hand fell away as she changed her position a little to smile up at him. She nodded and Kitredge moved away. The second set had been promised, Wulfric guessed.

He let his glass fall on its silken ribbon.

CHRISTINE HAD ALWAYS enjoyed dancing. She had not always enjoyed *balls*—not for the last few years of her marriage anyway. Oscar had started to object to her dancing with other gentlemen, though she had tried pointing out to him that the whole point of a ball was to dance with a variety of partners. He could not dance with her himself all night. It would not have been good etiquette. Besides, he had liked to spend time in the card room or socializing with his male friends, and then she had been caught in the dilemma of either being a wallflower by her own choice or displeasing her husband.

She really had found marriage far more of a trial than she had ever expected. For all his extraordinary good looks, Oscar had been very unsure of himself—and of her. He had become increasingly possessive and dependent. She had loved him dearly, but it had been hard not to resent his lack of trust in her. She even feared she had fallen out of love with him before the end, when his accusations had become more hurtful and even insulting.

But those difficult, unhappy days were over, and tonight she was free to dance every set if she wished—and if enough gentlemen asked her. She laughed her way through the opening set, guiding Hector through the patterns of the country dance and rescuing him more than once when he would have gone prancing off in one direction while all the other gentlemen were gliding gracefully in the other. He thanked her profusely afterward and even forgot himself sufficiently to kiss her hand.

She danced cheerfully through the second set with a sweating Earl of Kitredge and steered the conversation firmly away from the flirtatious banter with which he had been regaling her for the past week. When he would have drawn her through the French doors into the garden in order to enjoy the cool evening air for a few minutes, she assured him that it would break her heart to miss one single step of one single dance during such a splendid ball.

She danced with Mr. Ronald Culver—she had learned to distinguish him from his twin—and with Mr. Cobley, one of Bertie's tenant farmers, who had asked her three times during the past year and a half to marry him, and laughed and talked a great deal.

She noticed with some satisfaction that Hazel had been asked to dance each set and that even Eleanor, who despised dancing, had been persuaded to take the floor for two sets.

She smiled with warm pleasure whenever she saw Audrey and Sir Lewis Wiseman together. Although they were not at all ostentatious in their affection for each other, they nevertheless seemed very well suited. They were happy together. Happiness was such a rare commodity. She *hoped* it would last for them. She had always been fond of Audrey, who had been little more than a child when Christine had married Oscar.

Tomorrow, she recalled, she would be going home. What a glorious thought that was, even though in many ways the party had been enjoyable and most of the guests amiable. But three of them had not been, and that had made all the difference. There had been a terrible tension between Christine on the one hand and Hermione and Basil on the other since the day of the picnic. They had avoided one another whenever possible, though every day Christine had resolved to corner them somewhere and have out with them whatever it was that needed to be had out. But it was difficult at a house party to find a private moment—or perhaps she had not tried too hard.

And the Duke of Bewcastle had offered to make her his mistress—and then had been witness to her humiliation at the hands of her brother- and sister-in-law and to her show of bad temper and spite and indiscretion afterward. It was all very disturbing indeed.

She could hardly wait to get home.

Never, never, *never* again would she allow herself to be drawn into any entertainment that involved the *ton* in general and Hermione and Basil in particular. She did not include the duke in her resolution since there was no possible chance that they would ever meet again.

For which happy fact she would be eternally grateful.

Nevertheless, all the time in the ballroom—every single moment—she was aware of the Duke of Bewcastle, looking severe and immaculate and positively satanic in black evening coat and silk knee breeches with silver waistcoat and very white stockings and linen and lace. He also looked as if he despised every mortal with whom he was doomed to spend this final evening of a house party that appeared to have brought him no pleasure at all. It probably appalled him to be forced to share a ballroom with people who, though they all had some claim to gentility, were nowhere near his own elevated social rank. Her mother and Eleanor, for example.

He danced with Hermione and then with Melanie before strolling toward the open doorway into the card room. But Christine, watching him unwillingly as she took her place in the third set with Ronald Culver, was startled to see him take one step back into the ballroom, hesitate, look pained and supercilious, and then step forward again to bow over the hand of Mavis Page, the thin, plain daughter of a deceased naval captain, who was sitting with her mama as she had been all evening. No one ever danced with Mavis, who was unfortunate enough not to have a strong personality to compensate for her lack of looks.

Christine found herself with divided feelings. For Mavis's sake, of course, she was genuinely delighted—Mrs. Page would have something truly grand to boast of for the next year or two, perhaps even for the rest of her life. But it was annoying—and disturbing—to witness the duke behaving so out of character. Christine really had not wanted to find even one redeeming quality in him. Yet it appeared now that he had spotted a wallflower and had gone to her rescue.

Mr. Fontain, another of Bertie's tenants, led Mavis out for the next set. She looked almost pretty, with a glow of color in her cheeks.

After the third set the Duke of Bewcastle disappeared into the card room and Christine felt free to relax and enjoy herself. After tomorrow she would not have to think of him ever again. She would never have to look into his cold, arrogant face again. She would not have to be constantly reminded that he had made her a dishonorable proposal and that for a single, shameful moment she had been *disappointed* that it was not marriage he offered.

The very thought of being married to him . . .

Her relief at his absence was short-lived. After the fourth set she was making her way back to her family when Mr. George Buchan and Mr. Anthony Culver stopped her to exchange a few remarks with her. One of them would probably ask her to dance, she thought. She hoped *someone* would. The next set was to be a waltz. She had learned the steps back in her London days, though she had never danced them with anyone but Oscar.

She *hoped* someone would ask her to waltz here.

And then she felt a touch on the arm and turned to find herself gazing up into the silver eyes of the Duke of Bewcastle.

"Mrs. Derrick," he said, "if you have not promised the next set to someone else, I wish you would dance it with me."

He had taken her completely by surprise. Even so, it struck her that she could simply say no. But if she did, then she could not decently dance with anyone else. And this was to be the only waltz of the evening.

Bother, bother, bother, she thought. Five hundred botherations!

And yet her heart was pattering against her rib cage, and her knees were threatening to wobble beneath her, and she was close to panting, as if she had just run a mile without stopping. And all other considerations aside for the present mindless moment, he was truly, truly a gorgeous man.

It was the final evening of the house party. It would be her final encounter with him.

And it was to be a *waltz*.

"Perhaps," he said, "you do not waltz?"

She had, of course, been gawking at him like a fish hauled out of its natural element.

"I do," she said, unfurling her fan and wafting it before her hot cheeks, "though it is a long time since I last danced it. Thank you, your grace."

He offered his arm, and she snapped her fan closed, set her hand on his sleeve, and allowed him to lead her onto the dance floor. She remembered suddenly that he had danced with Mavis and glanced up at him with some curiosity. He was looking very directly back into her eyes.

They were like a wolf's eyes, she thought. Someone had mentioned a few days ago that his given name was Wulfric. How strangely appropriate!

"I thought," she said, "you would avoid me at all costs this evening."

"Did you?" he asked, his eyebrows arched upward, his voice haughty.

Well, there was no answer to that, was there? She did not attempt one but waited for the music to begin. *What* had she just thought? That he was a gorgeous man? *Gorgeous?* Did she have windmills in her head? She looked up at him again. His nose was too large. No, it was not. It was his prominent, slightly hooked nose that gave his face character and made it more handsome than it would have been with a perfectly formed nose.

How silly noses were when one really thought about them.

"I have amused you—again?" he asked her.

"Not really." She laughed aloud. "Only my own thoughts. I was thinking how silly noses are."

"Quite so," he said, a glint of something indefinable in his eyes.

And then the music began and he took her right hand in his left and set his other behind her waist. She set her free hand on his shoulder—and had to stop herself from panting again. He surely was holding her at the correct distance. But now suddenly she understood why many people still considered the waltz not quite proper. She had never felt *this* close to Oscar when she had waltzed with him. She could not remember feeling his body heat or smelling his cologne. Her heart was pattering again, yet they had not even moved yet.

And then they did.

And she knew within moments that she had never waltzed before. He danced it with long, firm steps and twirled her firmly about so that the light from all the candles blurred into one swirling line. She had not known what it was to waltz before tonight. Not really. It was pure sensual bliss. Light, colors, perfumes, body heat, a man's musky cologne, the music, the smooth, slightly slippery floor, the hand at her waist, the hand holding her own, the delight in her own body's lightness and movement—it was pure enchantment.

She looked into his face and smiled and for the moment felt utterly, mindlessly happy.

He gazed back at her, and in the flickering of the candlelight from the chandeliers overhead it seemed to her that his eyes glowed warm for once.

The enchantment did not last, alas.

He had just twirled her about a corner close to the French doors when Hector came lumbering around in the opposite—and wrong!—direction with Melanie. The Duke of Bewcastle hauled Christine right against his chest in what she realized afterward was a valiant attempt to save her from disaster, but he was too late. Hector trod hard on her left slipper, not missing even one of her five toes in the process.

She hopped on the other foot while the duke's arm wrapped very firmly about her waist, and sucked in her breath as she watched the proverbial stars wheeling in a black sky all about her person. Melanie exclaimed with dismay and informed Hector that she had *told* him he was dancing in the wrong direction. Hector apologized profusely and abjectly.

"I warned Mel that I do not waltz," he complained. "She knows I do not even *dance,* but she would insist I waltz with her. I am most awfully sorry, Christine. Did I hurt you?"

"A foolish question if ever I have heard one, Hector," Melanie said tartly. "*Of course* you have hurt her, you great looby."

"I daresay that soon the urge to scream will subside entirely," Christine said. "In the meanwhile I shall continue to count slowly—forty-seven . . . forty-eight . . . But don't worry, Hector, my toes needed flattening anyway."

"My poor Christine," Melanie said. "Shall I take you to your room and have a maid summoned?"

But Christine waved them on, gritting her teeth and trying not to look conspicuous. Why did such things always happen to her, even when she was quite innocently minding her own business?

Hector lumbered onward—in the right direction this time—with Melanie in tow. Christine became aware that she was still pressed right up against the Duke of Bewcastle's side. The pain had not even crested yet. She sucked in her breath again.

And then he stooped down, swung her up into his arms, and stepped out through the French doors with her. It was neatly done, she admitted even as her eyes widened in shock. She doubted that many of the guests had noticed either the collision or its aftermath—or her escape into the garden in the Duke of Bewcastle's arms. Though, if anyone *had* noticed that last point . . .

"Oh, dear," she said, "this is getting to be a habit." What normal woman had to be swept up into a gentleman's arms *twice* within two weeks?

He strode some distance from the doors and finally set her down on a wooden seat that circled the huge trunk of an old oak tree.

"But this time, Mrs. Derrick," he said, "the fault was entirely mine. I ought to have seen him coming sooner than I did. Has any real damage been done to your foot? Can you bend your toes?"

"Give me a few moments to stop silently screaming," she said, "and to reach one hundred. Then I will try wiggling them. I suppose that every time dancing lessons were on the agenda when Hector was a boy, he made sure he was safely hidden away somewhere with a book of Greek philosophy—in Greek. He really ought not to be let loose within two miles of any ballroom. He looked quite miserable too, did he not, the poor love? Ninety-two . . . ninety-three . . . Oh, ouch!"

The Duke of Bewcastle had gone down on one knee before her and was untying the ribbon bow about her leg and easing off her slipper.

He looked very picturesque. He looked as if he were about to spout a marriage proposal.

It was strange how one could feel amusement and excruciating pain at the same moment. Christine bit down on her lower lip.

WULFRIC WAS NO physician, but he did not believe any bones had been broken. There was not even any noticeable swelling in her foot, though she held it stiffly and he could tell from her ragged breathing that she was still in great pain. He set her stockinged foot flat on his palm, cupped the back of her heel with his other hand, and slowly lifted it upward, bending her toes as he did so before lowering her heel again.

One of her hands came to rest on his shoulder and gripped it. Her eyes were closed, he noticed, and her head bent forward. At first she grimaced and bit down harder on her lower lip, but as he repeated the action, she gradually relaxed.

"I do believe," she said after a minute or so, "I am going to survive. I may even live to dance another day." She chuckled—a low, merry, seductive sound.

It was a small, delicate foot, warm in its silk stocking. He set it down on top of her pink slipper and she continued to lift her heel and flex her toes on her own. After a few moments her hand moved away from his shoulder.

"What I fail to understand," she said as he stood up, clasped his hands behind him, and looked down at her, "is why Hector came here at all. He is unworldly and bookish and not at all socially inclined—not with ladies anyway."

"I believe," he said, "he thought it was to be a gathering of intellectuals."

"Oh, poor thing," she said as she slid her foot back inside her slipper, arranged the ribbon about her leg and retied the bow, and then flexed her toes a few more times. "I daresay Melanie thought a party of this nature would be good for him—just as she thought dancing would be good for him this evening. She probably misled him from the start without ever lying to him outright. He probably had not even noticed—or he had forgotten—that his sister had become recently betrothed and that Melanie was bound to throw one of her famous parties for her."

Wulfric did not say anything. A few lamps had been lit outdoors for the convenience of guests who wished to take the air beyond the stuffy confines of the ballroom. One of them was slanting its light across her and gleaming off her hair. And then she looked up at him, an arrested look on her face—and her eyes laughed.

"Oh, goodness," she said, "it was Hector who invited *you*. Did you too think this was to be a gathering of intellectuals? You *did*, did you not? I have wondered why you came, when Melanie said you never go anywhere beyond London and your own estates. How *horrified* you must have been when you discovered your mistake. You poor . . . duke."

"I assume, Mrs. Derrick," he said, the fingers of one hand finding the handle of his quizzing glass and curling about it, "there was no question in what you have just said that was not rhetorical?"

He was unaccustomed to being laughed at. He could not remember ever being *pitied*.

"But you do have some of the social graces—you waltz well," she said, clasping her hands in her lap and tipping her head slightly to one side as she continued to look at him. "Exceedingly well, in fact."

"It is possible," he said, "to be both bookish, as you call it, and accomplished in the social arts, Mrs. Derrick. I did not hide from *my* dancing lessons. Learning to dance correctly, even well, is an essential part of the education of a gentleman."

He was not even particularly bookish. Although he considered himself well read, he did not have the time to keep his head buried in books. There were more practical concerns with which to fill his days. He had not even *liked* reading as a boy.

"I always loved the waltz more than any other dance," she said with a wistful sigh, "though I rarely performed it when I lived in London. And now poor Hector has stamped out all my hopes of dancing it tonight."

"The set is not ended," he pointed out to her. "We will continue dancing if you are able."

"My foot is almost as good as new again," she said with a final wiggle of her toes inside the pink silk slipper. "I must be thankful that Hector weighs only one ton instead of two."

"Then let us waltz." He held out a hand for hers.

She set her own in it and got to her feet. "You must be sorry you asked me," she said. "Disaster seems to follow me around even when I am in no way to blame."

"I am not sorry," he told her—and made the mistake of not moving off immediately in the direction of the ballroom with her. The lamp was swaying slightly in the breeze, wafting light and shade over her.

Suddenly it seemed as though the air between them and all about them fairly sizzled.

"Let us waltz out here," he suggested.

"Out here?" Her eyebrows arched upward in surprise, but then she laughed softly. "Under the lamps and beneath the stars? How wonderfully rom— How delightful! Yes, do let's."

How romantic, she had been about to say. He grimaced inwardly. He was never romantic. He did not believe in romance.

But this had not been a practical suggestion, he thought as he set a hand behind her waist, took her hand in his, and led her off into the steps of the waltz again. Grass did not make for the smoothest dancing surface, and this particular lawn was not even perfectly flat. And it was not quite proper behavior to dance alone with her like this. Although they were not far from the house, and the ballroom doors were open and lamps had been lit as a deliberate invitation to guests to step outside, he ought not to have her alone, away from the sight of her mother and the rest of her family.

But the absurdity of the thought struck him almost immediately. She was, of course, a widow and surely far closer in age to thirty than to twenty. There was nothing even remotely improper in what they were doing.

And yet he was fully aware that being alone with her thus, waltzing with her thus, was more than slightly dangerous.

They danced and twirled in silence while the music from the ballroom curled about them—and it struck him after a few minutes that grass was the perfect surface to have underfoot and starlight the perfect ceiling to have overhead. The night smells of grass and trees were more enticing than all the combined perfumes in the ballroom.

And he held the perfect partner in his arms. She did not dance the steps stiffly and correctly. She followed his lead, she relaxed in his arms, and she felt the magic with him.

He drew her a little closer, the better to guide her over the uneven surface of the lawn. Then he tucked her hand palm-in against his heart and held it there with his own palm. And then somehow her face was lost in the folds of his neckcloth and her hair was tickling his chin. Her body, all soft and warm and feminine, rested against his, and her thighs touched his own and moved in perfect harmony with them.

The waltz, he thought, was a downright erotic dance.

He felt the distinct stirring of sexual arousal.

It had been so long . . .

The music had not stopped. But somehow their waltz had. They both stood very still for timeless moments, and then she tipped back her head and looked at him.

Moonlight rather than lamplight lit her face this time. She was, he thought, quite ethereally lovely. He framed her face with both hands, sliding his fingers into the softness of her hair. With his thumbs he traced the lines of her eyebrows, her cheekbones, her chin. He ran one thumb lightly across her lips, drew down the lower one, and moistened the pad by running it across the soft flesh within. She touched the tip of his thumb with her tongue, luring it into her mouth before sucking it deep. She was hot, soft, wet.

He withdrew his thumb and replaced it with his mouth.

But only briefly.

He drew back his head a few inches and gazed into her moonlit eyes.

"I want you," he said.

Even as he spoke he was aware that she could break the spell with one word. And part of him willed her to do just that.

"Yes," she said on a whisper of sound.

She regarded him with dreamy, lovely eyes, her eyelids slightly drooped over them.

"Come to the lake with me," he said.

"Yes."

The waltz tune played merrily on. The sounds of voices and laughter escaping the ballroom did not abate. The lamps continued to sway in the breeze. The moon was almost at the full. It beamed down its light from a clear sky, along with that from a million stars as he took Christine Derrick's hand in his and led her toward the line of trees and the grassy bank of the lake beyond.

9

*C*HRISTINE DELIBERATELY KEPT THOUGHT AT bay. The night held magic, and this was the final night of the two weeks before life resumed its normal—and admittedly rather dull—course tomorrow. She disapproved of the Duke of Bewcastle and all he stood for. He had insulted her with his arrogant assumption that money and jewels and a carriage of her own must be more enticing to her than genteel poverty and the life that was familiar to her. He was everything she did not want in a man.

But that was reason speaking, and she deliberately did not listen to its dreary voice.

There was this undeniable attraction between them, which was obviously mutual. Surely, she thought, it must be as unwilling with him as it was with her. But it was there nonetheless—this *something*—and tonight was all they had left in which to explore it before they went their separate ways tomorrow.

She was under no illusion, of course, about what that exploration would involve. They were not walking to the lake to gaze at the moonlight, or even to share a few chaste kisses.

I want you.

Yes.

He held her hand in his. She could almost have wept at

the intimacy of it. His grip was strong and hard. He did not lace his fingers with hers. There was no suggestion of tenderness or romance in his touch. But she would not have welcomed either. There *was* no tenderness between them and definitely no romance. Only this intimacy and the promise of more when they reached the lake.

She did not know why she had agreed to such a thing—she really had *no* idea. It was not a part of her nature to be in any way promiscuous or loose in her morals. She had shared no more than a few kisses with Oscar before their marriage, and during it, despite his accusations toward the end, she had never even dreamed of being unfaithful. She had lived chastely during the two years of her widowhood without feeling any temptation to stray, even though there were several gentlemen in the neighborhood who would have been only too pleased either to dally with her or to court her honorably.

Yet here she was walking among the trees on her way to the lake with the Duke of Bewcastle halfway through Melanie's ball because he had said he wanted her and she had agreed with one word that she wanted him too.

It defied understanding.

She did not even try to understand. She kept thought at bay.

He did not make conversation. Neither did she. Indeed, it did not even occur to her to do so. They walked in silence, the music and the sound of voices from the ballroom gradually receding behind them, only the hooting of a night owl and the faint rustling of leaves overhead and the scampering of unseen night creatures through the undergrowth breaking the absolute stillness. It was a warm night after a hot day. The moon was bright. Even among the trees there was enough light to see by.

Down by the lake it was almost as bright as day with

the branches gone from overhead and the moonlight shining in a bright band across the water.

It would have been a brilliant night for romance. But this was not a romantic tryst. Still holding her hand in his, the Duke of Bewcastle struck off to the right until they reached a grassy part of the bank that would be totally hidden from the path to the house in the extremely unlikely event that anyone else should have the idea of walking out here. Then he stopped.

He did not immediately release her hand. He stepped in front of her, and his mouth found hers.

There was nothing to inhibit them now. They were no longer within sight and sound of the ballroom. And there was no pretense between them. He had told her he wanted her, she had agreed, and here they were.

Their hands parted company. Her arms went up about his neck. His came about her waist. Their mouths opened. His tongue came into her mouth and clashed with her own tongue. Such a powerful, raw sexual longing stabbed downward through her breasts and her abdomen and womb and down along her inner thighs that she needed the support of his arms about her and his body pressed to her own to stop from falling. One of his hands spread over her buttocks, pressing her hard to him, and left her in no doubt that his need matched her own.

His arms left her then, though his mouth did not for a few moments. He was shrugging out of his very costly black evening coat. He lifted his head and turned to spread the coat over the grass.

"Come," he said. "Lie down."

The shock of hearing him speak made her realize that they were the first words he had uttered since he had invited her to come to the lake. And the refined accents and faint hauteur of his voice made her realize anew just who

it was with whom she was doing these things. But the realization only heightened her desire.

She lay down, her head and shoulders on his coat, and
he came down with her, sliding his hands under her skirt
and up along the outsides of her legs to raise the skirt and
withdraw undergarments. He undid the buttons at the
flap of his breeches. Then one arm came beneath her
head and the other beneath her chin to hold it steady
while he plundered her mouth with his tongue again.

There was no gentleness, no tenderness. She reveled in
the unabashed carnality of what was happening. She expected that within moments he would enter her and that
it would all be over very soon after that. She consciously
enjoyed every moment. She had been so very starved. Not
just for two years, but forever, it seemed.

She had always been starved.

Always.

His mouth left hers and trailed a hot path down over
her chin to her throat and her bosom. He hooked his
thumb inside the low bodice of her gown and brought it
beneath her breast on one side. His mouth suckled her,
his tongue circling over her nipple. At the same time his
hand roamed over her inner thighs and then came between them to invade her private places and to explore
and caress her there until, her head thrown back, her fingers tangled in his hair, she thought it might well be possible to go mad with the pain that pleasure brought with it.

When he came between her thighs, spreading them
wide on the grass and sliding his hands beneath her, she
was quite sure she was too sensitive and swollen for the
ultimate act to bring anything else but pain. And indeed
when she felt him at her entrance, hard and firm, she almost begged him to stop.

"Please," she said instead, her voice low and throaty

and almost unrecognizable even to her own ears. "Please."

He came inside. But she was wet and slick, and though he was hard and long, the only pain she felt was that of sexual pleasure ready to burst out of her at any moment.

A pain and a pleasure she had never felt before.

Or even dreamed of.

It burst from her almost as soon as he began to move in her, his thrusts long and deep and firm. She shuddered into something that felt very like ecstasy and lay open and relaxed beneath him for what might have been several minutes listening to the wet rhythm of their coupling, feeling the hard, utterly pleasing pounding of his body into hers. But after those few minutes her enjoyment became less passive again, and then it built to an ache and an urgency and a second bursting of sexual release just moments before his own came as he stilled in her suddenly and strained deeper before she felt the hot gush of his release at her core.

His weight relaxed down on her for a few moments before he rolled off her, sat up, and then got to his feet. He stood with his back to her, setting his clothes back to rights, and then walked to the bank of the lake a few yards distant and stood looking out, a tall, handsome figure of a man in evening knee breeches and embroidered waistcoat with white shirt and copious amounts of lace at his wrists and throat.

The Duke of Bewcastle, in fact.

Christine sat up and made herself as respectable as she was able without aid of brush or looking glass. She raised her knees, her feet flat on the grass, and wrapped her arms about her legs. Those legs were trembling slightly, she realized. Her breasts felt tender. Inside she was sore. Physically she felt absolutely wonderful.

And enlightened.

She had loved Oscar—for several years anyway, and surely she had never quite stopped loving him. She had never found the marriage bed distasteful. It was, after all, what happened between husbands and wives. If she had ever felt a niggling disappointment, considering the fact that she had been head over ears in love when she married, then she had consoled herself with the very sensible thought that reality never did quite match up to dreams.

But now she *knew*. Reality *could* match and even surpass dreams. It had just done so.

At the same time she was very aware that there had been no tenderness in what had just happened, no pretense of romance or love, no commitment to any future. It had been purely carnal.

She had enjoyed it anyway.

Were not only men supposed to be capable of enjoying *that* on a purely physical level? Was it not supposed to be a primarily emotional experience for women? She felt no emotion for the duke. Not even any negative emotions at this particular moment. Certainly she was not imagining that she was now in love with him. She was not.

How dreadfully shocking!

But she was, of course, feeling *upset*. She knew she would not escape so lightly once this was all over and she was alone with reality and her own thoughts again.

He turned to look at her. At least, she presumed he was looking at her. The moonlight was behind him and so his face was in shadow. He said nothing for a few moments.

"Mrs. Derrick," he said then, his voice as cold and haughty as ever, it seemed to her—or perhaps it was just his normal voice, "I believe you will agree with me that now you must reconsider—"

"No!" she said, cutting him off firmly midsentence. No, she could not bear to hear him say it. "No, I do *not* agree, and I will *not* reconsider. What just happened here was not the beginning of anything but rather the end. For some reason that perhaps neither of us fully understands, there has been this something between us. Now we have given in to it and satisfied it. Now we can say good-bye and go our separate ways tomorrow and forget each other."

Even as she spoke she realized what utter drivel she was mouthing.

"Ah," he said faintly. "Will we?"

"I will not be your mistress," she said. "I did this for myself, for my own pleasure. It *was* pleasant, I have satisfied my curiosity, and that is that. The end."

She gripped her legs harder. He had turned his face slightly to the left so that she could see it in profile— proud, aristocratic, austerely handsome. Even now, minutes after it had happened, it was almost impossible to realize that she had *lain* with this man, that all the physical aftereffects of a thorough bedding that she was experiencing had been provided by him—by the Duke of Bewcastle. She could suddenly see him in memory as he had looked in the hall on that very first afternoon when she had gazed over the banister at him and sensed the danger he posed.

She had not been wrong, had she?

"And has it occurred to you," he asked her, "that I might have impregnated you?"

She was glad she was sitting. Her knees turned suddenly weaker at the plain speaking. This man certainly did not speak in euphemisms.

"I was barren through seven years of marriage," she said, as bluntly as he. "I think I will have contrived to remain barren through one more night."

There was a rather lengthy silence, which she would have broken if she could have thought of something to say. But although her thoughts were now working, they were not anything she could share with him. Actually she was already beginning to realize how she had deceived herself a few minutes ago. Her feelings were very much engaged in this night's doings even if they had nothing to do with romance or love. The next few days and even weeks were going to be wretched, she knew. It was not an easy thing for a woman to give her virtue and her body in a casual encounter and then shrug carelessly and assure herself that it had been purely for pleasure with no serious aftereffects.

But it was too late now to realize that when he had said *I want you* she ought to have asked for ten minutes or so in which to consider her answer.

"There is nothing I can say, then," he said at last, "that will persuade you to change your mind?"

"Nothing," she assured him.

And that at least was perfectly true. She could conceive of no worse fate than being this man's mistress, subordinate to his power and arrogance, at his beck and call, his paid employee, nothing to him but a body with which to pleasure himself when the mood was on him. And all the time half despising him, half disliking him, repelled by his coldness, his lack of humor and humanity. And despising herself.

He strode toward her and she scrambled to her feet, reluctant now to accept even the touch of his hand to help her up. But it was his coat he had come for. He bent and retrieved it from the ground, shook out the grass that clung to it, and put it back on. He looked, she thought then, as immaculate as he had appeared when she first caught sight of him in the ballroom.

She clasped her arms behind her back as he turned to her, and he took the hint and led the way back to the path without offering his arm—or his hand. It was strange how two people could share the deepest of all intimacies and yet, just a short while later, shun even the slightest touch from each other.

Tomorrow she would return to Hyacinth Cottage.

Tomorrow he would be gone.

She would never see him again.

Yet her breasts were still tender and her inner thighs were still trembly and inside she was still slightly sore as a result of their lovemaking—though that particular word was a euphemism if ever she had heard one.

They walked back to the house in silence. But he stopped when they were still some distance from the French doors into the ballroom.

"It would be as well," he said, "if we were not seen to return together. I will remain out here for a while."

But before she could hurry onward, grateful for his thoughtfulness, he spoke again.

"You will write to me at Lindsey Hall in Hampshire if there is need, Mrs. Derrick," he said.

It was a statement, not a request. He did not explain his meaning. He did not have to.

Christine shivered, suddenly chilly as he strode off in the direction of the old oak where he had set her down when he carried her outside after Hector had trodden on her foot. How long ago that seemed now!

She hurried in the direction of the ballroom, feeling suddenly more depressed than she could remember feeling for a long time.

So much for no emotional involvement in what she had allowed to happen!

WULFRIC STAYED OUTSIDE for some time before making his way to the card room.

There was nothing in his experience before this night to account for what had just happened between him and

Christine Derrick. He had never been a womanizer. Rose had been his only other woman, and an agreement had been carefully drawn up between them and all practical details settled before he had bedded her for the first time.

He had always had a healthy sexual appetite, and he had satisfied his needs with regularity whenever he was in town, but he had never thought of himself as a passionate man.

Tonight he had felt passion.

He wondered what would have happened out there by the lake if she had allowed him to finish what he had begun to say after staring out across the lake for several minutes, thinking. She had assumed that the offer he was about to make was the same as the one he had made in the maze the week before. She had assumed wrongly—and truth to tell, he had been glad to be stopped. He had allowed her interruption to turn him from the course he had decided upon with very little consideration. Honor had dictated it, but honor had been swallowed up in her interruption.

He did not want a duchess.

More especially, he did not want a duchess who was not his social equal, who looked pretty at all times and startlingly lovely when animated but was not at all elegant or refined, who behaved impulsively and not always with proper decorum or gentility, who drew attention to herself every time she became enthusiastic about something and then simply laughed when things went wrong instead of being suitably mortified. There were huge responsibilities attached to the position of duchess. If he ever married, he would want—he would *need*—to ally himself to a lady who had been raised and educated to step confidently into just such a role.

Mrs. Derrick quite patently could not do so.

There was nothing about her—*nothing!*—that would qualify her for the role.

Aidan had married beneath himself. Eve, though she had been brought up and educated as a lady, was in fact no more than the daughter of a Welsh coal miner. Rannulf had married beneath himself. Judith was the daughter of an obscure country parson and the granddaughter of a London actress. Wulfric had not approved of either marriage, though he had given his blessing to both. Alleyne was the only brother to have made a respectable marriage—with the niece of a baron.

Was he, the Duke of Bewcastle, head of the family, to do no better than any of his brothers? Was he to subordinate everything he had ever lived for to a summer's passion that he could in no way understand?

It would have been a disaster if Mrs. Derrick had allowed him to finish his marriage proposal. For of course she would not have refused if he *had* finished. To scorn to be his mistress was one thing, but what woman in her right mind would turn down the chance to be a duchess, to be married to one of the wealthiest men in Britain?

It would have been a disaster.

And so he had allowed himself to be interrupted, to be misunderstood. He had held his peace.

Yet now he felt that perhaps he had missed one of the few chances life offered to step off the wheel of routine and familiarity and duty to discover if there was joy somewhere beyond its turning.

Joy?

He remembered that Aidan was happy with Eve, as was Rannulf with Judith—quite as happy, in fact, as Alleyne was with his baron's niece or Freyja with her marquess or Morgan with her earl.

But they were *free* to be happy. None of them was the

Duke of Bewcastle, who could expect almost everything of life except freedom and personal happiness.

Life for a while, he thought as his steps led him slowly back in the direction of the revelries, was going to seem bleak indeed without even a glimpse of Christine Derrick to look forward to.

But then, life *was* bleak. In reality there was nothing beyond the wheel's turning. Not for men like him, anyway. He had been told in no uncertain terms at the age of twelve that he was different, set apart, bound by privilege and by duty for the rest of his days. He had fought and railed against his fate for only a short while—perhaps not even a year—before accepting the truth of what he had been told.

After that he had learned his lesson well.

The child in whose body he had lived and dreamed for twelve years no longer existed.

Christine Derrick was not for him.

THE MUSIC STOPPED playing in the ballroom below while Christine was in her bedchamber packing her meager belongings. Justin was sitting on the bed. It was not at all proper for him to be there, of course, but she did not care. She had been relieved when she answered the tap at her door to discover that it was only he and not Melanie or Eleanor or . . . someone else.

"I thought," she explained, "that it would be a good idea to go home with my mother and Eleanor tonight and save Bertie the trouble of having to call the carriage out again tomorrow."

"And so here you are packing in the middle of a ball without summoning a maid to do it for you," he said. "Poor Chrissie. I saw Hector plowing into you when you were waltzing and Bewcastle carrying you outside. I saw you slip back inside an hour later and then skirt about the edge of the floor until you reached the door and could disappear again. Are you *sure* nothing happened to upset you? He did not repeat his dishonorable offer by any chance, did he?"

She sighed as she pressed a pair of slippers down the side of the bag. Justin had always had an uncanny ability to appear on the scene during the various crises of her life, sensing that something upsetting had happened, that she needed a friendly ear into which to pour out her anger or grief or frustration or whatever the negative emotion happened to be, finding ways to console her or advise her or simply make her smile. She had always considered herself to be marvelously fortunate to have such a friend. But tonight she did not really want to confide even in him.

"No, of course not," she said. "He was actually very gallant. He stayed with me until I could stand on my foot again, and then we waltzed a little and strolled outside until the music stopped. Then he went wandering off to the card room, I suppose, and I stayed outdoors for a few minutes. It was so cool and peaceful out there that I was reluctant to come back inside. Then I got the idea of coming up here to pack my things so that I can go home tonight instead of waiting until the morning."

He looked at her with a gentle smile and keen eyes, and she knew that he knew she had lied to him for once in her life. But being Justin and her dear friend, he would not push for more information than she chose to give.

"I am glad he did not upset you," he said.

"Oh, he did not," she assured him again, setting her brush on top of the bag and closing it. "But I will be very glad to be back home, Justin. I daresay Hermione and Basil will be happy to see me go too. Do you know what those wretched girls, Lady Sarah Buchan and Harriet King, did? They ran to them and told them about that silly wager."

"Oh, Chrissie," he said, interrupting her, "I'm afraid that was me. Audrey told me about it too after you had won, and I was so certain that word would spread to everyone else pretty soon that I went and told Hermione myself. I wanted to assure her that you had been drawn into the wager against your will, that you had put none of your own money into it, that it was *Bewcastle* who invited *you* to walk in the alley, not the other way around—I saw it happen, remember?—and that your manner toward him was in no way flirtatious. I really wanted her to understand that. I suppose I did the wrong thing. Perhaps she never would have heard about the wager after all if I had not told her."

She stared at him in some dismay. It was *Justin* who was responsible for that horrid scene out at the lake? She knew from old experience that he often took it upon himself to intervene in any altercation that involved her, to defend her, explain for her, intercede for her. She had always appreciated his efforts to be her champion, though they had not seemed to do much good. This interference she resented, though. It had actually caused trouble for her.

"Do forgive me," he said, looking so crestfallen that her heart melted.

"Well," she said, "I daresay someone else would have told if you had not. And it does not really matter, does it? I'll probably never see them again after tonight."

She would never again accept any invitation from Melanie that included them. And yet it broke her heart. Basil was Oscar's brother and had once seemed like hers for a few years. Hermione at one time had been like another sister.

"I'll talk to them again," he promised.

"I would really rather you did not," she said, leaving her packed bag where it was and making for the door.

"You spoke up for me so many times, Justin, that they stopped believing you. Leave well enough alone. There has been no music downstairs for some time now, has there? Supper time must be almost over. I suppose I ought to put in an appearance again, though there must be only another set or two left. None of the neighbors will wish to be too late leaving here, will they? And all the houseguests are to begin their journeys tomorrow and will not want too late a night."

"Come and dance with me, then," he said, getting up off the bed to open the door for her, "and smile as only you know how, even though I know Bewcastle said or did *something* to upset you, damn his eyes."

"Not at all," she said. "I am a little weary, that is all. But not too weary to dance with you."

It was hard to imagine feeling more depressed than she was feeling at this precise moment, Christine thought. Her spirits were lodged somewhere in the soles of her slippers. But she smiled anyway.

She informed her mother and Eleanor that she would be accompanying them home, and then she danced with Justin and with Mr. Gerard Hilliers. She smiled determinedly and made merry. It was an enormous relief to find that the Duke of Bewcastle was not in the ballroom.

She thanked Melanie and Bertie at the end of the ball and explained to them that she was leaving with her mother. She had hoped to slip away unnoticed after that, but Melanie spread the word, and the actual leave-taking became a grand public event, the very thing she had hoped to avoid by not waiting until the morning.

She hugged Audrey and shook hands with Sir Lewis Wiseman and wished them well at their wedding next spring and in their future life. She kissed Lady Mowbury's cheek and promised to write to her. She exchanged farewell greetings with a large crowd of the young people, all of whom were trying to talk at once—with a great deal of laughter thrown in.

Even Hermione and Basil must have decided that it was their duty to take a formal leave of her. Hermione kissed the air near her cheek and Basil bowed stiffly to her. Ignominiously, Christine felt a rush of tears to her eyes, and she startled Hermione—and herself—by hugging her sister-in-law tightly.

"I am so sorry," she said. "I am so sorry, Hermione. So *very* sorry."

She had little idea what she was talking about, but Hermione, she noticed before she turned and clambered into the waiting carriage, moved closer to Basil's side, and he set an arm about her shoulders.

The Duke of Bewcastle, at least, had absented himself from the small crowd gathered on the terrace. Christine felt enormous relief about that as she settled back into the well-upholstered seat, her chest tight with unshed tears. She was very, *very* glad of it.

"That was a fine entertainment," her mother said, taking her place on the seat opposite with Eleanor. "It was gratifying to see you made so much of, Christine."

"Well, and so she ought to be, Mama," Eleanor said. "She is, after all, a Derrick by marriage and related to Lady Renable and Viscount Elrick and Viscount Mowbury. Our Christine is an important lady." She winked across the carriage at her younger sister.

"It was most courteous of the Earl of Kitredge to ask to be presented to us," their mother said. "And he actually *danced* with you, Christine. So did the Duke of Bewcastle for a short while, though I must say I thought him a thoroughly disagreeable man. *He* did not come to be introduced."

"Too cold and haughty for his own good," Eleanor agreed. "I am *so* delighted that the evening is over and done with. I never could see the attraction of cavorting about a floor with dozens of other people, wearing out one's legs and one's conversation when one could be more pleasantly employed at home, reading a good book."

"And *I* am delighted the two weeks are at an end," Christine said. "I have missed the children at school and our niece and nephews and all the villagers and the garden. And both of you," she added.

"And yet," her mother said, "I always fear that life must seem dull to you, Christine, when you have known something far grander."

"It is never dull, Mama," she said, smiling and setting her head back against the cushions. "And it was never grand."

She closed her eyes and felt suddenly that she was back at the lake, the Duke of Bewcastle bending his head to kiss her before all passion broke loose between them. She had done such a careful job of convincing herself that it had all been just carnal and therefore meaningless, something to be experienced and enjoyed and then shrugged off.

Well, and so it had been!

She opened her eyes to rid herself of the images.

I thought him a thoroughly disagreeable man.

Too cold and haughty for his own good.

Why had those words hurt? She *agreed* with them. But they *had* hurt. They still did. She felt raw with grief, though she could not understand the reason.

He had been inside her. They had shared life's deepest intimacy. But only physically. There was no other connection between them at all, and never could be. There was nothing in him she could like and admire, and—to be fair—there was nothing in her that he could possibly like or admire either. And so they had been intimate without intimacy.

Her heart felt like a leaden weight in the middle of her chest.

She would never see him again.

Thank heaven.

But *never*.

It sounded like an awfully long time.

10

WULFRIC WENT HOME TO LINDSEY HALL IN Hampshire. For a whole week he reveled in the huge, silent emptiness of the place. It was home. It was where he belonged. For perhaps the first time in his life he realized that he loved it. He had not wanted it. As a boy, if there had been anything he could have done to change places with Aidan, to make *him* their father's heir instead of himself, he would have done it.

But when one was born the eldest son of a duke, of course, one was born with an unchangeable destiny. There was no freedom of choice allowed such a child.

As there was none to any child born to a chimney sweep, he supposed.

He had never been much of a one for self-pity. Why should he have been? There were thousands who would give a right arm for even a fraction of the privileges and wealth and power he took largely for granted.

He wandered from room to room in the house, far more than he usually did, and enjoyed the knowledge that there would be no people beyond every door, waiting to converse and be conversed with. He roamed about the large park surrounding the house, both on horseback and on foot, and was thankful that there was no one to suggest a picnic or an expedition by carriage.

Strangely, even though he prized his aloneness, he avoided the one small place on his estate where he always went when he wanted to relax into total solitude. He was too restless to relax.

He spent long hours with his steward, as he had not seen him in person since the Easter break from the House of Lords, and he rode with him about the vast home farm, checking that all was running smoothly according to his directions. He granted audience in the library to a number of his tenants and laborers and other petitioners, something he did conscientiously twice a week whenever he was home. He looked over the estate books and other business papers. He read all the reports that came from stewards on his other properties and dictated the appropriate responses to his secretary.

He wrote to each of his siblings, something he did regularly, at least once a month.

He received courtesy visits from some of his neighbors and returned most of them. Viscount Ravensberg and his lady and their children had just returned from a journey north that had taken them through Leicestershire. They had stayed for a week at Grandmaison with Rannulf and Judith and were able to bring Wulfric direct news of them.

He began to think that what remained of the summer might prove tediously long and planned visits to some of his other estates.

He read a great deal. Or, at least, he sat in his library a great deal, a book open in one hand, while he stared through it and brooded.

There were a score of women he already knew and doubtless scores more he did not who would jump at the chance of being his mistress. It was not a conceited thought. He did *not* think he was the answer to every woman's prayers. But he did know that he was a powerful and influential and enormously wealthy man, and he did not doubt that most such women were well aware that he had been generous with Rose.

If he were to choose one of them and set her up as his mistress, he would probably settle contentedly with her. His life would soon return to normal.

He missed Rose with a gnawing ache.

He kept his thoughts firmly away from the one woman with whom he had already tried to replace her.

She had rejected him. Just as Marianne Bonner had done when he had offered matrimony. Mrs. Derrick had rejected him when she had assumed he was offering the same thing again—even though she had just given herself to him.

A little rejection, he supposed, was good for the soul.

But his soul felt bruised, even crushed.

He planned visits to some of his other estates—but neglected to give the necessary orders that would have set the preparations in motion.

It was unlike him to procrastinate, to feel lethargic, to brood.

To feel lonely.

He did not think of Christine Derrick. But sometimes—or most of the time if he were to be quite truthful with himself—he discovered that bright, laughing blue eyes and tangled dark curls and sun-bronzed skin and a freckle-dusted nose could slip past thought and lodge themselves in unwelcome images in the brain and in a heavy feeling about the heart.

Soon he would visit some of his other estates. All he needed was something to keep him busy.

Soon he would be back to normal.

* * *

LOOKING BACK ON her fortnight at Schofield Park one week after the house party was over, it seemed to Christine that it might all have happened a year ago or a lifetime ago. Her life had resumed its usual semiplacid course and she was happy again.

Well, perhaps not exactly *happy*. But she was contented at least. Although she had been happy with both Oscar and his world for a few years, it was a world that had ultimately let her down and made her desperately miserable. Seeing Hermione and Basil again had not been a good experience. And being in company with people of *ton* again had reminded her of how easy it was to be scorned, sneered at, disapproved of. Not that it had happened much during her marriage, and not that it had happened much at Schofield. But the thing was that it *never* happened during her day-to-day life at Hyacinth Cottage and in the village beyond it. There she could relax and be herself and everyone seemed to like her for it. She had no enemies in the neighborhood, only friends.

And yet those years of her marriage and those years spent with the *ton*—and now the fortnight spent at Schofield Park—had left her restless and less satisfied with her life at home than she had been before. She felt like someone caught between two worlds and not quite belonging in either. She resented the feeling.

She *chose* to belong in her village. She enjoyed life here. There was always something to do. She liked teaching at the village school, even though she did it for only three hours a week. The schoolmaster had complained to her one day that he hated teaching geography, she had replied that it had always been her very favorite subject when *she* was a pupil, and the arrangement had been made. Even as a child she had visited the sick and elderly with her mother or with the old vicar's wife. It had become a habit, though never a dreary one. She still did it. She *liked* the elderly, and she had endless stories and smiles and cheerful conversation to share with both them and the sick—as well as two ears willing to listen and two hands willing to help out.

There were social visits to pay and receive, a few teas and dinners to attend, one assembly at the village inn. There were female friends with whom to share some confidences, gentlemen who would become her suitors if she wished.

She did not wish, even though perhaps it was a pity she did not. All she had ever really wanted was a home of her own and a husband and children to love. But she had lost the one—even before his death, if the truth were known—and never had the other. And her dreams had changed—or perhaps they had simply died.

There were her nephews and niece at the rectory, and Melanie's children at Schofield Park, though she did not visit the latter so often when Melanie and Bertie were in residence. She loved children. She quite passionately *adored* them. It had been the great disappointment of her marriage that she had never conceived.

There was Melanie to call upon and a long coze to enjoy together over the success of the house party. Melanie insisted that all the gentlemen had fallen in love with Christine and that the Earl of Kitredge had looked quite forlorn when he discovered that she had left Schofield after the ball instead of waiting until the following morning. In Melanie's opinion Christine could have been a countess before the summer was out if she had been so inclined.

"But I know," she had said with a sigh. "You have been unwilling to look at any man since poor Oscar died. He *was* a dear, was he not? And so very, very handsome. But *one* day, Christine, you will be able to let go of him and fall for someone else. I thought at one point that he might be the Duke of Bewcastle. You won that very naughty wager I heard about—*and* you were waltzing with him at the ball. But, splendid as he is, you know, and elated as I was to have him as a guest at my party, I certainly would not wish him upon my dearest friend. It is true, is it not, that he lowers the temperature of any room he walks into? Even so, I think he was the tiniest bit sweet on you, Christine."

Christine chose to laugh merrily as if a great joke had been made, and after a moment Melanie joined her.

"Well, perhaps not," she said. "I doubt there is any sweetness in him or any normal human sensibilities. I wonder if even the Prince of Wales cowers under his steely glance."

The Duke of Bewcastle was the one factor in Christine's life—in the past tense of her life—on which she chose neither to think nor to brood. There was pain in that direction, and she chose not to explore the pain.

She had plenty with which to occupy herself in the days following her return from Schofield, then—plenty to keep her busy and feed her natural ebullience of spirit. She was almost happy. Or, if not that, then she was definitely contented—provided she kept her thoughts carefully censored.

CHRISTINE WAS FEELING rather warm and flushed after one particular geography lesson. She had taken the children outside the schoolhouse, since it was a very warm day, and their usual game of flying on a magic carpet to the chosen country had taken them on an energetic course about the garden, all their arms flapping to the sides to keep them aloft—including her own. She could hardly be left behind when the carpet embarked on its journey, after all.

They had flown over a wide and blustery Atlantic

Ocean, spotting two sailing ships and a large iceberg on the way, and up the St. Lawrence Seaway to Canada, to Montreal, to be more precise, where they had touched down and rolled up the carpet before embarking inland with the colorful French voyageurs in their large canoes to trade for furs in the interior of the continent. They had rowed in near-perfect time with one another after practicing for a while and had braved rapids with noisy exuberance and negotiated rugged portages past the worst of them, the imaginary canoe held upside down over the heads of half of them while the other half staggered beneath the weight of the imaginary cargo. They had sung a rousing French song to keep their spirits high and spur them on their way.

By the time they had stopped to rest at the large trading post of Fort William on Lake Superior, from where they would embark at the beginning of the next lesson, they were all weary and fell back onto the magic carpet—which they had taken with them in the canoe—and crawled or staggered back in the direction of the schoolhouse with a great fuss of moans and groans and limp, flapping arms and giggles and complaints about having to go back inside for arithmetic.

Christine smiled after them until they were safely inside and she was free to return home to change her clothes and cool down in the quiet of the sitting room with some of Mrs. Skinner's freshly squeezed lemonade. She turned away from the building, the smile still on her face.

There was a man leaning on the fence, she could see. A gentleman, if she was not mistaken. She shaded her eyes with one hand and looked to see if he was someone she knew.

"Mrs. Thompson informed me I would find you here," the Duke of Bewcastle said. "I came to meet you."

Gracious heaven! Absurdly—*utterly* absurdly—her first thought was for her flushed cheeks, her damp, rumpled hair beneath her old straw bonnet, her dusty dress and shoes, and her generally bedraggled appearance. Her next thought—just as foolish—was that he must have seen some of that silly lesson—silly, but very effective in helping children learn and remember without their ever realizing that they were doing it. Her third thought was a blank question mark, which seemed to hang invisible in the air over their heads.

Her *feelings* were another matter altogether. She felt rather as if the bottom had fallen out of her stomach—or as if the journey by magic carpet had made her queasy.

"What are you doing here?" she asked him. It was a horribly rude question to ask of a duke, but who could think of good manners at such a moment? What *was* he doing here?

"I came to speak to you," he said with all the cool hauteur of a man who believed he had every right to speak to anyone he chose at any time he chose.

"Very well, then." The return flight across the Atlantic had also left her lamentably short of breath, she noticed. "Speak to me."

"Perhaps," he said, straightening up from the fence, "we may walk back in the direction of Hyacinth Cottage?"

He had been there already? But he had just said so, had he not? He had spoken with her mother. He had actually walked up the garden path to the cottage and knocked on the door. There was no sign of any servant trotting along in his shadow to perform such menial tasks for him.

She left the schoolhouse garden and fell into step beside him. And lest he get any idea about offering his arm, she clasped her own very firmly behind her back. She must look like a veritable *scarecrow*.

"I thought," she said, "you left here ten days ago like everyone else."

She *knew* he had. She had visited Melanie since then.

"You thought correctly," he said haughtily. "I went to Lindsey Hall. I have come back."

"Why?" she asked. Anyone would think she had never even *heard* of good manners.

"I needed to talk to you," he said.

"About what?" It was beginning to strike her fully that the *Duke of Bewcastle* was in the village and walking along the street at her side.

"Were there any consequences?" he asked her.

She felt a rush of heat to her cheeks. There was no misunderstanding his meaning, of course.

"No, of course not," she said. "As I told you at the time, I am barren. Is *this* why you returned? Do you always show such solicitude for the women with whom you—" Ignominiously, she could not think of a suitably euphemistic word with which to complete the sentence.

"I could have sent my secretary or another servant if that were all I wished to ascertain," he said. "I noticed a private-looking garden beside your house. Perhaps we may talk there?"

He was going to ask her again, she thought incredulously. How dared he? How *dared* he? And how dared he come back like this to disturb her peace all over again. Determined as she had been not to think of him, her nights were still filled with vivid dreams of him, and even her days were not yet free of unwilling memories that seemed quite beyond her power to banish. She did not *want* this.

Being a duke did *not* give him any right to harass her.

They did not proceed unseen. It was a warm day. Half the villagers—at *least* half—were sitting quietly or standing in gossiping groups outside their cottages. And every last one of them turned to wave a hand or call a greeting to her. And every last one of them gave the duke a good looking-over. Even if some of them did not know who he was, they would soon find out from those who did. It would be the sensation of the hour—of the decade! The Duke of Bewcastle was back and walking along the street and disappearing into the side garden of Hyacinth Cottage with Christine Derrick. Word would get back to Melanie and she would be here at the crack of dawn tomorrow—or as close to dawn as she could rise from her bed and submit to her elaborate toilette—to worm an explanation out of her friend.

Melanie would think she had been right all along. She would think the Duke of Bewcastle was sweet on Christine. But instead he was hot for her and determined to employ her as his mistress.

He did not say another word while they were on the street. Neither did she. She really thought that if he was too arrogant to accept that no meant no this time, she was going to have to slap his face. She had never slapped any man's face and disapproved of it as a feminine weapon of annoyance, since the man concerned—if he were a gentleman—could not retaliate in kind. But her palm itched with the urge to dole out punishment to the ducal cheek.

She was *not* pleased to see him.

Eleanor was in the sitting room window, peering over the tops of her spectacles, but she disappeared when Christine glared at her. Mrs. Skinner opened the front door unbidden but closed it again when Christine glared at *her*. She could only imagine the excitement and speculation going on within.

She led the way through the low garden gate, diagonally across the front garden, which was ablaze with the colors of numberless flowers, and up the stone steps and through the trellised arch into the square side garden, which tall trees partially secluded from both the house and the street and flower borders made lovely and fragrant. She went to stand behind a wooden seat and set one hand on its back. She leveled a gaze on the Duke of Bewcastle. Dressed in a charcoal gray coat and paler pantaloons and white-topped Hessian boots, he looked quite overwhelmingly male. Not many men came into this garden.

"Mrs. Derrick," he said, removing his hat and holding it at his side while the sunshine tangled in his dark hair. His voice was haughty and abrupt. "I wonder if you will do me the honor of marrying me."

Christine gawked. Thinking back afterward, she was sure she had not just stared in genteel surprise—she had gawked.

"What?" she said.

"I find myself unable to stop thinking about you," he said. "I have asked myself why I offered to make you my mistress rather than my wife and can find no satisfactory answer. There is no law to state that my position demands I marry a virgin or a lady who has not been previously married. There is no law that states I must marry my social equal. And if your childless state after a marriage of several years denotes an inability to conceive, then that is no prohibitive impediment either. I have three younger brothers to succeed me, and one of them already has a son of his own. I choose to have you as my wife. I beg you to accept me."

She stared at him, speechless for several moments. She gripped the back of the seat with both hands. Her head always seemed to fill with the most ridiculously absurd thoughts at the most serious of moments. This occasion was no exception.

She could be the *Duchess of Bewcastle,* she thought. She could wear ermine and a tiara. At least she thought she could. She had never really investigated the privileges of being a duchess, having never expected to be offered the role.

And then she found herself being restored to cold sanity as some of his words fell into place in her mind.

. . . a virgin . . . my social equal . . . your childless state . . . an inability to conceive. I choose to have you.

She gripped the back of the seat more tightly as anger welled in her and almost broke free.

"I am honored, your grace," she said, her nostrils flaring. "But, no. I decline."

He looked arrested, surprised. His eyebrows arced upward. She expected his infernal quizzing glass to materialize in his hand—and *that* would have made her temper finally snap—but he appeared not to have it about his person today.

"Ah," he said. "I daresay I offended you when I offered you something less than matrimony."

"You did," she said.

"And when I allowed you to believe after we had coupled that it was the same offer I was about to make," he said.

Her brows snapped together. It had not been? He had been about to offer her marriage then? She did not believe it. A man did not propose marriage to a woman who had just freely given him everything he wanted of her. But why had he come back now to do just that?

"You offended me," she said.

He looked at her with what appeared to be cold disdain. "And an apology will not suffice to soothe your wounded pride, ma'am?" he asked. "You are resolved to reject my marriage offer because you cannot forgive me for the other? I *do* apologize. I did not mean to offend."

"No," she said, moving around the seat to sit on it before her legs gave way under her and she sank to the ground in an ignominious heap from which he would have to rescue her again. "No, I suppose you did not. It is a marked distinction to be offered the position of mistress to the Duke of Bewcastle."

His eyes pierced through her own to the back of her skull.

"I have already begged your pardon," he said.

"I could do another woman a great favor," she said. "I could be your wife and leave the position of mistress vacant for someone else."

She was being worse than ill-mannered. She was being *vulgar*. But she was only just getting launched.

. . . a virgin . . . my social equal . . . your childless state . . . an inability to conceive. I choose to have you.

His eyes hardened, if that were possible.

"I believe in fidelity within marriage, Mrs. Derrick," he said. "If I ever take a wife, she will be the only woman to occupy my bed for as long as we both live."

She was glad she was sitting then. Her knees became boneless.

"Perhaps," she said. "But she will not be me."

She had nothing but ancient, faded, and patched clothes to wear, she had scarcely two ha'pennies to rub together, she was almost totally dependent upon her mother, she lived a rather tedious life, she had no dreams left to dream—and yet here she sat refusing the chance to be a *duchess*. Did she have a whole arsenal of windmills in her head?

He turned as if to leave. But then he paused and looked back at her over his shoulder.

"I did not think you indifferent to me," he said. "And contrary to popular belief, one coupling does not kill physical attraction. Your prospects of living a fulfilled life here seem slender. Life as my duchess would offer you infinitely more. Do you say no, Mrs. Derrick, only to punish me? Will you perhaps punish yourself too in the process? I can offer you everything you can ever have dreamed of."

The fact that she was tempted—drat her, she was *tempted*—fanned the flames of her anger.

"Can you?" she asked sharply. "A husband with a warm personality and human kindness and a sense of humor? Someone who loves people and children and frolicking and absurdity? Someone who is not obsessed with himself and his own consequence? Someone who is not ice to the very core? Someone with a heart? Someone to be a companion and friend and lover? *This* is everything I have ever dreamed of, your grace. Can you offer it all to me? Or any of it? Any one thing?"

He pierced her with those eyes of his for so long that she had to exert great control over herself to stop from squirming.

"*Someone with a heart,*" he said very softly then. "No, perhaps you are right, Mrs. Derrick. Perhaps I do not possess one. And, if I do not, then I lack everything of which you dream, do I not? I beg your pardon for taking your time and for offending you yet again."

And this time when he turned away he kept going— beneath the trellis, down the steps, out through the garden gate, which he closed quietly and precisely behind him, and down the street, presumably to the inn, where he had probably left his carriage. She doubted he would stay somewhere so humble.

Christine gazed after him until he was out of sight. And then she looked down at her hands, which were clasped very tightly in her lap, the knuckles white.

"Bother," she said aloud. "Bother, bother, bother, bother, bother."

And then she burst into noisy tears, which she could not seem to control even though she feared they might be audible from the sitting room or from the street.

She wept until her nasal passages were swollen and her throat and chest were sore and her face, no doubt, was puffy and blotchy and ugly. She wept until she could weep no more.

Bother, bother, bother.

She hated him!

Someone with a heart.

No, perhaps you are right, Mrs. Derrick. Perhaps I do not possess one.

There had been a look in his eyes when he spoke those words.

What did she mean by that? A *look*?

It had broken her heart, that was what she meant.

It had broken her heart.

She hated him, she hated him, she *hated* him.

11

*W*ULFRIC WAS NOT REALLY SURPRISED BY HIS invitation to the wedding of Miss Audrey Magnus to Sir Lewis Wiseman at the end of February. The nuptials were to take place in London, at St. George's on Hanover Square, at a time of year when not every member of the *ton* was back in town. The Season would not begin in earnest until after the Easter holiday. It was understandable, then, that Lady Mowbury and her son would invite everyone of any distinction who *was* there. Besides, Wulfric was a friend of Mowbury's and would probably have merited an invitation under any circumstances.

With the exception of ten days spent in Oxfordshire with Aidan and Eve and their family over Christmas, he had been back in town since late autumn, though there had been no good reason for returning even before the House began its session. He had spent a few months traveling about the country, visiting and inspecting a number of his estates, consulting with his stewards, receiving petitioners, and being feted by families of distinction in the various neighborhoods. He would normally have been so thankful to be back at Lindsey Hall that he would have stayed there until the last possible moment before the new session began.

But as soon as he was back there, he had been assailed

again by that dual reaction of love for the place and an unbearable restlessness. It had seemed so alarmingly empty—a strange thought when it was its very emptiness that he yearned for when he was away from it. But even Morgan, the youngest of his family, and her governess had been gone for more than two years. She was married, with two children—the second one, another son, born early in February. She had been a mere infant of two years when he inherited his title. She had always seemed more like his daughter than his sister, though he had not realized that until after she was gone—or, more accurately, until her wedding day.

He had come to town, where at least there were his clubs and a few other carefully chosen diversions to distract his mind.

Besides, he had needed to set up a new mistress. Not that he had had a great deal of heart for the task, but he did have needs that demanded satisfying, and he was too fastidious to relieve them in any casual encounter with a whore. His sexual preferences had always leaned toward regularity and monogamy.

But by the end of February he had still not acquired a mistress, though he had taken a certain much-sought-after actress to dinner one night after admiring her performance at the theater and making an unexpected appearance in the green room afterward. He had fully intended discussing terms of a contract with her, and she had indicated quite clearly that she would welcome such a discussion and even a consummation of their arrangement before the final details had been worked out. But he had talked about acting and drama with her instead and then escorted her home and paid her handsomely for her time. And though the beautiful, accomplished, very discreet Lady Falconbridge had signaled her availability to him and he had spent some time with her socially, he had not broached the topic that they both knew he might broach at any moment.

He had procrastinated—something he rarely did.

He was not surprised when the wedding invitation came, but he did hesitate before answering it. Mowbury's family included the Elricks and the Renables, and it was highly likely that they would be in attendance too. They were people he had known for years. He would not normally scruple to meet them again, since he had never particularly disliked any of them. But most recently—though it was in fact more than six months ago—he had spent two weeks with them at Schofield Park. And of course the bride and groom had been there too as well as the bride's mother and brothers.

He would really prefer to have no reminder of the unfortunate lapse from his usual habits that he had allowed to happen there. He had chosen to forget, and he believed he had been quite successful. Why would he not, after all? It had all been sheer madness, that business with Mrs. Derrick, and he was quite happy that he had escaped with his familiar way of life still intact. But he wanted no reminder.

It *was* his habit, however, to be polite and to do as he ought in any given situation. He wrote a brief acceptance and directed his secretary to send it off to Lady Mowbury.

MUCH AS SHE was fond of Melanie and Hector and Justin and Audrey as well as Lady Mowbury, Christine would certainly not have accepted her invitation to Audrey's wedding in February if something quite extraordinary had not happened. How could she, after all? The wedding was to be in London. Not that the distance would be any great impediment, she realized. Melanie and Bertie would of course be going and they would surely agree to take her along with them in their carriage. They would probably even invite her to stay with them, though Lady Mowbury had added a note to the bottom of her invitation assuring her that she would be quite welcome to stay with *them*.

But how could she go when she had nothing decent to wear—and, more important, when Hermione and Basil would be there too? In the months since the house party her heart had been heavy over their hostile, even spiteful treatment of her. Their bitterness and hatred had not abated in two years—now closer to three. Neither had their resentment at having to claim her as kin. She would not wittingly put herself in their way ever again.

But then, just an hour after she had written an affectionately worded refusal to Lady Mowbury and propped it beside the clock on the mantel in the sitting room, ready to be sent on its way, something extraordinary really did happen. A letter from Basil was delivered to Hyacinth Cottage, and with it a draft on his bank for a rather large sum of money—indeed, it seemed like a vast fortune to Christine, whose only source of personal income was her teaching, and to call that income pin money was somewhat to exaggerate its significance.

The money was to be spent on new clothes and other personal items, Basil explained in the brief, rather terse note that accompanied the bank draft. Christine would doubtless wish to attend the wedding of their cousin and must be decently clothed, but even besides that she was his sister-in-law and therefore his responsibility. Hermione had brought it to his attention that her summer wardrobe had been on the shabby side last year.

There were no expressions of affection or forgiveness, no apology, no greetings to her family or from Hermione, no news of their doings or of their sons, no questions about her life or situation—just the brief explanation of what he wished to say and the money.

Christine's first instinct was to return it with a note that was even terser and more dispassionate than Basil's. But Eleanor came into her room while she held the letter in one hand and the bank draft lay in her lap. Eleanor was looking for embroidery silk of a color she did not have in her own workbox.

"You are looking as if you had seen a ghost," she said after making her request.

"Look at this." Christine held out the letter to her and then the bank draft.

Eleanor read the former and glanced at the latter before raising her eyebrows.

"At Schofield last summer," Christine said, "they both treated me as if they would dearly like to rid the universe of my presence in it if only they could find a legal way of doing so."

"And so you intend to return the money, I suppose," Eleanor said, "with all the injured pride you can drag about yourself. They were very polite to Mama and me during the ball at the end of that fortnight. They sat with us at supper, I remember, and made themselves very agreeable."

Christine had not even known that.

"I cannot accept money from them," she said.

"Why not?" Eleanor asked. "You *are* the widow of Viscount Elrick's only brother, and you *do* need new clothes. You have been most stubborn in your refusal to allow Mama to pay for new ones for you."

It was true. Oscar had left her nothing, and yet it did not seem right to be dependent upon her mother, whose income from Papa's estate was adequate for her needs and Eleanor's but only barely.

"There is enough money here to clothe all three of us in some luxury for the summer," she said. "But I cannot accept it, Eleanor. They do not even *like* me."

"The money is for *you*," her sister told her, tapping the letter with one finger. "Viscount Elrick has made that very clear here. And if they do not like you, why have they sent this? It looks to me like some sort of peace offering."

"They still blame me for Oscar's death," Christine said. "Basil adored him, and because Hermione adores Basil, then *she* loved Oscar too."

"But how could they blame you?" Eleanor asked, exasperated. "I have never understood that, Christine. He was out hunting and you were not. Were you supposed to have stopped his going?"

Christine shrugged. She had never been able to tell the truth about Oscar's death, and the inability to confide in even her favorite sister and her mother had always weighed heavily on her.

"Is that what it is?" She frowned. "A peace offering?"

"Why else would he have sent it?" Eleanor asked.

Why indeed? Perhaps they regretted certain things they had said to her and of her during those two weeks at Schofield and wanted to extend some sort of an olive branch. If she sent the money back, she would offend them and thus keep alive an enmity that had never been of her choosing. In some way Christine felt they deserved it. But she had never been one to hate or hold grudges. She did not want to hate them any longer. And she certainly did not want to hurt them any more. Perhaps Basil had suddenly realized that she was his only remaining link with his brother.

She swallowed against a lump in her throat.

Or perhaps Hermione feared that she would turn up at the wedding in rags to shame them. Perhaps that was *all* this bank draft was about.

But why always think the worst of people? What would she be doing to herself if she adopted that attitude to life? It was better to think the best and be wrong than to think the worst and be wrong.

She sighed. "If I am to keep it," she said, "I must also go to Audrey's wedding—if Melanie will agree to take me with her and Bertie."

"*If!*" Eleanor clucked her tongue and tossed a glance at the ceiling. "You know very well that within the next day or two Lady Renable is going to be bearing down upon you here anyway, Christine, to talk you into accepting your invitation. Even if you had already decided against going, even if you had actually sent a refusal, you would end up going anyway."

"Am I really so weak-willed?" Christine frowned.

"No, but she is the most stubborn woman it has ever been my misfortune to know," Eleanor said, "in addition to being the most frivolous and the most pretentious." She chuckled. "I cannot help but like the woman, though—especially as she has chosen *you* as a friend rather than me. *Do* you have any embroidery silk in this particular shade of green, Christine? If not, I will have to walk all the way to the shop to purchase some and the rain is still tipping down."

And so Christine decided to keep the money and to spend it on herself—though that latter point she decided only after both Eleanor and her mother had flatly refused to take even a single penny from her. She also decided that she must attend the wedding, since the money had surely been sent primarily to buy her clothes suitable for that grand occasion. She would, she decided, bring back gifts for her mother and Eleanor—as well as for Hazel and the children.

Ah, the wonderful luxury of being able to think about purchasing gifts!

She tore up her letter of refusal to Lady Mowbury and replaced it with an acceptance. And she labored for upward of an hour over a suitable reply to Basil.

Less than an hour after she had finished it, the unmistakable sounds of horses' hooves and carriage wheels approaching along the village street heralded the arrival of Melanie, despite the rain, girded for battle. But no battle was required. Christine was able to inform her that she had already accepted her invitation to the wedding and had been planning to walk to Schofield as soon as the rain stopped in order to beg a ride to London.

"You would have *walked*, Christine, all the way to Schofield after a *rain*?" Melanie said, her lorgnette suspended in the air, her free hand pressed to her heart. "Just in order to beg a ride with Bertie and me? *Beg*? I would have had my brawniest footman carry you bodily out to the carriage on the day of our departure to London if you had shown any resistance to coming voluntarily. But you would have walked through *mud* to *beg*?"

Christine chuckled and Eleanor dipped her head behind her book.

She was going to London, then, it seemed, and to Audrey's wedding at St. George's. She did not know whether to feel excited or dismayed, but decided upon the former. It was not even quite spring, after all, and not the most fashionable time to be in London. There were not likely to be any social entertainments *except* the wedding, and Lady Mowbury in her invitation had called it a *family* wedding.

Besides, she was to have some new clothes and would be able to purchase them in London from plates of the latest fashions. She surely would not have been human if that prospect had not cheered her.

IT WAS STRANGE, Wulfric thought as he took his place in the church pew and concentrated his attention upon Sir Lewis Wiseman, who was waiting at the front for the

arrival of his bride and looking as if his valet must have
tied his neckcloth too tightly—it was strange that he had
expected all of Miss Magnus's family to attend and had
even hesitated about coming himself because he did not
want to be reminded of those two weeks at Schofield
Park. But it had not once occurred to him that perhaps
Christine Derrick—*who was a member of that family by
marriage*—might also be here.

But she was.

He had almost not recognized her as he passed the
pew she was occupying with the Elricks. She was dressed
neatly and smartly in dove gray and pale blue. She had
glanced up at him as he passed, and for one ghastly moment until she dipped her head hastily and he averted his
head just as sharply, their eyes had met.

If he had known, he most certainly would not have
come.

He really had not wanted to set eyes upon Christine
Derrick again this side of eternity. He had no kind
thoughts for her. And it embarrassed him to remember
that he had traveled all the way from Hampshire to
Gloucestershire in order to offer marriage after all to a
widow, daughter of a schoolmaster and a teacher herself,
who half the time did not know how to behave and who
found her embarrassing scrapes *funny*. A woman less eligible to be his duchess he could scarcely have chosen.

Yet she had refused him!

Only belatedly did it strike him that both of them had
behaved uncharacteristically this morning. He almost
never looked away from another person merely because
that person was looking back at him. And at Schofield she
had always engaged him in staring matches rather than
have him believe she was being meekly obedient to his
silent and arrogant command that she lower her gaze in
his august presence.

The old irritation against her returned just as if he had not forgotten about her in the intervening months.

He would sit through the service, Wulfric decided, and then make some excuse to Mowbury for missing the wedding breakfast. He would wait in his pew until everyone behind him had left and then slip out unnoticed.

Perhaps he was behaving like a coward—*certainly* he was behaving out of character—but then he would be doing her a kindness too. She was doubtless as dismayed to find him here as he was to find her—and she had had less reason to expect that he might be a fellow guest.

A husband with a warm personality and human kindness and a sense of humor.

He could hear her voice speaking the words, almost as if she had spoken them out loud now, in St. George's, for all to hear. There was scorn in her voice and trembling passion.

He had no warmth of personality, no compassion or kindness, no laughter inside himself. That was what she had accused him of. That was part of her reason for rejecting him.

No warmth.

No kindness.

No humor.

Why was it that that little speech of hers had imprinted itself indelibly upon his memory? And the image of her as she delivered it, dusty, even grubby, from that remarkable lesson she had been giving the village schoolchildren, her floppy-brimmed straw bonnet doing little to hide the dampness and unruliness of her hair, her face flushed and even glistening with perspiration, her eyes flashing.

What the devil was it about her that had made him decide that he must have her as his bride? Even after what had happened between them down at the lake he might have considered carte blanche a sufficient price to pay—

and she could have expected no more. Her very reaction
to his uncompleted words proved that. Why matrimony,
then? What was it that had discomposed him for weeks,
even months, after her unexpected refusal?

Wounded pride?

Fortunately, he had made a full recovery and was now
very thankful indeed for her refusal.

*Someone who loves people and children and frolicking and ab-
surdity.*

Of course he was not such a person. The very idea—
frolicking and *absurdity*! But there were people he loved—
even children.

*Someone who is not obsessed with himself and his own conse-
quence. Someone who is not ice to the very core. Someone with a
heart.*

His mind shied from the memory. He had never been
able to cope with that particular part of her rejection. But
it was the part that had caused most pain—in the days before he had recovered from such foolishness.

Fortunately, Miss Magnus arrived at the church only a
minute or two late, and Wulfric was able to concentrate
his attention upon the nuptial service. He could identify
with Mowbury's rather sheepish pride as he gave his sister
away to her new husband. It was two and a half years
since Morgan's wedding and more than three since
Freyja's. On both occasions he had been startled by the
pain of loss, especially with Morgan, the baby of the family, the one they had all most adored. Even he . . .

Someone with a heart.

He could *feel* Christine Derrick several pews behind his
own, almost as if she held a long feather and was brushing
it up and down his spine. Soon it would touch his neck
and he would shrug his shoulders defensively.

He gazed sternly at the bride and groom and at the

clergyman and listened carefully to everything that was said without hearing a word.

Unfortunately he delayed too long after the nuptials were over. By the time he left the church, Sir Lewis and the new Lady Wiseman had already driven away in the wedding carriage, but Mowbury and his mother had gone too, as had most members of the two families, Mrs. Derrick included. Her disappearance was a vast relief, of course, but how could he now avoid going to the breakfast, Wulfric thought, when he had not had a chance of a word with either Mowbury or his mother? It would be ill-mannered, and he was never discourteous if he could help it.

A hand grasped his shoulder.

"Bewcastle," the Earl of Kitredge said, "I will ride with you if I may and leave my own carriage to the young people."

"It would be my pleasure," Wulfric assured him.

He would, he decided, sit at his appointed place for the breakfast, pay his compliments to the newly married couple afterward, express his thanks to Lady Mowbury, and slip away at the earliest opportunity. He would confine his movements for the next few days to the House and White's when he must leave Bedwyn House. It occurred to him that such a decision might be cowardly, but he convinced himself that he would merely be doing what he usually did. At this time of year there were not a great many social events to be avoided anyway.

Although most of the guests to Magnus House on Berkeley Square had not yet taken their places in the ballroom, which had been converted into a dining hall for the occasion, but were milling about there, greeting and conversing with one another, Wulfric was not tempted to join any of them. He was adept at distancing himself from such social intercourse. He would have found his place, taken it, and looked about him with cool ease had it not been for the fact that he had entered the house and the ballroom with Kitredge.

"Ah," the earl said, setting a hand on Wulfric's sleeve, "there is the very person I want to have a word with, and you have an acquaintance with her too, Bewcastle. Come."

Too late, Wulfric realized that he was being drawn in the direction of Christine Derrick, who was standing with the Elricks and the Renables and Justin Magnus.

She had removed her bonnet. Her hair looked newly cut. It framed her round, pretty, wide-eyed face in short, soft, shining curls. The dove gray dress with its blue trimmings and ribbons suited her. Many ladies would sink into insignificance behind such muted colors, but her vitality shone past them and dominated them. She was laughing at something Magnus was saying and looking animated and quite incredibly lovely.

And then she saw them coming—and her animation vanished, though her smile remained fixed in place.

"Mrs. Derrick," Kitredge said after greeting the others with hearty good humor. He took her hand in his, bowed over it with a slight creaking of his stays, and raised it to his lips. "You are looking lovelier than ever, if that can be possible. Is she not, Bewcastle?"

Wulfric ignored the question. He bowed to the others and to her.

"Ma'am," he said stiffly.

"Your grace." She looked very directly into his eyes when he had expected that she might fix them on his chin or cravat. But how foolish of him—she had clearly recovered from her surprise in the church, and would not give him the satisfaction of showing embarrassment, if she felt any.

"I trust," he said, "that you left your mother well?"

"I did, thank you." She held his gaze.

"And your sisters too?"

"Yes. Thank you."

"Ah." The fingers of his right hand found the handle of his quizzing glass and closed about it. "I am gratified to hear it."

Her glance did drop then—to his hand and his glass—before coming back to meet his own. But now there was a change. Now her eyes *laughed* at him, though she was no longer actually smiling. He had forgotten that extraordinary look.

"Mowbury's ballroom has been done up quite splendidly for the occasion," Kitredge said. "Perhaps you would care to take a turn about the room with me, Mrs. Derrick, so that we may admire all the floral decorations."

She moved her gaze to Kitredge, and this time she did smile—quite dazzlingly.

"Thank you." She took his offered arm and moved off with him.

She sat with her family during the breakfast. Wulfric sat some distance away, making polite conversation with Lady Hemmings to his left and Mrs. Chesney to his right. As soon as the meal was over and he had offered his congratulations and expressed his thanks, he took his leave and walked home, having waved away his carriage, which was drawn up in the square with many others.

He was feeling irritated. It was not a feeling he allowed himself with any frequency, and when he *did* feel it, he went instantly about relieving himself of its cause with the appropriate action.

But how did one deal with one's irritation over a woman who stubbornly refused to leave either one's thoughts or one's blood—even when one had believed one had purged her memory and influence long ago? And a woman, moreover, who smiled far too brightly and talked with far too much animation, even to people who sat *across* the table from her?

She simply did not know how to behave.

How did one deal with a woman who insisted upon holding one's glance every time she caught one watching her and outmaneuvered one by raising her eyebrows— and then laughing at one?

He was still infatuated with her, Wulfric thought in some amazement as he strode out of the square and a couple of coachmen who had been lounging on the corner jumped out of the way of his stern glance and pulled at their forelocks.

And *infatuated* be damned. He was near to being blinded by his attraction to her. He was *in love*, damn it all. He disliked her, he resented her, he disapproved of almost everything about her, yet he was head over ears in love with her, like a foolish schoolboy.

He wondered grimly what he was going to do about it.

He was *not* amused.

Or in any way pleased.

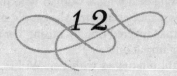

*C*HRISTINE HAD ARRIVED IN LONDON ONE WEEK before Audrey's wedding and had taken up residence with Melanie and Bertie. She had enjoyed the week. It had included numerous shopping trips to Oxford Street and even the more exclusive Bond Street, since she needed new clothes, and for once in her life had money to spend on them—and since shopping was one of Melanie's passions. Soon Christine had a new wardrobe of spring and summer clothes, all chosen with an eye to color and fashion and practicality—and economy. She did, after all, want to have some money left with which to purchase gifts to take home to her family. And she was not extravagant by nature.

She had enjoyed visiting Lady Mowbury with Melanie and seeing Hector and sharing some of the excitement of the approaching wedding with Audrey. She had taken a drive in the park with Justin.

She had even gone with Melanie and Bertie to dine with Hermione and Basil two days before the wedding, an occasion she had not looked forward to with any eagerness at all. But they had been civil, if not exactly affectionate, and Basil had taken her aside during the evening to explain to her that he intended to make her a quarterly allowance, since she was Oscar's widow and therefore his financial responsibility. When she had tried arguing with him, he had insisted. He and Hermione had talked about it, he had told her, and come to the decision that it was what Oscar would have wanted. Christine had seen that it was important to him that she accept, and so she had argued no more.

Hermione had kissed the air near her cheek as they were leaving and submitted to Christine's hug.

Some sort of peace had been made, Christine supposed. It was more than she had expected after last year. Their two sons, Oscar's nephews and therefore Christine's too, had greeted their aunt with enthusiasm and she had remembered that she had always been a great favorite with them.

She had done the right thing to come to town for the family wedding, she had decided. She had still thought so even when she arrived at St. George's on Hanover Square and discovered that there were obviously going to be far more guests than just family. At least by then she had been clad in the smartest of her new clothes and was with Hermione and Basil and the boys.

She had thought it right up to the moment when she had looked up to see who the gentleman was who was important enough to be seated in front of Viscount and Viscountess Elrick, cousins of the bride, and had realized that he was the Duke of Bewcastle.

To say that she had felt seriously discomposed at that moment would be greatly to understate the case. She had almost panicked, if the truth were known, and jumped out of her pew and blundered back along the nave of the church to make her escape—and a public spectacle of herself. Instead, she had looked sharply away from him at just the moment when their eyes met and had completely missed the wedding of Audrey and Lewis, even though it had been solemnized right before her eyes.

She had been aware only of the proud, rigid, broad-shouldered, handsomely clad back of the Duke of Bewcastle. And memories of that dreadful fortnight at Schofield Park had come flooding back—as well as of the final evening by the lake. And of his return ten days later to call upon her at Hyacinth Cottage.

She had never for one single moment considered the possibility of his being at Audrey's wedding. She had thought it was to be an intimate family affair. She would not in a million years have come within a million miles of London if she had known.

She might as well have been in an empty barn rather than a splendidly decorated ballroom and have eaten straw rather than sumptuous banquet fare during the wedding breakfast for all she had concentrated upon either after the wedding was over. She was aware that she had smiled rather too brightly at the Earl of Kitredge and conversed rather too animatedly with him. She was also aware that she had recovered some of her aplomb during the meal and had not looked meekly downward whenever her gaze and the duke's had happened to lock, but even so it had been one of the most uncomfortable days of her life.

She had been enormously relieved when he left early.

And then she had been mortally depressed for the rest of the day even though she had chattered and laughed and sparkled until she had arrived back at Melanie and Bertie's quite late in the evening and was safely shut up in her own room.

She believed she had quite effectively forgotten the Duke of Bewcastle in the six months or so since she last saw him. Her reaction to seeing him again, therefore, shook her considerably. How could she *ever* have believed that lying with him by the lake on that final night was something that could be casually done and easily forgotten? Would her reaction have been any less intense, though, if that had *not* happened? And if he had not come back after ten days to offer her marriage?

It was impossible to know. She had never understood any of her feelings of attraction to a man who was simply *not* attractive. Handsome, yes, but not attractive—not to her anyway.

It did not matter. She was to return home a day or two after the wedding and would simply have to work on forgetting again. If her emotions were far more involved than she had supposed, then she had no one but herself to blame. No one had forced her to walk in the laburnum alley with the duke. It had been her idea to go into the maze. And no one had forced her to go to the lake with him.

And then Melanie changed her mind. About returning home, that was. The original plan had been to come up to town for the wedding and then return to Schofield until after Easter when the Season would begin, bringing with it an endless round of entertainments. Christine would not be returning with them for the Season, of course.

"But the thing is, Christine," Melanie said at breakfast the morning after the wedding, "that there are more families back in town than there usually are at this time of year, and each morning the post brings with it a number of invitations to events one would really hate to miss. And of course one feels it almost one's civic duty to attend as many as possible, since no one can expect a great squeeze of a crowd this early in the year. And it does seem a shame to have come all this way only to go back before we have had a chance to enjoy ourselves. It seems a shame to deprive Bertie of his clubs so soon."

Bertie, who was partaking of breakfast with them, cut into his juicy beefsteak and rumbled. He had perfected the art of making that sound to serve as a suitable answer to whatever Melanie asked or suggested, Christine had noticed, and had thereby released himself from the necessity of listening to everything she said.

"And you have all your new clothes," Melanie said, "and are looking pretty enough for a girl half your age. You simply must have occasion to wear them. Mama and Justin will be disappointed if we leave so soon, and Hector would be too, the poor dear, if he had noticed that we had arrived. Besides all of which, the Earl of Kitredge is quite smitten with you, Christine, and is surely within an inch of declaring himself. And though I know you cannot possibly want a husband who is all of thirty years your senior and who is portly even *with* his stays, it is nevertheless vastly diverting to watch him pay you court—and it cannot hurt your consequence for the *ton* to watch it too, at least that portion of the *ton* that is in town."

A few times Christine had opened her mouth to speak, but, as usual, it was impossible to get a word in edgewise when Melanie was launched upon an enthusiastic monologue—especially when she sensed that the answer at the end of it all might be no.

"We will stay for another week," she continued, setting down her coffee cup and laying a hand over the back of Christine's on the table. "We will be busy from noon until the early hours and have a thoroughly enjoyable time. I can have your company in town for a whole week, or a fortnight if you count the week we have already been here. It will be so marvelously diverting. What do you say? Do agree to stay. Do say yes."

It was really not the time to be firm, Christine thought in some dismay. How could she say no? She had come here in the Renable carriage and she was staying in the Renable town home and eating the Renable food. How could she dictate when they were to return to the country? It did occur to her that she might return alone on the stagecoach, but she knew that if she even suggested such a thing Melanie would threaten a fit of the vapors—and she might well be genuinely offended. Even Bertie would probably exert himself enough to speak actual words.

But a whole week? With the *ton* again? It was a horrible thought. But it was *only* a week—only seven days. And at Schofield it had been generally agreed that the Duke of Bewcastle did not attend many social events. Had not Lady Sarah Buchan said that she had not seen him at all last spring even though she had been making her come-out and must have gone everywhere where the *ton* was gathered in large numbers? And, indeed, Christine herself had not set eyes on him during the seven years of her marriage.

"If you wish to stay, of course, Melanie," she said, "then I must."

Melanie tapped her arm sharply before picking up her coffee cup again.

"That is no answer," she said. "There is no *must* about it. If you would prefer to go home, then we will deprive Bertie of his clubs and go. But we will miss Lady Gosselin's soiree the evening after tomorrow, and she is a particular friend of mine and will be vexed if I go home instead of waiting and going there first. And we will miss—"

"Melanie." Christine leaned toward her across the table. "I would be delighted to accept your hospitality and stay one more week."

"I knew you would." Melanie beamed at her and clasped her hands with delight. "Bertie, my love, you will be able to go to your clubs and to Tattersall's. You will be able to play cards at Lady Gosselin's, where the stakes are always high enough to be to your liking."

Bertie, more than halfway through his beefsteak, rumbled.

And so she was stuck, Christine thought with glum resignation, not only in London, but also with the obligation to attend any social event that Melanie chose for their amusement. It soon became apparent that there was a formidable number of such events despite the earliness of the season. There were teas to attend and a private concert and a dinner—and of course the soiree at Lady Gosselin's.

CHRISTINE WORE ONE of her new gowns to the soiree—a midnight blue lace on velvet that she particularly loved because its design was flowing and elegant yet not fussy. She felt that it suited her age as well as her coloring. She borrowed a pearl necklace at Melanie's insistence but wore no other adornment, only her white evening gloves and an ivory fan Hermione and Basil had once given her for a birthday gift.

She smiled brightly as she entered Lady Gosselin's drawing room, the first of several adjoining chambers that had been thrown open for the convenience of guests. And the very first person she saw—of course!—was the Duke of Bewcastle, looking dark and elegant and toplofty as he stood at the opposite side of the room conversing with a handsome raven-haired lady who was seated and sipping from a glass of wine. She was Lady Falconbridge, a marquess's widow, whom Christine remembered from past years.

If she could have retreated in good order and returned to the Renable house—or all the way to Hyacinth Cottage— she would have done so. But Melanie had linked an arm through hers, and the only way to go was forward.

Bother, bother, bother, Christine thought, noticing irrelevantly the elegance of Lady Falconbridge's upswept curls and the fineness of the plumes with which they were adorned.

She felt like a country cousin again.

There must surely have been a dozen people in the

room whom Melanie knew. Better yet, there must have been a dozen people in the *next* room. But she brightened noticeably at sight of just the one person, lifted both her chin and her lorgnette, and swept across the room with Christine in tow in a manner that would have had Eleanor in stitches of mirth if she could just have witnessed it. Bertie had already disappeared, presumably in the direction of the card room.

"Bewcastle!" Melanie exclaimed, tapping him on the arm with her lorgnette. "It is not often one sees *you* at such events."

He turned, his eyebrows arching upward, his eyes meeting Christine's before they moved on to Melanie. He inclined his head stiffly.

"Lady Renable," he said. "Mrs. Derrick."

Christine had forgotten just how arctic those silver eyes could look—and how they could penetrate one's own eyes to the back of one's skull.

"Your grace," she murmured.

He did not deign, Christine noticed, to justify his appearance at this particular entertainment to Melanie. Why should he? He fingered the handle of his quizzing glass while Lady Falconbridge tapped one impatient foot on the floor.

"We have stayed in town for an extra week," Melanie announced, "because London is full of superior and agreeable company despite the earliness of the season. And Lilian's soirees are always worth attending."

His grace inclined his head again.

"Melanie," Christine said, "I see Justin in the next room. Shall we move on?"

The ducal eyes rested on her for a moment, and the ducal quizzing glass was raised to the level of the ducal chest. Christine silently dared him to raise it all the way to his eye.

"I will not keep you, then," he said, turning back toward Lady Falconbridge.

The next room was a music room, and someone was playing the pianoforte—it was Lady Sarah Buchan, Christine could see. She smiled happily at Justin, who came and took her arm while Melanie swept onward toward a group of ladies who opened ranks to admit her and swallow her up into their midst.

"I saw you and Mel paying homage to Bewcastle," Justin said with a grin.

"I never would have come here," Christine assured him, "if I had suspected that he would be here too."

He chuckled. "For someone who protested last year that he had been merely polite and gallant," he said, "you are reacting rather strongly, are you not? But you have nothing to fear from him this year. He is in determined pursuit of Lady Falconbridge, and since she is also in determined pursuit of him, no one expects many more days to pass before they have come to a satisfactory and discreet arrangement. I do believe there are wagers on the exact number of days in some of the betting books at the clubs."

"Dear Justin," she said, smiling brightly at him. "You are always willing to fill a lady's ears with everything she ought not to hear." And everything she really did not want to know.

"But I know you are not missish, Chrissie." Justin laughed and drew her closer to the pianoforte.

She was not allowed to relax there with him for long, though. The Earl of Kitredge soon joined them, and, having applauded his daughter on her musical performance and then ascertained that Christine had never seen the famous Rembrandt that hung in the salon beyond the refreshment room, he offered his arm and informed her that he would be delighted to show it to her.

There was no one else in the salon, which was poorly lit and had probably not even been intended to be used during the soiree. After gazing obligingly at the painting for all of five minutes, Christine would have maneuvered her way back to the other rooms, but the earl took her firmly by the arm and led her toward a bench at the far side of the salon. He stood before her as she seated herself, his hands behind him. She suspected that his stays prevented him from joining her there and was thankful for it.

"Mrs. Derrick," he began after clearing his throat, "you must have suspected even last summer the depth of my admiration for you."

"I am honored, my lord," she said, instantly alarmed. "Shall we—"

"And this year," he said, "I feel constrained to tell you openly of the violence of my attachment to you."

Was she a flirt? Christine wondered. *Was* she? Oscar had come to believe that she was, and Basil and Hermione had finally been convinced of it too. But if she was, then it was really quite unconscious. She had never said or done anything to encourage the earl to conceive a violent attachment to her—or even a mild one, for that matter. She had never done anything to encourage *anyone*—except Oscar, almost ten years ago.

"My lord," she said, "much as I am gratified, I must—"

But he had seized one of her hands in both his own. One of his rings dug painfully into her little finger.

"I beg you, ma'am," he said, "to tease me no longer. I am too old for you, the world will say. But my family is grown, and I am free to pursue my heart's desire again. And you, ma'am, are my heart's desire. I flatter myself that—"

"My lord." She tried to snatch her hand away and failed. He had too strong a grip on it.

"—you must have a regard for my person," he continued. "I lay it and my title and fortune at your feet, ma'am."

"My lord." She tried again. "This is a very public setting. Please release—"

"Tell me," he said, "that you will make me the happiest of—"

"*My lord,*" she said firmly, embarrassment turning to annoyance, "I find this insistence that I listen to you discourteous, even offensive. I—"

"—men," he said. "I beg that you will allow me to make you the happiest of—"

"One wonders," a haughty, rather languid voice said to no one in particular since there was no one with the owner of the voice, "if daylight does more justice to the canvas in its present setting than candlelight does. Rembrandts are notoriously dark canvases and need to be very carefully displayed. What do you think, Kitredge?"

So the Duke of Bewcastle was not talking to himself, was he?

Christine slid her hand free of the earl's and smoothed her skirt over her knees. If she could have died of mortification at that moment, she probably would have counted herself fortunate.

"I never had much use for the man myself," the earl said, looking ruefully and perhaps apologetically down at Christine before turning toward the duke and the picture. "Give me a Turner any day—or a Gainsborough."

"Yes, quite so." The duke had his quizzing glass to his eye and was examining the painting through it from a distance of two feet. "Nevertheless, I would like to see this one in the appropriate light."

He lowered his glass then and turned to look at Christine.

"This is a quiet place to be sitting, ma'am," he said,

"when most of the guests are in the other rooms. May I take you for some refreshments?"

"I was about—" the Earl of Kitredge began.

"*Yes.*" Christine jumped to her feet. "Thank you, your grace."

He bowed stiffly and offered his arm. When her hand was safe upon his sleeve, she turned her head to smile at the earl.

"Thank you, my lord," she said, "for showing me the Rembrandt. It is indeed impressive."

He could do nothing but nod and allow her to leave.

Though, really, she thought, she had just been juggled between the proverbial devil and the deep blue sea, though she was not quite sure which man fit which role. And here she was with her hand upon the sleeve of the Duke of Bewcastle and suddenly feeling a little as if she had just grasped a lightning bolt.

"It appeared to me," he said, "that perhaps you needed rescuing, Mrs. Derrick. Forgive me if I was wrong."

"I daresay I would have rescued myself in a little while," she said. "But for once in my life I was quite delighted to see you."

"I am flattered, ma'am," he said.

She laughed. "Of course," she said, "there was no one to rescue me from you, was there?"

"I hope," he said, looking sidelong at her, "you are referring either to the scene in the maze or to the one in the garden of your mother's cottage."

Ignominiously she felt herself flush hotly at the only other possible scene she might have been referring to.

"Yes, to those," she said. "Both of them."

"And both times," he said, "you did admirably well in convincing me that my addresses were *not* welcome to you. May I fill a plate for you?"

They were in the refreshment room, where food had

been set out on a long table and footmen waited to help guests with their selections. A few tables and chairs had been set out, though most guests had carried their plates into the music room or the drawing room.

"I am not hungry," she said.

"May I fetch you a drink, then?" he asked.

It would have been churlish to refuse that too.

"A glass of wine, perhaps," she said.

He went to get it for her and came back with a glass of something for himself as well. He indicated one of the tables, a vacant one in the corner.

"Shall we sit?" he asked her. "Or are you plotting your escape from me too? If so, you may simply leave and rejoin your relatives. I shall not attempt to detain you against your will."

She sat.

"If I had known you were to attend that wedding," she said, looking directly at him, since the temptation was to fix her gaze on her glass, "I would not have come to London."

"Indeed?" he said. "Is the world not large enough for the two of us, then, Mrs. Derrick?"

"Sometimes," she said, "I wonder. And I do not suppose you have many kindly thoughts of me. It cannot be every day that a lowly commoner refuses two very different but equally flattering offers from a duke."

"You assume, then," he said, "that I have *had* thoughts of you, ma'am?"

Her terrible discomfort fled, and she leaned a little toward him and laughed aloud.

"I love it," she said, "when you can be provoked into spite. Or perhaps I insult you by accusing you of that. A more genteel word would be *setdown*. It was a rather magnificent one and certainly put me in my place."

He gazed haughtily at her.

"And I love it, Mrs. Derrick," he said softly, "when you can be provoked to laughter—even when you do it with just your eyes."

That silenced her. She sat back in her chair feeling as if a lightning bolt had shot through her even though she was no longer touching him. She could not think of a thing to say, and he did not jump in to fill the silence.

"Are you saying," she asked him at last, "that I am a flirt?"

"A flirt." He set down his glass with some deliberation and sat back in his chair. He regarded her with those penetrating silver eyes. "That is a word that seems to be used with tedious frequency about you, Mrs. Derrick—usually in denial. I would not use it at all."

"Ah, thank you," she said, and another silence ensued while he looked steadily at her and she dared not lift her glass lest her hand shake and she be horribly mortified.

"You do not need to flirt," he told her. "You are extraordinarily attractive and need to use no wiles."

"*Me?*" She spread a hand over her bosom and looked at him in astonishment. "Have you taken a good look at me, your grace? I have none of the beauty or elegance of any of the other ladies here tonight. Even with my new gown I am well aware that I look like—and *am*—someone's country cousin."

"Ah, but I did not call you either beautiful or elegant," he said. "The word I used was *attractive. Extraordinarily attractive,* to be more precise. It is something your glass would not reveal to you because it is something that is most apparent when you are animated. It is difficult for any man who looks at you once not to look again. And again."

From any other man the words might have sounded ardent. The Duke of Bewcastle spoke them matter-of-factly, as if they were discussing—well, the Rembrandt in the next room. She was suddenly acutely aware that she had once lain with this man. And yet it seemed impossible to believe, just as it was that he had just said what he had. They were not the sort of words one expected of the Duke of Bewcastle.

She was saved from having to make some sort of reply when someone stopped beside their table. Christine looked up to see that it was Anthony Culver, grinning broadly.

"Bewcastle?" he said. "*Mrs. Derrick?* Are you still in town? I thought you were returning to Gloucestershire right after Wiseman's wedding. Ronald and I were talking about you just yesterday and remembering what a good sport you were and how you were the life and soul of the party at Schofield last summer. Come and see him—he is in the music room. And come and meet some other fellows. They will be delighted to know you."

Christine offered him her hand and a bright smile.

The Duke of Bewcastle's quizzing glass was in his hand.

"I beg your pardon, Bewcastle," Anthony Culver said with a grin. "Will you release her? Have I interrupted something?"

"I claim no ownership over Mrs. Derrick's time," the duke said.

"His grace was kind enough to procure me a glass of wine," Christine said, getting to her feet. "But, you see? I have already drunk it. I will be delighted to see your brother again and to meet some of your friends."

But she turned back to smile at the duke before moving off on the arm of the younger man.

"Thank you, your grace," she said.

She was actually feeling severely shaken.

He considered her *extraordinarily attractive*.

She had refused to be his mistress.

She had refused to be his wife.

But he still thought her *extraordinarily attractive*. She despised herself for feeling flattered. How could she after some of the things he had said to her while offering her marriage last year? He considered her his inferior in every way. He had believed he was conferring an irresistible honor on her.

After tonight it was very unlikely she would ever see him again.

How was she going to forget him—again? It had been hard enough last year. Indeed, if she were quite honest with herself—and she had been remarkably *dis*honest where he was concerned—she had not succeeded then either.

There was nothing about him she could either like or admire—except his looks. Though it was more than just those that disturbed her peace during the last six months, she knew.

She was horribly in love with him.

Horribly, she supposed, being the operative word.

Ignominiously might be even better.

13

WULFRIC HAD JUST COME FROM PICKFORD House, where Morgan, the younger of his two sisters, and Rosthorn were in residence. They had brought the children up from Kent with them, hoping that the London air would agree more with the older boy this year and that the baby would not know any different.

Jacques, brought from the nursery to greet his uncle, had gazed solemnly from a distance until Morgan had placed the sleeping Jules along Wulfric's free arm. Then the child had come closer in order to examine the tassels hanging from his uncle's Hessians and had finally grown bold enough to pat his knee.

"I wish you could see yourself now, Wulf," Morgan had said, laughing.

He had sat very still, afraid of dropping the baby, afraid of frightening away the boy. He was very aware that they were his nephews, children of his beloved Morgan, to whom motherhood had added a glow of maturity to enhance her lithe, youthful beauty—she was still not quite twenty-one.

"I wish the *ton* could see you," Gervase had added dryly. "But I daresay they would not believe the evidence of their own eyes."

Wulfric had gone there to invite them to come to

Lindsey Hall for the Easter holiday. Freyja and Joshua, who had also recently arrived in town, had already agreed to come, and letters had been sent to Aidan and Rannulf and Alleyne. The last time they had all been together in one place was for Alleyne and Rachel's wedding two and a half years ago. It was time they were together again. Although Wulfric had seen them all since then, he had found himself recently longing to have all his family about him at home. It was a considerably expanded family now, of course, with all the children and babies, but Lindsey Hall was a large place.

Morgan and Gervase had accepted the invitation and Wulfric rode away from Pickford House satisfied that he would have at least some of his family with him for the holiday. He would invite his aunt and uncle, the Marquess and Marchioness of Rochester, too, he had decided, but not today. Today—this afternoon—he had another destination in mind.

He was riding through Hyde Park, along the Serpentine. There were a surprising number of people out, either riding or walking. It was early in the year after all, though it was a lovely spring day. The sun was shining and there was warmth in the air.

He was riding to Renable's house, though there was no assurance, of course, that the ladies would be at home. He was not expected. They were to stay for one week after the wedding of her sister, Lady Renable had said at the soiree. Five days of that week had passed and Wulfric had made a decision.

Part of the decision involved Lady Falconbridge, who had been his reason for attending the soiree. He had gone in a determined effort to put out of his mind a certain ineligible country schoolmistress—whom he had assumed was back in the country—and to press forward with the consummation of an affair with a lady of the world who would expect nothing of him except sensual pleasure.

He had been celibate for too long—for more than a year with one memorable exception.

But as soon as he had seen Lady Falconbridge, as soon as she had beckoned him to her in the Gosselin drawing room and sent him to fetch her wine and then engaged him in conversation, he had known that he could not after all choose a mistress with his head. The lady was everything he could possibly want in a mistress except for one thing.

She was not—damn it!—Christine Derrick.

And then, just as he was realizing it with some annoyance at the illogic of his own will, he had heard Lady Renable's voice and felt her lorgnette tap his arm, and he had turned and seen the very woman who had brought disorder into his life again since that infernal wedding.

He had felt deeply resentful toward her even as he had pursued her and rescued her from Kitredge's clutches and then spoken to her with unaccustomed unguardedness.

And now, three days later, he was riding toward a deliberate meeting with her—*if* she was at home, that was. If she was not—well, he would have to come back at another time, unless in the meanwhile he returned to his senses.

A couple of little boys were sailing wooden boats on the Serpentine under the eagle eye of their nurse. Wulfric nodded to several acquaintances as they rode by and touched his whip to his hat when he passed ladies he knew. Mrs. Beavis—a courtesy title, since she was one of London's more famed courtesans yet no one had ever known or known of any Mr. Beavis—was strolling close to the water with her abigail, looking like a particularly flamboyant bird of paradise. She was also preening herself at the approach of Lord Powell, who was reputed to be in hot pursuit of her.

Wulfric watched idly as the lady drew off her glove, extended her arm over the water, smiled beguilingly at the approaching baron, and dropped the glove in blatant invitation. It fluttered down into the water six inches from the bank.

Lord Powell minced forward in response to the mating call and would have fished out the glove with the silver tip of his cane if someone else had not ruined the game for both him and his potential light-of-love.

That someone else came hurrying up behind Mrs. Beavis, calling out to her that she had dropped something and at the same time bending over to retrieve it. There had been no rain in days. It was hard to know how the grass could be slippery unless on this relatively windless day some of the water had slopped over the edge of the bank. However it was, the lady rescuer's right foot slipped toward the edge, she made a clumsy effort to transfer her weight to the left in order to regain her balance, failed, flailed her arms, shrieked loudly enough to draw the attention of every single mortal in the vicinity who was not already watching her, and pitched sideways into the water with a resounding splash.

Wulfric drew his horse to a halt and watched with pained resignation as Lady Renable and Lady Mowbury exclaimed in horror and Powell, doubtless seething with wrath, played the gallant and hauled Mrs. Derrick out of the Serpentine.

Mrs. Beavis strolled onward as if oblivious both to the scene of disaster playing itself out behind her and to the fact that she now wore only one glove.

Mrs. Derrick meanwhile stood with chattering teeth on the bank of the Serpentine, her new bonnet with its pink and lavender plumes dead on her head, her pink walking dress and darker rose spencer clinging to her like the flimsy drapery of a Greek goddess. She dripped water everywhere while Powell withdrew a handkerchief from his pocket and swiped ineffectually at her.

Lady Renable and Lady Mowbury fussed about her.

The numerous spectators gaped and exclaimed.

"S-someone should r-return this g-glove to that l-lady," Mrs. Derrick said, holding it aloft.

Wulfric, tempted for only half a moment to ride on, sighed instead, swung down from his horse's back, and left it to its own devices while he approached the scene with firm strides, shrugging out of his long drab coat as he did so.

"Lord Powell will doubtless be glad to do it," he said, taking it from her hand and dangling it between his thumb and forefinger before the nose of the baron, who was only too delighted to be released from the necessity of having to cope with one half-drowned lady and her two ineffectual companions while his lady-love walked out of his future.

"Oh, I say, Bewcastle," he said. "I say." He made his escape.

"Allow me, ma'am," Wulfric said briskly, tossing the coat about Mrs. Derrick's shoulders and overlapping its edges at the front. He gazed grimly into her eyes. There was not another lady of his acquaintance—including Freyja—who was so adept at getting herself into the most ghastly public scrapes. Why he had been fated to be on the spot when this one happened he could not imagine.

And how he could have chosen this woman—though there had been no conscious choice in the matter—to fall in love with he would never understand even if he lived to be one hundred.

"H-how excruciatingly m-mortifying!" she said, huddling inside the coat and gazing back at him from beneath the former brim of the dead hat while the plumes drooped forlornly about her shoulders. "It s-seems inevitable that you should be c-close by to witness my humiliation."

"It would seem to me, ma'am," he said curtly, "that you ought to be thankful for it. Lord Powell's handkerchief would not suffice to wrap about you."

He turned toward Lady Renable, since she still seemed in no state to take charge of the situation.

"I shall take Mrs. Derrick up before me on my horse, ma'am," he said, "and convey her home without further delay."

He did not wait to listen to her thanks or to hear Mrs. Derrick's reply. He strode grimly back to his horse, which was quietly cropping the grass, supremely indifferent to a scene that had every human within sight riveted. He mounted and rode the short distance to the bank. He reached down one arm.

"Set your hand in mine and one foot on my boot," he instructed her.

It was not easy, of course. She needed both hands to clutch the coat to herself, since she had not had the sense to slide her arms into the sleeves, and the bottom six inches or so of the garment bunched on the grass around her. But with a little help from Lady Renable, who held the coat, and with a little inelegant pushing and hauling from Lady Mowbury and himself, Mrs. Derrick was finally seated sideways before his saddle, the coat still about her to preserve her modesty and provide a little warmth.

"I would suggest," he said as two soggy plumes threatened to drip Serpentine water down inside his shirt collar, "that you remove your bonnet, ma'am."

"Oh, yes, indeed," she said, one arm coming out from inside his coat and undoing the wet ribbons. She gazed at the bonnet when she had taken it off, and he gazed at her wet, squashed curls. "Oh, dear, I suppose it is ruined."

"I know it is." He took it from her, looked around until he saw a hopeful-looking serving maid close by, and held out the offending garment to her. "Here, you girl, dispose of this for me."

He handed her a guinea to go with it, but from the look on her face, he guessed that the dead bonnet was the greater prize to her. She bobbed a series of curtsies and showered him with thanks—or what he supposed were thanks, since she spoke in an atrocious and almost unintelligible cockney accent.

Mrs. Derrick chose that moment to start laughing. At first it was a shaking of the shoulders that might have been a fit of the ague caused by her dunking, but then an explosion of mirth burst out of her, and he could see that her eyes were dancing with merriment. Before he could give his horse the signal to move, almost all the gathered spectators chose to join her and she poked out one hand yet again to wave to the crowd.

And—damn it!—swathed though she was in his drab coat and with squashed wet curls, she looked suddenly quite dazzlingly lovely.

At last they were on their way. Wulfric found himself in unfamiliar waters—with no pun intended. Unlike Mrs. Derrick, he was *not* accustomed to finding himself in the middle of an undignified, farcical scene that would doubtless be the topic of every drawing room conversation for days to come—especially as Mrs. Beavis had had a part in it. And more especially since *he* had had a part to play in it too.

But how could he have left her there to shiver on the bank when it did not appear that anyone else had been about to offer her any practical assistance? She would not have been laughing then—though he suspected that he might be wrong about that.

"Do you wonder," she said, "that Oscar often viewed me as a distinct liability?"

"I do not wonder at it at all," he said cruelly.

But the strange thing was—the *very* strange thing— that annoyance was beginning to be displaced by something far different. He found himself wanting to laugh as she and the crowd had just done—to throw back his head and bellow with mirth, in fact. Even the incident with the yew tree in the churchyard last summer could not compete with this. He had never in his life witnessed anything so hilarious.

He did *not* laugh. For one thing they were within view of a number of people every step of the way to Renable's house and drew enough curious glances without his adding fuel to the inevitable gossip by presenting his audience with the unheard-of picture of a merry Duke of Bewcastle. And for another thing she must be feeling cold and miserable despite her laughter, and courtesy dictated that he not be seen to mock her.

"I suppose," she said, "I did not present a graceful picture as I fell in, by any chance?"

The arm that he had about her waist to hold her steady was growing distinctly damp. His drab coat was probably going to be ruined.

"I am not sure," he said bluntly, "there *is* a way to tumble gracefully into water, since by no stretch of the imagination could it be called a dive."

She sighed. "And I suppose," she said, "I drew considerable attention to myself. While it was happening, I mean. I *know* I did afterward."

"You shrieked," he said.

"At least," she said, "I rescued that poor lady's glove. She did not even realize she had dropped it."

For a woman who had been married for years before being widowed and who must be very close to thirty if not past it, she seemed to be a dangerous innocent. He might have left her with her illusions, but he was back to feeling annoyed with her. How could she possibly have tumbled into the water? The glove had been no farther than a few inches from the bank.

"She dropped it deliberately," he told her. "Lord Powell was to fish it out—without falling in."

She turned her head and looked at him wide-eyed. "But why?"

"She is . . . not quite respectable," he told her. "And Powell is doing all in his power to court her favors. She is playing hard to get."

She stared at him while he guided his horse out of the park and onto the street. That frank gaze was considerably disconcerting when her face was less than a foot from his own. And he had forgotten how very blue her eyes were—and how they could suddenly laugh, as they did now.

"I spoiled his moment of gallantry and triumph, then," she said. "Oh, the poor gentleman."

He might really have laughed outright then if he had not had to concentrate upon maneuvering his horse past a crossing sweeper who had darted across the road to snatch up a penny a pedestrian had just dropped for him.

She was still looking at him after he had completed the maneuver. Laughter still lurked in her eyes.

"And I have embarrassed you horribly," she said. "You see now how fortunate you were that I rejected your rash proposal last summer?"

"I do indeed see," he admitted curtly.

She turned her head at last to look front again.

"Well, I am glad about that," she said after a brief little silence. "But though I am deeply mortified that you had to witness what happened this afternoon, I am also grateful that you were there. Wet as I am, it would have been a very cold and a very long walk home."

She also would have been ogled every step of the way—as she would realize for herself if she looked in a mirror before stripping off her clothes in her dressing room. Her dress had looked like a second skin. It was even pink, for God's sake.

They were approaching Renable's house.

"I *do* thank you for your assistance," she said. "And you do not have to worry that I will ever embarrass you again. We will be returning to Gloucestershire the day after tomorrow. This is good-bye."

He held her in place as he dismounted and then lifted her down, a soft, wet bundle inside his damp coat. She would have taken it off to return to him before running up the steps to the house, but he held it firmly in place.

"I will come inside with you," he said. "You must wear the coat up to your room and then send it down with a maid."

"That is very kind of you," he said.

"It is very *practical* of me, ma'am," he said pointedly, preceding her up the steps and rapping the brass knocker against the door.

"Yes," she said. "Oh, yes, I see."

And she did too, apparently—her cheeks were flaming when he turned back to look at her.

"Good-bye," she said when they were inside the hall and the butler and one footman regarded her wooden-faced. "You will be very glad to be rid of me once and for all." But for once, he noticed, her eyes were focused on his chin rather than on his own eyes—and they held none of their usual sparkle.

"Will I?" He bowed to her as she made her awkward way to the stairs, clutching his coat about her with one hand and lifting it off the floor with the other.

Would he?

Embarrassing as this afternoon had been, had it also turned out to be something of a fortunate escape? She was a truly dreadful woman. It was no wonder her dead husband had considered her a liability. It was no wonder the Elricks were hostile to her and had even warned him against her. She had an inappropriate sense of humor— she had *waved* to the crowd instead of hanging her head in shame. She attracted disaster like iron to a magnet. She was a *schoolmaster's* daughter.

Yes, it was indeed fortunate that she was leaving town the day after tomorrow and that it was very improbable he would see her ever again. It was fortunate that she had not been at home to his call this afternoon and that he had come upon her at just the moment he had.

He should have used the word she had used. He should have said good-bye.

Yes, he would be very glad to be rid of her once and for all.

Now, if he could just rid her from his mind too and his . . . heart?

A maid brought his soggy coat down to him after a few minutes and he left the house, mounted his horse, and rode away—out of her life.

He rejoiced at being saved from a very serious disaster.

CHRISTINE WAS FEELING a touch depressed.

Well, it was more than a touch, if the truth were known. Hermione and Basil had called during the morning. They had *said* they came to satisfy themselves that she had not taken a chill from yesterday's dunking—about which they had heard, of course. They would surely have had to be deaf in all four ears *not* to have heard. Their real reason for coming, though, Christine had known, was to satisfy themselves that she was really and truly leaving the next day.

She was.

Melanie had bemoaned the fact that they could not stay longer, but then she had remembered that Phillip—her eldest child and only son—was to have a birthday within the week and she would only just have time to make the journey and plan his party.

They were leaving. Christine had never been happier in her life—or more depressed.

No sooner had her in-laws taken their leave than the Earl of Kitredge had arrived, also to ascertain that Mrs. Derrick had taken no lasting harm from her unfortunate accident in Hyde Park. But then he had asked with a great deal of pomp and head-nodding and winking if Lady Renable would grant him a moment or two alone with Mrs. Derrick, and Melanie, the fiend, with a merry smirk for her friend, had whisked herself out of the room.

Christine had rejected his offer of marriage, though he had made it four separate times in four different ways within fifteen minutes and even then refused to believe that she could be serious. He promised himself a journey into Gloucestershire after the parliamentary session was adjourned for the summer, when he hoped to renew his acquaintance with Mrs. and Miss Thompson and to find Mrs. Derrick in a kinder frame of mind.

It was all very vexing, even though Melanie laughed merrily over an account of it afterward and Christine joined her.

"You are just too attractive for your own good, Christine," Melanie said, dabbing at her eyes with a lace-edged hand-kerchief. "If Kitredge were only thirty years younger and handsome—and intelligent and sensible. But he is none of those things, is he, and I daresay he never was. I thought you looked very romantic riding off with Bewcastle yesterday, except that you were all bundled up inside his coat with your hair dripping about your ears, and he had a brow of thunder. I do not suppose he was at all amused at being forced to ride to your rescue."

"No," Christine said with a sigh. "He was not."

And then they both went off into whoops of laughter again, though Christine's spirits were down somewhere in the soles of her slippers.

Thank heaven they were returning home tomorrow. But that thought only succeeded in making her feel more depressed.

And then, in the middle of the afternoon, when she was upstairs packing her own bags even though Melanie had tried to press the services of a maid on her, a footman tapped on her door and informed her that her ladyship requested her company in the drawing room below. When she went to see what it was that Melanie wanted, she discovered her friend seated on one side of the fire, smirking with self-satisfaction, and the Duke of Bewcastle just getting to his feet from the chair at the other side.

Christine's spirits, firmly lodged in the soles of her slippers, did an uncomfortable little flip-flop.

"Mrs. Derrick." He bowed.

"Your grace." She curtsied.

Melanie remained silent and continued to smirk.

"Ma'am," he said, directing his silver gaze on her, "I trust you took no harm from yesterday's adventure?"

"That is a very kind euphemism," she said. "I assure you I took none—except to my dignity." She had almost collapsed into a fit of the vapors when she had taken off his coat and caught sight of herself in the pier glass in her room.

But surely he had not come just to ask after her health. They had said good-bye yesterday. At least, she had. She had noticed that he had not. It had inexplicably saddened her that he had not said at least that much to her when they were parting for the rest of their lives.

"I wonder, Mrs. Derrick," he said, "if you would care for a stroll in the park with me?"

"A stroll?" With her peripheral vision she could see that Melanie's smirk now looked as if it had been painted on her face.

"A stroll," he repeated. "I will escort you back here in time for tea."

Melanie was tapping her lorgnette against the wooden arm of her chair.

"That is remarkably civil of you, Bewcastle," she said. "Christine has not had any fresh air today. We had visitors all morning."

But his grace kept his eyes on Christine, his eyebrows raised. If she said no, she would be teased to death after he had left. And if she said yes, she would be teased to death after she returned. She really had not wanted to see him again. She *really* had not.

"Thank you," she heard herself say. "I will fetch my bonnet and pelisse."

Five minutes later they were out on the street walking in the direction of the park, her arm through his. She had forgotten how tall he was, how forbidding his presence. She had forgotten how powerful an aura he projected. But she had not forgotten that she had shared deep intimacies with this man. She suddenly felt robbed of breath. And really she had nothing to say to him that she had not said yesterday, and he could have nothing to say to her.

Why on *earth* had he asked her to come walking with him?

At least while they were out on the street there were plenty of people and activities on which to fix her attention. But soon enough she found herself alone with the Duke of Bewcastle in a silent and empty Hyde Park—at least it seemed empty where they were, a fact that the chilly, blustery weather may have accounted for.

She turned her head and looked up at his profile.

"Well, your grace," she said.

"Well, Mrs. Derrick."

At least, she thought with foolish vanity, she was wearing her new blue dress with the matching pelisse and the gray bonnet she had worn to the wedding. She particularly liked the bonnet. The underside of its brim was lined with pleated blue silk and tied with blue ribbons that matched her outfit. *At least* she was not dressed like a scarecrow as she had been during the summer. Or in dripping, clinging finery as she had been yesterday.

They walked for what seemed like half a mile in absolute silence. It was ridiculous—as well as unnerving. She could be back at the house now packing her bags. He could be wherever he usually went on an afternoon in early March. They could both be comfortable.

"Sometimes," she said, "people engage in the game of staring each other down, the object being not to be the first to look away. You and I have indulged in it once or twice, though I daresay it was never a game to you. You simply expect that lesser mortals will lower their gaze when it encounters yours. But is *this* another of those games, your grace? Out-silencing each other? Each determined not to be the first to speak?"

"If it is," he said, "then I believe you would have to agree, Mrs. Derrick, that I have won."

"And so you have." She laughed. "Why on earth did you ask me to come walking with you? After yesterday— and after last summer—I really would have thought myself to be the very last person on earth you would wish to spend time with."

"Then perhaps you would have thought wrongly, ma'am," he said.

They walked another hundred yards or so in silence.

"This at least," she said at last, "is a game I will never win. I confess myself curious. Why *did* you ask me? It was obviously not for conversation."

Two gentlemen were riding toward them. They both drew their horses off the path, exchanged greetings with the duke as they passed, and touched the brims of their hats to Christine.

"My brothers and sisters and their families will be joining me for Easter at Lindsey Hall," he said abruptly.

She stole a glance at him. "That will be pleasant for you," she said, wondering if it would be. She could not really imagine him surrounded by brothers and sisters and nephews and nieces. What were they like? She could not remember meeting any of them. Were they like him? It was a thought that for the moment amused her.

"I have considered," he said, "inviting your brother- and sister-in-law too and your cousins by marriage."

She did not just glance at him this time. She gazed fully at him, all amazement. She knew he was a friend of Hector's, but she had not realized he had any close acquaintance with the others.

"But I need you to help me decide," he said.

"Me?" She continued to stare at his stern, cold profile.

"I will invite them," he said, "if you will come too."

"*What?*"

She stopped walking and turned to gaze fully and wide-eyed at him. But there were four people approaching this time, again on horseback, and the duke took her arm and drew it through his again before walking on with her until the riders had passed, again after a flurry of greetings. Then he released her arm and they both stopped walking.

"I cannot invite you alone," he said. "It would be grossly improper, even though my own family will be with me. I cannot invite you with your mother and sisters and brother-in-law. We are not betrothed. And so I must invite you simply as a peripheral member of a family I wish to have join me and my family for the holiday."

Anger was beginning to curl its fist about her stomach.

"Do you mean to seduce me, then?" she asked him. She did not add the word *again*. What had happened between them one night last summer had not been seduction.

"At my home?" he said stiffly. "With my family and your late husband's in residence there? You presume to think to know me, Mrs. Derrick. If you can ask such a question, you know nothing about me at all."

"And for the same reasons, I suppose," she said, "you will not renew your offer there that I become your mistress."

"I will not," he said. "I ought never to have made it. I have no wish to make you my mistress."

"Then what?" she asked him. "Then *why*? You *cannot* still wish to marry me."

"I wonder," he said, "if you presume to know the thoughts and intentions and wishes of all your acquaintance, Mrs. Derrick. It is an annoying character trait."

She clamped her lips together, stung. She turned and walked slowly onward. The wind was blowing in her face, but she lifted her chin and welcomed the cold blast.

"I would like your assurance," he said, falling into step beside her again, "that if I invite your late husband's family to Lindsey Hall, Mrs. Derrick, you will accept your own invitation."

"But why?" she asked him again. "Do you wish me to see what I missed by refusing you?"

"I am not a great deal given to spite," he said. "Besides, I am convinced that you would take one look at my home if that were my motive and laugh at me."

"*Now*," she said, "you are presuming to know *me*."

"When you rejected my marriage offer," he said, "you gave a lengthy list of all my disqualifications to be your husband."

"Did I?" She could scarcely remember what she had said to him that day. She could only remember the terrible longing to run after him down the street after he had left—and the tears that had left her limp with grief.

"I have them by heart," he said. "Any man who hopes to marry you, you told me, must have a warm personality, human kindness, and a sense of humor. He must love people, particularly children, and frolicking and absurdity. He must be a man who is not obsessed with himself and his own consequence. He must be someone who is not ice to the core. He must be someone who has a heart. He must be capable of being your companion and friend and lover. You asked me if I could be all those things to you—or any of them. You implied, of course, that I could be none."

She could not remember saying any of those things. But she must have done so. They were exactly what she would have wished to say. But *he* had remembered. And in great detail.

She licked her lips. "I did not mean to be cruel," she said. "Or rather, I suppose I did because I can remember feeling upset at the manner of your proposal. But I do not mean to be cruel now. I married once because I tumbled into love and was young and foolish enough to believe that that first euphoria of romantic bliss could carry me happily through the rest of my life. I do not intend to marry again. But if I do, it could only be to a man who has all those qualities you have just repeated to me. It is an impossibility, you see. No man could ever be all those things or quite fit that dream. And so I choose to remain single and free. I am sorry if I offended you. You do not seem like the sort of man who could be offended, especially by someone as lowly as me. But if I offended you, I am sorry."

"I want to prove to you," he said, "that I have at least some of those attributes you dream of finding in a man."

"*What?*"

She stopped and spun to face him again. There was no one else in sight this time. Somehow, she half realized, they had strayed from the main carriage path and were on a more secluded footpath.

"I do not believe," he said, "I am so lacking in all humanity as you believe I am."

"I did not say—"

"*Human kindness* was your exact phrase," he said.

She stared at him and suddenly remembered something that she had forced herself to forget. She remembered the look in his eyes as he left her in the garden outside Hyacinth Cottage, and some of the words he had spoken then—*Someone with a heart. No, perhaps you are right, Mrs. Derrick. Perhaps I do not possess one. And if I do not, then I lack everything of which you dream, do I not?* She remembered feeling as if her heart had broken.

"I was wrong to suggest that," she said. "I beg your pardon. But you are very far from fulfilling my dream, you know. I do not say that to be offensive. You are as you are, and I am sure that in your own world you do very well indeed. You command respect and obedience and even awe. They are necessary attributes, I daresay, for an aristocrat in your position. They are just not attributes that I look for in a lifelong companion."

"I am a man as well as a duke, Mrs. Derrick," he said.

She wished he had not said that. She felt as if a giant fist had caught her a blow in her abdomen, robbing her of all breath and strength in her legs.

"I know." She was whispering. She cleared her throat. "I know."

"And you have not been indifferent to that man," he said.

"I know."

He touched the gloved knuckles of one hand to her cheek for a brief moment, and she closed her eyes and frowned. Much more of this and she would be bawling— or casting herself into his arms and begging him to propose marriage to her again so that she could have the pleasure of living unhappily ever after with him.

"Give me a chance," he said. "Come to Lindsey Hall."

"It would be pointless," she said, opening her eyes. "Nothing can change—not you, and not my feelings toward you. And I cannot change."

"Give me a chance," he said again.

She had never heard him laugh. She had never even seen him smile. How could she marry a man who was eternally grim? And stiff and haughty and cold? He looked all those things now at this moment while begging her to give him a chance to prove otherwise.

"I would be consumed by you," she said, and blinked her eyes furiously when she felt them fill with tears. "You would sap all the energy and all the joy from me. You would put out all the fire of my vitality."

"Give me a chance to fan the flames of that fire," he said, "and to nurture your joy."

She turned sharply away from him, one hand over her mouth.

"Take me back," she said. "Take me to Melanie's. I ought not to have agreed to this. I ought not to have come to London. I ought not to have gone to that house party."

"It is precisely what I have been telling myself," he said curtly. "But I did and you did. And there is this something between us that has not yet been resolved even though we intended to do just that on the night of the ball at Schofield. Come to Lindsey Hall. Promise me that you will accept your invitation and not leave me with other guests whom I will invite only for your sake."

"You want me to come," she said, rounding on him, "only that I may show you how very unsuited we are, how very much we do not belong together, how utterly miserable we would be if we committed our lives to each other?" But had not yesterday proved that to him once and for all?

"If necessary, yes," he said. "If you can convince me of those things, ma'am, you would, perhaps, be doing me a great favor. Perhaps you would help me rid my blood of you."

"It will not," she said, "be a happy Easter. Not for either of us."

"Come anyway," he said.

She sighed aloud and thought of Eleanor. If ever she needed a will of iron, now was definitely the occasion.

"Oh, very well, then," she said. "I will come."

For a moment his silver eyes blazed with something that looked very like triumph.

"Take me back to Melanie's now, if you please," she said.

This time he did not ignore her request. They walked the whole distance in silence. He did not offer to come inside with her and she did not invite him. He took her gloved hand in his outside on the pavement, bowed over it, and raised it to his lips before fixing his eyes very intently on her own.

"You will remember that you have promised," he said.

"Yes." She withdrew her hand. "I will remember."

14

*N*O LONGER COULD WULFRIC STEP INTO ANY
room of Lindsey Hall and enjoy emptiness and silence. The house was full of Bedwyns and their spouses
and children, and other people connected with them. The
Bedwyns had never been a quiet lot. But now that their
numbers had multiplied and they had not seen one another for a while, they made their former selves seem like
cloistered nuns and monks.

Freyja and Joshua, the Marchioness and Marquess of
Hallmere, were the first to arrive from London, bringing
their son, Daniel, now two years old, and three-month-
old Emily with them. Freyja had recovered well from her
latest confinement. Her favorite activity seemed to be
wrestling with her giggling son on the floor—not necessarily in the nursery. When Daniel was not occupied thus,
he was far more likely to be found galloping about the
house on his father's shoulders than decently shut up inside the nursery with his nurse.

Alleyne and Rachel, Lord and Lady Alleyne Bedwyn,
and Morgan and Gervase, the Countess and Earl of
Rosthorn, arrived on the same day, the former couple
with their twin girls, Laura and Beatrice, now a year and a
half old, and with Baron Weston, Rachel's uncle, who had
made a good recovery from the heart problems he had

suffered last summer, and Morgan and Gervase with their sons—Jacques, who was almost two, and Jules, who was two months old. Rachel was apparently increasing again, though her condition was not noticeable yet.

Rannulf and Judith, Lord and Lady Rannulf Bedwyn, came the following day with their son, William, now almost three, and Miranda, one year old. Not many hours passed after their arrival before William demanded to be like his younger cousin and ride his father's shoulders all about the house. The good-natured way in which Rannulf complied with this imperious demand spoke volumes about the sternness of his paternal rule over his household. And Jacques was not to be outdone, though he asked *his* papa more politely by tugging at the tassel on one of his Hessian boots until he was noticed and then stretching both arms over his head.

Stampeding human steeds and their squealing riders became a common sight and sound in the hallways and on the staircases of Lindsey Hall. Occasionally one of the latter was a twin girl, though Wulfric was having difficulty telling them apart.

Aidan and Eve, Lord and Lady Aidan Bedwyn, came with Mrs. Pritchard, Eve's aunt, and their three children—Davy, aged ten, Becky, aged eight, and Hannah, almost one. Davy and Becky were actually their foster children, but neither Eve nor Aidan would tolerate hearing them referred to as such. Davy called them *Aunt* and *Uncle*, while Becky called them *Mama* and *Papa*. But as far as Eve and Aidan were concerned, both children were *theirs* as surely as Hannah was.

Davy became the new favorite with the boys, who callously abandoned their fathers for the marvel of an elder cousin who actually slid down banisters when no adult was looking. And Becky was adored by all, though it was mostly the girls who clustered about her like chicks with their mother.

It was all a little bewildering, not to say trying, for Wulfric. And the chatter among his siblings and their spouses only grew louder and more animated with each new arrival. He retreated to his library, his own personal domain, as much as he had done when they all lived there. He went to his private retreat in the park too, though only once.

Last to arrive of his own family were his uncle and aunt, the Marquess and Marchioness of Rochester. His aunt was a Bedwyn by birth and as formidable as any of them. She brought with her—somehow it seemed unlikely that the marquess had had any hand in the bringing—a niece of Rochester's, who had been languishing somewhere in the north country until at the age of twenty-three she had been brought to the attention of her relatives in London and Aunt Rochester had decided to take the girl under her wing and introduce her to both the queen and polite society during the upcoming Season.

Aunt Rochester also made no secret of the fact that she intended to promote a match between Miss Amy Hutchinson and her eldest nephew.

"We will attach a husband for Amy before the Season is over," she announced quite frankly to the whole table at dinner the evening of their arrival. "Or perhaps even before it begins. Twenty-three is too old for a girl to be unmarried."

"I was twenty-five, Aunt," Freyja reminded her.

Aunt Rochester picked up her jeweled lorgnette from beside her plate and waved it in Freyja's direction.

"You waited dangerously long, Freyja," she said before changing the direction of the lorgnette to indicate Joshua. "If that boy had not come along to tame you and charm you out of your stubbornness, you would have ended up a spinster. That is no desirable fate for a girl even if her brother *is* a duke."

Joshua waggled his eyebrows at Freyja, and she glared haughtily back at him as if it were *he* who had just claimed superior charm and accused her of wildness and stubbornness.

Less than five minutes later Aunt Rochester broke into the general conversation with another observation.

"And it is high time *you* married, Bewcastle," she said. "Thirty-five is both the perfect age and the dangerous age for a man. It is the perfect age to marry and a dangerous age at which to procrastinate. A man does not want to be crippled by gout before his son and heir is even in the nursery."

Five pairs of Bedwyn eyes—not to mention all the non-Bedwyn ones—focused upon Wulfric with unholy glee.

"She has you there, Wulf," Alleyne said. "You are thirty-five now. You cannot afford another moment's delay—it might prove fatal."

"Take my word for it, Wulf," Rannulf added, "gouty papas make inferior horses and sons will not appreciate them."

"Thank you, Aunt," Wulfric said, well aware that her implications concerning himself and Miss Hutchinson were as obvious to everyone else at the table as they were to him. "I do not begin to feel any symptoms of gout yet. And if and when I should select a bride to be my duchess, my family will certainly be informed of my choice and my intentions."

The Bedwyns collectively grinned at him—joined by Joshua and Gervase. Eve smiled kindly. So did Rachel. Judith spoke up.

"Do you plan any special activities for the holiday, Wulfric?" she asked in an obvious attempt to turn a subject that was merely annoying to him but was probably quite distressing for Miss Hutchinson, who, though she was a pretty and elegantly turned-out young lady, was also shy and clearly in awe of the company in which she found herself. "May we organize some? There will be church over Easter itself, of course. But may we plan some sort of party for later? A concert, perhaps? Amateur theatrics? A picnic if the weather will cooperate? Even a ball?"

"Which of those questions would you like Wulf to answer first, my love?" Rannulf asked her.

"Amateur theatrics." She laughed. "May we arrange some?"

"If we do," Freyja said, eyeing her sister-in-law askance, "I am going to be quite out of sorts, Judith. You will outact us all and make us look very amateurish indeed."

"We must plan an entertainment at which Judith can act and you can warble a duet with me, then, sweetheart," Joshua said. "None of us would willingly put you out of sorts."

"I do not see any need for organized entertainment," Morgan said. "We never failed to entertain ourselves without any organization, did we? I have my painting things with me and look forward to taking my easel outside. I was never allowed to paint the park here as I wished—Miss Cowper was forever hovering over my shoulder with suggestions of how I *ought* to paint. I do believe she feared Wulf would be angry with her if she did not teach me properly and would hang her in chains in the dungeons. Until the day she left here, I am convinced she believed there really *were* dungeons beneath Lindsey Hall."

"There are not, Morg?" Alleyne asked, all shocked surprise. "You mean Ralf and I *lied* when we told her about the secret stairway leading down to them? Dear me."

"The children will certainly be happy to play in this lovely park," Mrs. Pritchard said in her thick Welsh accent. "And they all have so many cousins to play with."

"But *may* we organize something special, Wulfric?" Judith asked.

"I am expecting more houseguests," he said.

He instantly had everyone's attention. Although he had always done his share of entertaining, as courtesy dictated, he had never been one for inviting guests to stay at the house.

"I have invited Mowbury to come down from London with the viscountess, his mother," he said. "And his brother and his sisters will be coming too—Justin Magnus, Lady Renable with the baron and their children, and Lady Wiseman with Sir Lewis. And Elrick, Mowbury's cousin, with the viscountess and their widowed sister-in-law, Mrs. Derrick."

"Mowbury?" Aidan said. "Is he as bookish and absent-minded as ever, Wulf? *And* his whole family? I did not realize you were so particularly acquainted with them."

"And they are all coming *here*?" Rannulf added. "Why on earth, Wulf?"

Wulfric's fingers curled about the handle of his quizzing glass as he set down his dessert spoon.

"I am unaware," he said, "that I need to account to my brothers and sisters for the guests I choose to invite to my home."

"Be fair, Wulf," Freyja said haughtily. "Morgan and I did not utter a word. But is not Mrs. Derrick the woman you fished out of the Serpentine and took home dripping on your horse?"

"No!" Alleyne laughed heartily and then continued to grin. "Wulf did *that*? I say! Do tell more, Free."

So much for slipping her name unobtrusively into the list of guests he was expecting, Wulfric thought as Freyja, helped along by Joshua and Gervase, proceeded to give a more or less accurate but decidedly lurid account of what had happened that day in Hyde Park.

"I'll wager," Rannulf said after they had all stopped laughing, "you were not amused, Wulf. And now you have felt obliged to invite the lady here with the rest of her family. Hard luck, old chap! But never fear—we will all protect you from her."

"We will make a wall of bristling Bedwyns," Alleyne promised, chuckling again. "She will never get past us, Wulf. You may recover your dignity at your leisure."

Wulfric raised his quizzing glass halfway to his eye.

"All my guests," he said, "will be treated with the proper courtesy. But to answer your question, Judith, there is to be a ball here. My secretary has already sent out the invitations and is seeing to the other arrangements. Doubtless other activities will suggest themselves as the days go by."

He dropped his quizzing glass, picked up his spoon again, and addressed his attention to his custard.

What on earth had possessed him?

Give me a chance, he had begged her. A chance for what? To prove he was something he was not? And he never begged. He never needed to.

Nothing can change, she had told him. And, of course, she was right. How could he change his very nature? Did he even want to? She was *perfectly* right. There was nothing that could draw them together into a happily ever after.

I would be consumed by you, she had said. *You would sap all the energy and all the joy from me. You would put out all the fire of my vitality.*

He did not know what joy was. He did not know much about vitality either—at least, not the sort of vitality that gave her that inner glow he could never quite describe in words.

Did he have *anything* to offer her that she might want? And—to look at the other side of the coin—was there anything in her that could make her suitable to be his duchess? Not just his woman or his wife, but his *duchess*?

He set down his spoon, ascertained that everyone else had finished eating, and looked at his aunt with slightly raised eyebrows. She took her cue immediately and rose to lead the ladies from the dining room.

IT WAS A cold and windy day even though it was almost April. Gray clouds hung low over the land and occasionally drizzled rain down onto a bleak world below. But fortunately the heavens held back the bulk of their load, and the highway remained passable throughout the long journey.

Christine almost wished for a prolonged deluge of rain that would strand them at a country inn somewhere until the holiday was over. But it was far too late for that now. They must be nearing Lindsey Hall. In fact, even as she thought it the carriage slowed and turned between two towering gateposts onto a straight driveway lined with elm trees.

"Gracious!" Melanie exclaimed, waking with a start from a lengthy doze and pulling her hands from beneath her lap robe in order to adjust her bonnet. "Are we here? Bertie, do wake up. I have suffered your snores for long enough. How anyone can fall asleep in a carriage I do not know. I am shaken and bounced to shreds. Are you not, Christine?"

"I have found the journey quite comfortable," Christine said.

When she set her head closer to the window beside

her, she could see a vast mansion up ahead. It was not medieval or Elizabethan or Georgian or Palladian, though it seemed to have elements of them all. It was magnificent. It was awe-inspiring.

She had never noticed before that she suffered from motion sickness. But her stomach was feeling decidedly queasy. It was a good thing their journey was at its end. But *that* thought caused her stomach to turn a complete somersault inside her.

The carriage turned and she could see that it was moving about a huge circular garden, bright with tulips and late-blooming daffodils, with a great stone fountain at its center, shooting water at least thirty feet into the air. It made for a magnificent approach to the house, she decided.

She could also see that once the carriage had made the half-circle about it, they would be on the terrace before the great front doors. She watched them both swing open before the carriage made its final turn and cut off her view of the house.

Melanie had been chattering away ever since she awoke, but Christine had heard scarcely a word. If only she could go back, she thought, and say no instead of yes in Hyde Park—so simple really! She could be quiet and content at home now, this day like any other, looking forward to Easter with her family.

But she had not said no, and so here she was. Her heart thumped loudly in her ears as the carriage door was opened by a servant wearing gorgeous livery and the steps were set down. There was no going back now.

She despised her nervousness. She absolutely *despised* it. She had told him that all this was pointless, that nothing was going to change, that nothing *could* change. She had told him they would both be doomed to a miserable holiday if he insisted that she come here.

He had insisted anyway and she had come.

So why be nervous? What was there to be nervous *about*? And why should she expect misery and therefore draw it down upon herself? Why not simply enjoy herself? She could sit in a corner again and laugh at the foibles of humanity, could she not? It was a tactic that had not worked particularly well at Schofield, but that was no reason for it not to work here.

Only servants met them outside the house, though a butler she might have mistaken for the duke himself if she had not already known that gentleman bowed to them with dignified formality and invited them to follow him inside, where his grace awaited them.

Melanie and Bertie followed him decently inside.

Christine did not.

The carriage bearing Melanie's children and their nurse had drawn up behind the baron's, and it was instantly apparent that all was not well inside it. Pamela, aged six, had probably been sick again, as she had been almost from the moment of their departure, and had therefore taken all of the nurse's time and attention and patience. The sound of her scolding voice—clearly at the end of its tether or perhaps even a little beyond the end—emerged into the outdoors as soon as the carriage door was opened. Phillip, aged eight, was laughing in the sort of jeering, hyena-like way that little boys have when they wish to be particularly obnoxious to their elders, and Pauline, aged three, was alternately bawling and screeching complaints against her brother. It did not take a genius to understand that he had been teasing her—always a favorite sport with big brothers. It was also apparent to Christine that the nurse was going to be quite unable to cope with the situation unless someone came to her assistance quickly.

Christine strode off in the direction of the second carriage.

"Phillip," she said, smiling brightly at him and preparing to lie through her teeth, "the funniest thing just happened! Do you see that very grand butler?" She pointed at his retreating back. "He asked me who the elegant gentleman in this carriage was. I suppose he mistook you for an adult. How do you like that!"

Phillip seemed to like it very well indeed. He stepped down onto the terrace with all the airs of a jaded town dandy, and Christine leaned into the carriage and swept Pauline up into her arms.

"We have arrived, my pet," she said, flashing a grin at the nurse, who was cuddling a green-faced Pamela on her lap and looking harried and grateful. "And very soon now you are going to have a whole new nursery to explore. Will that not be exciting? I am almost certain there are going to be other children there too—new friends for you."

Melanie and Bertie and the butler, she noticed with an inward grimace, had disappeared inside the house. But someone else had appeared from the opposite direction—a woman of bustling middle age who was obviously coming to take the children and their nurse inside by another door. Phillip inclined his head regally to her and informed her that the older of his two sisters was travel-sick and the younger was tired and their nurse would be obliged for her assistance.

"What a perfect gentleman you are," the woman said with an approving smile. "And so concerned for your sisters too."

Christine almost expected a halo to sprout out about his head.

"I'll take her, ma'am," the woman said, reaching out her arms for Pauline while the children's nurse descended slowly from the carriage with Pamela.

But Pauline would not go. She clung tightly to Christine's neck, pushing her bonnet slightly askew, buried her face in the hollow of Christine's shoulder, and showed distinct signs of gathering up her flagging energies for a full-blown tantrum.

"She is tired and feeling very strange," Christine said. "I'll bring her up to the nursery myself in a short while."

And she turned and hurried back to the front doors, which she half expected to find already shut and bolted against her. They were not. But as she stepped inside, she felt suddenly and horribly conspicuous and disheveled.

She only half noticed her surroundings, but even half her attention was sufficient to make her aware that the entrance hall was vast and magnificent and medieval. There was a huge fireplace opposite the front doors, and in front of it and stretching almost the whole length of the hall was a great oak table surrounded by chairs. The ceiling was oak-beamed. The walls were whitewashed and hung with banners and coats of arms and weapons. To one side was an intricately carved wooden screen with a minstrel gallery above. At the other end was a wide staircase leading upward.

Perhaps she would have noticed with far more attention if it had not been for the fact that a large number of people were drawn up in a receiving line between the front doors and the table. And they were all—ghastly realization!—waiting for her, since Melanie and Bertie were already being ushered away in the direction of the staircase.

It took a few moments for Christine's eyes to adjust fully to the light of indoors. But when they did so, she could see that the Duke of Bewcastle himself was at one end of the line. Actually, he was stepping forward from it and welcoming her with a formal bow and a quite unfathomable look on his face—not that she had often seen any look there that was *not* unfathomable, it was true. He opened his mouth to speak, but she forestalled him.

"I am so sorry," she said, her voice sounding horribly loud and breathless. "Pamela had been sick, and Phillip was being obnoxious, and Pauline was well on the way to having a fit of hysteria. I left Pamela to her nurse, persuaded Phillip to act the part of gentleman for at least five minutes, and lifted Pauline from the carriage to comfort her. But she is feeling tired and strange, poor lamb, and insisted upon staying with me. And so . . ." She felt suddenly tangled in words. She laughed. "And so here I am."

Pauline burrowed closer, twisted her head to peep at the duke, and knocked Christine's bonnet slightly more off center as she did so.

"Welcome to Lindsey Hall, Mrs. Derrick," the Duke of Bewcastle said, and for a moment it seemed to her that his pale silver eyes burned with a curious light. "Allow me to present my family."

He turned and indicated the first in line, a haughty, elderly lady whom Christine instantly recognized as one of society's most formidable dragons even though she had never before been presented to her.

"The Marchioness of Rochester, my aunt," the duke said. "And the marquess."

Christine curtsied as best she could with a three-year-old in her arms. The marchioness inclined her head and swept Christine from head to foot with one glance that suggested she had been seen and firmly dismissed as of no account whatsoever. The marquess, who appeared to be about half the size of his wife, bowed and murmured something unintelligible.

"Lord and Lady Aidan Bedwyn," the duke said, indicating a grim-looking, dark-haired gentleman of military bearing, who looked very much like him except that he was broader in build, and a pretty, brown-haired lady who smiled at her while her husband bowed.

"Mrs. Derrick," she said. "That child is going to be asleep in a few more minutes."

"Lord and Lady Rannulf Bedwyn," the duke said.

Lord Rannulf looked quite different from his brothers except for some similarity of facial features, especially the nose. He was something of a giant of a man with thick, wavy fair hair worn rather long. He brought Saxon warriors to mind. His wife was sheer, luscious, feminine beauty with vibrant, flame-colored hair. She smiled kindly while Lord Rannulf bowed.

"Mrs. Derrick," he said, a twinkle in his eye. "Lady Renable thought you had run away."

"Oh, no." Christine laughed. "But the children's nurse might well not have survived the day if I had not hurried to her rescue. Travel and children—especially *three* children shut up together for hours on end two days in a row—are not a good mix."

"The Marquess and Marchioness of Hallmere," the Duke of Bewcastle said.

It was clearly the marchioness who was the Bedwyn. She was small and looked like her brother, Lord Rannulf. She also had the family nose—and the family hauteur.

"Mrs. Derrick," she said, inclining her head formally while her husband, a tall blond god, bowed and smiled and asked if she had had a comfortable journey.

"Yes, I thank you, my lord," she said.

"Lord and Lady Alleyne Bedwyn," the duke said.

Lord Alleyne, Christine concluded immediately, was the handsome brother. Dark and slender and with perfect features even though he had the family nose, he also had eyes that laughed—perhaps with mockery, perhaps with simple pleasure in life. They were roguish eyes. He bowed elegantly to her and asked her how she did. Lady Alleyne too was lovely—she was all golden beauty.

"My uncle believes that he had an acquaintance with your late husband, Mrs. Derrick," she said. "I will present you to him later if I may—after you have taken that poor child to the nursery and settled in."

"The Earl and Countess of Rosthorn," the duke said, indicating the couple at the end of the line.

"I am delighted to make your acquaintance, madame," the earl said with a faint and attractive French accent as he made her a bow.

"Mrs. Derrick," the countess said, "how kind of you to pick up this little one, who looks very, very tired indeed."

She touched one of Pauline's cheeks with the backs of two fingers and smiled at her when the child peeped.

Lord Alleyne might be the handsome brother, Christine thought, but the very young Countess of Rosthorn was clearly the beauty of the family. Dark and youthfully slender, she was perfect in every feature.

The Duke of Bewcastle must have given an unobtrusive command—a raised eyebrow, perhaps?—and a female servant came into the hall and waited silently a few feet away.

"You will be escorted to the nursery and then to your room, ma'am," the Duke of Bewcastle said. "And someone will come to escort you to the drawing room for tea in half an hour's time."

"Thank you," Christine said, turning to look at him.

"And when Wulf says half an hour," Lord Alleyne said with a low chuckle, "he means thirty minutes."

The duke was looking stern and impassive. Was it possible he could have pressed her so hard to come here? Or that he had invited all of Oscar's family simply as an excuse to invite her too? There was no glimmering of anything in his eyes now except cool courtesy.

Oh, how she *despised* herself for being glad to see him again. She had felt starved for a sight of him, if the truth were known. Was she so determined, then, to set herself up for misery? Seeing the outside of his home and this great hall, seeing his very aristocratic family, seeing him in his proper milieu, she was more than ever aware that even if they suited in every personal way—which they most certainly did not—they could never make a match of it anyway.

The idea of her becoming a duchess was ludicrous, to say the least.

She followed the silent servant in the direction of the staircase—and felt suddenly very vexed. She had pictured herself arriving at Lindsey Hall, smart and aloof and dignified in some of her new clothes, very much the gracious lady, greeting the Duke of Bewcastle in company with Melanie and Bertie, smiling distantly at him, very much in control of the situation.

Instead . . .

Well, she seemed to have got all hot and flushed somewhere between Bertie's carriage and the front doors of Lindsey Hall. And her bonnet was very definitely askew—she could see several more inches of the underside of the brim on the left side than on the right. And now that she was walking again she could feel that her cloak had got twisted awkwardly about her, bringing her dress with it so that when she glanced downward she could see that far too much ankle—fortunately encased in her new half-boots—was showing on one side.

And hadn't she *prattled* at him when she entered the house instead of waiting for him to greet her and then smiling at him with cool, gracious dignity?

Yes, indeed she had. She had prattled—loudly enough for them all to hear every word. And then she had met every brother and sister he possessed as well as their spouses and the impossibly arrogant Marchioness of Rochester with twisted clothes, a bonnet askew, hot cheeks, and a child in her arms who was not even her own.

It was enough to make one want to weep.

It was enough to convince the Duke of Bewcastle without further ado that *no* man, least of all himself, would *ever* want to be her dream man.

And then *that* thought made her want to weep even harder.

15

*W*ULFRIC WAS VERY CAREFUL DURING TEA IN the drawing room to focus the bulk of his attention upon every newly arrived guest except Christine Derrick. He was careful to have her seated far from the head of the long table during dinner, between Alleyne and Joshua, while he had Lady Elrick on his left and Lady Mowbury on his right.

He did not want any of his family suspecting that she was, in fact, the guest of honor.

Characteristically, she was dressed simply, in a high-waisted, short-sleeved evening gown of pale green with but a single flounce at the hem and a modestly low neckline. She wore no jewelry and no adornments in her hair. She was decently, prettily clad, but even his partial eyes could see that she did not match in splendor any of his sisters or sisters-in-law or, indeed, any of the other ladies present. Yet her section of the table, as first Joshua and then Alleyne conversed with her, fairly sparkled with wit and humor—or so it seemed to Wulfric, who could not actually hear a word of what was being said.

When the gentlemen joined the ladies in the drawing room after dinner, Mrs. Derrick was sitting in one corner of the room, away from the fire, with Eve, Rachel, and Mrs. Pritchard. Her eyes met Wulfric's briefly, and he was not surprised when they laughed at him as if to say that her attempt to be unobtrusive and to observe humanity rather than be one of its number had been foiled.

He did not hold her gaze but gave his attention to his other guests and somehow found himself after a few minutes performing the unspeakably tedious task of turning pages of music for Miss Hutchinson while she played the pianoforte—competently but somewhat nervously, it seemed to him. After she had finished and he had complimented her, he strolled away in order to accept a cup of tea from Judith, who was pouring, and then found himself in conversation with his aunt and Miss Hutchinson again, though the former, after a mere couple of minutes, suddenly claimed that Rochester was beckoning her and swept away with all her hair plumes nodding.

Rochester, Wulfric could see, was playing cards with Weston, Lady Mowbury, and Mrs. Pritchard and was probably unaware that his wife was even in the room.

Miss Hutchinson, who had already been showing signs of nervous discomfort, looked as if she were on the verge of swooning quite away as he addressed his conversation exclusively to her. Morgan approached them, a smile on her face, but almost before Miss Hutchinson could turn to her in relief like a drowning person being thrown a rope, Aunt Rochester came swooping back down upon them and bore Morgan away on some slim pretext.

This, Wulfric, decided, was quite intolerable. It was more than a decade since he had last been the object of his aunt's matchmaking efforts.

"Miss Hutchinson," he said, "I see that a group of young people is gathering about the pianoforte. Would you care to join them?"

"Yes, please, your grace," she said.

His aunt, he thought, must have taken leave of her senses if she believed a match was possible between this girl and himself, but he knew that when she made up her mind to something, she was not easily deterred. If he did not wish to find himself tête-à-tête with Miss Hutchinson again in five minutes' time or less, he had better take an active role in his own salvation and find some alternative. And so he did what he wished to do.

He strolled toward the corner of the room where Christine Derrick was for the moment sitting alone. He stood before her, looking down at her and marveling anew that she was actually here at Lindsey Hall. For a few ghastly moments after the Renables had entered the house alone this afternoon, he had thought she must have changed her mind and not come after all. And then when she had stepped inside, flushed and breathless, her bonnet askew, her dress and cloak bunched up on one side, the child clutched in her arms, and had immediately launched into speech, he had thought the old thought— she simply did not know how to behave. But at the same time he had had the curious feeling that if there were any sunshine outside at all on such a gloomy day she must have brought it all inside with her.

He had never expected to fall in love. He had certainly never expected to develop an attachment to someone so very ineligible. And so he was quite unprepared to deal with the emotional turmoil that doing both had brought with it.

"Well, Mrs. Derrick," he said now.

"Well, your grace."

"I trust," he said, "all is to your liking? Your room? The service?"

"I have the loveliest room," she said, "with the loveliest view. Your housekeeper has been exceedingly kind to me. She has even insisted on assigning me my own personal maid, even though I assured her that I did not need one."

He inclined his head. His housekeeper, of course, had

taken her orders from him. He had chosen that room specifically for Christine Derrick, partly because he had thought the Chinese silk wallpaper and screens and the cheerful green and gold bed and window hangings would please her, and partly because he had wanted her to be able to look out upon the fountain surrounded by spring flowers, and upon the long, straight driveway beyond. It was, he always thought, a particularly stately view of the park. It was also the view he had from his own windows, though there were three rooms separating his apartments from hers. And he had guessed that she would not have a maid with her. She would be the only lady in his home who would not. It simply would not do.

He seated himself on a chair close to hers and arranged the tails of his coat neatly behind him.

"I trust," he said, "you had a pleasant journey."

"Yes," she said. "Thank you."

"And I trust," he said, "you left your mother well? And your sister?"

"Both, thank you," she said.

"And your sister at the vicarage?" he said. "And your nephews and niece?"

"They are all well, thank you." She half smiled at him and her eyes laughed outright. "So is Charles—the vicar."

When had he begun to take delight from that way she had of laughing at him?

"I am glad to hear it." The fingers of his right hand found the handle of his quizzing glass, and for a moment her eyes followed the gesture and made him conscious of it.

He was not a particularly sociable man. He avoided entertainments and trivial conversation whenever he could. He was, nevertheless, a gentleman and therefore adept at making polite conversation when he needed to do so.

This evening there was certainly need. He was entertaining houseguests in his own home. And they had all—even his brothers and sisters—been invited here because of this woman, because of his need to have her here and somehow woo her.

He could not think of a thing to say to her.

"I was surprised," she said, "to find the nursery so full of children, many of them very young."

"My brothers and sisters," he said, "have been somewhat prolific during the past few years. But you must not fear that the house will be overrun with them or that you will be called upon again to tend any of their needs. They belong in the nursery and will be kept there by their nurses."

His own family, he had decided, must make less free of the house with their offspring now that his other guests had arrived.

"I must not fear," she said softly. "They will be kept in the nursery. How convenient it is for the very wealthy to have nurseries and nurses to help them forget that they even have children—except for the succession."

"You would prefer to have them constantly underfoot, then?" he asked her. "Forever interrupting adult conversation and trying adult patience?"

"In my experience," she said, "the situation is more like to be reversed. Adults constantly interrupt a child's conversation and try a child's patience to the limit. But adults and children *can* coexist to the mutual happiness and benefit of both."

"And so," he said, "adults must board magic carpets with children and flap their arms with them as they fly over the Atlantic Ocean without getting their feet wet?"

"Oh, dear," she said, flushing, "so you *did* see some of that lesson, did you? It was unkind of you to stand against the fence at just the place where the sun would be behind you and make you virtually invisible. Did you disapprove, then? Did you think me undignified? Would it have been better to have the children sit in disciplined rows on the grass while I stood to assert my physical and intellectual superiority? Would it have been better to give them a verbal history of the fur trade in the interior of the North American continent beyond Canada and to describe to them the canoe routes taken by the voyageurs and the riverbed they follow and the flora and fauna they pass? To give the children a list of the food they take with them and the trading goods they carry to exchange for furs? And would I then have been justified the next day in my annoyance over discovering that not a single child remembered a single detail of the lesson?"

Many people spoke with their lips alone. Mrs. Derrick spoke with her lips, her eyes, her whole face, her hands, and her body—and with everything that was inside herself. She spoke as she appeared to live—with eagerness, even passion. He watched her and listened to her with fascination.

"Actually, Mrs. Derrick," he said, "I was charmed."

"Oh." Clearly he had taken the wind out of her sails. She had been preparing to argue with him. Perhaps, he thought belatedly, he should have baited her. "And yet you believe children belong in the nursery?"

"I wonder," he said, "what the children upstairs would think if we invaded their domain at will. Would they perhaps come to the conclusion that in the main adults belong downstairs?"

She laughed. "That is a novel thought, I must confess," she said. "At the vicarage Hazel is forever shushing the children because Charles is invariably writing and rewriting next Sunday's sermon, and she is forever correcting their grammar or criticizing their posture or directing their activities. Perhaps they would be delighted to have a nursery as their very own domain."

"I am not after all, then," he said, "the monster you first thought me, Mrs. Derrick?"

"But we must compromise," she said. "We adults must be allowed to enjoy ourselves free of children, and they must be allowed to enjoy *themselves* free of *us*. If we never see them, though, how can we learn from them? How can they learn from us?"

"*We* can learn from *children*?" he asked her.

"Of course we can." She leaned a little more forward in her chair. "We can learn to see the world anew through their eyes. We can learn spontaneity and joy and wonder and silliness and laughter. And love."

"All of which attributes," he said, "I believe I lack, Mrs. Derrick."

She sat back again and looked at him warily.

"I would not know," she said.

"But I believe you do." He half raised his quizzing glass. "Or so you once told me."

"I ought not to have done so," she said. "You ought not to have goaded me."

"By asking you to marry me?" he asked softly, his eyes narrowing on her. "I was *goading* you?"

"In your nightly prayers, your grace," she said, "you should give fervent thanks that I did not say yes."

"Should I?" Her eyes were pure blue, he saw again. Like the sea on a summer's day. He could easily drown in them.

"Look about you, your grace," she said. "Look at all the ladies."

He did so to oblige her. He even raised his glass to his eye. Freyja, he noticed, was looking quite magnificent tonight in a flowing gold gown with gold hair plumes and diamonds sparkling at her neck and ears and wrists and on several fingers. But she was only one of many. All the other ladies looked similarly elegant and richly clad.

"I have done so," he said, lowering his glass and turning back to Christine Derrick.

"And now look at me," she said.

He saw what he had already seen at dinner. Her gown was obviously new. It was more stylish than the clothes she had worn last summer. But it was simply styled and unadorned, and she wore no jewelry. Her shining dark curls had no ornament. Her cheeks were slightly flushed. Her eyes were dark-lashed and widely spaced and intelligent. Her freckles seemed to have disappeared. Her lips were soft and generous and slightly parted.

"I have done so," he said softly.

"Now tell me," she said, "that you do not see the difference."

"I see all the difference in the world," he told her. "None of those other ladies is you."

"Oh." The color in her cheeks deepened. "You are very clever this evening, your grace."

"I beg your pardon," he said. "Was there a script? Was I intended to say something else?"

"I am not of your world," she said. "I once married into it, though only as the wife of a younger son. We never had much money, especially in later years, and Oscar died in debt. These new clothes, which I chose with great care and consideration to cost, were bought from a money gift my brother-in-law sent me when he knew I had been invited to Audrey's wedding. I live contentedly in a small village. I teach. I am the daughter of a man who was a gentleman in name and education but not in substance. His father was a baronet, but my mother's father was a physician. You can be *very* thankful, your grace, that I said no. And I can be equally thankful. I would rather be dead, I believe, than be the wife of a duke."

He was rather taken aback by the firm assurance of her statement.

"Those are strong words, Mrs. Derrick," he said. "Would you rather be dead than marry a man who had engaged your affections, whether he were a duke or a chimney sweep?"

"But my affections are *not* engaged," she said.

"There is a way some people have," he said, "of seeming to answer a question without actually doing so at all."

"I do not believe," she said, "that I could be happy married to either a duke or a chimney sweep, your grace. It thus behooves me to be very careful that I do not develop an affection for either. For of course the dilemma would be a nasty one, would it not? Would I rather be dead than marry the man I loved—only because he was a chimney sweep or a duke? Would I become the heroine of a grand tragedy in the style of Shakespeare if the answer were yes, do you suppose? But I would not even know it, alas. I would be dead and floating down a river with my hair spread over the surface all about me—if I had not cut it all off."

His heart plummeted.

She did not mean to have him, and she was warning him—as she had done in Hyde Park—that there was nothing he could do to persuade her to change her mind. It was a rare challenge she presented to him. He could not dangle either his title or his enormous wealth before her, and he did not know how to woo a woman simply as a man. And, even if he could do it, she would still be immune to him just *because* he was also a duke and a very wealthy man.

She was a supreme realist, Christine Derrick—though perhaps she was wrong too. If there were practicality on the one hand and a dream on the other, why choose practicality? Just because it was sensible? Why not the dream? Why not live dangerously?

And was this really he, Wulfric Bedwyn, who was having these thoughts and dreaming of rebelling against all that had ordered his life for more than twenty years? And living dangerously?

But he had invited her here, had he not?

He feared that he was a little more than just in love with Christine Derrick. He very much feared that she had become essential to his happiness. And that in itself was a strange, alarming thought. He had never looked for happiness. He had never considered it important. He had never even really believed in it. Or perhaps he had. During the past three years he had seen each of his siblings find it and live with it. He had seen the wild and sometimes cold, even heartless, Bedwyns grow into the still wild, but contented, almost domesticated Bedwyns. And, without fully realizing it, he had felt left behind and ever so slightly resentful.

And lonely.

The silence had stretched for too long, and it was clear that she was not going to break it.

"It is to be hoped, then, Mrs. Derrick," he said, "that if you are ever the subject of a drama, it will be as the romantic heroine rather than as a tragic one. Perhaps there is a schoolmaster somewhere who will attach your admiration and the undying love of your heart. I wish you happy with him. In the meanwhile I shall do my best to give you and your fellow guests a memorable holiday here."

All traces of laughter had gone from her eyes. She leaned forward in her chair again.

"I think," she said, "you wear a mask that is at least a foot thick. It is virtually impenetrable. Have I offended you?"

"I beg your pardon?" His glass was halfway to his eye.

"Your eyes are like ice chips again," she said. "The eyes are usually the weak point in any disguise, you know, because the wearer has to see out into the world and must leave them exposed no matter how thoroughly he covers up every other part of his person. But your eyes *are* your disguise, or at least a large part of it. I cannot see even a glimmering of your soul by gazing into them."

If his eyes were ice, then they were freezing his whole person. He looked back at her in the only way he knew how—with cold hauteur. How could he look at her any differently? How could he risk . . .

"Perhaps, Mrs. Derrick," he said, "I should wear my heart on my *sleeve*, and you would not be obliged to look into my eyes at all. But I forget—I have no heart."

"I do believe, your grace," she said, "we are quarreling. But you are doing it in your own inimitable fashion by growing colder and more toplofty rather than more heated like the rest of us lesser mortals. It is a pity."

"You would like to see me in a rage, then?" He raised his eyebrows.

"I think I would like it very much," she said.

"Even if it were directed at you?"

She regarded him thoughtfully, her head tipped to one side, a smile lurking in the depths of her eyes.

"Yes, even then," she said. "I could fight you if you were in a rage. You would be horribly dangerous, I suspect, but I could perhaps communicate with the real man if you were to lose your temper—if there is a real man and not just a duke through to the very core of your being."

"You become offensive, ma'am," he said softly, and felt unmistakable anger tighten inside him like a hard ball.

"Do I?" Her eyes widened. "Have I hurt you? Have I angered you? I think I hope I have done both. I did not invite myself here, your grace. I did not wish to accept your invitation, and I was quite candid with you about that. You asked me to give you a chance to prove that there is more to you than you have yet revealed to me. I have not seen anything yet. But when I accuse you of wearing a mask, of hiding yourself behind icy eyes and an arrogant demeanor, you become colder still and throw my own words back at me so that I will squirm with discomfort—*but I forget—I have no heart,* you say. Perhaps you are right, then. Perhaps there *is* no mask. Perhaps I have been right about you all along."

He leaned a little closer to her.

"By God," he said, "we *are* quarreling. And though you are sitting there half smiling and talking softly and I am my usual icy self, we will be drawing attention to ourselves if we continue. We *will* continue, but not here and not now. If you will excuse me, I must mingle with my other guests. May I escort you to someone's side? Lady Wiseman's, perhaps, or Lady Elrick's?"

"No, thank you," she said. "I am quite contented here."

He got to his feet and bowed to her before moving to one of the card tables, where he stood looking down at Lady Renable's hand without at all seeing it.

He had certainly bungled that encounter, he thought. He had intended spending ten minutes or so with her, making her feel comfortable in his home and in his company, beginning to show her that he was human, and he had ended up . . . *quarreling* with her. Was that what they had been doing? He never quarreled and no one ever tried quarreling with him. No one *dared.* Was that part of her fascination to him—that she did dare?

But did he still find her fascinating? She *had* been offensive. She knew nothing about civility, about leaving well enough alone. She had talked about masks and eyes and ice chips. She had implied that he was not only without heart, but without soul too—*I cannot see even a glimmering of your soul.*

He felt—he drew a sharp, almost hissing breath—rather like weeping.

Lady Renable looked back over her shoulder at him and laughed as she replaced into the fan of cards she held in one hand the card she had been about to throw down. She selected another instead.

"You are quite right, Bewcastle," she said. "That was definitely not the card to play."

Justin Magnus had joined Mrs. Derrick in her corner, he could see. They were talking and laughing together. She looked happy and at ease again. Wulfric clamped his teeth together so that he would not grind them, and fought jealousy.

That would be the final humiliation.

16

AFTER EVERYONE ELSE HAD RETIRED TO BED, the Bedwyn siblings and their spouses remained behind in the drawing room—with the exception of Wulfric, who had withdrawn to the library, his own private domain.

"I wish Wulf had stayed here with us," Morgan said.

"The only marvel," Freyja said, "is that he stayed all evening until everyone else withdrew without finding some excuse to slip away."

"Well, I would think he *would* stay," Rannulf added, lowering himself to the floor at Judith's feet and tipping his head back onto her lap, "after inviting a houseful of guests here. Does anyone understand why he chose Elrick and Renable and all the rest? I have no objection to any of them, but they don't seem quite Wulf's type, do they?"

"Does Wulf *have* a type?" Alleyne asked.

"He is probably very thankful now that he *did* invite a houseful and not just family," Aidan said, squeezing onto a large chair beside Eve and setting one arm about her shoulders. "Aunt Rochester is in full matchmaking mode. It is hard to know for whom one ought to feel more sorry—Amy Hutchinson or Wulf."

"He would devour her for breakfast the morning after their wedding," Freyja said scornfully. "Josh, do come and help me get these absurd plumes out of my hair. They are hopelessly tangled."

"You are supposed to say please, Free," Rannulf told her.

"You needn't glare at me, sweetheart," Joshua said, grinning at her as he sat on the arm of her chair and batted her hands out of the way before setting to work on the plumes. "I am not the one who just accused you of bad manners."

"Perhaps," Eve suggested, "we ought to do something to help out—to keep Amy out of Wulfric's way and Wulfric out of hers."

"Aunt Rochester would fight back with every weapon in her arsenal," Alleyne said. "She means business."

"Might I suggest," Gervase said, taking up a stand before the fire, his back to it, "that Wulfric is a match for the dragon aunt? The idea of our taking a hand in his salvation seems mildly absurd, does it not?"

Most of his in-laws snickered their agreement.

"What we would need to do," Morgan said, frowning in concentration, "is find a diversion—someone else for Amy or someone else for Wulf."

"I cannot like Mowbury for the part," Aidan said. "I have never known a man with his head so lost in the clouds. I doubt he has noticed the girl's existence. And his brother must be shorter than she is by a whole head—*and* he is a younger son and would not fit Aunt Rochester's expectations."

"Which does not entirely exclude him as a possible suitor," Judith pointed out.

"He is also thin and balding," Freyja said bluntly, "and would surely not fit *Amy's* expectations."

"It has to be Wulf, then," Morgan said. "We have to find someone else for *him*."

"*Chérie,*" Gervase said fondly, "we would have as much

chance of success as King Canute did with holding back the tide."

"And," Freyja said, "Mrs. Derrick would seem to be the only candidate available for the diversion."

That silenced them all for a few moments. Then Joshua chuckled, handing the last of the gold plumes to Freyja as he did so.

"I would have paid a fortune to witness Wulfric fishing her out of the Serpentine," he said, "and then taking her home on his horse. I would wager he was *not* delighted."

"She made rather a grand entrance this afternoon too," Aidan said. "I thought Aunt Rochester's eyeball was going to pop right out through the lens of her lorgnette."

"I was afraid that Wulfric would freeze her into an icicle," Morgan said. "But she took no notice of him, did she? She looked a fright, but she had gone to the rescue of that child instead of coming to make her curtsy to us all and then she greeted us with the greatest good cheer."

"One has to admire her spunk," Freyja said. "Joshua says we are a formidable lot when we are all lined up together. He says we could be as effective as a firing squad without any of the mess of guns and blood."

"Mrs. Derrick is a jolly good sort actually," Alleyne said. "She has some lively conversation and a healthy sense of humor."

"She is as far from being Wulf's sort as it is possible to be, though," Freyja said, feeling her unruly coiffure with one hand now that the plumes were all gone and grimacing over the tangles. "Can you imagine him allowing himself to be paired with her even if Amy were the only alternative?"

There was general laughter as they all attempted to picture just that.

"He did spend some time talking with her this evening, though, Free," Rannulf pointed out, "and the very reason was that he was running away from Amy—or rather from our aunt."

"But he would not let it happen again," Freyja said. "No, we have to find someone else for him."

"But there is no one else, Free," Morgan pointed out, "unless the Earl of Redfield has invited guests to Alvesley for the holiday. Perhaps Lauren's cousin is staying there."

"Lady Muir?" Rannulf said. "I once fancied her myself." He tipped back his head and grinned upside down at Judith. "But then I met Jude and forgot her very existence."

Judith shoved at his head.

"I am not so certain that Mrs. Derrick is wrong for Wulfric," Rachel said suddenly. "She is a widow and far closer to him in age than Amy is. I think she is pretty, though not in any *tonnish* sense. And we must all have noticed how lively she is, how warm in manner, how ready to laugh. There is a certain sparkle about her that might be just what Wulfric needs."

"*Wulf?*" Rannulf looked blankly at her. So did everyone else.

"Wulfric loves very deeply," she said. "He just needs someone who can help him show it openly."

Rannulf laughed and Joshua chuckled.

Alleyne went to sit beside Rachel, took her hand in his, and laced their fingers together.

"Rachel has held this strange belief about Wulf," he said, "from the moment she first set eyes on him."

"I was the only one who saw his face," Rachel explained, "when he set eyes upon Alleyne for the first time after believing for several months that he was dead. The rest of you saw only that he hurried across the terrace at Morgan's wedding and hugged Alleyne. I saw his *face*. And if anyone wants to say in my hearing that Wulfric is a cold man and feels no deep emotion, I am here to argue with that person."

"And Rachel's wrath is a terrible thing." Alleyne raised their clasped hands to his lips and kissed hers.

"Oh, bravo, Rachel!" Freyja exclaimed. "I always admire anyone who has the courage to scold us Bedwyns."

"And you are absolutely right, Rachel!" Morgan cried. "I have never told anyone this before except Gervase. It seemed disloyal somehow, and at the time I must admit I was horrified. After the memorial service we held for Alleyne when we thought he was dead, I went to the library at Bedwyn House just for the comfort of being in the same room as Wulf. Luckily he did not see me. He was standing before the fireplace weeping."

There was an appalled, rather embarrassed silence.

"I do not suppose, *chérie*," Gervase said, "that you would endear yourself to Bewcastle if he knew you were telling such a dreadful story about him."

"Of course Wulfric loves," Eve said. "He had a hand in bringing Aidan and me together even though we were already married when he did it. And I believe he did as much for Freyja and Joshua and for Rannulf and Judith as well. It would be easy enough to say he did it simply for the family name and pride, but I have long believed he really cares. And what other possible motive than love could he have had for coming to Oxfordshire to make sure I did not lose Davy and Becky when my cousin would have taken them from me? But do you *really* think Mrs. Derrick is the woman to break down all of Wulfric's defenses, Rachel?"

Freyja snorted. "Of course she is," she said unexpectedly. "I cannot understand why we did not all see it sooner. Was he not at one of Lady Renable's house parties last summer? Mrs. Derrick was probably a guest there herself. And have we not wondered why Wulf would deign to rescue her from the Serpentine disaster when according to all accounts half the fashionable world was there to lend her assistance if he did not? It is quite unlike him to so expose himself to gossip and laughter. And why did he invite her family here for Easter when none of us are aware of any deep friendship he has with any of them except perhaps Lord Mowbury? Why did he invite *us* here? It is usually we who invite ourselves."

"You are not saying—" Alleyne began.

"And *why*," Freyja continued, sawing at the air with one hand, "did he line us all up in the hall this afternoon when it was merely Lord Renable's carriage that had been spotted approaching? We were all mystified at the time."

"Deuce take it," Alleyne said, "you *are* saying. Women have marvelous imaginations, I must say. They leap from point A to point D without even a sideways glance at points B and C. You believe Wulf already has a *tendre* for Mrs. Derrick, Free?"

"It is altogether likely," Rachel said, turning her head to gaze into his eyes.

"Well," Aidan said briskly, "I believe we are all agreed that Aunt Rochester's ill-conceived notion that Amy Hutchinson and Wulf would suit needs to be foiled—for both their sakes. And, if putting Mrs. Derrick more in his way will accomplish that purpose, then I am all for it. If he should also happen to fall head over ears for her—though I do believe *that* is something of a stretch even for the most active of imaginations—then I am very prepared to buy Eve new clothes for the wedding."

"What I think," Joshua said, "for what it is worth when I am talking to Bedwyns and know perfectly well that they invariably do the opposite of what one suggests— what *I* think is that we should leave well enough alone. I cannot think of anything much more ludicrous than a band of well-meaning Bedwyns plotting together to save Wulfric—*Bewcastle*, for the love of God!—from one unlikely marriage prospect only to thrust another even more unlikely one in his way."

"My point exactly." Gervase laughed.

"Ludicrous?" Freyja said haughtily. "You are accusing us of being *ludicrous*, Joshua? And you think it *funny*, Gervase?"

Aidan got to his feet.

"I believe," he said, "it is time we all went to bed. There is only one thing more alarming than matchmaking Bedwyns and that is squabbling Bedwyns. Fists will be flying next, and there *are* two or three ladies present."

"Two or—" Freyja jumped to her feet, her eyes sparking.

But Aidan held up one hand and silence fell. He could be almost as formidable as Wulfric when he chose, and he had the added advantage of having been a cavalry colonel for several years.

"You know very well, Freyja," he said, "that in any fight yours would be the first fists flying. To bed now, and we will see what tomorrow brings. My guess is that Wulf will foil Aunt Rochester *and* avoid Mrs. Derrick without any effort whatsoever more strenuous than the raising of an eyebrow and without the slightest assistance on our part." He offered his arm to Eve.

"*Some* people," Freyja said with a toss of her head, "always have to have the last word."

Rannulf and Alleyne looked pointedly at each other and then at her, their lips pressed tightly together.

Joshua grinned and wrapped one arm about her waist.

WHILE THE BEDWYNS were meeting in the drawing room, Christine was entertaining Hermione in her bedchamber. Her sister-in-law had caught up with her on the stairs as they all retired for the night and had then invited herself inside.

Christine looked warily at her and offered her a chair while she went to perch on the side of the bed.

"Oh," Hermione said, looking about, "what a perfectly delightful room. It must be one of the largest and best bedchambers in the house."

Christine had not considered that. She had assumed that all the upper rooms were similarly grand. But Hermione did not pursue the topic. She sat down on the chair and regarded her sister-in-law gravely.

"Christine," she said, "Basil and I have talked and wondered about this invitation. Our acquaintance with his grace is really quite slight, and he has never been known to host a house party at Lindsey Hall. Why us? It is true that he has a friendship with Hector, but Melanie and Bertie are no more his close associates than we are, despite the fact that Hector brought him to Schofield last summer. No—we have been drawn to the conclusion that *you* are the reason for our being invited here."

"Me?" Christine said.

"Strange and almost incredible as it seems," Hermione said, "I do believe—and Basil agrees with me—that his grace is *infatuated* with you."

Christine bit her lower lip.

"It is clear," Hermione continued, "that the Marchioness of Rochester has other plans for him, and she has considerable influence. And his family would never countenance such a match, you know. Neither would he. If he *is* infatuated, he will offer only dalliance."

"You are trying to warn me, then," Christine asked, "not to get my hopes too high?"

Her sister-in-law's brows snapped together.

"I am *asking* you," she said, "not to make a fool of yourself, Christine—or of us. You will never be the Duchess of Bewcastle—the very idea is absurd. But if you get up to any of your usual tricks, your ambition will soon be quite obvious to the marchioness and all of his grace's brothers and sisters and the embarrassing vulgarity of it will reflect upon us."

"My usual tricks." Christine felt herself grow cold.

"Pretending to fall out of a tree when he was close by," Hermione said, her voice bitter and unhappy. "Pretending to fall accidentally into the Serpentine when he just happened to be riding by. Just happening to be sitting in the laburnum alley when he chose to walk there. Pretending to be badly hurt when Hector had merely stepped on your foot and not returning to the ballroom for a whole hour. And attracting the admiration of almost every other gentleman at that house party at the same time. The Earl of Kitredge even proposed marriage to you in London. But you refused him, I hear. Why be a countess when you believe you could be a duchess?"

"I think," Christine said, "you had better leave, Hermione."

Her sister-in-law got to her feet and crossed to the door without another word. But it had always been like this, Christine thought suddenly—at least, it had been for the last few years of Oscar's life and after his death and last summer and again now. They always avoided really speaking with each other.

"Wait!" she said, and Hermione looked back at her over her shoulder.

Christine got up off the bed and crossed to the window. She threw back the curtains, but of course there was nothing to see outside—only fine drops of drizzle on the windowpanes and darkness beyond.

"There was a time," she said, "when you used to delight in my not-infrequent disasters. You used to tell me that the *ton* was delighted with me despite the laughter I provoked. You told me that laughter was good for the soul and the *ton.* You used to tell me that I had a gift of attraction—that ladies liked me, that gentlemen liked and even admired me because it was safe for them to do so, my being a married lady. Oscar loved me and I loved him, and we really were a happy family. You told me I was the sister you had never had but had always wanted. You were the sister I needed to replace my own, who were far away. What changed? I never understood it. It was like a nightmare from which I could not awake. Suddenly all my social gaffes were embarrassing and humiliating for you all. And suddenly every gentleman with whom I conversed or danced or exchanged smiles was a victim of my flirtatious wiles. And not even just flirtation. Suddenly I acquired a whole string of clandestine lovers. Why did that change happen?"

Hermione was still looking at her over her shoulder. There was a short silence.

"You tell me, Christine," she said at last. "You tired of Oscar, I suppose. You realized your power to attract larger fish. You had no feeling for him—or us."

Christine blinked back tears.

"I always loved Oscar," she said. "Even in the last years, when he became difficult and when he started to gamble too recklessly and lost all his fortune, I never stopped caring for him. I was his *wife.* I never *ever* thought of straying."

"Well," Hermione said. "I would like to believe you, Christine. But we both know that is a lie. If it were not, Oscar would still be alive."

"You *cannot* believe I was guilty on that occasion," Christine said. "I begged you at the time to ask Justin. Why did you not do so? He could have confirmed my innocence."

"Of course we asked Justin," Hermione said wearily. "And of course he protested your innocence—over and over again and with great indignation over the fact that we could doubt you for a moment. But he always did defend you, did he not? No matter what, Justin was always there to be your champion, to deny every charge against you. Justin has always been in love with you, Christine. He would perjure himself to the grave rather than have anyone believe ill of you."

"I see," Christine said. "And so I am guilty. His very defenses have made me so. Poor Justin. His efforts on my behalf have always had the opposite effect than the one he intended. You must believe what you will, then. But I can relieve your mind of one concern. I am *not* here out of any ambition to be the Duchess of Bewcastle. I have already refused the position and will refuse again if the offer is renewed. I am perhaps even more sensible than you and Basil of the fact that it would be a match made in hell—for both of us. I am longing for the day when I can go back home and resume the life that has made me happy for almost three years—though I mourned Oscar deeply for the first of those years."

"Christine." Unexpectedly Hermione's eyes too filled with tears. "I *do* wish to believe the best of you now. Basil and I both do. You are Oscar's widow."

Christine nodded. There seemed to be nothing to say. Some sort of peace was being offered, she supposed— again.

Hermione left the room without another word, leaving Christine with the unenviable task of trying to get to sleep in a strange bed in a strange house while her conversation with Hermione—*and* her quarrel with the duke— buzzed around endlessly in her brain.

17

*T*HEY ALL WENT TO CHURCH THE FOLLOWING
morning for the Good Friday service. A few of the
older people went by carriage, but most of them walked,
since the weather had taken a distinct turn for the better.

Christine walked with Justin. The duke, she noticed,
had Miss Hutchinson on his arm, though Lord and Lady
Aidan stayed close to them. The Marchioness of
Rochester was, of course, promoting a match between
the pair. Christine heartily sympathized with Miss
Hutchinson, who was both a pretty and a sweet-natured
young lady—but no match for the duke.

It was as if Justin sensed her thoughts.

"Poor lady," he said, nodding in their direction. "I wonder if she realizes that being a duchess comes at a high
price. But I daresay her aunt will explain before the
nuptials—*if* Bewcastle can be brought to the point, that is."

Christine did not comment. She did not want to discuss the duke even with her dearest friend—especially
after last night. But he continued.

"Lady Falconbridge will certainly understand," he
said. "I daresay she does not really expect that he will
marry her anyway. And I suppose his mistress will learn
to understand—she will not have much choice, will she,

short of leaving his employment, which I daresay is rather lucrative."

"Justin!" Christine said sharply. "Do you usually speak to ladies about such things?"

He looked instantly contrite. "I do beg your pardon," he said. "But you knew about Lady Falconbridge, and he has had his mistress for so many years that I assumed everyone knew. Foolish of me—you are indeed a lady. But you were the wise one, Chrissie." He patted her hand on his arm. "You would have none of him. I don't suppose he liked that."

"I am going to change the subject *now*," she said firmly. "Hector tells me he is going on his travels again soon and that you may be going with him. Is that true?"

He pulled a face. "Only if he decides to go somewhere civilized," he said. "Italy, perhaps."

Christine listened with only half an ear. She really had not needed to know about the Duke of Bewcastle's women. How very annoying of Justin to treat her like a male comrade rather than as a lady. What the duke did was none of her business, of course, even if he employed a whole harem of women. But she could not help remembering his saying that if he ever married, his wife would be the only woman to share his bed for the rest of his life. Somehow she had believed him. But it did not matter anyway, did it? She was never going to be his wife. She was quite determined about that even if he had brought her here to court her.

Was that why he had invited her? It seemed just too incredible.

She avoided him all morning and sat far from him at both breakfast and luncheon. She was, however, thrown unexpectedly into his company again during the afternoon. Lord and Lady Aidan announced their intention of taking their children for a walk outside, Lord and Lady

Rannulf decided to join them with theirs, and before another minute had passed almost everyone had decided to go out. They all dispersed to fetch their outdoor things and their children, having agreed to meet downstairs in the hall. Christine was delighted at the prospect of some fresh air and at the discovery that the Bedwyns shared her love of the outdoors.

She joined Audrey and Sir Lewis in the hall and smiled at all the young children, who darted about with caged energy that was about to be unleashed. She hugged Pauline and Pamela, who came dashing up to greet her before darting off again to rejoin some young companions. Justin, who was in conversation with Bertie, indicated that he would join her in a moment. The Marchioness of Rochester, who was not going out with them, had come down to the great hall anyway to see them on their way—and to do some organizing.

"I have been telling Amy about the pretty path that connects the wilderness walk with the lake, Wulfric," she said in a voice that was clearly accustomed to command. "You must be sure to show it to her."

He bowed stiffly to her and to poor Miss Hutchinson, who almost visibly shrank from the prospect of spending the afternoon in his company.

"That will have to wait for another day, I am afraid, Aunt," the Countess of Rosthorn said, tucking her arm firmly through Miss Hutchinson's and smiling apologetically at both the marchioness and the duke. "I have promised Amy that we will talk about her presentation to the queen in a few weeks' time. I shall pass along to her my own experiences and advice, for what they are worth."

The countess's husband, the earl with the attractive French accent, had a little boy astride his shoulders—his son Jacques. Christine had visited the nursery before church and got to know all the children, including the babies.

"Oh, poor Wulfric!" Lady Alleyne cried. "Now you have no partner. Perhaps Mrs. Derrick will take pity on you."

Justin, who had been threading his way through the crowd toward Christine, stopped short, and the Duke of Bewcastle turned and inclined his head to her.

"Ma'am?" he said, offering his arm. "Will you? Though it would appear that you have been given little choice."

Neither had he, she thought, casting a rueful glance at Justin as she took his grace's arm and they led the way from the house. She very carefully did *not* look Hermione and Basil's way.

"It would also appear," he said, "that the ladies in my family are in league against my aunt. I wonder if it is on Miss Hutchinson's account or mine."

"Undoubtedly Miss Hutchinson's," she said. "She is clearly terrified of you."

He gave her a sidelong glance but she did not respond to it.

"It is, of course, for your sake," he said, "that I agreed to participate in this walk at all. However, I do not intend to be overrun with infants or to have my eardrums assaulted by their shrieks every step of the way. They and their parents are heading toward the lawns and the trees. We will lead those people who are not so encumbered to the wilderness walk."

"I suppose," she said, "you never allow your peace to be disturbed."

"Not if I can help it," he agreed. "And I usually can. I have been looking forward to showing you the park. I suppose it is even more picturesque during the summer, but there is a certain fresh beauty about it in the spring— and the weather is kind today."

"I love winter landscapes too," she said. "They have all the appearance of death but all the potential for resurrection. One understands the full power and mystery and glory of life during winter. And then comes spring. Oh, how I *adore* springtime! I cannot imagine your park looking lovelier than it does now."

As they turned off a long lawn to the west side of the house in order to move uphill into what must be the wilderness walk, they passed some cherry trees that were in bloom. The children and their parents, a noisy, ebullient group, continued along the grass.

"I believe, Mrs. Derrick," the duke said, "you are an eternal optimist. You find hope even in death."

"The whole of life would be a tragedy if one did not understand that it is, in fact, indestructible," she said.

They followed a path upward through trees sporting their new, bright greenery and some darker evergreens until they turned onto a more level path that wound its way between rhododendron bushes and taller trees. Wild daffodils and primroses carpeted the ground in more open places. Occasionally a break in the trees gave them a view down to the house or the park or surrounding countryside. There was a large lake to the east of the house, surrounded by trees, an island in the middle of it.

A few of the other guests had turned onto the wilderness walk too, but they soon fell behind as Christine and the duke strode briskly onward. She felt her spirits rise after the depression she had felt last night. It was true what she had just said. Easter began with mourning for a death and was gloomy for a while. But then came the glory of resurrection.

At the end of a gradual climb the path reached the top of a rise, on which a folly had been built—a picturesque ruined tower.

"Can one get to the top?" Christine asked.

"There is an unobstructed view for miles around from up there," he told her. "But the stairs inside are steep and narrow and winding—and rather dark. Perhaps you would prefer to walk onward rather than stop."

Christine gave him a sidelong glance.

"And then again," he said, "perhaps you would not. You enjoy climbing to the battlements of old castles, I seem to remember."

She laughed.

She climbed the staircase carefully, keeping to the outer wall, where the spiraling steps were at their widest, holding up the hem of her skirt so that she would not trip over it. But the view from the top was well worth the climb. From up here she could see just how vast and magnificent the park of Lindsey Hall was and how extensive the farmlands surrounding it. The house was huge and imposing.

And with a simple yes when she had said no, Christine thought, she might have been mistress of it all—and of those other properties he had told her about last summer. And *he* might have been hers too. Perhaps he still could. *Was* he courting her?

Could he not see the impossibility of it all?

He was standing at the top of the steps, looking at her more than at the view, she could see when she turned her attention to him. His eyes were narrowed against the sunlight.

"It is all quite magnificent," she said, twirling slowly once about.

"Yes," he said, "it is." But it was at her he looked.

And *he* was magnificent too, she thought. He was dressed immaculately in brown and buff and white with shining black Hessians. His austere, handsome face perfected the picture he made of the refined and consummate aristocrat. He would surely be a portrait painter's dream.

They were stuck then within a few feet of each other, staring at each other, he with narrowed gaze, she wide-eyed, with nothing to say.

He stepped forward after a few moments and pointed and she turned to look at what he indicated.

"Do you see the small building among the trees there to the north of the lake?" he asked her.

It took her a moment to find it, but then she could see a round, thatched roof. The stone building beneath it was round too.

"What is it?" she asked. "A dovecote?"

"Yes," he said. "I would like to show it to you, but it is some distance away."

"Am I incapable of walking so far?" she asked, laughing.

"Will you come?" He had turned his head to look at her, and their glances met and held again.

"Yes," she said, and felt that she was somehow agreeing to something far more significant than was apparent to her.

The other group of walkers was approaching the tower as they came down—Mrs. Pritchard and Lord Weston, Lady Mowbury and Justin, Hermione and Basil. Audrey and Sir Lewis were lagging far behind.

"I will be taking Mrs. Derrick down off the walk," the Duke of Bewcastle told them. "But do not let us disturb anyone else. This path eventually winds its way back to the house and there are several resting places along the way."

They walked a short distance in silence and then turned sharply to their right onto a grassy slope that would take them down among the trees that surrounded the lake. The duke offered his arm again since it was a long, rather steep slope and would be difficult to descend without slipping and sliding. Indeed, Christine thought, ignoring the offered arm, there was only one sensible way to do it. She gathered her skirts above her ankles and ran.

The slope was longer and steeper than she had estimated. By the time she reached the bottom she was close to flying. The brim of her bonnet had blown back, her curls were bouncing about her face, and she was shrieking. But how wonderfully exhilarating it had been! She also realized as she arrived there that the families with children were approaching from among the trees—and most of them had witnessed her undignified descent of the hill. She laughed and turned to watch the Duke of Bewcastle descend with the utmost dignity, as if he were strolling on Bond Street.

"What a splendid hill this would be for rolling down," she called up to him.

"If you cannot resist the temptation, Mrs. Derrick," he said as he reached the bottom, "I will wait here while you trudge back up then roll down. I'll be a spectator."

And then he turned with raised eyebrows as exuberant children came running out into the open with adults behind them.

"Are we going up?" young William Bedwyn shrieked to Lord Rannulf. "I want to go up, Papa."

"Up," young Jacques demanded of his own papa.

Daniel did not even ask. He dashed upward, turned partway up the slope, and dashed down again, his little legs pumping just fast enough to land him safely in Lady Freyja's arms before he toppled over. He wriggled free and went up again.

The hill was obviously going to be the chosen playground for some time to come. The Duke of Bewcastle looked at his nieces and nephews with his usual unreadable expression before turning to offer his arm to Christine, but he was forestalled by Pamela and Pauline, who grabbed one of her hands each, both speaking—or rather yelling—at once and demanding that she watch them despite the fact that Melanie and Bertie were not far off. Christine laughed and watched as they darted away to join the game of running down the hill before they fell down. Beatrice Bedwyn was the first to come to grief and set up a wailing until her father grabbed her up, set her astride his shoulders, and went galloping off among the trees with her. Miranda Bedwyn, who was little more than a toddler, persuaded Lord Rannulf to go up a little way with her and run her down. He swung her up into the air with a loud roar as they neared the bottom and had her shrieking with delight and demanding more. Hannah Bedwyn was toddling about in circles, clapping her hands and laughing up at Lord Aidan as she lost her balance and landed on her well-padded bottom.

The noise was deafening.

"Phillip and Davy are going to the very top," Pamela screeched full volume as she came to grab Christine's hand again, "and my friend Becky and I want to go too. Come with us, Cousin Christine."

It did not occur to Christine as Becky caught hold of her other hand to say no even though she had just come down that long slope. She trudged up it with the two young girls, stopping halfway to watch the two older boys hurtle downward with bloodcurdling whoops of delight.

"You know," she said as they neared the top, "it would be far more fun to roll down than to run."

"*Roll?*" Becky giggled. "How?"

"You lie flat along the top of the hill with your legs together and your arms above your head," Christine explained, "and let yourself roll over and over to the bottom. I have never seen a more splendid hill for rolling down."

"Show us," Pamela demanded.

"I will," Christine promised. "I'll show you how it is

done, but I'll not actually do it. It would be very undignified for a grown lady, would it not?"

The two girls giggled with glee and Christine joined them. But when they were at the very top she stretched out on the grass to demonstrate the ideal position for rolling.

"It is quite easy," she assured them. "If you have trouble getting started, I will give you a little push. But once you *have* started, there will be no need for any more—"

The sentence ended on a shriek. Two little voices had giggled again, four mischievous little hands had given her a push, and she was rolling downward. For one moment she thought of trying to stop herself, but she knew from past experience that she might hurt herself if she tried, especially on such a steep slope, and that even if she did not, she would look enormously undignified as arms and legs flailed for hand- and footholds to slow her progress. And then in the next moment trying to stop was no longer an option. She rolled over and over down the slope at an alarming speed, shrieking as she went.

By the time she reached the bottom her thoughts were no longer coherent at all, and her shrieks had turned to laughter. Two strong arms caught her and two grim silver eyes looked down at her. When her thoughts *did* become coherent, she realized whose arms and eyes they were and noticed that everyone else seemed to be laughing except him.

There were more shrieks as the two girls came rolling down the hill after her, and then the nature of the game changed as all the children demanded to roll rather than run. Phillip and Davy were taking the hill up at a run.

"And so you had your wish, Mrs. Derrick," the Duke of Bewcastle said.

"Jolly good show!" Lord Rannulf said, grinning and looking ruggedly handsome.

"Now I am mortally jealous," Lady Freyja said. "I have not done that in years. But today I will. Wait for me, Davy!"

Christine was hastily checking that her legs and head were decently covered and wondering if she had left any grass on the slope or if she had brought every blade of it down with her on her person. She brushed vigorously at herself as she got to her feet.

"Wulfric," Lord Aidan said, "now that Mrs. Derrick has shown the children how to *really* enjoy themselves and set a challenge for Free, why do you not take her to show her the lake?"

"I will do that, thank you, Aidan," the duke said curtly, "if Mrs. Derrick wishes it. Ma'am?"

"I do indeed," she said, laughing and taking his offered arm. "I have made enough of a cake of myself for one day."

The Earl of Rosthorn, she noticed, winked at her.

The duke led her off through the trees, and soon they had left the noise and the frolicking behind them.

"I was merely showing the girls how to do it," she explained after the silence had stretched between them. "They *pushed* me."

He did not comment.

"It must have been a most undignified spectacle," she said. "Your brothers and sisters must think me the most dreadful of creatures."

Still he made no comment.

"And *you* must think it," she added.

She was not quite sure what he did with her arm then. But whatever it was, she found herself the next moment with her back against a tree trunk and the Duke of Bewcastle standing in front of her, looking grim and very dangerous indeed. One of his hands was propped on the bark beside her head.

"And do you care, Mrs. Derrick?" he asked her. "Do you *care* what I think?"

It was obvious what he thought. He was furious with her. He thought her vulgar and unladylike. She had just put on a shocking display of both traits for his family. And she was his invited guest. Her behavior reflected badly upon him. She suddenly thought of Hermione's warnings of last night.

"No," she said, though she did, she realized. She did care.

"As I thought." He looked arctic.

"You just do not like children, do you?" she said. "Or anything suggestive of childhood or exuberance or sheer enjoyment. Cold, sober dignity is everything to you—*everything*. Of course I do not care what you think of me."

"I will tell you anyway," he said, his eyes blazing with a curious cold light that she recognized as anger. "I believe you were put on this earth to bring light to your fellow mortals, Mrs. Derrick. And I believe you should stop assuming that you know me and understand me."

"Oh." She pressed the back of her bonnet against the tree. "I hate it when you do that. Just when I think we are launched on a satisfactory quarrel, you take the wind out of my sails. What on earth do you mean by it?"

"You do not know me at all," he said.

"The other thing," she said. "About my being here to bring light."

He moved his head one inch closer, but his eyes were still like two blazing ice chips—a curious anomaly!

"You do things that are impulsive and unladylike and clumsy and even vulgar," he said. "You chatter too much, you laugh too much, and you sparkle in a manner that is in no way refined. And yet you attract almost everyone within your aura as a flame does a moth. You think people despise you and scorn you and shun you, when the opposite is true. You have told me that you did not take well with the *ton*. I do not believe it. I believe you took very well indeed—or would have done if you had been allowed to. I do not know who put the idea into your head that you did not, but that person was wrong. Perhaps he could not bear the power of your light, or perhaps he could not bear to share it with his world. Perhaps he mistook the light for flirtation. That is what I *think*, Mrs. Derrick. I was digesting the wonder of the fact that Lindsey Hall was alive with the presence of children again, most of them the offspring of my own brothers and sisters—and then you came hurtling down the hill into my arms. You will not *dare* tell me now that I do not like children or exuberance or enjoyment."

She felt considerably shaken. At the same time she felt a certain elation—she had made him angry! He was clearly furious with her. And his anger had spilled over. She had never, since her first acquaintance with him, heard him string together so many words at one time.

"And *you* will not dare tell me what I may or may not say," she said. "You may have almost total power over your world, your grace, but I am not of it. You have no power over *me*. And, after hearing your description of me, we must both be glad of it. I would shame you every day of your life—as I did in Hyde Park, as I did this afternoon."

"Unlike your late husband or his brother, or whoever it was that convinced you that you are nothing more than a flirt," he said, "I believe I *could* stand the power of your light, Mrs. Derrick. My own identity would not be diminished by it. And *yours* would not be diminished by my power. You once told me I would sap your joy, but you belittle yourself if you truly believe it. Joy can be sapped only by weakness. I am not, I believe, a weak man."

"What nonsense you speak!" she said as he finally

leaned back away from her and removed his hand from the tree trunk. "No one else exists for you except as minions to run and fetch for you and obey your every command. And you command with the mere lifting of a finger or an eyebrow. Of *course* you would have to control me too if I were unwise enough to put myself into your power. You know no other way of relating to people."

"And you, Mrs. Derrick," he said, taking a few steps away from her and then turning to look back at her, "know no other way of fighting your attraction to me than to convince yourself that you know me through and through. Have you decided, then, that I wear no mask after all? Or that you were right last evening when you said that perhaps I was simply the Duke of Bewcastle to the core?"

"I am *not* attracted to you!" she cried.

"Are you not?" He raised one supercilious eyebrow and then his quizzing glass. "You have sexual relations, then, with every dancing partner who invites you to accompany him to a secluded spot?"

Fury blossomed in her. And it focused upon one object.

"*That*," she said, striding toward him, "is the outside of enough!"

She snatched the quizzing glass out of his nerveless hand, yanked the black ribbon off over his head, and sent the glass flying with one furious flick of her wrist.

They both watched it twirl upward in an impressively high arc, reach its zenith between two trees, and then begin its downward arc—which was never completed. The ribbon caught on a high twig and held there. The glass swung back and forth like a pendulum a mile off the ground—or so it seemed to Christine.

She was the first to speak.

"And this time," she said, "I am not going up for it."

"I am relieved to hear it, ma'am," he said, his voice sounding as frosty as she had ever heard it. "I would hate to have to carry you all the way to the house in another ruined dress."

She turned her head to glare at him.

"I am *not* attracted to you," she said. "And I am *not* promiscuous."

"I did not believe you were," he assured her. "That, in fact, was my very point."

"I daresay," she said, looking ruefully up at the quizzing glass, which was now swaying gently in the breeze, "you will raise an eyebrow when we return and an army of gardeners will rush out here to rescue it. You will not be able to raise your quizzing glass, will you? Though I daresay you have an endless supply of them."

"Eight," he said curtly. "I have eight of them—or will have when that particular one is back in my keeping." And he strode away from her.

For a moment Christine thought that she was being abandoned for her sins. But then she realized that he was headed for the old oak tree in pursuit of his quizzing glass. He went up the tree as he had come down the slope from the wilderness walk—with ease and elegance. Her heart was in her mouth by the time he was high enough to reach for his glass, but it was too far from the trunk, and he had to sit on a branch and edge his way out toward it.

"Oh, do be careful!" Christine cried, and set both hands over her mouth.

"I always am." He unhooked the ribbon, dropped it and the glass for her to catch, and sat there looking down at her. "Always. Except, it would seem, where you are concerned. If I were careful, I would stay here, just where I am, until you had returned safely to Gloucestershire. If I had been careful, I would have avoided you at Schofield

Park as I would avoid the plague. Earlier this year I would have shut myself up inside Bedwyn House after Miss Magnus's wedding until I was sure you were at least fifty miles on your journey home. After one aborted plan to marry when I was twenty-four, I gave up all idea of marriage. I have not looked for a bride since then. If I *had*, she most certainly would not have been you. I would have been very *careful* to choose altogether more wisely. Indeed, you are the very antithesis of the woman I would have chosen."

"Of course you do not wish to marry," she said tartly, "when you have two mistresses."

Too late she realized that she had been goaded into the ultimate vulgarity. But how dared he tell her so bluntly that she was the very antithesis of the woman he would want for a duchess.

He gazed down at her from his high perch, looking surly and gorgeously handsome.

"Two," he said. "One for the week and the other for Sundays? Or one for the country and one for town? Or one for the day and one for the night? Your informant is misinformed, Mrs. Derrick. My long-term mistress died more than a year ago, and I know of no other. And you *will* forgive the vulgarity of my mentioning such a person to you, no doubt, since you were the first to refer to her."

More than a year ago. At Schofield last summer, then, he had been trying to replace that mistress—with *her*.

"I find myself constantly infuriated and enchanted by you," he told her. "Often both at the same time. How can one explain that?"

"I do not *want* to enchant you," she cried. "I do not even want to infuriate you. I do not want to be *anything* to you. You have no business having feelings for a woman you so obviously despise. Imagine how much more you would come to despise me if you were forced to live with me for the rest of your life."

He speared her with his cold glance.

"Is that what happened to you the last time?" he asked her.

"It is no *business* of yours what happened to me last time or any time," she said. "I am none of your business. Are you planning to sit there all day—or until I leave for Gloucestershire? It is remarkably foolish to be quarreling thus when you might fall at any moment and I might acquire a stiff neck."

He made his way down without another word. She watched him in silence. He was a marvelously muscular and virile man, she thought resentfully. He was also a very disturbing presence. This afternoon she had seen that there was more to him than power and ice. She had seen him angry and frustrated. He had told her that she enchanted him—and infuriated him.

Why was it, she wondered, that opposites attracted? And they were such very extreme opposites. But opposites surely could never progress beyond mere attraction. They could never coexist in harmony and happiness. She would not—oh, she *would not*—give up her freedom ever again on the mere whim of an attraction.

Even though it felt like love.

He slapped his hands over his coat and pantaloons while she looped the ribbon of his quizzing glass over her head. He was not going to use it on her again this afternoon if she could help it.

"It is too late to walk to the dovecote today," he said. "It will have to wait for another occasion. Let me take you to walk back beside the lake—as Aidan suggested."

His eyes came to rest on his quizzing glass, but he made no comment or demand for its return.

"Yes," she said, clasping her hands behind her. "Thank you."

I believe you were put on this earth to bring light to your fellow mortals, Mrs. Derrick.

Would she ever forget his saying those words? Such strange words. They made her want to weep.

He made her want to weep, nasty, horrid man.

18

They walked along the shore of the lake back in the direction of the house. The wind came directly across the water and, though it was a lovely day, one could feel now that it was still only early spring.

Wulfric felt shaken by the fact that he had lost his temper with her. It was something he never did. But then, falling in love was something he never did either—until now. He had told her the truth—he was constantly irritated with her and enchanted by her. Even now he was tempted to let her go, to back off, to turn on the chill again—according to her he never turned it off anyway—and to forget all about this madness of wooing her.

Whoever had heard of a Duchess of Bewcastle rolling down a long hill with a large audience of Bedwyns and Bedwyn children looking on, and shrieking with exuberance and laughing with glee as she did it? And looking so vibrantly beautiful that he had almost scooped her right up into his arms at the bottom of the hill and covered her face with kisses.

He wondered how his brothers and sisters—and the Renables—would have reacted if he had done so.

They walked in silence. It was he who broke it at last—half unwillingly. He did not know what he might unleash with his question. He was not sure he wanted to know the answer—*if* she was prepared to give one. But how could he love her if he did not *know* her?

"Tell me about the years of your marriage," he said.

She turned her face toward the lake. Looking down, he could see his quizzing glass about her neck. For several moments he thought she was not going to answer him.

"He was blond and beautiful and sweet and charming," she said. "I fell in love with him on sight, and, incredibly, he fell in love with me. We married within two months of our first meeting, and for a while it seemed that we would live happily ever after. I loved all his family, and they loved me, even his brother and sister-in-law. I adored his nephews. Life with the *ton* was never easy, but somehow I was accepted, even welcomed—you were right about that. I even made my curtsy to the queen and was granted vouchers to Almack's. I considered myself the most fortunate woman in the world."

She would have been about twenty at the time—young and lovely and filled with dreams of romance and a handsome husband and happily-ever-after. He felt a wave of tenderness for the girl she must have been. If he had met her then, would he have fallen in love with her too?

"What went wrong?" he asked.

She shrugged her shoulders and kept them hunched, though she did not complain of the cold.

"Oscar surprised me when I got to know him better," she said. "For all his looks and charm and rank and fortune, he was very insecure. He leaned heavily on me emotionally. He adored me and was scarce willing to allow me out of his sight. I did not mind—*of course* I did not mind. For me, the sun rose and set on him. But then he started openly to fear that he would lose me. He started to accuse me of flirting with other gentlemen. It got to the point at which if I spoke or smiled or danced with someone else, he would be in the mopes for days. And then, whenever

I went out without him—though I was always with some other lady or my maid—he suspected that I was keeping a secret tryst with another man. He even accused me of—well, never mind."

Oscar Derrick, Wulfric realized, had been a weak man, and as such he had been possessive. He had measured his worth by the amount of attention his wife paid him. And when it had not been enough—as it never could have been—he had turned petulant and even cruel.

"Adultery?" he suggested.

She drew a slow breath. Her face was still averted.

"Eventually Hermione and Basil came to believe it too," she said. "It must be a dreadful thing to be accused of wrongdoing when one is guilty. When one is innocent it is intolerable. No, that is not a powerful enough word. It is . . . soul-shattering. For the last few years of my marriage every last particle of joy was drained out of me. And out of Oscar too. He started drinking heavily and gaming for high stakes. We were never wealthy, but he had a comfortable competence. By the time he died he was so deeply in debt that he would never have extricated himself. I am not sure I would have survived with my sanity intact if it had not been for Justin. He was the only friend I had left, it seemed. He always believed me, always trusted me, always consoled me. But though he tried, he never seemed to have much influence with his cousins."

She had stopped walking and was squinting out in the direction of some waterfowl that were bobbing on the surface of the water close to the island. It was a good thing for her, he thought, that Oscar Derrick had died young.

"Your husband died in a hunting accident?" Wulfric asked her.

"Yes." The answer came quickly.

"You once told me," he said, "that you had been accused of killing him even though you were not with him when he died."

"He died in a hunting accident." The words were very precisely spoken. The wind was pulling at the brim of her bonnet and sending her pelisse fluttering out behind her.

He had thought that perhaps he could get to know her better this afternoon. He had planned to take her to the dovecote, but too much time had been spent at the hill and then quarreling in the woods. Now she had told him some things that he suspected she did not tell many people, but it was obvious that she still harbored some secret concerning the death of her husband. He felt disappointed. He had wanted, he realized, to be her friend. He had wanted her to be his.

Foolish of him! He had never inspired real friendship in other people.

He walked slowly on, turning his steps up the slight slope away from the lake and back through the trees to the house.

"He was shot in a duel," she said quickly.

He stopped in his tracks but said nothing.

"We were at Winwood Abbey," she told him, her hands balling into fists at her sides, he saw when he looked back toward her. She had turned to face him. "Hermione and Basil were away for a few days, and Oscar had gone to play cards with a neighbor. Another neighbor called on him when he was gone, a young, single gentleman. He and Oscar had been friends since they were boys. I met him outside, but he would not come in because Oscar was not there. I walked back down the driveway with him, since I had gone out for exercise and he had come on foot. And then, at the end of the driveway, we met Justin—he often came to stay for a few days. He knew Mr. Boothby too. He dismounted, and the three of us stood there talking for what I suppose was quite a while. Justin had just remounted and I was waving Mr. Boothby on his way when Oscar came riding into sight. I can still remember what Mr. Boothby called out to him, laughing as he did so—*There you are, Derrick,* he said. *You have been neglecting your wife, and I have been entertaining her this past hour or more. And here is your cousin arrived to catch me with her. And now you.*"

"Ah," Wulfric said. "Not a wise joke to make to any husband. A disastrous joke to make to a *jealous* husband."

"He would not believe either my protestations of innocence or Justin's assurance that he had been there to play chaperon almost the whole time," Christine said. "That same evening Oscar rode over and challenged Mr. Boothby, dragging poor Justin with him, and the next morning they fought it out with pistols. It was dreadful, horrible." She shivered. "Mr. Boothby said that he aimed for Oscar's leg and shot him there. But he hit an artery and Oscar bled to death since they had not taken the precaution of having a physician on hand. Hermione and Basil arrived home just as he was being carried into the house. They . . ." But she waved a hand in his direction suddenly and turned her back. "I am sorry. I cannot . . ."

She was obviously fighting tears and memories.

"They would not believe you either?" Wulfric said after a while.

She shook her head. "He looked so beautiful . . . so peaceful. I . . ."

But she could not go on.

Inclination told him to go back down to her and gather her into his arms. Instinct warned him that she probably needed to stand alone. If Oscar Derrick still lived, he thought, he would be very tempted to pound some sense into his head.

"Have you told anyone this story before?" he asked her.

She shook her head again. "It was agreed that we all say

it was a hunting accident," she said. "Mr. Boothby avoided trouble with the law that way, and we avoided disgrace."

"But you were innocent," he said.

"Yes." She looked back at him then over her shoulder. "I cannot believe I have told you of all people. But you cannot know how I have longed to tell *someone*."

He gazed back at her. Oscar Derrick's reaction to events he could perhaps understand. The man had been a jealous fool, doubtless weakened by drink and disastrous debts. It was harder to understand the part the Elricks played in the story. They seemed like sensible people. But then, of course, Derrick had been Elrick's brother. One could not always see events or people objectively when one's siblings were involved. Blood, as the old saying went, was thicker than water.

"Thank you," he said at last, feeling strangely gifted by her telling him the true story. "Thank you for telling me. You can trust my discretion."

"Yes," she said. "I know."

She walked toward him, her hands clasped behind her, his quizzing glass swinging on its ribbon about her neck. They walked back to the house side by side and in silence.

Never become emotionally involved with any other person.

Never seek to know or share the emotions of another person.

Remain aloof.

Deal with facts.

Always seek out the reasonable course of action in any situation, avoiding impulse and emotion.

They were all rules that had been drilled into him by the two tutors his father had hired for him when he was twelve. And eventually he had learned and followed the rules, made them his own, lived by them without conscious thought. Aloofness and reason had become second nature to him.

He had just broken the rules. He had entered the

emotional life of another person. And—God help him—
he was very much emotionally involved with her.

"SHE THREW HIS glass up into a tree, I tell you." Alleyne
stretched out on his back on Aidan and Eve's bed, set the
back of one hand over his eyes, and gave way to a gust of
laughter. "She must have done. Wulf certainly would not
have tossed it up there and it did not get up there by itself.
They were definitely quarreling."

"Oh," Morgan said, perching on the side of the bed and
clasping her hands to her bosom, "I like her. She is really a
creature after our own hearts, is she not?"

They had all crowded into Aidan's room after returning their children to the nursery, Alleyne having indicated
after his return from galloping about the woods with
Beatrice that he had something of great import to share
with them.

"I cannot imagine anyone having the temerity even to
touch one of Wulfric's quizzing glasses, let alone wrest it
from him and toss it," Gervase said, laughing. "This is
marvelously diverting."

"And did he send her up to get it?" Joshua asked. "Lady
Renable told me at the beginning of our walk that last
year Mrs. Derrick climbed a tree in a churchyard and left
half her dress behind when she jumped down again—in
full view of most of the Schofield houseguests. Wulfric
was the one who went to her rescue."

"I like her more and more," Freyja declared. "When I
saw her rolling down the hill I knew she was the very one
for Wulf. *Did* she go up the tree after the quizzing glass,
Alleyne? *Do* answer in your own good time, after you
have stopped guffawing."

"No, she did not," Alleyne said. "Wulf went—and then

sat on a branch glaring down at her while they resumed their quarrel."

But the mental image of their eldest brother climbing a tree to rescue his quizzing glass and then sitting in the tree to conduct a quarrel was too much for the Bedwyns and their spouses. They were convulsed with merriment for a few minutes.

"I did not eavesdrop," Alleyne assured them all when he had recovered a little. "It would not have been sporting and I daresay Bea would not have cooperated. All I actually heard was Wulf saying that she was the very opposite of any woman he would choose and Mrs. Derrick saying with the utmost scorn that of course he would not think of marrying when he had two mistresses."

There was a fraction of a second of silence and then laughter again.

"Dear Wulfric," Rachel said, dabbing at her eyes with a handkerchief. "He must be in love if he has been goaded into being so dreadfully discourteous."

The men found the idea of Wulfric's being in love cause for more hilarity, but the ladies clearly agreed with Rachel.

"I simply must have her as a sister-in-law," Freyja declared. "I will not be thwarted."

"Poor Wulfric," Joshua said. "He does not stand a chance, sweetheart."

"Poor Aunt Rochester!" Rannulf said with a grin. "She is so determined to have Wulf for Rochester's niece that she can scarcely see the nose on her face—which is saying something for a Bedwyn by birth."

"We should go down to the drawing room for tea," Eve suggested, "or we will be thought unsociable—and poor Amy will find herself on a sofa, tête-à-tête with Wulfric."

"We must make an effort," Judith said, "to see to it that he and Mrs. Derrick are thrown together more often."

"I believe they can safely see to that on their own, Jude," Alleyne told her, sitting up on the bed.

"Not so," she said. "They would not have been together this afternoon if Morgan had not had the presence of mind to say she had agreed to talk to Amy about her presentation. And, if they had not been together, they would not have had the chance to quarrel."

"Which, according to female logic, is a good thing?" Rannúlf asked, grinning fondly at his wife.

"If I had thought I would ever be part of a conspiracy to matchmake for Wulfric," Aidan said sternly, opening the door to usher everyone out, "I would have shot myself on some battlefield and blamed the French."

But of course it was the Bedwyns who persuaded Christine, despite all her protests, to go riding with them the next morning. Since some of the other houseguests were going too, they trusted that Wulfric's duties as a host would impel him to accompany them.

THIS WAS NOT something she ought to have let herself be talked into, Christine thought as she set her foot in Lord Aidan's cupped hands and allowed him to toss her up into the sidesaddle.

The Bedwyns, without exception, all looked as if riding came as naturally to them as walking. So did Miss Hutchinson. And Christine knew that Melanie, Bertie, and Justin were excellent riders.

She was not.

For one thing, she did not possess a riding habit but wore a dark green carriage dress and hat instead. For another, she had to humiliate herself by asking in the hearing of them all for the quietest horse in the stable—something lame and half blind would suit her admirably, she told Lord Aidan, who was making the selection. And, for yet another, once she was in her sidesaddle, she sat there tense and grimly determined not to fall off. She clutched the reins, which she knew would not have saved her anyway, as if they were the only things that kept her safely suspended above the ground. Naturally enough, her mount, which was neither lame nor blind, but which Lord Aidan had assured her was as docile as horses come, was skittish from the first moment.

She understood these things but seemed powerless to do anything to correct them. It did not help that she had not ridden for almost three years—her soggy ride from the Serpentine to Bertie's town home did not count.

The Bedwyns and their spouses seemed charmed nevertheless. They called greetings and encouragement and advice to her and laughed when she laughed. They rode out of the stable yard with her in a body that for a few moments gave her the illusion of safety.

And then they abandoned her.

One group of them bore Miss Hutchinson off in their midst, though the Marchioness of Rochester had commended her to the duke's keeping. Another group of them bore off Melanie and Bertie, Audrey and Sir Lewis, and Justin.

The only person left for Christine to ride with was the Duke of Bewcastle. And the reverse was true too, of course.

She felt more than ever self-conscious in his company. She still could not believe that she had poured out the true story of her marriage and Oscar's death to him. She had never told any of those things even to Eleanor, the sister to whom she was closest. She had felt strangely comforted afterward even though he had offered no words of consolation. This morning, though, she felt simply embarrassed—and a little chilled. He had offered no words of comfort. *Of course* he had not. He was probably disgusted, even though he had thanked her for telling him. He had kept his distance from her all last evening, and this morning he had not uttered one word to her at breakfast.

"If we are to keep up with the others and reach Alvesley before dark," he told her now, "you had better coax that horse to a walk instead of a dance, Mrs. Derrick."

Now that her mount had been abandoned by the group, it was doing just that—dancing in place.

Christine laughed, though she felt somewhat chagrined too.

"We need to become acquainted," she said. "Give me a moment."

"Trixie," he said, "meet Mrs. Derrick. Mrs. Derrick, meet Trixie."

"I am delighted to know that I inspire you to such flights of wit," she said. She tightened her grip on the right rein and Trixie obediently danced about in a complete circle.

"Relax," the duke instructed her. "Relax your body— she can feel your tension and it makes her nervous. And relax your hands. She is a follower rather than a leader. She will follow Noble if you leave her to her own devices."

It sounded so simple—*relax*. Yet when she tried it, it worked and Trixie plodded obediently after the magnificent black stallion on which the duke was mounted.

"Now I must only hope," she said, "that no hedge looms suddenly before us. I suppose Noble would go soaring over it, and since Trixie is a follower, she would soar after him. I fear I might be left behind on the ground on the other side."

"I promise," he said, "to come back for you."

She laughed, and he looked across at her with his steady, inscrutable eyes.

"Tell me about Alvesley Park and the people there," she

said. That, she had learned, was their destination. "It is the Earl of Redfield's home?"

"It is," he said.

She thought that was all he was going to say and was determined that she would not bother herself with making labored conversation as they rode. If he was content with silence, then so was she.

But he proceeded to tell her about the earl's three sons, the eldest of whom had died some years ago, while the youngest was the steward at his Welsh estate. He had been terribly maimed in the Peninsular Wars and was apparently determined to prove that he was not useless. Kit Butler, Viscount Ravensberg, the middle son, was now the Earl of Redfield's heir and lived at Alvesley with his wife and children.

"Have your two families always been close?" Christine asked.

"Most of the time," he said. "Redfield's sons and my brothers and Freyja were always playmates—Morgan too when she was old enough."

"But not you?"

"For a while." He shrugged. "I outgrew them all."

The words were coldly, disdainfully spoken. Had he never known human joy, this man, even as a child? How could she ever imagine that she might be in love with him? How could she have confided in him yesterday? And *quarreled* with him? She had almost forgotten the quarrel. He had not been cold then. Ah, how provokingly complex he was.

"You said *most* of the time," she said. "Have there been some disagreements, then?"

And then he told her an extraordinary tale about his plan and the Earl of Redfield's to arrange a marriage between Lady Freyja and the eldest of the earl's sons, a plan that had proceeded smoothly until Kit returned from the wars one summer and he and Lady Freyja fell in love. She had renounced him and announced her betrothal to his brother anyway, and Kit had returned to the Peninsula, but only after engaging in a vicious bout of fisticuffs with Lord Rannulf on the lawn outside Lindsey Hall one night. And then three years later, after the eldest brother had died, the duke and the earl had tried to arrange a match between Lady Freyja and Kit, assuming it would be to the liking of both. But when Kit returned home that summer, presumably for the betrothal celebrations, he had brought the present Lady Ravensberg with him as his betrothed.

"Oh," Christine said. "And was Lady Freyja very upset?"

"Angry," he said. "If she was upset, she was not admitting it. But none of us, if the truth were told, were pleased with Kit—and we let both him and his lady know it in our own peculiar way. The hard feelings have passed by now, though. Freyja even made her peace with Lady Ravensberg after she met Joshua."

It was a complicated tale and not at all the sort of story he would have told her last year, Christine realized, remembering how he had spoken of his properties and his family without any unnecessary details and no emotion at all. He was, she realized, trying to open up to her as she had to him yesterday. He was trying to establish some sort of relationship with her. He was, in a sense, wooing her.

He talked almost all the way to Alvesley with very little prompting on her part. He even told her things she had not asked about. He told her a little about the courtships of all his siblings and about the dreadful summer months of 1815, when they had believed Lord Alleyne to be dead, killed at the Battle of Waterloo, where he had gone to deliver a letter to the Duke of Wellington from the British ambassador, to whose embassy he had been attached at the time.

"And then," he said, bringing the story to its end,

"when we all drove back to Lindsey Hall from the church after Morgan's wedding, there he was, standing on the terrace waiting for us."

Christine felt as if she had a lump in her throat.

"It must have been an amazingly wonderful moment," she said.

"Yes," he said curtly. "He had fallen from his horse after being shot in the leg at Waterloo, and had banged his head so hard it is amazing he survived at all. He lost his memory for a few months. It was Rachel who found him and nursed him back to health."

She gazed at him as Trixie plodded docilely after his horse. And she realized something about him that she was not at all sure she wanted to know. Despite the curtness of his tone and the usual severity of his expression, he was reliving something that had been deeply emotional to him.

And then . . . there he was, standing on the terrace waiting for us.

Did he realize how he had betrayed himself with just those bare words?

She blinked her eyes furiously and turned her head to face front. How would she explain tears to him if he saw them?

They reached Alvesley, another grand mansion, soon after that, and the duke helped her dismount, turned over the horses to a groom's care, and escorted her after the others into the house. It was a great relief not to be alone with him any longer. He was beginning to disturb some of her firmly held preconceptions and she really did not want that to happen. She wanted her safe life back. More than that, she wanted it back without regrets, without any doubts that it was what she chose with both her head and her heart.

For someone who had been very reluctant to mingle

with members of the *ton* at Schofield Park last year and even more reluctant to mingle with society in London after Audrey's wedding earlier this spring, Christine thought ruefully over the next hour, she had really allowed her control over her world to slip alarmingly. First all the Bedwyns, and now this.

After being presented to the Earl and Countess of Redfield and Viscount and Viscountess Ravensberg—whom she looked at with some interest after the story about them she had just heard—she then had to be introduced to all their houseguests and there was not a person among them without a title—the Earl and Countess of Kilbourne, the Duke and Duchess of Portfrey, Lady Muir, the Earl and Countess of Sutton, the Marquess of Attingsborough, and Viscount Whitleaf, all of them relatives of Viscountess Ravensberg.

It was really quite overwhelming. But fortunately there were so many in the visiting party and so many voices attempting to talk at once that Christine was able to find a window seat in the drawing room that made her relatively inconspicuous, and set about recapturing her long-held ambition to be an amused spectator of humanity rather than a participant in its follies.

The Duke of Bewcastle sat in a group with the Earl of Redfield, the Duke of Portfrey, and Bertie, and was soon deep in conversation with them. It was strange how he looked the most aristocratic of anyone present—and also the most handsome. Which was a silly thought, really, when she had already admitted that Lord Alleyne was the best-looking of the Bedwyn brothers and when Viscount Whitleaf was a remarkably good-looking young man with devastatingly attractive violet eyes—whose effect he was now demonstrating on Amy Hutchinson. And the Marquess of Attingsborough, tall, dark, handsome, and charming, was enough to make any warm-blooded female trip all over her feet and her tongue. Not to mention the Earl of Kilbourne and Viscount Ravensberg . . .

"Wool-gathering, Chrissie?" Justin asked, coming to perch beside her. "I am sorry I had to abandon you to your fate with Bewcastle on our way here. I seemed to have no choice. I'll try to do better on the way back."

She smiled at him. He had promised her last evening that he would stay by her side whenever he could and protect her from what he was sure were the unwelcome attentions of the duke. She had not contradicted him. Neither had she agreed with him.

She had slept with his quizzing glass beside her pillow— the duke's, that was—so that she would not forget to return it to him this morning. She could feel it now, rather heavy inside the pocket of her carriage dress.

"I did not mind," she said. "I learned all sorts of interesting things about his family. They really are pleasant people, are they not, Justin?"

"*Pleasant?*" He chuckled. "If you like your people arrogant and overbearing, Chrissie, yes, I suppose they are. And if you like them going off on their own now and then to laugh at us all. I *heard* them yesterday after that walk— they were all in a room together. They did not like your behavior, you may be sure. But don't worry about that." He patted her hand. "I like it, even though I did not witness the roll down the hill. And I like *you.* I am going to come to Schofield for the summer, as soon as the Season is over. We will spend some time together, you and I. We will go for long walks and drives, and we will laugh at the fashionable world."

Why, she wondered, had she not been able to fall in love with someone safe like Justin nine and a half years ago—or one year ago? She did not believe he had ever been in love with her either, despite what Hermione had said a few nights ago and even though he had offered her marriage, but even so . . .

"Mrs. Derrick."

Christine looked up, startled, to find herself being regarded by Lady Sutton, a young lady who gave the impression that she thought herself of enormous consequence. "Was it not you who caused such a stir by falling into the Serpentine a few weeks ago?"

"Oh, dear." Christine felt herself blushing as everyone in the room turned to look at her, though just a moment before there had been several group conversations in progress. "I am afraid I do have that dubious distinction."

The Marquess of Hallmere chuckled. "She stooped to pick up a glove a certain, ah, *lady* had dropped in the water," he said, "and fell headlong in. Lord Powell fished her out, but it was Bewcastle who played knight errant and wrapped his coat about her and took her home on his horse."

"The story was all about London within hours, as you may imagine," Lady Rosthorn added, suddenly looking quite as haughty as her eldest brother. "Everyone enjoyed a hearty laugh and was charmed with a lady who had put her own safety at peril in such a cause."

"We were greatly disappointed," Lady Hallmere added, also looking decidedly formidable, "as were many other people, that Mrs. Derrick disappeared from town so soon after. She would have been much in demand at various entertainments. But we were fortunate enough to meet her here as one of Wulfric's houseguests."

"And yesterday," Lord Hallmere said with a flashing of his handsome smile, "we all had the privilege of witnessing Mrs. Derrick's unconventional and exuberant approach to life when she rolled down the hill from the wilderness walk to delight our children, who then all had to copy her, of course."

"As did Free," Lord Rannulf added.

"Dear me," Lord Sutton murmured.

"The children all adore her," Lady Aidan added. "They positively mobbed her in the nursery before breakfast this morning."

"I can well imagine," the very lovely Viscountess Ravensberg said with a warm smile for Christine. "Children always choose the right people to love. Have you had much to do with children, Mrs. Derrick? Do you have any of your own?"

What they had all just been doing, Christine realized as she stumbled through an answer, was *defending* her against the undoubted spite of the Countess of Sutton. The Duke of Bewcastle had not said a word, but he had directed one of his frosty stares at the countess and raised his quizzing glass—one of the remaining seven—to his eye.

For what remained of the hour's visit, Christine was forced to abandon her role as spectator. She was drawn into various conversations and somehow ended up with the Marquess of Attingsborough seated beside her instead of Justin. And an extremely charming gentleman he was too. He was the one who escorted her outside when it was time to leave and helped her mount Trixie, who eyed her with patient resignation while she was still on the ground and behaved with magnificent docility after she was in the saddle, her body and her hands determinedly relaxed.

"Mrs. Derrick," the marquess said before moving back, "may I hope that you will save a set for me at the Lindsey ball? The first, perhaps?"

"Thank you." She smiled down at him. "I will indeed."

Justin, she could see, had attached himself to the Duke of Bewcastle and held him in conversation. Doubtless he was keeping his promise to defend her from his company as much as possible. Sometimes, she thought disloyally—and for the first time since she had known him—Justin could be rather tiresome.

But she did not have to fear that Trixie would act up without the steadying, dominating influence of Noble. Lord Aidan fell in beside her, and Christine, remembering that he had been a cavalry colonel, felt as safe as it was possible to feel when perched sideways on the back of a horse a mile off the ground.

19

$\mathcal{A}$LTHOUGH JUSTIN MAGNUS WAS MOWBURY'S brother and Wulfric felt the greatest respect for his friend, who was enjoying the chance to potter about in the library at Lindsey Hall this morning, he had never felt any affinity with the younger man. He had even wondered with considerable distaste if jealousy might partly account for his dislike, since Magnus was so clearly a close friend of Mrs. Derrick.

But he had lain awake half the night, thinking. Then he had got up very early and gone for a brisk walk and thought some more. And since it was still early when he returned to the house, he had sat in his library, thinking.

It was, in fact, Wulfric who had maneuvered Magnus into riding back to Lindsey Hall with him, though the younger man was probably under the impression that it was the other way around.

"Attingsborough is taking his time with his farewells," Wulfric commented frostily. "He ought to have found time enough in the drawing room to say all he needed to say."

He wondered if those few words would be cue enough. If they were not, then he was doomed to a tedious ride back when his brothers and sisters had been just as eager to pair him with Mrs. Derrick this time as they had on the way here. And it could not be for Amy Hutchinson's sake on this leg of the journey, since Aunt Rochester was not here to try to force the girl on him. His siblings were *matchmaking*, by thunder.

"Attingsborough has been one of London's most notorious rakes for years," Magnus said pleasantly as they rode off, a little apart from the rest of the group.

It was the first Wulfric had heard of it. Attingsborough had undoubtedly been one of the greatest matrimonial prizes on the market for years past, and it was unlikely that he lived like a monk in the meanwhile. But a rake?

He did not offer any comment beyond a noncommittal grunt. He waited to see what might come next.

"It would be unfair to accuse Chrissie of flirting with him, though," Magnus said. "For all that she has been married and has some experience of life with the *ton*, she is really no match for someone like Attingsborough, is she? And I suppose it was natural that he pick her out of the crowd since Lady Muir is his cousin and Whitleaf was monopolizing Miss Hutchinson and there *was* no other unattached lady. Besides which, Chrissie is rather pretty and far more charming than she realizes."

"Quite so," Wulfric said, sounding bored.

"I suppose you are annoyed with her for paying so much attention to him," Magnus said. "One cannot fail to notice—if you will forgive my saying so —that you admire her yourself. I don't blame you for being a trifle irritated. But she is my dearest friend, and I must speak up in her defense. You must not blame her when men like Kitredge and Attingsborough want her too. It is not her fault. She has always had that effect on men. She cannot help it. Oscar made her life miserable by accusing her all their married life of flirting and even going beyond flirtation. Hermione and Basil accused her of the same thing. And, of course, there was all the cover-up over Oscar's

death, which they blamed on her too. It was *not* her fault.
I just want to make sure that you understand that."

"It would appear to me," Wulfric said coldly, "that you
protest too much. In my experience there is rarely smoke
where there is not also fire."

Magnus sighed. "What do you expect me to say?" he
asked. "Chrissie is my friend. And of course she is innocent. I would defend her with my last breath. Even if there
had been hundreds of instances since I have known her
instead of just dozens, I would have believed her every
time. That is what friends do."

Wulfric, who had taken the safest route to Alvesley for
the sake of Mrs. Derrick, who was not a good rider, felt
no such inhibitions on the way back. They were trotting
across a field and might have turned their course slightly
to pass through an open gate, but he did not swerve from
his path. He spurred his horse forward and made for the
highest, thickest part of the hedge. Noble soared over it
with at least a foot to spare. Wulfric gritted his teeth and
waited for the other man to clear the hedge too and catch
up with him.

"Goodness," Magnus said with a laugh, "I have not
done anything so reckless for a long while."

"I believe," Wulfric said, his voice steely, his cold eyes
resting on the other man, "you are in love with Mrs.
Derrick yourself. I believe you would say anything in her
defense. I believe you would even perjure yourself if it
were necessary."

Justin Magnus rode in silence for a while. "Trust is as
essential to friendship as it is to love, you see," he said. "I
trust Chrissie. I always have and always will. If you love
her, Bewcastle, or are in any way fond of her, then you will
trust her too—even when she appears to have been indiscreet. You are a man of the world. Oscar was not, and neither was he strong. He wanted her all to himself. *Not* that

she would ever actually *do* anything indiscreet. I am not saying that—quite the contrary, in fact. Chrissie is the soul of honor. But sometimes it just seems otherwise—as it did the day before Oscar died, when she was alone with a man at Winwood Abbey for a whole hour with no one else there to chaperon her. I tried to give her an alibi because I *trusted* her when she said nothing had happened. But even so, she had been indiscreet, you see—*innocently* indiscreet. But I am talking too much. You would not be interested in that particular incident."

"Quite so," Wulfric said faintly.

"I have promised to keep you from her as much as I can," Magnus said with a frank, rueful grin. "That is why I am riding with you now. I suppose the idea of being a duchess tempts her—just as the chance of being the Countess of Kitredge did. It would be quite a coup for a schoolmaster's daughter after all, would it not? But at the same time, you see, she is afraid of you—afraid that you would be stricter with her than Oscar was. She needs to be free to . . ."

"Flirt?" Wulfric suggested.

"That is a word I do not like." Magnus sounded annoyed. "Chrissie never flirts. She needs to be free to be herself."

"Free to pursue her, er, friendships with other gentlemen," Wulfric said.

"Well, yes, if you like," Magnus conceded. "But *innocent* friendships."

"Quite so." The ride from Alvesley had never seemed half so long, Wulfric thought as Lindsey Hall came into sight at last. "But I find this conversation tedious, Magnus. Contrary to what you seem to believe, my interest in Mrs. Derrick is really quite minimal. And of course I do not believe one word in ten of what you say about her. Your loyalty is admirable, but the woman is clearly a strumpet."

He turned his horse thankfully onto the elm drive leading up to the house.

"*Your grace!*" Magnus sounded shocked to the core. "I would have you know that you are speaking of my cousin by marriage and my *friend*."

"Whom you would defend with your life," Wulfric said. "I understand perfectly. A man who is besotted will believe anything he wishes to believe—or rather will ignore anything he does *not* wish to believe. If you have ridden home with me not only to protect Mrs. Derrick from my oppressive company but also to plead her case with me, you have failed miserably. And that is my final word on the matter."

"But—"

Wulfric spurred his horse on ahead of the other and made for the stable block.

Never feel anger. It is counterproductive. It is also unnecessary.

If something needs to be said, say it. If something needs to be done, do it.

Never feel anger. Above all else, never show anger.

Anger is a mark of weakness.

The old lessons had been well learned. But today his mastery of them was being severely tested. Today he felt the urge to kill—with his bare hands.

Today he was very, very angry.

THE MARQUESS AND Marchioness of Hallmere were about to sing a duet, though the marchioness had protested when it was first suggested until goaded into it by two of her brothers.

"Lord love us," Lord Rannulf said, grinning, "you have never taught Free to *sing*, Joshua?"

"I have heard, Ralf," Lord Alleyne said, "that in the damp climate of Cornwall saws quickly become rusty."

Bertie and Hector laughed heartily, the Marchioness of Rochester raised her lorgnette to her eyes, Mrs. Pritchard, her face wreathed in smiles, wagged a finger at Lord Alleyne and reminded him that the Welsh were renowned for their singing *and* their damp climate, and Lady Freyja got to her feet with awful dignity.

"Josh," she said, "we will sing. And then, if anyone has more rusty saw jokes, I will poke a few noses."

"No one does it better, sweetheart," he said, laughing. "Singing, I mean."

They were all entertaining themselves for the evening. Miss Hutchinson had played the pianoforte, Lady Rannulf had brought Desdemona alive for them with a startling talent for acting, Hector had given one of his rare performances of magic and sleight of hand, and now the duet was about to begin.

Christine was trying to enjoy herself. There was really no reason why she should not. It had been a full, active day. After the morning ride and visit and luncheon spent in conversation with Baron Weston, she had gone back outside with most of the younger people and their children. She had frolicked on a spacious lawn with them, playing a ball game with the older children and a few adults while others played ring-around-the-rosy with the infants and the Earl of Rosthorn rocked his baby in his arms and Lady Alleyne cuddled the Hallmeres'. Then she had gone for a long walk with Justin.

She had certainly been wise in avoiding Bewcastle and ignoring his attentions, Justin had told her with a sympathetic pat on her hand. The man was downright morose and would make a horribly jealous husband to some poor lady. He had been irritated over the fact that the Marquess of Attingsborough had escorted Chrissie out of the house and helped her into the saddle and then spoke a few words of farewell to her.

"Which was grossly unfair of him," he had added, "since Whitleaf was doing as much for Miss Hutchinson. But he fancies you, you see, Chrissie, and so wants all your attention for himself. I told him in no uncertain terms that you are a free spirit, that you need to be free to be you. I don't care if he liked it or not."

The duke had remained at the house all afternoon—as far as Christine knew anyway. And though he had appeared at the dinner table—looking arctic and taking almost no part in the conversation—he had not come to the drawing room when the gentlemen joined the ladies there.

It did not matter to Christine. Of course it did not. It had been foolish of her to quarrel with him yesterday and then to confide in him. His own revelations this morning about his family and neighbors meant nothing at all. He had merely been making conversation.

And then, just as the marquess and marchioness were seating themselves on the bench before the pianoforte, Christine felt a light touch on her shoulder and looked up to find a footman bending over her to speak softly in her ear.

"His grace begs the favor of your company in the library, ma'am," he said.

Christine looked at him in surprise. But then she could see that Hermione and Basil were on their feet and making their way toward the door. They had been invited too? She rose and made her way from the room as the music began.

The three of them went downstairs together after exchanging somewhat embarrassed looks. Although there had been no open hostility during the past couple of days, they had kept aloof from one another as if by mutual consent.

"What is this about?" Hermione asked.

"I daresay Bewcastle wishes to be sociable but does not wish to sit in a crowded drawing room," Basil said.

Christine said nothing.

The same footman who had come to fetch them went on ahead of them and opened the library doors when they arrived there.

"Lord and Lady Elrick and Mrs. Derrick, your grace," he said.

It was an enormous apartment, Christine saw, smelling of leather and wood and candles. There must be thousands of books here, she estimated. They filled bookshelves from the floor to the high ceiling. There was a huge desk close to the windows and a circle of large chairs about the fireplace, in which a fire burned.

The Duke of Bewcastle stood before the fire, his back to it, looking cold and forbidding in his black and white evening clothes. He was not alone. Justin was rising to his feet from one of the leather chairs beside the fireplace, looking surprised. But then he smiled.

The duke bowed and greeted the new arrivals and offered them seats, all without moving from his place or in any way relaxing his frosty demeanor. But then, he rarely did.

Christine looked very directly at him. How *dared* he be irritated this morning at her speaking with the Marquess of Attingsborough and allowing him to help her mount her horse. How *dared* he! For a moment his glance met hers, and hers did not waver. He was the one who looked away.

As well he might, nasty man! Did he believe he owned her merely because she had agreed to come to Lindsey Hall and had been in private conversation with him a few times?

"We have just been marvelously entertained in the drawing room," Hermione said. "Lady Rannulf is a magnificent actress. For a few minutes I quite forgot that she was not indeed poor Desdemona about to be murdered by Othello. And Hector performed some of his magic tricks. I always watch with the greatest concentration, determined that *this* time I will see exactly how he does them, but I never can. How can a piece of string become two pieces and then one again when he never puts his hands near his pockets and has his sleeves rolled back?"

"Hector has had that skill since he was a boy," Justin said with a laugh. "He used to drive Mel and Audrey and me to distraction in the nursery, but he would never let us in on the secret."

"It is all illusion," the Duke of Bewcastle said. "The acting and the magic. It is the trick of making the beholder take the appearance for the reality. It is something that takes dedication and skill."

"Well," Justin said, "it is beyond my understanding. But I am sorry to have missed Lady Rannulf's performance. Perhaps she will repeat it some other evening."

"Some people, for example," the duke said, ignoring Justin, "have the skill of saying one thing and meaning another."

"Irony can frequently be amusing," Basil said. "You are right, Bewcastle. Some people are masters of the art, and some of our greatest writers use it to perfection. Alexander Pope leaps to mind. 'The Rape of the Lock' has always set me to chuckling."

"And some people," the duke continued as if Basil had not spoken at all, "have the gift of speaking the truth and convincing their listeners that it is a lie."

Hermione, Basil, and Justin looked politely at him, having nothing to say this time. Christine continued to stare steadily and coldly at him. He was arrogant and self-absorbed, she thought. She did not know now why she had come to think that perhaps there was more to him. Some of the illusion of which he spoke, perhaps?

She had no idea why she had been invited here.

"It has been my distinct impression," the duke said, "that Mrs. Derrick is generally considered a flirt."

"The devil!" Justin jumped to his feet.

Hermione's hand went to the pearls about her neck.

"I believe you owe my sister-in-law an apology, Bewcastle," Basil said stiffly.

Christine sat frozen to her chair.

The duke grasped the handle of an evening quizzing glass in his long fingers.

"I trust you will all hear me out," he said, sounding almost bored. "Do be seated, Magnus."

"*Not,*" Justin said, "until you have apologized to Chrissie."

The ducal glass was raised all the way to the ducal eye.

"Did I say that *I* considered her a flirt?" he asked haughtily.

Justin sat, but it was clear to see that he was furious. Christine smiled reassuringly at him before returning her gaze to the duke again, hoping it was as steely as his own.

"It is what you called her yourself, ma'am," he said with a slight inclination of the head in Hermione's direction, "at Schofield last year. However, I must confess that that was the only occasion on which I have heard her actively called a flirt. I have, however, heard a tedious number of times that she is *not* a flirt."

His silver eyes came to rest on Christine for a few moments. She glared steadily back. She would dearly have liked to jump to her feet and crack her hand across his cheek, but she doubted her legs would support her. And she was so short of breath that she was almost gasping.

"You told me, ma'am," the duke said to Hermione, "that Mrs. Derrick had flirted with every gentleman at the house party and that she had flirted with *me* by walking in the laburnum alley with me in order to win a wager she had with the other young ladies. I beg you to try to recall what put both ideas into your head. Was it entirely your own observation and conclusion? Or did someone so forcefully and passionately assure you that she was *not* flirting that your suspicions were aroused and your conclusion drawn?"

"You see?" Justin cried before Hermione could answer. "I told you this morning that this is the way it has always been, Bewcastle. You are referring to me, are you not? I wish I had *never* spoken up in Chrissie's defense. I always seem to have done more harm than good. *Always!* But this is it! I'll never do it again." He looked across at Christine, apparently on the verge of tears. "I am sorry, Chrissie."

But she was looking at him, arrested.

"We all know," Hermione said gently, "that Justin is very fond of Christine. Perhaps even in love with her. And we have always known that he can see no wrong in her. He would defend her even if he had actually witnessed some blatant indiscretion. It is an endearing quality in him. But he hardly inspires belief. Pardon me, Justin. I know you have always meant well."

"If there is one word apart from *flirtation* that seems to have become associated with Mrs. Derrick through all the stories I have heard of her marriage and through all that I have known of her in the last year," the duke continued, "it is the word *Justin*."

"What are you suggesting?" Justin jumped to his feet again. "You filthy—"

The Duke of Bewcastle, quite unperturbed, had his glass to his eye again.

"I am suggesting that you sit down, Magnus," he said, and, incredibly, Justin sat.

"I would ask you to think, Elrick," the duke said, "about all those occasions during her marriage when Mrs. Derrick was perceived by her husband and by you and Lady Elrick to have been flirting or behaving in an indiscreet manner with other gentlemen and ask yourself whether you or your brother or your wife ever saw incontrovertible evidence that she was guilty or ever received any complaint from another person. I ask you to remember if you ever directly heard any unsavory gossip about her."

Christine was feeling cold even though she was well within range of the fire's heat. And she was no longer looking at the duke. She was watching Justin.

"I hardly think our private family business is your concern, Bewcastle," Basil said.

Christine could hear Hermione swallowing. "It was Justin who always told us," she said. "He brought the news from the gentlemen's clubs and other places, gossip that would not be spoken when Basil or Oscar was present. He was always angry and upset. He always defended Christine and insisted that there was no truth in any of the stories or rumors. He always . . ."

She set one hand over her mouth.

"Justin," Christine said, "what have you done?"

It was all very simple really. Very, very simple. And almost undetectable.

"I was told this morning," the duke said, "as I rode home from Alvesley with Magnus that Mrs. Derrick must not be blamed for responding to the attentions of the Marquess of Attingsborough or accused of being a flirt, since the man concerned is an experienced rake. I was told she cannot help the effect she has on men like Attingsborough and Kitredge and myself. That is just the way she is—though she *is* understandably ambitious to win for herself the highest-ranking title she can acquire. I was told that if he knew of hundreds of indiscretions of Mrs. Derrick's instead of dozens, he would defend her every time because that is what friends do. I was told that though Mrs. Derrick was alone for more than an hour with a gentleman the day before her husband's death, he had willingly provided her with an alibi because he trusted her."

"Justin." Christine had not taken her eyes from his face. "You quite deliberately wrecked my marriage? You drove Oscar out of his mind? You actually drove him to his death?"

"You cannot believe that, Chrissie!" he cried, his eyes wild. "I am your friend. I am the only one who understands you. I *love* you!"

Basil cleared his throat.

Hermione held the fingertips of one hand against her forehead. Her eyes were closed.

"This is too much like a nightmare," she said. "It *cannot* be true. It surely cannot. And yet I know it is. You were so convincing, Justin. We always felt *sorry* for you. And we did not believe a word you said."

"You!" Justin pointed accusingly at the duke. "You, Bewcastle! You called Chrissie a strumpet this morning."

"And then rode on to the stables," the Duke of Bewcastle said, raising his glass to his eye once more, "so that you could savor your triumph in private."

"And then you came and told me," Christine said, "that his grace would make a horribly jealous and possessive husband since he had been irritated by the fact that the Marquess of Attingsborough had escorted me outside the house and helped me mount. Justin! Oh, Justin. Poor, poor Oscar!"

She spread her hands over her face and felt a cool hand come against the back of her neck—Hermione's.

"Nobody loves you as I do, Chrissie," Justin said. "But of course, you are always dazzled by looks. First Oscar and now Bewcastle and a whole host of other handsome men in between. And look at me—or rather *don't* look. No woman ever does, least of all you. You never took me seriously. I can't bear to see you with other men who don't appreciate you properly. Chrissie, I *love* you."

Christine removed her hands in time to see the Duke of Bewcastle lean over Justin's chair and then straighten up again, without any apparent effort, Justin's neckcloth in his firm grasp and Justin's person dangling above the floor so that he could touch it only with his toes.

"I share your skill in one particular way, Magnus," his grace said so softly and so coldly that Christine shivered. "I have never been quite sure what love is, but I certainly know what love is *not*. Love does not destroy the beloved or cause her endless suffering."

Christine's hands were over her face again. But the hot tears oozed between her fingers and dripped onto her lap.

"I would like to shake you like the rat you are until you are limp and lifeless," the duke said in the same voice, "but you are a guest in my home, as are other members of your family, including your mother. Your family may deal with you as they see fit later, but for now you will make any reasonable excuse you can invent to leave my house before breakfast tomorrow. And, if you are wise, you will keep yourself for the next decade or two as far away from my sight as you are able."

Christine was aware of Basil getting to his feet.

"But before you leave, Justin," Basil said, "before you leave both Lindsey Hall and England, that is, I will see you outside the house. Now."

"Basil—" Hermione said as Christine looked up.

"You will remain here, Hermione," he said. "And you too, Christine. Justin? Outside!"

Justin stopped before Christine's chair, his face ashen and distraught. There were tears in his eyes.

"Chrissie?" he said.

A truly amazing and shocking thing happened then. The Duke of Bewcastle's foot came up and caught him in the seat of his breeches, lifting him half off his feet and sending him staggering after Basil, who was stalking from the room.

There was a moment of silence after they had left. Then the duke bowed to them.

"I will leave you alone," he said. "You will not be disturbed."

But before he left the room, he paused before Christine's chair, as Justin had done, and set a large linen handkerchief in her hand.

Christine and Hermione sat side by side for a few moments.

"Christine," Hermione said at last, "how can I ever expect you to forgive us?"

"I was as deceived as you were," Christine said. "He was *my* friend. For those few years before Oscar died, he was the only person I trusted."

They were both in tears then, crying their eyes out in each other's arms, crying for the lost years and the lost friendships, for the unnecessary death of a weak, tormented man, for their own gullibility in falling for a scheme that was so fiendishly simple it had succeeded utterly.

When their tears were spent Christine blew her nose in the borrowed handkerchief.

"I do hope Basil will not get hurt," she said. "How foolish of him to take Justin outside."

"Basil is a man," Hermione said fondly. "How else can a man react to such a revelation? I hope he pounds Justin to a pulp."

They both laughed rather nervously and then shed a few more tears.

20

SUNDAY—EASTER SUNDAY—PASSED IN RELA-
tive peace. There was church in the morning, family
activities in the afternoon, and a quiet evening of music,
conversation, and reading.

No one remarked a great deal on the sudden disappearance of Justin. He was reputed to have made his
apologies to the Duke of Bewcastle over a suddenly remembered engagement in town, and, as his mother said,
Justin had come and gone as he pleased all his adult life,
so doubtless he had a good reason for leaving now. Everyone accepted Basil's sheepish explanation that he had hit
his right cheekbone and grazed his knuckles when he fell
out of the bathtub in his dressing room—or, if some did
not believe him, they kept their suspicions to themselves.

Justin, Basil had assured both Christine and Hermione
when he had rejoined them in the library, looked far
worse than he. After saying it, he had hugged first
Hermione and then Christine—very tightly and for a long
while.

"Oscar loved you, Christine," Basil had said, his voice
sounding rather choked. "He did love you to the end, even
if he stopped trusting you."

"Yes, I know." It was all she had been able to say.

"And so," he had said, "we had no business not looking

after you for him when he was gone. I don't ask forgiveness—only your permission to make up for lost time."

She had sniveled into the duke's handkerchief again.

"And if you should choose to marry Bewcastle," he had said, "then you will have my blessing, and Hermione's too, I daresay."

"Oh, yes," Hermione had said. "I believe he cares deeply for you, Christine, else why would he have spoken so murderously to Justin tonight?"

They had left it at that, and Christine had returned to the drawing room, where Mrs. Pritchard was singing a quavering but very sweet rendition of a Welsh ballad. Hermione had gone with Basil to their room to bathe his cheek in cold water.

Monday dawned cloudy and blustery and chilly. A sizable group rode over from Alvesley and was given a boisterous welcome. It was time for luncheon soon after they left. Lord Aidan announced his intention of launching the boats on the lake afterward despite the weather, and there was a chorus of enthusiastic agreement from around the table and a general exodus from the dining room to the nursery to get the children ready.

"You must row Amy to the island, Wulfric," the Marchioness of Rochester said. "There are some pleasant prospects from there."

He stood up from his place at the head of the table.

"I am sure someone else will be pleased to take her there, Aunt," he said. "I have already arranged to take Mrs. Derrick for a stroll—unless she finds herself unable to come after all, that is."

His eyes alighted on Christine for what must surely be the first time since he left the library two evenings before, leaving his handkerchief in her hand. Normally she would have laughed back at him, since they both knew he had just told a barefaced lie. But her heart was pattering in her chest and she felt decidedly breathless again. And she was very aware of the marchioness's sudden scrutiny.

"Oh, no, your grace," she said, "I have been looking forward to it."

The marchioness made a sound that was very like a harrumph, and Christine got to her feet lest she be stranded in the dining room, alone with the woman.

"I will go and fetch my bonnet and pelisse," she said.

And so a mere ten minutes later she was stepping out of the house, having just met a whole army of Bedwyns on the stairs with their children. They had invited her to join them, and she had been forced to decline and tell them that she was going out with his grace.

She would swear that they had all greeted her announcement with a collective smirk.

"I suppose," she said, taking the duke's offered arm, "you were hoping for a quiet afternoon in your library?"

"Do you?" he asked her. "How well you claim to know me, Mrs. Derrick."

They walked for a while in silence. It was still cloudy and blowy, more like late winter again than early spring. But at least the wind was behind them.

"I have to thank you," she said at last, "for what you did for me on Saturday evening. I feel foolish for not having ever suspected. It seems so obvious now that I know the truth."

"Very often," he said, "the most fiendish and the most successful schemes are the most simple ones. Why *should* you have suspected? He offered you friendship and sympathy and support when you needed them. And why should your husband or your brother- and sister-in-law have suspected? He was their relative, and they knew—quite correctly—that he was very fond of you. And so it seemed quite believable to them that he would defend you against all reason and truth. It was perhaps easier for me as an outsider to discover that those two words—*flirt* and *Justin*—always seemed to go together with tedious regularity. And yet I have never once seen you flirt. Are you very upset?"

"Over the loss of Justin?" she asked him. "No. I am only sad that Oscar lost his life before knowing the truth, that he died thinking I had betrayed him. He was not a strong man emotionally. He was, I suppose, the perfect dupe for such a scheme and Justin must have realized that when he concocted it. But he was also a sweet-natured man when I first knew him, and we could have had a good marriage even though he was very different from what I had made him out to be in my girlish romantic dreams after I met him. Yes, I am upset, but I am at peace too. Hermione and Basil know the truth, and I *do* care about that. There was always a deep affection between us until the trouble started. I have a great deal to thank you for. You had no need to exert yourself as you did on my behalf."

"I had every need," he said quietly.

He did not explain and she did not ask. They walked on in silence, across the lawn above the lake and the tree line, beneath the wilderness walk, past the hill she had rolled down a few days before, in among the trees where they had quarreled and where she had snatched his quizzing glass—which she had *still* not returned to him. She realized that they must be on their way to where he had wanted to take her that afternoon—the dovecote north of the lake.

Silence between two people, she discovered, did not have to be an uncomfortable thing. Not when there was a certain harmony of mind. And there *was* some harmony. She was, she realized, growing to like him, and though the knowledge partly distressed her—because, of course, the differences between them were still too huge to be bridged—she decided to relax into the liking just for this afternoon. She had, after all, accepted his invitation here. And he had recently done something unimaginably wonderful for her.

I had every need.

To exert himself on her behalf, that was.

She stole a glance at his stern, aristocratic profile. Strangely, though it looked no different from usual, it was coming to seem like a rather dear profile.

Finally they came to a clearing in the woods, in the middle of which was the old stone building he had pointed out from the tower. It was tall and round, with a pointed, thatched roof and small windows high in the walls. A flight of steps led down to a sunken wooden door.

"Ah, the dovecote," she said. "How pretty it is. Is it occupied?"

"By birds?" he said. "No, it fell out of use and into disrepair in my father's time. I always liked the look of it, but it was only a couple of years ago that I decided to have work done on it, mostly on the inside. I did not want to draw attention to it by changing the outside, though I did have it reroofed. Let me show you."

He went down the steps, turned a key in the lock of the door, and opened it inward before standing aside to allow her to precede him inside.

She did not know what she had expected. But what she saw caught at her breath and made her stand stock-still and gaze about her in wonder. And she *could* see perfectly clearly though not in white light. There were six windows in all, she could see, all of them well above the level of her head. They were all made of stained glass in rich, translucent colors.

She could see upward to the point of the roof. The walls were of plain stone, but they were pigeonholed from floor to roof, as they must have been in the time when hundreds of birds had lived in them. But the pigeonholes were all clean now, and many of them on the lower levels held candles in holders, or books. In one she could see an inkwell, in another a tinderbox.

In the single round room itself there was a low bed covered with a sheepskin blanket, a plain desk and chair, a large leather armchair, and a fireplace, which had obviously been built recently, together with the chimney that climbed the wall opposite the door. A pile of logs lay in a wooden box beside the hearth, a set of fire irons next to it.

It was an exquisite little hermitage, made magical by the multicolored light in which it was bathed.

She spun around to look at him. He was standing just inside the door, his hat in his hand, looking steadily back at her. It was a dreadful moment. It was the moment she would have far preferred to avoid. It was the moment at which she finally and quite consciously *knew*. She knew that she was deeply entangled with the Duke of Bewcastle with no safe way out—and surely no possible way in.

But it was already too late to guard or deflect her feelings.

He moved past her before she could frame any suitable words to say. She took off her bonnet and gloves even though it was cold inside the dovecote, and set them down on the desk while he stooped and lit the fire that was ready laid in the hearth. It sprang to instant life, though she doubted that it ever had the power to heat such a high building completely.

"Why?" she asked him. "When all of Lindsey Hall is your own and you have other large homes too, why this?"

But she somehow knew the answer. It was as if she had lived this moment before and knew just what he was going to say. She felt stupidly frightened, as if a whole mountain of snow were about to avalanche down upon her.

"One can get lost in vastness," he said. "Sometimes even I forget that I am anything else but the Duke of Bewcastle."

She swallowed awkwardly.

"Here," he said, "I can remember. Yet curiously I have not been here for a whole year—not until last week anyway, when it occurred to me that I must bring you here."

And then she knew—that this had been inevitable, that this was the chance he had asked for, that this visit here to the tiny hermitage on one corner of his vast estate was what he had dreamed of and planned for. All was clean and comfortable, yet no one came here but himself. He had cleaned and tidied the room and set the fire ready to be lit.

She looked around for somewhere to sit and decided upon the wooden chair before the desk. She sank onto it and clutched the edges of her pelisse.

"And what is it," she asked him, "that you remember when you are here?"

"That I am also Wulfric Bedwyn," he said.

The avalanche crashed down onto her head.

Yes. Ah, yes. Yes, he was. During the few days she had been at Lindsey Hall she had already discovered that there was a real person lurking behind the formidable figure of the Duke of Bewcastle. They were one and the same, of course, the man and the duke. Not for a moment did she suspect that he was somehow mad, that there were two quite different persons living within the same body. But she was not sure she wanted to see any more of the man or *know* any more about him. Her life had been so very safe again for almost three years—and now she had Hermione and Basil back as well.

And yet her heart ached at his words—*I am also Wulfric Bedwyn*.

"Tell me about . . . yourself," she said. She had almost

said *about him,* as if Wulfric Bedwyn were indeed a different person from the man she saw standing before the fire, stern and aloof and apparently very much in command of his world. "No, that is a poor question. There is nothing more calculated to tie the tongue. Tell me about your childhood."

If she was to know him—though she shied away from the knowledge—she would have to begin with his childhood. It was so nearly impossible to imagine that he had ever been a baby, a child, a boy. Yet, of course, he had been all three.

"Move to the armchair," he said, indicating it with one hand, and when she did so, he brought the sheepskin blanket from the bed and settled it over her lap before going to sit on the desk, one booted foot braced against the dirt floor, the other swinging free. He had removed his greatcoat and thrown it over the back of the desk chair. Blue and purple light played over him.

"What were you like?" she asked him.

"I was a bundle of energy and restlessness," he said. "I was going to travel the world when I grew up. I was going to push back the American frontier. I was going to go beyond it and then sail across the Pacific to China. I was going to penetrate the mysteries of Africa and experience the allure of the Far East. I was going to be a pirate of the Robin Hood variety, or I was going to hunt for pirates. With greater maturity—when I was nine or ten, I suppose—I was going to captain a ship of my own and become the admiral of a fleet or else I was going to be a military officer and become a general and command the British armies wherever they fought and lead them to brilliant victories. But while I waited to grow up to my life of glory, I raised hell at home and about the park here. I was the terror of every gardener and groom and indoor servant, the greatest challenge my father ever faced, and the despair of my mother."

He got to his feet again and crossed to the fire, where he nudged a log with his booted foot so that it would burn more easily.

"Aidan and I once had a plan," he said. "I suppose we were still close to infancy at the time. We would change clothes and therefore identities, we agreed, and our father would never know the difference. Aidan would stay at home and become the duke one day, and I would sail the seven seas and grasp whatever adventure the world and life had to offer."

Christine kept quiet, startled and fascinated. He was staring into the fire and into a long-gone past. After a minute or two he looked over his shoulder at her and came back from that place.

"But from the moment I was born," he said, "I was set for the dukedom and for all the duties and responsibilities that came with it, and from the moment *he* was born, Aidan was marked for the army. We dreamed of changing places, but it could not be done, of course. In the end I betrayed him."

Beneath the cozy sheepskin, under which she had pushed her hands, Christine felt herself turn cold.

"He did not want his chosen career," he said. "He was a peace-loving, placid boy. He used to follow our father around like a shadow when he was on farm business, and he used to spend a great deal of time with the steward. He pleaded with our father and enlisted our mother's aid to plead his case for him. All he ever wanted was to live quietly on the land and farm it and administer it. By what cruel fate he was born second and I first I do not know. After our father died, of course, I might have given him his reprieve. I was only seventeen, he fifteen. He was at school for a few years after that, but when he came home he threw himself into farm business again with great enthusiasm. He knew the farms surrounding Lindsey Hall intimately. He knew how to run them. He had a better instinct for it than I. He tried to advise me—with eminently good advice. He wanted me to retire our father's steward, who had grown rather old for the job, and let him take over. He tried to point out to me some of the ways in which I could improve what was being done and some of the things I was doing wrong. He meant well—he loved this place, he knew it better than I did, and I was his *brother*. I purchased a commission for him and summoned him to the library to tell him. He had almost no choice but to obey me. Such was my power as the Duke of Bewcastle even when I was still a very young man. I wielded it unflinchingly. I have wielded it ever since."

"And you have never forgiven yourself," she said—she did not have to phrase it as a question. "Even though you did the right thing."

"I did," he agreed. "But I had to choose between my role as Duke of Bewcastle and my role as brother—to the boy who had once been heart of my heart. It was the first notable occasion on which I faced the conflict and had to choose. I chose the duke's role, and have been making similar choices ever since. I will continue to do so until I die, I suppose. I am, after all, that aristocrat, and I have duties and responsibilities to hundreds, perhaps even thousands, of people that I cannot and will not shirk. And therefore, you see, I cannot assure you that I will become a changed man in order to fit your dream. You find me cold, reticent, hard, and I am all those things. But I am not *only* those things."

"No," she said, though she was not sure that any sound had escaped her lips.

He stood before the fire, his hands behind his back, his booted feet slightly apart, his expression haughty and cold, at variance with what he was saying—or perhaps not. He had chosen to make his role as Duke of Bewcastle the dominant one in his life.

"I cannot offer you anything I am not, you see," he said. "I can only hope you are able to see that any person who has lived for almost thirty-six years is vastly complex. You accused me a few evenings ago of wearing a mask, and you were wrong. I wear the mantle of Duke of Bewcastle over that of Wulfric Bedwyn, but both mantles are mine. I am not less of a man because I choose to put duty first in my life. And then you wondered if I am a cold, unfeeling aristocrat right through to the very core. I am not. If I were, would I ever have been first enchanted by you and then haunted by the memory of you? You are not at all the sort of person Bewcastle would even notice, let alone choose to woo."

Christine sat very still.

"But I get ahead of myself," he said. "I had a good childhood. It was boisterous and happy. I had good parents, though it did not seem to me during my later boyhood that my father cared for me."

"What happened?" she asked. He had found her enchanting. He had been haunted by the memory of her? *Haunted?*

"He had a heart seizure when I was twelve," he said. "He survived it, but he was warned that his heart was weak, that it could stop beating at any moment. He was one of the wealthiest, most powerful men in Britain. He owned more property than almost any other man. His duties and responsibilities were enormous. And yet his eldest son—his heir—was a wild, rebellious hellion."

It was almost impossible to realize that it was of himself he spoke.

"Although I remained at Lindsey Hall," he said, "I was almost totally separated from my family. I was put under the care of two tutors. I saw my father infrequently, my mother rarely. Aidan and then Rannulf and finally Alleyne went off to school, as I had expected to do, and I almost never saw them—even during the holidays, when they came home. I was virtually isolated. I fought, I ranted, I pouted, I sulked—and I learned. I had five years in which to learn everything there was to know about the rest of my life. No one knew that there would be even five, of course. There might have been only one, or even less. My father died when I was seventeen. On his deathbed he kissed my hand and told me that sometimes love hurts even though it is nonetheless love. He had had no choice, you see. I was his son and he loved me. I was also his heir. I had to learn to take his place."

It struck Christine suddenly that he had probably never told this story to anyone else—just as she had never told the story of the events surrounding Oscar's death to anyone but him. It was a realization that frankly terrified her—and threatened to bring tears to her eyes. He was baring his soul to her. Because . . . because he had been enchanted with her and then haunted by the memory of her. Because he had brought her here deliberately—here to Lindsey Hall, here to the dovecote, his private hermitage, for just this purpose. Because he had begged her to give him a chance.

She was, she realized, terribly in love with him. And yet . . .

And yet she no longer believed in happily-ever-after. She was no longer the girl she had been ten years ago, when she had rushed headlong into a relationship that she surely would have avoided if she had only given herself more time to get to know Oscar better. She *had* loved him to the end, but in her heart she knew that she had detected quite early in their marriage his essential weakness of character. Theirs had not been the grand, lifelong passion of her dreams.

This time she was wiser and far more cautious. This time she was well aware that no happily-ever-after danced merrily just beyond a proposal of marriage and its acceptance. And yet . . .

And yet he was a man whom, against all the odds, she had grown to like. And he was a man she was unwillingly coming to admire. How could she *not* admire a man to whom honor and duty meant everything? Whose sense of responsibility to hundreds or even thousands of dependents was more important to him than personal gratification? His education might have been oppressive, even brutal, but his father would have seen to it that it did not actually break his spirit. He could, then, after his father died, have turned his back on everything he had been taught. He could have become a wild, extravagant young man, as so many other men in similar circumstances did. He had had the power and wealth to get away with it, after all.

But he had held firm. From the age of seventeen on, he had donned the mantle of the Duke of Bewcastle and worn it unflinchingly.

How could she *not* admire him? And, God help her, how could she not *love* him?

She smiled at him. "Thank you," she said. "I understand that you are a very private person. Thank you for showing me this enchanted private place and for telling me about yourself."

He gazed at her, as stern and formidable as ever, his eyes as inscrutable as they ever were.

"I have dreamed," he said, "for almost a year I have dreamed of seeing you here, sitting there, just as you are. I am not going to ask any questions today. The time is not right. I will tell you something, though. I did not bring you here to seduce you. But I want you. You know that. I want to have you now, here on that bed. I want it as a free expression of what I feel for you and what perhaps you feel for me. No commitments, no obligations—unless there are consequences, which you told me once before are unlikely. *Will* you lie with me? Ah, I have asked a question after all."

Her mind went numb though it raced with a million thoughts at the same time. Her body felt anything but numb. Her breasts tightened with instant desire, and a sharp ache stabbed downward through her womb and along her inner thighs. She felt robbed of breath. Here? Now? *Again?* Memories of the night out by the lake at Schofield came flooding back. And she said exactly what she had said that night when he had asked basically the same question.

"Yes," she said.

He took the three steps that separated them and held out his right hand, palm up. She pushed the sheepskin aside and set her hand in his.

He raised it to his lips.

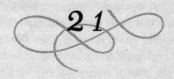

21

WULFRIC PICKED UP THE SHEEPSKIN AND tossed it over the bed before pulling back one corner with the bedsheets. When he turned back to her, she was standing where he had left her, watching him, though she had taken off her pelisse and thrown it over the back of the chair.

She was wearing a dress of pale yellow wool, though one side of it looked more apricot in the red light from one of the windows overhead. It was a high-waisted, high-necked, long-sleeved dress with no adornments. It hugged her trim, shapely figure and needed no other allure.

"Come closer to the fire," he said, walking back toward her, setting a hand at the small of her back, and moving her nearer to the hearth, where they would feel the full benefit of the heat from the burning logs. He did not want this to be a simple outpouring of sexual hunger as it had been last time. Although he had not used the word to her and *would* not, he wanted to make love to her.

He did not immediately kiss her. He framed her face with his hands and ran his thumbs over her eyebrows. Her eyes were wide and bright. Pink and lavender light from the windows overhead gave a glow to her complexion. She had a lovely mouth, with soft, smooth lips that were almost always curved upward at the corners. He ran his fingers through her hair. It felt soft and clean. The short curls bounced back into place after the passage of his fingers. The style suited her to perfection.

He moved his hands down over her shoulders and behind her, felt the row of buttons at the back of her dress, and undid them one at a time until he could draw the edges back off her shoulders and down her arms to her waist. It fell the rest of the way to the floor on its own. She was not wearing stays. Her shapely body was her own, as nature had intended it to be. She wore a plain linen shift, which covered her from her bosom to just above her knees.

He took a step back from her and went down on one knee to remove her shoes one at a time and then her garters before rolling her stockings down her legs and off her feet.

He kissed the side of one foot before setting it back on the floor, and then the inside of her knee.

She had not, he noticed as he stood again, touched him yet. And yet he knew from her slightly parted lips and drooped eyelids that she wanted this as much as he did.

He set his lips to her shoulder and licked its warm, smooth, slight saltiness. She shivered despite the heat from the fire. He drew down the strap of her shift, uncovered one breast, and cupped it in his hand as he kissed his way down to it. It was perfect—soft and heavy, yet firm and uptilted too. He parted his lips over the nipple, breathed in through his mouth and then out again, and then suckled her. For the first time she touched him. Her fingers tangled in his hair, her head came down to touch his own, and she made a low sound in her throat.

It occurred to him that though he had been intimate with her once before, he had never seen her unclothed. He wanted to see her now. He wanted to make love to her with no barriers between them.

Need, desire, longing throbbed in him with every pulse beat. He could feel the heat from the fire all down his left side.

He lifted his head, and her hands fell to her sides again.

"Come to bed," he said.

He undressed her completely after she lay down. A band of pink light from one of the windows slanted across the upper half of her body, blending into red across her legs and one hip. But though he could have stood there for a while just drinking in the sight of her, they were some distance from the fire here and it had not yet taken the chill from the whole space. He covered her with the sheet and the sheepskin and sat on the side of the bed to pull off his Hessian boots before standing again to remove the rest of his clothes. When he was naked, he lifted the covers and lay down beside her.

She was enticingly warm. He turned to her, burrowed them both deeper beneath the covers, and touched her again.

He set about arousing her with all the skill and patience of which he was capable, using his palms, his fingers, his lips, his tongue, his teeth. And all the while he burned for her and for the moment when he could mount her and consummate his passion for her again.

She was not idle. Her hands moved over him, tentatively at first, with growing boldness as he felt her body grow hotter and heard her breathing become more labored.

The time had come, he knew at last—and the temptation was to roll over to cover her, to dip his hands beneath her, to spread her legs with his own, to mount her, and to ride them both to completion.

But he wanted to make *love* to her.

He lifted his head and looked down into her face.

"Christine," he whispered, and he kissed her for the first time, lightly, brushing parted lips over hers.

Her eyes opened wider.

"Oh," she murmured.

"Christine," he said again, "you are so very beautiful." And he kissed her deeply.

But they were both far gone into sexual passion. He moved onto her, and she opened to him, spreading her legs wide, lifting them from the bed, and twining them about his. He slid his hands beneath her, positioned himself, and entered her with one glad, slow thrust. At the same moment she tilted to him and drew him deeper with tightly clenched inner muscles.

He slid his hands free, took some of his weight onto his forearms, and lifted his head to look down into her face again. Her eyes laughed rather dreamily into his.

"Wulfric," she said. "A powerful name for a powerful man. *Very* powerful." She laughed softly and wickedly.

He lowered his head to the soft spot beneath one of her ears and growled. She laughed again, and her legs tightened about his and her inner muscles clenched about him again.

He loved her slowly and for a long time beneath the warm cocoon of the covers, while the fire crackled in the hearth and red, pink, and lavender light danced over the surface of the sheepskin blanket. He loved her until they were both gasping for breath and their bodies slid damply and hotly together. He loved her until she moaned to his every thrust and strained up harder against him.

He brought them both to a swift, pounding climax.

"Wulfric," she protested sleepily as he rolled away to lie beside her after realizing that his full weight was bearing her down into the mattress. He felt a sudden chill down his damp front, but the bedcovers soon settled warmly over him.

He turned to watch her with narrowed gaze as she slept. Pale colored lights were catching one side of her face, while the other side lay in shadow. Her curls were tousled.

He was, as she had just reminded him, a powerful man. He had, it seemed, everything any man could possibly want in this life. But there was something else that he wanted, and he was not at all sure he would ever have it. He was certainly not going to ask today. Maybe not even tomorrow or the next day.

He was afraid to ask.

He was afraid the answer would be no. And, if it was, he could never ask again.

So the question must wait.

He wanted her love.

THE CLOUDS HAD moved off and the sun was shining by the time they left the dovecote. The wind was still blowing, though, and it was still a chilly day.

They walked back in the direction of the house as they had walked back from the lake at Schofield—not touching and not talking. But it felt different this time. This time their silence and proximity felt companionable. Though perhaps that was not quite it either. There was a *knowledge* between them. They had shared far more than they had at Schofield. They had shared bodies there. Here they had shared themselves.

Christine still felt weak-kneed and vulnerable. She

was deeply in love. At the same time, she was trying to convince herself that since being in love and loving were two quite different things, she must be sensible. She was relieved that he had not asked the question. She hoped he would not ask it—ever. For if he asked, she would have to answer and she honestly did not know what she would say.

She knew what she *ought* to say, but not what she *would* say.

But what if he never did ask? How could she bear it?

He had asked once and she had said no. Surely he would not humiliate himself by asking again.

Then what was this visit to Lindsey Hall all about? What was this afternoon all about?

He had called her *Christine*. It was absurd to remember that as perhaps the most tender and precious moment of all. But it *had* been precious—*Christine*, spoken in his very cultured, very aristocratic voice. Though he had whispered it the first time. And when she had called him *Wulfric*, he had growled at her.

She turned her head to look at him and discovered that he had his head turned too and was looking at her. She looked sharply away.

"What?" he said. "I have won the game so easily today?"

But she could feel herself blushing.

"There are too many trees," she said. "If I do not look where I am going, I will no doubt walk slap into one and embarrass myself."

She had initiated their second lovemaking in the dovecote, she thought and felt the heat deepening in her cheeks. She had woken up, feeling warm and snug and delicious and turned her head on the pillow to find him looking at her. And she had lifted herself up onto one elbow, leaned over him, and kissed him open-mouthed. And then, when he had turned onto his back, she had followed him and climbed right on top of his warm, naked, splendidly muscled male body and rubbed herself against him in a blatant invitation he had not been slow in accepting.

She had never done anything like it before.

Making love with the Duke of Bewcastle—with Wulfric—was by far the most exciting, most exhilarating experience of her life.

But she must *not* equate being in love or even making love with love itself.

He took her back by a different route. They came out of the trees at the far end of the lake, the wilder end, where the trees grew to the water's edge. And there, just ahead of them, was the party from the house, adults and children, obviously engaged in a game of hide-and-seek among the trees.

Pamela spotted Christine and came skipping toward her, Becky at her side.

"Cousin Christine!" she screeched. "We went in a boat and I trailed my hand in the water and Phillip wanted to try rowing but Becky's papa said no, not today because the water was choppy and Laura was sick over the side and we stopped at the island and then Laura was not willing to get in again but Becky's papa told her that if she kept her eyes on the horizon she would not be sick again and she was not and I was not sick at all even though Phillip said I would be because I always am when I am in the carriage."

Christine laughed. "What an exciting afternoon you have had," she said. Becky, she noticed, had taken the duke's hand and was swinging his arm with her own.

"Uncle Wulf," she said, "Pamela and I want to play school, but we cannot with so many children in the nursery. May we borrow your library when we get home?"

"If you promise not to take it too far away," he said.

Both little girls burst into delighted laughter.

"Silly!" Becky said. "We are not going to *take* it anywhere, Uncle Wulf, only *use* it."

"Ah," he said. "Then you may."

The game of hide-and-seek must have run its course. Adults and children were gathered on the bank, and the girls drew Christine and the duke in that direction too.

"We have just been telling the children," Lord Rannulf explained, "that though swimming was always allowed farther along, it was forbidden here."

"That was because the temptation to dive off a tree branch would have been too strong," Lord Alleyne said.

"But it would be great fun," young Davy cried, pointing. "Look at that branch, Uncle Aidan. I could dive off that, I bet."

"It looks very dangerous, Davy," Lady Aidan said.

"Strictly forbidden, lad!" Lord Aidan said at the same time.

"It always was, Davy," Lord Rannulf said. "More is the pity."

"That never stopped you doing it, though," the Duke of Bewcastle said. "All of you. Even Freyja—*especially* Freyja, in fact. And even Morgan."

Melanie laughed and all the Bedwyns turned to look at their eldest brother in some surprise.

"Uh-oh," Lord Alleyne said. "You *knew*, Wulf? And we thought we were being so sly."

"Kit trod water under the branch the first time I tried it and offered to catch me," Lady Rosthorn said. "I was eight, if I remember correctly, and would have died rather than have him think me a coward. I was desperately in love with him."

They all laughed with her. Lord Rosthorn draped an arm about her shoulders.

"That is *my* age," Becky cried. "Papa, I want to try it when it is a warmer day."

"Now see what you have all started by talking in front of the children," Lady Aidan said, exasperated.

"It was Wulf who started it," Lady Hallmere pointed out. "How did you know we used to dive here, Wulf?"

"Because I used to do it myself as a child," he said. "Aidan and I did. We never brought Rannulf with us because we were afraid he would knock his head on a stone or a tree root and we would have our bottoms whipped."

The children all whooped with delight.

"Uncle Wulf said *bottom*," William cried, and they all shrieked with laughter again.

"Wulfric *diving*?" Lord Hallmere said, grinning. "And *against the rules*? I don't think I believe it."

"Neither do I," Lord Rannulf said derisively. "I would never have agreed to be left behind."

The Duke of Bewcastle raised a quizzing glass to his eye. "Do I understand that I am being called a *liar*?" he asked.

But his question seemed only to provoke more derision and hilarity.

Becky, Christine could see, was pulling at his hand, which she still held.

"Show them, Uncle Wulf," she whispered. "Show them!"

He looked down at the child and Christine heard him sigh.

"There is no other way, is there?" he said.

And to Christine's stunned amazement—and everyone else's—he took off his hat, his gloves, and his greatcoat and handed them to Becky.

"Oh, I say," Lady Hallmere said. "Wulf is going diving. Stand behind me, Josh. I am about to swoon."

"Wulfric," Lady Aidan warned, "the water will be icy cold."

"It is icy cold even *out* of the water," Melanie said.

Bertie rumbled.

"Oh, this is splendid of him," Lady Alleyne said.

The duke had removed his coat and waistcoat and quizzing glass and cravat and handed them to Christine. He dragged his shirt off over his head and set it on the pile.

"Wulfric," Lady Rannulf said, "don't let yourself be goaded into this. It is dangerous. You will hurt yourself."

The children were prancing about in irrepressible high spirits.

"This," Lady Rosthorn said, patting her husband's hand on her shoulder, "I have to see."

Lord Rannulf and Lord Alleyne stood side by side, almost identical grins on their faces.

The duke managed to remove his boots without sitting down. He set them side by side on the grass.

He must be half frozen, Christine thought. But she was watching him with wonder.

His stockings came off and were stuffed inside his boots.

All that was left to him were his pantaloons and the drawers she knew he wore beneath them.

He strode away from them all in his bare feet and went up the oak tree as if he climbed one every day of his life. Of course, he *had* had some practice a few days before when he had gone to the rescue of his quizzing glass.

He walked out along the branch that extended over the water, holding onto another branch for balance as long as he could and then doing it on his own. He went to the very end of the branch, tested it for strength, bent his knees a few times, flexed his arms. He was, Christine realized, playing up to his audience, which was loving it.

And then he dived in headfirst, his arms stretched above his head, his legs straight and together, his feet pointed. There was hardly a splash as he went in.

There *was*, however, a collective gasp from the bank, followed by a cheer. Christine clapped her free hand over her mouth until his head broke above the surface and he shook the water out of his eyes.

"Someone," he shouted, "should have warned me that the water is cold."

It was the moment at which Christine slid all the way—irretrievably—in love.

And then something extraordinary happened—something *else* extraordinary, that was. Lady Hallmere stepped up in front of her, frowning ferociously, and hugged her hard, the duke's clothes squashed between them.

"If *this* is what you have done for him," she said, "I will love you all my life."

And then she was off to watch the show with everyone else as the Duke of Bewcastle swam the few strokes to the bank, hoisted himself out, and stood dripping like a sleek seal on the grass.

"And diving into *this* lake from *these* trees," he said to all the children with something of his usual sternness though his teeth were chattering, "is *still* strictly forbidden."

"That was a bit extreme, was it not, Wulf?" Lord Aidan asked him. "If they all wanted to know whether you spoke the truth, all they had to do was ask me." He smiled one of his rare smiles and looked very handsome indeed.

Christine hurried toward the duke with his clothes, but he handed them to Lord Aidan rather than fuss around him herself.

The duke's eyes, very silver beneath his wet, sleek hair, met hers.

"I am happy to remember, ma'am," he said, "that I did not laugh at you that day beside the Serpentine. I now understand the discomfort you were suffering."

But *she* laughed at *him*. Not out loud. She laughed with her eyes.

He had done it for her, she was sure.

To prove to her that he was Wulfric Bedwyn as well as the Duke of Bewcastle.

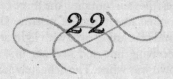

22

$\mathcal{T}$HE BALL AT LINDSEY HALL WAS WELL AT-
tended, most of the neighboring families still being
in the country for the Easter break. And grand balls
hosted by the Duke of Bewcastle were rare events. Everyone came from miles around.

Wulfric had certainly not organized the event himself.
He had a secretary to see to all the mundane details and
sisters and sisters-in-law to fuss over others, like the floral
arrangements in the ballroom and the choice of particular foods for the supper and the refreshment room. However, he took a more than usual interest in proceedings on
the day of the event, wandering from the library to the
great hall to the ballroom, unable to settle to any particular activity.

His guests were to leave the day after tomorrow. Even
his family was leaving, some for town, some for their own
homes in the country. And he was going to let them all
leave. He was going to let *her* leave. He had decided that.

But he wanted this evening to be special.

And so he wandered restlessly and stayed away from
the drawing room and refused to participate in any of the
activities anyone had planned.

The ballroom, he thought when the evening came and
he stood in the receiving line with his aunt and uncle

dressed in his customary black and white, really did look rather magnificent, with baskets of spring flowers hanging from the walls and above doorways, and great pots of fern and Easter lilies surrounding the three central pillars.

And *she* looked lovely too—Christine Derrick, who was smiling and brimming over with light and joy as she passed the receiving line and had her first sight of the room. Her gown was white. The delicately scalloped hem and short, puffed sleeves were embroidered with buttercups and daisies and greenery. She looked like a piece of the springtime.

Wulfric's heart lifted at the sight of her.

He had asked her as they left the dining room after luncheon if she would reserve the first waltz for him. They were almost the first words he had spoken to her since the day before yesterday after he had dived into the lake.

He was feeling absurdly shy.

Or perhaps it was terror. He wanted to believe that all was now well between them, that she felt as he felt, and that—most important of all—she could now see the possibility of a future with him. But he was not certain. And since his adult life had not held many uncertainties, he did not know quite how to cope with this one.

He opened the dancing with Viscountess Ravensberg who had cleverly discovered a violet gown to match exactly the color of her lovely eyes. Then he danced with the blond and pretty Lady Muir, sister of the Earl of Kilbourne, and wondered as he had before why she had not remarried though she had been widowed for a number of years and was extremely eligible. Strangely, perhaps, he had never considered courting her himself. He danced the third set with Amy Hutchinson by his aunt's maneuvering. Aunt Rochester had swept into his library unannounced the day before and lectured him on dut and what he owed the family name. He did *not* owe it, according to her, a schoolmaster's daughter who smiled too much and did not always know how to behave. He had listened to her without comment, raised his glass almost to his eye, thanked her for her concern, and really had given her little choice but to turn tail and leave him master of his domain, taking her ruffled feathers with her. But she had still not given up hope of pushing her niece on him, it seemed.

The fourth set was to be a waltz.

Christine Derrick had danced with Attingsborough, Kit, and Aidan. She was looking flushed and bright-eyed, and not at all the way a lady ought to look at a ball—aloof and slightly bored. She looked really quite adorable. She was standing at the opposite side of the ballroom from where Wulfric stood, with Lady Elrick and the Duchess of Portfrey.

Her eyes met his across the empty floor.

He could not resist. His fingers grasped the jeweled handle of his quizzing glass and raised it all the way to his eye before lowering it slightly. Even across the distance he could see the laughter well up into her eyes.

And then she reached down into a little cloth reticule that hung from her wrist and brought something out of it. For a moment all he could see of it was black ribbon. She brought the object slowly up to her eye and regarded him—through the lens of his own quizzing glass.

Wulfric Bedwyn, the oh-so-toplofty, oh-so-frosty Duke of Bewcastle, was shocked into uttering a short bark of laughter. Then he smiled at her slowly until his whole face beamed his amusement and affection.

She was no longer smiling, he saw as he set off across the empty floor toward her—it did not occur to him that it would have been far more correct to walk unobtrusively about the perimeter of the room. But her eyes were huge and translucent, and her teeth were biting into her lower lip.

"I believe, Mrs. Derrick," he said, making her a bow when he came up to her, "this is my dance?"

"Yes, your grace," she said. "Thank you."

It was only then, when he extended a hand toward her, that he became aware of the near-hush that had descended on the ballroom. He turned his head and looked about in some surprise, his eyebrows raised, to see what had happened. But as he did so, everyone rushed back into conversation.

"Did I miss something?" he asked.

Christine Derrick set her hand in his—the quizzing glass had disappeared inside her little reticule again.

"Yes," she said. "A looking glass. You missed seeing yourself smile."

What the devil? He frowned at her.

"I understand," she said, and she was *laughing* at him again, the minx, "that it is as rare as a rose in winter."

How foolish, he thought. How very foolish! But he made no comment.

For half an hour he waltzed with her and the world receded. There was no Hector this time to come lumbering into them from the opposite direction—he had been firmly established in the card room since well before the first set began. There was nothing at all to harm her or take his attention from her. She sparkled. He felt as if he held joy itself in his arms. He kept his eyes on her, marveling at her beauty, breathing in the fragrance of her, doing nothing to hide his admiration somewhere deep behind his eyes.

"Thank you," he said when the set was finally over and he was forced to return to reality. And then, more softly, "Thank you, Christine."

Duty called. He was the host of the ball. His home was

filled with guests. His half-hour of self-indulgence was over.

CHRISTINE COULD NOT remember feeling more depressed in her life. Of course, one always thought that when one was depressed. But even so, this was a depression to beat them all.

He had wanted to prove a point to her. He had brought her here in order to do so—and he had *succeeded*. But that was all he had ever intended.

She had been given her chance last year and had rejected it—with firmness and scorn. He would not ask again. *Of course* he would not. He was the Duke of Bewcastle.

And of all things, it was *raining* today. Oh, not enough to stop them all traveling and keep them at Lindsey Hall for an extra day. Thank *heaven* it was not raining that heavily. But it was enough to make the world gray and gloomy and to steam up the carriage windows when they were on their way.

Christine took one last look around the lovely Chinese bedchamber that had been hers during her stay. Her bag had already been taken down and stowed in the carriage.

Just two evenings ago she had been happier than she had ever been before. He had smiled at her across the ballroom floor after she had looked at him through his quizzing glass—which was now weighting down the pocket of her pelisse, nestled for safety within the folds of his handkerchief. He had smiled, and she would swear that her heart had performed a complete somersault in her chest. And then he had waltzed with her, and his eyes had devoured her the whole time. She was certain there had been a smile in their depths. Silver had suddenly seemed warm and light-filled to her. She had felt as if her slippers had scarcely touched the ballroom floor all the time they danced.

All doubts had fled, all barriers had simply ceased to exist.

And then the waltz had ended—and he had hardly spoken to her since.

Yesterday she and all the others had been busy enjoying themselves from morning to night. But the Duke of Bewcastle had kept to his library, only Bertie and Basil and Hector and Lord Weston admitted to the hallowed precincts.

And now she was leaving. Bertie's two carriages were already drawn up on the terrace. The children were scrambling with their nurse into the second one. Melanie and Bertie were probably in the hall below wondering where she was.

She took a deep breath and left the room without a backward glance. She pasted a smile on her face.

There was a crowd down in the hall.

"Oh, *there* you are, Christine," Melanie said.

She was caught up in handshakes and hugs then. They were the first to leave, though everyone else was also going today. Hermione was actually crying, and that threatened to start Christine off too. She stretched her smile wider.

Melanie and Bertie hurried out to the carriage.

"Mrs. Derrick." It was the duke's cool, haughty voice. "Allow me to hold an umbrella over your head so that you will not get wet."

She added a sparkle to her eyes.

"Thank you," she said.

She put her head down as they stepped out through the front doors and he hoisted a large black umbrella over her. She tried to hurry. But he took her arm in a firm grasp.

She turned and smiled at him.

"How unmannerly the rain has made me," she said. "I did not say thank you for your hospitality, your grace. It really has been a splendid stay."

"But your mother is not here, Mrs. Derrick," he said, "and neither are your sisters or your brother-in-law. There is a question I wish to ask you, but courtesy dictates that I speak at least to your mother first. It is something I did not do last summer. *May* I speak to her? And *may* I ask my question afterward? I will not trouble either her or you if you would rather I did not."

The umbrella gave the illusion of seclusion and privacy. Christine could hear the rain drumming lightly on its fabric. She looked into his eyes, and suddenly depression fled and a blazing happiness took its place.

"Yes," she said, her voice breathless. "You may call on my mother. She will be honored. And you may call upon me. I will be . . ."

"Christine?" he prompted softly.

"Pleased," she said, and whisked herself out from under the umbrella and up the steps into the carriage without waiting for him to hand her in.

And now the stupid tears came, filling her eyes and blurring her vision, and threatening to spill down over her cheeks.

Melanie patted her hand as the door shut with a firm click and the carriage bounced and lurched into almost instant motion.

"I am so sorry, Christine," she said. "I expected some announcement during the ball. *Everyone* did. But no matter. He is a haughty, disagreeable man anyway, is he not, and we will find someone else for you. It will not be difficult, you know. You are amazingly attractive to men."

There had been no announcement at the ball, Christine thought, *because her mother had not been there*, or

Eleanor or Hazel and Charles. And he had felt—so different from last year!—that it would be discourteous to proceed without the formality of consulting them first.

She was not in love, she thought. Not at all.

She *loved*!

It was Wulfric's guess that Christine Derrick had not told her family that he was to be expected. He was seated in the sitting room at Hyacinth Cottage making labored conversation with them, and it was perfectly clear to him that they were terrified. At least, Mrs. Thompson and Mrs. Lofter were—the latter had come to call just after Wulfric and looked, after she had entered the sitting room, as if she would have withdrawn again if only she decently could. Miss Thompson looked at him over the tops of her spectacles, which she had not removed even though she had closed the book she had been reading when he arrived. There was a faint look of amusement on her face, somewhat reminiscent of her youngest sister.

It was eight days since Christine had left Lindsey Hall with the Renables. And of course he had had to arrive on an afternoon when she was not at home, though she was expected home at any moment for tea. Mrs. Thompson kept glancing nervously at the window as if she could thus precipitate the arrival of her youngest daughter.

Actually it was a good thing she was not at home, Wulfric decided. And he had made enough small talk.

"There is a matter I wish to discuss with you, ma'am," he said, addressing Mrs. Thompson, "before I speak with Mrs. Derrick. And it is, perhaps, as well that your other daughters are present too. I wonder if you would have any objection to my making Mrs. Derrick the Duchess of Bewcastle?"

Mrs. Thompson gaped at him. Mrs. Lofter slapped

both hands to her cheeks. It was Miss Thompson who answered him after a short silence.

"Is Christine expecting you, your grace?" she asked.

"I believe," he said, "she is."

"Then if it is the prospect of that that has put an extra spring in her step and an even warmer smile than usual on her lips since she returned from Hampshire last week," she said, "I believe we would be delighted, your grace. Not because she will be the Duchess of Bewcastle, but because she will be happy again."

"But Eleanor," Mrs. Lofter said, "Christine is always happy."

"Is she?" Miss Thompson asked, though she did not pursue the question.

"Oh, bless my soul," Mrs. Thompson said, "Christine a duchess. It is remarkably civil of you to ask us, your grace. You do not need to do so, I am sure, you being a duke and all and Christine being quite old enough to decide for herself. If her father could only have lived to see this day."

But there was the sound of voices from the hallway beyond the sitting room.

"I am late for tea, Mrs. Skinner," Christine Derrick was saying. "I was reading to Mr. Potts and he fell asleep as he usually does by the time I reach the third paragraph, the poor lamb. But as I got up to tiptoe out and home, he woke up and entertained me for half an hour without stopping with all his old stories. I wish someone would give me a shilling for every time I have listened to them. But it gives him so much pleasure to hear me exclaim and laugh in all the right places."

She was laughing at the memory as she opened the sitting room door and came tripping inside, the old, floppy-brimmed straw bonnet on her head, and wearing the green-and-white-striped poplin dress Wulfric remembered from last year, and looking quite as pretty as she had looked in all her new finery in London and at Lindsey Hall.

"Oh," she said, the smile arrested on her face.

Wulfric had risen to his feet and was making his bow to her.

"Mrs. Derrick," he said.

"Your grace." She curtsied.

Mrs. Thompson got to her feet too.

"His grace wishes to speak with you in private, Christine," she said. "Come along, Eleanor. Come along, Hazel. We will go elsewhere."

"I would far prefer to take Mrs. Derrick into the side garden, ma'am," Wulfric said. That was where he had gone most terribly wrong last year. It seemed important to him that it be there he try to made amends.

And so no more than a minute or two later they had stepped out through the front door and climbed the shallow steps to the trellis arch, and walked beneath it into the quiet, square garden that he had seen in his nightmares for some weeks after the last time he was here.

"Mrs. Skinner ought to have said something before I went into the sitting room," she said. "I could have made myself more presentable."

"For one thing," he told her, "I do not believe you allowed your housekeeper to get a word in edgewise. And, for another, you look adorable as you are."

"Oh." She had scurried around behind the wooden seat again, as she had done last time. She gripped the back with both hands.

"First," he said, setting his hands behind his back, "I must tell you that I can never be the man you dream of—"

"Yes, you can," she said quickly, interrupting him. "You can and you are. I am not sure what was on that list I gave you last year, but it does not signify. You are *everything* I could ever dream of and more."

There went the speech he had so carefully prepared.

"You will have me, then?" he asked her.

"No." She shook her head, and he closed his eyes.

"I cannot possibly be the sort of woman you need as your duchess," she said.

He opened his eyes.

"You are not planning to spout nonsense at me, are you?" he asked her. "I have it on the highest authority—Freyja's—that none of my brothers and sisters *or* their spouses *or* their children will ever speak to me again if I do not offer you just that position *and* persuade you to accept. And no members of the *ton* are higher sticklers than the Bedwyns."

"The Marchioness of Rochester is," she said.

"My aunt," he told her, "is like the rest of us—she likes to have her own way. She had the silly notion that my uncle's niece and I would suit. But she will get over her disappointment. She adores me. I am her favorite. None of my siblings, by the way, have ever been jealous of that fact."

She laughed, as he had intended. She came around and sat on the seat.

"Your grace," she said, "I—"

"*Must* you *your grace* me?" he asked her. "Must you, Christine?"

"It seems presumptuous to call you Wulfric," she said.

"You did not think so when you were in bed with me at the dovecote," he said.

She blushed quite rosily, though she would not look away from him. It was amazing to think that it was that very fact that had first caused him to notice her at Schofield Park.

"Wulfric," she said, "I am thirty years old. I had my thirtieth birthday three days ago."

"Ah," he said. "For a few weeks, then, I can pretend that

I am only five years older than you. I am not yet quite thirty-six."

"Oh, you must know what I mean," she said. "Even if I were not barren I would be approaching the end of my fertile years. But I *am* barren. I ought to have said no when you asked if you could come here. But I was not thinking straight. I was thinking only of how wonderful those days at Lindsey Hall had been and of—"

"Christine," he said, "*do* stop talking nonsense. I have told you before that I have three brothers, any of whom I would be happy to have succeed me. You have met them for yourself. And, if Aidan produces no sons, I could happily think of young William eventually taking over the title. I did not really expect to marry. After trying and failing to make a dynastic marriage when I was twenty-four, I knew that I could never marry unless I met the woman who could be soul of my soul. Frankly, I did not expect ever to meet her. I am not a man who has inspired much love."

"Your brothers and sisters love you dearly," she said.

"Christine," he said, "you are light and joy and the embodiment of love. If you were to agree to be my wife, I would *not* expect you to shape yourself into your image of what a duchess should be—or into anyone else's image either. Aunt Rochester would have a good try. I would expect—I would demand—only that you be you. If anyone does not like your style of duchess, then to hell with that person. But I would not expect it to happen. You have a gift for attracting love and laughter, even from people who have no intention of loving you or laughing with you."

She looked down then at the hands in her lap, and her face was hidden beneath the brim of her bonnet.

"I will always be the stern, aloof, rather cold aristocrat you so despise," he said. "I have to be. I—"

"I know," she said, looking up quickly. "I would neither expect nor want you to change. I love the Duke of Bewcastle as he is. He is formidable and magnificent and dangerous—especially when he hauls villains to their feet with one hand and dangles them above the floor and throws terror into them with a few soft words."

The familiar laughter lurked in her eyes.

"But I will always be Wulfric Bedwyn too," he said. "And he has discovered that it can occasionally be fun to dive into lakes out of forbidden trees."

The laughter spread to the rest of her face.

"I *love* Wulfric Bedwyn," she said, and there was a wicked inflection in her voice.

"Do you?" He closed the distance between them and took both her hands in his. He raised them one at a time to his lips. "Do you, my love? Enough to take a chance on me? I had better warn you. There is a Bedwyn tradition that we do not necessarily marry early in life but that when we *do* marry we give our whole devotion and fidelity to our spouse. If you marry me, you must expect to be adored for the rest of your life."

She sighed. "I think I could bear it," she said, "if I try very hard. But only if I can do the same to you."

She laughed at him, and he smiled slowly back at her.

"Well." He gripped her hands more tightly. "Well."

He knelt on the grass before the bench and kissed her hands in her lap again.

"You will marry me, Christine?"

She leaned over him and kissed his cheek.

"Yes, I will," she said. "Oh, yes, I will, Wulfric, if you please."

He turned his head and their lips met.

*   *   *

SITTING IN A pew in St. George's, Hanover Square, when the church had been half full for Audrey's wedding to Sir Lewis Wiseman at the end of February had inspired Christine with awe.

Viewing it from the end of the nave when it was full to capacity with almost every member of the *ton* who was still drawing breath for her own wedding in the middle of June filled her with such terror that she was afraid that her knees would forget how to lock themselves in place and her legs would forget how to move one at a time and she would collapse in an ignominious heap as soon as the organ started to play—which it was doing *now*—and Basil would have to drag her down to the altar so that she would not lose her chance of becoming a duchess.

Charles was helping at the altar, and so there had been no conflict about which brother-in-law would give her away.

"Oh, dear," she murmured, in deep distress.

"Steady." Basil patted her hand. "Everyone is waiting to see you, Christine."

That, she thought, was the whole point.

Wulfric had given her the choice of where she wanted their nuptials to be solemnized. She would have been very happy with the church in the village, with Charles officiating. She would have been equally happy with the church at Lindsey Hall. And *he* would have been too. He had said so. But no, she had had to be noble about the whole thing. He was the Duke of Bewcastle, after all, one of the most powerful and wealthy men in the land. Surely, then, it was important for him that their wedding be solemnized with all the pomp and ceremony due to his position. And so she had settled on St. George's, where all the fashionable weddings of the beau monde took place during the Season.

So there was really no one to blame for this terrifying moment but herself.

And then Basil patted her hand once more and they began to walk toward the altar—and she discovered that her legs and her knees *did* remember how to function. But it was not her legs or her knees that she had to thank for that fact.

She had looked ahead—down the long aisle to the altar rail.

He was wearing cream and brown and gold and looked quite astonishingly gorgeous. There was one moment—perhaps even two—of unreality and disbelief. He could not possibly be waiting for *her*. She must have stumbled into someone else's dream and would wake up any moment in the schoolroom or in Hyacinth Cottage.

But then his face came into focus. It was handsome in a cold, austere way, with stern jaw, thin lips, high cheekbones, and a prominent, slightly hooked, finely chiseled nose. The face of the Duke of Bewcastle.

The face of the man she loved with all her heart.

Wulfric's face.

Through the veil of her moss green bonnet, she smiled at him.

But finally, as she drew closer on Basil's arm, it was only his eyes she saw—his silver eyes, glowing with an intense light as he watched her come, oblivious, it seemed, to Lord Aidan at his side and everyone else in the church.

And then he smiled slowly at her in that way he had of transforming himself into surely the most handsome man who had ever lived.

She was at his side then, and it no longer occurred to her to be nervous. There was no one else in the world except Wulfric and herself—and the clergyman who would make them into man and wife for the rest of their lives.

"Dearly beloved," he began in the sonorous tones peculiar to the clergy on all solemn occasions.

WULFRIC HAD HIS first taste of what was to come for the rest of his married days when the service was over and the register signed and the organ playing for the solemn procession out of the church, past all their guests, who sat with quiet dignity in their pews.

Christine clung to his arm and he looked down at her with warm sympathy. He knew she had chosen St. George's and a large, very public wedding for his sake. He guessed that she was very nervous, facing their guests for the first time.

She was smiling sunnily and happily, the veil thrown back over the brim of her bonnet. She was smiling right and left, at her family, at those few of his who were in evidence, at other acquaintances.

Ah, he need not have been concerned.

And then, when they were halfway out and the organ had reached a crescendo of the stately anthem, she pointed with one outstretched arm to the far corner of the church.

"Oh, look, Wulfric," she said aloud, "the children are here."

They were too—all the younger ones, with their nurses, close enough to the back that they might have been taken out if they had proved troublesome.

"That's Aunt Christine," William said quite distinctly.

"And Uncle Wulf," said Jacques.

And Christine raised her arm and waved gaily at them—with all the *ton* looking on.

Wulfric paused and waited until she was ready to resume the solemn procession. And since there was noth ing much else to do while he waited, he raised a hand and waved too. And grinned.

Life, he guessed, was going to be an adventure now that he was thirty-six. This was, in fact, his birthday.

"I had better warn you," he murmured as they reached the outer doors. "I am not sure if you noticed a few empty pews at the front of the church on the way out. The people who ought to have been occupying them are waiting for us outside."

And, sure enough, there were all the Bedwyns and their spouses and their older children lined up between the doors and the waiting carriage, armed with rose petals.

There were hordes of other people out there too—the curious masses, who had come to view a society wedding. Someone set up a cheer, and the crowd picked it up.

"Oh, Wulfric," Christine said, "this is so exciting."

He laughed and took her hand and ran with her. Petals rained down on them. But inevitably she stopped halfway to the carriage and stooped down to scoop up a handful of the petals, which she threw back at Rannulf and Rachel and Gervase with a delighted laugh.

They were in the open carriage then and she settled her very smart cream, green-trimmed dress about her while he picked up bags of coins from the seat and tossed their contents by handfuls over the heads of the gathered crowd. One liveried footman joined the coachman on the box and two others jumped up behind, and the carriage drove off—making a huge clatter as it did so, since it had to drag an assortment of old boots and other clutter behind it as well as cascades of bright ribbons.

Wulfric looked across at his bride, his wife, his duchess, and took her hand in his.

"At last," he said. "I would not believe in our happily-ever-after until now."

"Oh, not happily-ever-after, Wulfric," she said. "That is such a static thing. I don't want happily-ever-after. I want *happiness* and life and quarreling and making up and adventure and—"

He leaned across and kissed her on the lips.

"Well, and that too," she said with a laugh while the crowd about the church set up another cheer and the two footmen on the back of the carriage stared woodenly ahead.

EPILOGUE

*I*T WAS THE DUKE OF BEWCASTLE'S BIRTHDAY—
his thirty-seventh. He had never, however, been in
the habit of celebrating the occasion with a great show of
guests at Lindsey Hall.

It was also his first wedding anniversary. But though he
would undoubtedly have celebrated the occasion with his
duchess, it was doubtful that he would have invited guests
to share it with them.

It was far more probable, he thought as he sat patiently
for his valet to tie a perfect knot in his neckcloth, that they
would have gone to the dovecote, where they had spent
much of the Christmas holiday.

Nevertheless, there was a crowd of guests staying at
the house—even more than there had been over Easter
last year. And more guests were expected back at the
house after the church service that they were all about to
attend.

The occasion was neither the birthday nor the anniversary. The duke and duchess did not even expect to be the
focus of attention.

James Christian Anthony Bedwyn, Marquess of Lindsey,
had that distinction.

But one hour after the Duke of Bewcastle's neckcloth
had been successfully tied and the rest of his attire

donned, and after the Duchess of Bewcastle was properly clad in a new blue dress to match her eyes and a new bonnet to match both, the marquess seemed quite prepared to relinquish the center of attention to them.

He was sleeping.

He *did* awake with a start when water that was supposed to be tepid but which felt icy cold to him landed on his forehead and trickled back over his head. And for two or three minutes he gave lusty expression to his wrath.

But the water was soon wiped away, and he was soon handed into the keeping of someone whose arms told him quite firmly that while he was unconditionally loved, he nevertheless must learn not to disgrace himself by bawling over nothing.

Rather than argue the point, Lord Lindsey went back to sleep.

He had just been christened. He was wearing the gorgeous christening robe that all children of the Dukes of Bewcastle had worn for generations past.

He had aunts and uncles galore to fuss over him, as well as a grandmother and a great-aunt, the handle of whose lorgnette got tangled up in the lace of his skirt for one anxious moment. He also had cousins, most of whom demanded to be allowed to hold him after he had been carried back to the house in his papa's arms—much to the surprise and chagrin of his nurse. Almost the only ones who did not make such a demand were the eldest, Davy, who considered such a thing beneath his male dignity, and the youngest Robert, son of Uncle Alleyne and Aunt Rachel, who was asleep in a crib in the nursery. All the cousins were denied permission except for Becky and Marianne, who were made to sit down first and hold out their arms just so in order to hold the Marquess of Lindsey for one minute each.

There were neighbors to coo over him.

There was his mama to kiss his chubby little cheek and

his papa to kiss the other after they had taken him up to the nursery so that he would not be bothered by the crowd.

He was not bothered. He was supremely indifferent, wrapped up in blankets and sleep as he was.

Nevertheless, he was beginning to distinguish the two voices that spoke over him as he settled into his crib. They were the two voices that he would have thought most dear to him if his mind had been capable of such reasoning at the tender age of six weeks and two days.

"Our little miracle," his mama said foolishly and fondly.

"Our little ball of trouble," his papa said more firmly but just as fondly. "He was not just cross at church, Christine. He was furious. We are going to have our hands full with him, I do believe."

The Marquess of Lindsey would have felt the backs of two fingers rub gently against his cheek if he had not been too far sunk in sleep.

"I hope so, Wulfric," his mama said even more foolishly than she had spoken before. "Oh, I do hope so. And I hope he has brothers and sisters to fill our hands even fuller."

"Well," the Duke of Bewcastle said, sounding haughty and even slightly bored, "if there is anything I can do to assist you in bringing your wish to fulfillment, my love, do let me know."

The Duchess of Bewcastle laughed softly.

The marquess did not even know what brothers and sisters were.

But he would . . .

ABOUT THE AUTHOR

Bestselling, multi-award–winning author Mary Balogh grew up in Wales, land of sea and mountains, song and legend. She brought music and a vivid imagination with her when she came to Canada to teach. Here she began a second career as a writer of books that always end happily and always celebrate the power of love. There are over four million copies of her Regency romances and historical romances in print. She is also the author of the Regency-era romantic novels *No Man's Mistress*, *More than a Mistress*, *A Summer to Remember*, *Slightly Married*, *Slightly Wicked*, *Slightly Scandalous*, *Slightly Tempted*, and *Slightly Sinful*, all available in paperback from Dell. Visit her website at www.marybalogh.com.

And don't miss the first in a dazzling
new quartet of novels!

Mary Balogh invites us into a special world—a select
academy for young ladies—a world of innocence and
temptation. Drawing us into the lives of four women,
teachers at Miss Martin's School for Girls, Balogh
introduces this novel's marvelous heroine: music teacher
Frances Allard—and the man who seduces her with a
passion no woman could possibly forget. . . .

Simply Unforgettable

A Delacorte hardcover on sale in April 2005

Read on for a preview. . .

MARY BALOGH

SIMPLY UNFORGETTABLE

on sale April 2005

His mother had warned him that it would snow before the day was out. So had his sisters. So had his grandfather.

So indeed had his own common sense.

But since he rarely listened to advice—especially when offered by his family—and rarely heeded the dictates of common sense, here he was in the midst of a snowfall to end snowfalls and looking forward with less than eager zeal to spending the night at some obscure country inn in the middle of nowhere. At least he *hoped* he would spend it at some inn rather than in a hovel or—worse yet— inside his carriage.

And he had been in a black mood even before this journey began!

He looked hard at his woman passenger after he had climbed inside the carriage with her, everything that needed tending to having been accomplished. She was huddled beneath one of the woolen lap robes, the muff he had rescued from the other carriage and tossed in a couple of minutes ago under there with her, and he could see that her feet were resting on one of the bricks. *Huddled* was perhaps the wrong word to describe her posture, though. She was straight-backed and rigid with hostility and determined dignity and injured virtue. She did not even turn her head to look at him.

Just like a dried-up prune, he thought. All he could see of her face around the brim of her hideous brown bonnet was the reddened tip of her nose. It was only surprising that it was not quivering with indignation—as if the predicament in which she found herself was *his* fault.

"Lucius Marshall at your service," he said none too graciously.

He thought for a moment that she was not going to return the compliment, and he seriously considered knocking on the roof panel for the carriage to stop again so that he could join Peters up on the box. Better to be attacked by snow outside than frozen by an icicle inside.

"Frances Allard," she said.

"It is to be hoped, Miss Allard," he said, purely for the sake of making conversation, "that the landlord of the next inn we come to will have a full larder. I do believe I am going to be able to do justice to a beef pie and potatoes and vegetables and a tankard of ale, not to mention a good suet pudding and custard with which to finish off the meal. Make that several tankards of ale. How about you?"

"A cup of tea is all I crave," she said.

He might have guessed it. But good Lord—a cup of tea! And doubtless her knitting with which to occupy her hands between sips.

"What is your destination?" he asked.

"Bath," she said. "And yours?"

"Hampshire," he said. "I expected to spend a night on the road, but I had hoped it would be somewhat closer to my destination than this. No matter, though. I would no have had the pleasure of making your acquaintance o you mine if the unexpected had not happened."

She turned her head then and looked steadily at him. I was quite obvious to him even before she spoke that sh could recognize irony when she heard it.

"I believe, Mr. Marshall," she said, "I could have lived quite happily without any of the three of those experiences."

Tit for tat. Touché.

Now that he had more leisure to look at her, he was surprised to realize that she was a great deal younger than he had thought earlier. His impression when his carriage passed hers and again on the road outside had been of a thin, dark lady of middle years. But he had been mistaken. Now that she had stopped frowning and grimacing and squinting against the glare of the snow, he could see that she was only perhaps in her middle twenties. She was almost certainly younger than his own twenty-eight years.

She was a shrew, nevertheless.

And she *was* thin. Or perhaps she was only very slender—it was hard to tell through her shapeless winter cloak. But her wrists were narrow and her fingers long and slim—he had noticed them when she took the muff from his hand. Her face was narrow too with high cheekbones, her complexion slightly olive-hued, apart from the red-tipped nose. Put together with her very dark eyes, lashes, and hair, her face invited the conclusion that she had some foreign blood flowing through her veins—Italian, perhaps, Mediterranean certainly. That fact would account for her temper. Beneath her bonnet he could see the beginnings of a severe center part with smooth bands of hair combed to either side and disappearing beneath the bonnet brim.

She looked like someone's governess. Heaven help her poor pupil.

"I suppose," he said, "you were warned not to travel today?"

"I was not," she said. "I hoped for snow all over Christmas and was convinced it would come. By today I had stopped looking for it. So of course it came."

She was not, it seemed, in the mood for further conversation. She turned her face firmly to the front again, leaving him no more than the tip of her nose to admire, and he felt no obligation—or inclination—to continue talking himself.

At least if all this had had to happen fate might have provided him with a blond, blue-eyed, dimpled, wilting damsel in distress! Life sometimes seemed quite unfair. It had been seeming that way a great deal lately.

He turned his attention back to the cause of the black mood that had hung over him like a dark cloud all over Christmas.

His grandfather was dying. Oh, he was not exactly at his last gasp or even languishing on his deathbed, and he had made light of the verdict his army of London physicians had passed on him when he had gone to consult them in early December. But the fact of the matter was that they had told him his heart was fast failing, that there was nothing any of them could do to heal it.

"It is old and ready to be turned in for a new one," his grandfather had said with a gruff laugh after the news had been forced out of him and his daughter-in-law and granddaughters were sniffling and looking tragic and Lucius was standing deliberately in the shadows of the drawing room, frowning ferociously lest he show an emotion that would have embarrassed himself and everyone else in the room. "Like the rest of me."

No one had been amused except the old man himself.

"What the old sawbones all meant," he had added irreverently, "was that I had better get my affairs in order and prepare to meet my maker any day now."

Lucius had not had a great deal to do with his grandfather or the rest of his family during the past ten years, having been too busy living the life of an idle man about town. He even rented rooms on St. James's Street in London rather than live at Marshall House, the family home on Cavendish Square, where his mother and sisters usually took up residence during the London Season.

But the shocking news had made him realize how

much he actually loved his grandfather—the Earl of Edgecombe of Barclay Court in Somersetshire. And with the realization had come the knowledge that he loved all this family, but that it had taken something like this to make him aware of how he had neglected them.

Even his guilt and grief would have been quite sufficient to cast a deep gloom over his Christmas. But there had been more than that.

He just happened to be the earl's heir. He was Lucius Marshall, Viscount Sinclair.

Not that that in itself was a gloomy fact. He would not have been quite normal if he had hated the thought of inheriting Barclay, where he had grown up, and Cleve Abbey in Hampshire, where he now lived—when he was not in London or somewhere else with his friends—and the other properties and the vast fortune that went with them, even though they must come at the expense of his grandfather's life. And he did not mind the political obligations that a seat in the House of Lords would place upon his shoulders when the time came. After all, ever since the death of his father years ago he had known that life followed its natural course he would one day inherit, and he had educated and prepared himself. Besides, even an idle life of pleasure could pall after a time. Being actually engaged in politics would give his life a more positive, active direction.

No, what he *really* minded was that, in the opinion of his mother, his married sister and possibly her husband too—though one could never be quite sure with Tait—his three unmarried sisters, and his grandfather, a man who was soon to become an earl also needed even sooner to become a married man. In other words, an earl needed a countess.

Lucius needed a bride.

It had been as plain as the noses on all their faces, it seemed, except his. Though even that was questionable. He knew all about duty even if he had spent a large part of his life ignoring and even running from it. But up until now he had been free to do as he pleased. No one had even objected too loudly to his way of life. Normal young men were expected to sow wild oats, provided they did not descend too deeply into vice, and he had done what was expected of him.

But now everything was to change. And if one was to be philosophical about it, one would have to admit that duty caught up with most young men sooner or later—it was the nature of life. It had caught up with him now.

His relatives had all separately expostulated on the theme throughout the holiday whenever one, or sometimes two, of them could maneuver him into what they were all pleased to describe as a comfortable coze.

He had enjoyed more comfortable cozes over Christmas than ever in his life before—or in his life to come, he sincerely hoped.

The consensus was, of course, that he needed a bride without delay.

A perfect bride, if there were such a paragon available—and apparently there was.

Portia Hunt was far and away the most favored candidate, since it was next to impossible to find any imperfection in her.

She had remained single to the advanced age of twenty-three, his mother explained, because she fully expected to be his viscountess one day—and his countess eventually, of course. And the mother of a future earl.

She would make him an admirable wife, Margaret Lady Tait, Lucius's older sister, assured him, because she was mature and steady and had all the accomplishments a future countess would need.

She was still a diamond of the first water, Caroline and Emily, his younger sisters, pointed out—quite correct as it happened, even if they did choose to express themselves in clichés. There was no one more beautiful, more elegant, more refined, more accomplished, than Portia.

Miss Portia Hunt was the daughter of Baron and Lady Balderston and the granddaughter of the Marquess of Godsworthy, his grandfather reminded him—Godsworthy was one of his oldest and closest friends. It would be an eligible and highly desirable alliance—*not* that he was trying to put undue pressure on his grandson.

"Your choice of bride must be yours alone, Lucius," he had said. "But if there is no one else you fancy, you might seriously consider Miss Hunt. It would do my heart good to see you wed to her before I die."

No undue pressure, indeed!

Only Amy, his youngest sister, had spoken up with a dissenting voice, though only on the question of the candidate for perfect bride, not on the necessity of his finding such a creature somewhere within the next few months.

"Don't do it, Luce," she had said when they were out riding alone together one day. "Miss Hunt is so very *tedious*. She advised Mama just last summer not to bring me out this year even though I will be eighteen in June, just because Emily's broken arm prevented *her* from coming out last year and so her turn was delayed. Miss Hunt might have spoken up for me since she intends to marry you and become my sister-in-law, but she did not, and then she smiled that very patronizing smile of hers and assured me that I would be glad next year when the focus of family attention will be on me alone."

The trouble was that he had known Portia forever—her family had frequently come to stay at Barclay Court, and sometimes, when his grandparents had gone to visit the Marquess of Godsworthy, they had taken Lucius with them, and as like as not the Balderstons would be there too with their daughter. The desire of both families that they would eventually make a match of it had always been quite evident. And while he had never actively encouraged Portia after her come-out to sacrifice all other offers in favor of waiting for him to come to the point, he had never actively discouraged her, either. Since he was not of a romantical turn of mind and had always known that he was going to have to marry one day, he had assumed that probably he would end up married to her. But knowing that as a vague sort of future probability was altogether different from being confronted now with the expectation that it was actually to happen—and soon.

Indeed, a vague sort of panic had assailed him at frequent intervals all over the holiday. It happened particularly when he tried to picture himself in bed with Portia. Good Lord! She would doubtless expect him to watch his manners.

And yet another small fact that had darkened his mood even further was that he had distinctly heard himself promise his grandfather—it had happened when they were sitting together in the library on Christmas evening after everyone else had retired for the night, and a few glasses from the wassail bowl had mellowed his sense and made him really quite maudlin—that he would look seriously about him this coming spring during the Season and choose a bride and marry her before the summer was out.

He had not exactly promised to marry Portia Hunt, but her name had inevitably come up.

"Miss Hunt will be happy to see you in town this year," his grandfather had said—which was a strange thing really as Lucius was *always* in town. But what the old man had meant, of course, was that Portia would be happy to see him dancing attendance on her at all the balls and routs and other faradiddle of social events that he normally avoided as he would the plague.

He was a doomed man. There was no point in even trying to deny it. His days as a free—as a *carefree*—man about town were numbered. Ever since just before Christmas he had felt the noose tightening ever more firmly about his neck.

"That coachman of yours deserves to be led in front a firing squad," Miss Frances Allard, that charmingly ge tle lady, said suddenly and sharply, and at the same moment her hand clamped like a vise about Lucius's sleeve. "He is going *too fast* again."

The carriage was indeed slithering and sliding as it plowed its way through the heavy snow. Peters, Lucius thought, was probably enjoying himself more than he had in many a long day.

"I daresay you *would* say that," he said, "since you have your own coachman trained to proceed at about half the walking speed of a gouty octogenarian. But what have we here?"

He peered out through the window and saw that the slithering had been occasioned by the fact that the carriage was being drawn to a halt. They had arrived at what appeared to be an inn, though it was a decidedly poor specimen of its type if this first glimpse of it was anything to judge by. It looked more as if it might be a community center for the drinkers of the village that must be close by than a stopping place for respectable travelers, but, as the old adage went, beggars could not be choosers.

The inn also looked somewhat deserted. No one had cleared any snow away from the door. The stables to the back of the building were shut up. No light flickered behind any of the windows. No reassuring plume of smoke was billowing from the chimney.

It was something of a relief, then, when the door opened a crack after Peters had yelled something unintelligible, and a head complete with unshaven jaws and chin and a voluminous nightcap—in the middle of the afternoon— peered out and bellowed something back.

"Time to wade into the fray, I believe," Lucius muttered, opening the door and jumping out into the knee-deep snow. "What is the problem, fellow?"

He interrupted Peters, who was in the process of informing the man of his startling and quite uncomplimentary pedigree from his perch on the box of the carriage.

"Parker and his missus has gone away and not come back yet," the man shouted. "You can't stop here."

Peters began to give his unbidden opinion on the absent Parkers and on unshaven, bad-mannered yokels, but Lucius held up a staying hand.

"Tell me that there is another inn within five hundred yards of this one," he said.

"Well, there ain't, but that ain't my problem," the man said, making as if to shut the door again.

"Then I am afraid," Lucius said, "that you have guests for the night, my fine fellow. I suggest that you get dressed and pull your boots on unless you prefer to do some work as you are. There is baggage to carry inside and horses to attend with more on the way. Look lively now."

He turned back to hand down Miss Allard.

"It is a relief at least," she said, "to see your ill humor turned upon someone else."

"Do not try me, ma'am," he warned. "And you had better set your arm about my shoulders. I'll carry you inside since you did not have sense enough this morning to don proper boots."

She favored him with one of her shrewish glares, and it seemed to him that this time the reddened tip of her nose did indeed quiver.

"Thank you, Mr. Marshall," she said, "but I shall walk inside on my own two feet."

"Suit yourself," he told her with a shrug and had the great satisfaction of watching her jump down from the carriage without waiting for the steps to be set down and sinking almost to her knees in snow.

It was very hard, he observed with pursed lips, to stalk with dignity from a carriage to a building several yards distant through a foot or more of snow though she did attempt it. She ended up having to wade, though, and flail her arms in order to avoid falling after one inelegant skid just before she reached the door, which the night-capped occupant of the inn had left open.

Lucius grinned with grim amusement at her back.

"We picked up a right one there, guv," Peters commented.

"You will keep a civil tongue in your head when referring to any lady in my hearing," Lucius said, bending a stern gaze on him.

"Right you are, guv." Peters jumped down into the snow, looking quite uncowed by the reproof.

"It looks as if I may indeed have my ale," Mr. Marshall said. "And it looks as if you may have your tea if we can get a fire going and if there is tea hidden away somewhere in the kitchen. But I despair of my beef pie—and my suet pudding."

They were standing in the middle of a shabby, cheerless taproom, which felt no warmer than the carriage since there was no fire burning in the hearth. The servant who had opened the door to them and then not wanted to allow them inside despite the inclement weather came lumbering in with Frances's portmanteau and deposited it on the floor just inside the door together with large clumps of snow.

"I don't know what Parker and the missus will have to say when they hears about this," he muttered darkly.

"Doubtless they will hail you as a hero for hauling in extra business and double your wages," Mr. Marshall told him. "You have been left here all alone over the holiday?"

"I have," the man said, "though they didn't leave till the day after Boxing Day and they are supposed to be back tomorrow. They give me strict orders not to let no one in here while they was gone. I don't know about no double wages, but I do know about missus's tongue. You can't stay here the night and that's flat."

"Your name?" Mr. Marshall asked.

"Wally."

"Wally, *sir*," Mr. Marshall said.

"Wally, *sir*," the man repeated sullenly. "You can't stay here, sir. The rooms ain't ready and there ain't no fires and there ain't no cook here to cook no victuals."

All that was painfully apparent to Frances, who was about as deeply sunk into misery as it was possible to be. Her only consolation—the *only* one—was that she was at least alive and had solid ground beneath her feet.

"I see that a fire is ready laid in the hearth here," Mr. Marshall said. "You may light it while I go outside to bring in the rest of the baggage. Though first you will provide the lady with a shawl or blanket so that she may remain moderately warm until the fire catches. And then you will see about getting two rooms ready. As for food—"

"I will step into the kitchen myself to reconnoiter," Frances said. "I do not need to be treated like a delicate burden. I am no such thing. When you have finished lighting the fire in here, Wally, you may come and help me find what I will need to produce some sort of meal that will satisfy five people, yourself included."

Mr. Marshall looked at her with both eyebrows raised.

"You can cook?" he asked.

"I do need food and utensils and a stove if I am to succeed," she told him. "But I have been known to boil a kettle without causing the water to turn lumpy."

For the merest moment she thought that the gleam in his eyes might be amusement.

"That was *beef pie* in case you did not hear it the first time," he said, "with plenty of onions and gravy—without lumps."

"You may have to settle for a poached egg," she said, "*if* there are any eggs."

"At the moment," he said, "that sounds like a worthy substitute."

"There are eggs," Wally said, his voice still sullen as he knelt to his task of lighting the fire in the taproom hearth. "They are supposed to be for me, but I don't know what to do with them."

"One would hope, then," Mr. Marshall said, "that Miss Allard does know and is not merely indulging in idle boasting when she promises poached eggs."

Frances did not bother to reply. She pushed open the door that she guessed led to the kitchen while he went back out into the snow to help his coachman unload the carriage.

The building was chilly and cheerless. The windows were small and let in very little light even though there was so much whiteness outside. Her feet inside her boots were wet and cold. The inn was not dirty, but neither was it sparkling clean. She dared not take off either her cloak or her bonnet lest she freeze. There was no one to see to her needs except for one slovenly, lazy serving man. There was no one to prepare a hot meal—or even a cold one for that matter. And she was alone here with one bad-tempered, ill-mannered gentleman and three crotchety menservants.

The situation was decidedly grim.

She was expected back at the school today. The girls would be returning for the new term the day after tomorrow. There was much work to do before then if she was to have her classes all ready for the following morning—she had deliberately not worked over Christmas. There was a pile of French essays by the senior class waiting to be marked and an even larger pile of stories—in English—from the junior girls.

This whole turn of events with its resulting delay was more than grim. It was a total disaster.

But as Frances first looked about the kitchen and then explored tentatively and then more boldly in drawers and cupboards and pantry, and finally went in search of Wally and ordered him into the kitchen to clean out the ashes in the large grate and build another fire and light it, she decided that practicality was the only sane way of dealing with the situation.

And perhaps looking back on this day from the safety

of school once she finally got there, she would see it after all more in the light of an adventure than a disaster. She might even find something funny in the memories. It was hard to imagine such an outcome now, but she supposed this might well be considered an adventure of the first order.

Now if only she were stranded here with a handsome, smiling, charming knight in shining armor . . .

Though this man was certainly one of the three, she was forced to admit. Her first impression of him had been wrong in one detail. He was exceedingly large, but he did have a handsome face, even though he liked to ruin it by frowning and sneering and cocking one eyebrow.

He doubted she could poach an egg. He had spoken of beef pie as if it might be something she had never even heard of. Ha! How she would love to deal him his come-uppance. And she would too. She had amused her father and everyone else in his household by spending hours in the kitchen, watching their cook and helping her when-ever she had been allowed to. It had always seemed to her a marvelously relaxing way of using her spare time.

She examined a loaf of bread that she found in the pantry and discovered that though it was not fresh enough to be eaten as it was, it would be appetizing enough if toasted. And there was a wedge of cheese that someone had had the forethought to cover with the result that it looked perfectly edible. There was a slab of butter on another covered dish.

She sent Wally outside to the pump to fetch some wa-ter, filled the kettle, and set it to boil. It would take some time, she estimated, since the fire was only now crackling to life, but it would be worth waiting for. In the mean-while, there was probably enough ale in the inn to slake the thirsts of four men. Indeed, it was her guess that Wally had consumed little else in the time since he had been left alone at the inn. Certainly there was no sign of any dishes having been used or any food handled. And he had probably done nothing else but stay warm in his bed, too lazy even to light a fire for comfort.

Mr. Marshall was in the taproom when Frances went back in there. A fire now burned in the hearth, making the room look altogether more cheerful though nothing could save it from ugliness, and he was in the process of moving a table and chairs closer to the fire. He straightened up to look at her.

He had removed his greatcoat and hat since she last saw him, and she almost stood and gaped. That he was a large gentleman she had seen from the first. She had also thought of him as a heavyset gentleman. But she could see now that he stood before her, clad in an expertly tailored coat of dark green superfine with fawn waistcoat and pantaloons and dry Hessian boots with white shirt and neatly tied cravat, that he was not heavyset at all but merely broad with muscles in all the right places. His powerful thighs suggested that he was a man who spent a great deal of time in the saddle. And his hair without the beaver hat looked thicker and curlier than she had imagined. It hugged his head in a short, neat style.

He was a veritable Corinthian, in fact.